A Book of CANADIAN STORIES

JOSEPH HOWE

THOMAS CHANDLER HALIBURTON

SUSANNA MOODIE

EDWARD W. THOMSON

CHARLES G. D. ROBERTS

DUNCAN CAMPBELL SCOTT

STEPHEN LEACOCK

NORMAN DUNCAN

FREDERICK PHILIP GROVE

A Book of CANADIAN

MARJORIE PICKTHALL

MAZO DE LA ROCHE

ETHEL WILSON

WILL R. BIRD

RAYMOND KNISTER

THOMAS H. RADDALL

MORLEY CALLAGHAN

SINCLAIR ROSS

ERNEST BUCKLER

RALPH GUSTAFSON

DAVID WALKER

IRVING LAYTON

HUGH GARNER

DESMOND PACEY

BRIAN MOORE

HENRY KREISEL

JACK LUDWIG

MORDECAI RICHLER

ALICE MUNRO

ALDEN A. NOWLAN

STORIES

Edited by

DESMOND PACEY

McGRAW-HILL RYERSON LIMITED

Toronto   Montreal   New York   London   Sydney
Mexico   Panama   Düsseldorf
Rio de Janeiro   Kuala Lumpur   New Delhi   Singapore

Published, July, 1947.
Revised Edition, March, 1950.
School Edition, April, 1952.
Revised Edition, January, 1962.
Reprinted, 1964, 1965.
First Paperback Edition, 1967.

ISBN 0-7700-6018-8

*This book is published with assistance
from the Lorne Pierce Fund for
Canadian Literature established by
The Ryerson Press.*

PRINTED AND BOUND IN CANADA

Dedication

To the Canadian writers who
made this book possible.

ACKNOWLEDGMENTS

For permission to include coyprighted material, grateful thanks are due to the following authors, publishers and owners of copyright: Ernest Buckler for "The First Born Son" reprinted from *Esquire*, copyright 1941 by Esquire, Inc.; Morley Callaghan for "The Blue Kimono"; Mazo de la Roche for "Come Fly With Me" first published in *The Atlantic Monthly*; Doubleday & Company for "The Fruits of Toil" from *The Way of the Sea* by Norman Duncan; Hugh Garner for "One, Two, Three Little Indians" published in *The Yellow Sweater and Other Stories* by William Collins & Sons; Mrs. Christie Grace for "The Strawstack" by Raymond Knister published in *The Canadian Forum*; Frederick Philip Grove for "Snow" from *Queen's Quarterly*; Ralph Gustafson for "The Pigeon" first published in *Northern Review* and reprinted in *The Best Short Stories, 1950*; Hodder and Stoughton (Canada) Ltd. for "The Worker in Sandalwood" from *Angel's Shoes* by Marjorie Pickthall; Henry Kreisel for "Two Sisters in Geneva" published in *Queen's Quarterly*; McClelland and Stewart Ltd. for "The Speculations of Jefferson Thorpe" from *Sunshine Sketches of a Little Town* by Stephen Leacock, "The Amulet" from *Tambour and Other Stories* by Thomas H. Raddall, "The Lamp at Noon" by Sinclair Ross and "A Plausible Story" from *The Swinging Flesh* by Irving Layton; Alice Munro for "Sunday Afternoon" first published in *The Canadian Forum*; Alden A. Nowlan for "True Confession"; Desmond Pacey for "The Boat" first published in *Queen's Quarterly*; L. C. Page & Company for "The Young Ravens that Call Upon Him" from *Earth's Enigmas* by Charles G. D. Roberts; Mordecai Richler for "Benny, the War in Europe, and Myerson's Daughter Bella"; The Ryerson Press for "Movies Come to Gull Point" from *Sunrise for Peter* by Will R. Bird and "Paul Farlotte" from *In the Village of Viger* by Duncan Campbell Scott; David Walker for "Storms of Our Journey" reprinted by special permission of *The Saturday Evening Post*; Ethel Wilson for "Hurry, Hurry!" first published in *The New Statesman and Nation*; Willis Kingsley Wing for "Lion of the Afternoon" copyright 1957 by Brian Moore from *The Atlantic Monthly*; and Willis Kingsley Wing and McClelland and Stewart for "Requiem for Bibul" copyright 1960 by Jack Ludwig, first printed in *The Atlantic Monthly*.

Every reasonable care has been taken to trace ownership of copyrighted material. Information will be welcomed which will enable the publishers to rectify any reference or credit.

PREFACE

IT IS GRATIFYING to know that the reception of this book has been sufficiently favourable to necessitate the publication of a fourth edition. The first edition appeared in 1947, the second in 1950 and the third, only slightly modified for the use of schools, in 1952. This fourth edition represents a more radical revision of the book than was previously thought necessary. A whole new group of Canadian writers of fiction has appeared in the fifties, and their work is represented for the first time. This has necessitated dropping a few of the earlier stories, although the omissions have been made with great reluctance.

My hope is that this book will continue to serve as a useful introduction to the art of the short story as practised in Canada, and that reading it will encourage students and the general public to read other stories and novels by the authors represented.

I wish to thank those authors who have replied so promptly and kindly to my enquiries, and Mrs. Helen Moore and Miss Nan Gregg, of the staff of the University of New Brunswick, who have been so helpful in the preparation of this revised manuscript.

DESMOND PACEY

CONTENTS

CONTENTS

INTRODUCTION

"THE PEOPLE which ceases to care for its literary inheritance becomes barbaric." This statement by T. S. Eliot is as applicable to a young country such as Canada, whose literary history extends back only a century and a half, as to England or France. The process by which a country becomes increasingly civilized is, like the growth of a child towards mental and emotional maturity, a progress toward greater self-awareness. By self-awareness I do not mean mere passive self-contemplation, and still less the kind of awkward involution which we speak of as "self-consciousness"; I mean the intelligent and purposive comprehension of one's nature and circumstances, of one's strengths and weaknesses, the understanding of one's past which makes possible the informed direction of one's future. Literature is to the nation what memory coupled with intelligence is to the person.

Appreciation of Canadian poetry has been relatively keen, both at home and abroad, and has been nourished by frequent anthologies; but little attention has been paid to Canadian prose fiction, and least of all to the short story branch of it. For a score of poetry anthologies there have been only two or three designed to present readers with a cross-section of our best short stories. It is often alleged that the form has been little cultivated in Canada, but this allegation, I believe, is as much a result of the dearth of anthologies as an explanation of it. I hope that this book will do something to correct that impression.

The stories have been chosen on the grounds of their literary and artistic merit, and I am prepared to defend them on that ground alone. It would be pretentious to claim for all or any of them "greatness", in the full sense of that word; but I believe that they are all good stories and that of none of them need we be ashamed. They are of many different kinds: there are didactic stories in the eighteenth century manner, satirical sketches, romantic tales of adventure, superstition and horror, and realistic transcriptions of the episodes of everyday life. Some will appeal to one taste, some to another; but all have in common a genuine narrative interest, careful workmanship, sincerity and singleness of mood.

They are all Canadian stories, written by Canadians mostly about the Canadian scene, but their documentary or national significance was a secondary consideration in choosing them. Their reading is not urged upon the public as a duty or a patriotic exercise but as a pleasure—the pleasure which results from witnessing the imaginative re-creation of experience, from seeing the material of life moulded to significant form. It is nevertheless interesting to perceive, now that the stories have been collected, the extent to which they do reflect and interpret the nature of Canadian life. As an agency in the process referred to in the opening paragraph they are at least as effective as Canadian verse.

To begin with the simplest point, the reader of these stories cannot fail to become more sharply aware of the geographical diversity of Canada. The small, scattered farms and thick woods of the Maritime Provinces, the relatively close-set villages and small towns of Ontario and Quebec, and the great cities of those provinces, the immense flat distances of the midwestern prairies, the far western cities of Vancouver and Victoria—all of these areas form the settings of stories included in this volume.

Each of these areas has its distinctive culture and its own pattern of social behaviour, both of which the stories reveal to some extent. The mixture of envy and contempt with which the early Maritime settler regarded his shrewd republican neighbours is the theme of Haliburton's *Sam Slick*. In Thomson's "Privilege of the Limits" we see the humour and high jinks of the early Scottish settlers in Ontario, and in Duncan

Campbell Scott's "Paul Farlotte" the quiet life of rural Quebec, its serenity slightly ruffled by nostalgia for the ancestral France. With Leacock, of course, the case needs no arguing: *Sunshine Sketches of a Little Town* is as unmistakably Canadian as maple syrup or corn on the cob—more so, indeed, for we share these latter with the Americans. Fishing is one of Canada's basic industries, and in "The Fruits of Toil" Norman Duncan has written a parable of the lives of all fishermen. Frederick Philip Grove and Sinclair Ross give us neat complementary pictures of the main hardships of prairie life—summer dust and winter snow—and the stubborn courage with which the settlers meet them. In contrast, the bustle and crowded streets of metropolitan Montreal and Winnipeg form the background of Mordecai Richler's and Jack Ludwig's stories.

One can see reflected also the social development of Canada and the chief forces which have shaped it. Canada's transition from a largely agricultural to a strongly industrial nation is paralleled by a similar trend in the settings of the stories. The rebellions of 1837, and the general pressure for responsible government are not directly reflected in any of the stories, but it is certain that the degree of national consciousness which these movements aroused was a cause of the intense literary activity centred in *The Literary Garland*. In Leacock's story of Jefferson Thorpe's unfortunate investments we witness one of the waves of financial speculation which have periodically swept over this continent in the twentieth century. Such examples could be multiplied.

Perhaps more significant is the change of temper and outlook which can be discerned in the stories as we approach the present. The change is not a simple one, and could be treated from many points of view, but its essence is a gradual shift from an individualistic conception of experience towards a sense of collective responsibility and common danger. In Howe's story of the locksmith, the latter's suffering is looked upon as a purely personal affair: there is little effort on Howe's part to relate the mechanic's persecution to the hostility of one section of the population to another. In the E. W. Thomson story, similarly, the single eccentric individual is the hero, and it is taken for granted that the state should be the ally of his creditor: neither the debt, the debtor, the creditor, nor the legal means employed to recover it are conceived or intended to have any social or collective significance. When we turn to the more recent writers, however, the case is altered. Sinclair Ross's farmer and wife are representative specimens of a generation of prairie farmers who were trapped in the dust bowl; Mordecai Richler's hero is the hapless pawn of forces he can neither understand nor control. This is not to say that the characters in the more recent stories are mere types; but their fate as individuals is recognized to be bound up with the fate of others like them and to be in part the responsibility of us all.

This keener social consciousness and sense of collective responsibility in the new writers is the answer to those who would charge them with morbidity. It is true that, generally speaking, the contemporary stories are less cheerful than the early ones, that there is in them more suffering, more bitterness, more fear. But this change is largely the effect of the social chaos of our time, and when we realize that in all such modern stories there is a more or less implicit appeal to collective remedial effort the final result is not to dispirit but to hearten us.

The pleasure, then, which these stories can give as works of art is supplemented, for Canadians, by the enrichment which comes from the fuller and more direct comprehension of the nation's past and present. To non-Canadians, these stories will serve as an introduction to a nation which is slowly but surely evolving a culture commensurate with its material wealth and power.

II

The first short stories to develop in Canada were the legends, folk tales and myths narrated orally on special occasions by members of Indian tribes. We owe their present existence in printed form to the efforts of such scholars as Marius Barbeau,

W. H. Mechling and T. F. McIlwraith, who have painstakingly transcribed them and sought to retain their distinctive flavour. The stories are, in a stricter sense than those in this volume, social and cultural products. They were not invented by a single author, but represent the accumulation of tradition.

With stories by French-speaking Canadians we are not here concerned. It is fortunate, however, that in two of the stories in this volume — Scott's "Paul Farlotte" and Marjorie Pickthall's "Worker in Sandalwood" — there are sympathetic portrayals of French-Canadian life. We turn now to the Maritime Provinces where English-Canadian literature had its origins.

In the late eighteenth century the outbreak of the American Revolution brought to the Maritimes a large group of settlers who were determined to remain loyal to the British Crown and to live under the Union Jack. Among them were many men of considerable education, and it is from their arrival that we must date the real beginnings of literary activity in what is now Canada. The Loyalists gave to the Maritimes a distinctive social and cultural tone which the area has never completely lost, and their concern for literature and education was immediately fruitful and of permanent worth. Among their number was John Howe, a Boston editor, who in 1776 brought his printing press to Halifax and established a newspaper. John Howe was a journalist and printer and nothing more; but his son, Joseph, who became owner and editor in 1828 of a weekly newspaper called the *Novascotian*, was a man of many parts. Orator, essayist, poet, political pamphleteer, literary critic and short story writer, Joseph Howe might be said, without undue exaggeration, to have laid the essential foundations for the subsequent development of all phases of Canadian literature. This claim receives added force from the fact that he was able to generate literary enthusiasm in others. As editor of the *Novascotian* he gathered around himself Canada's first literary coterie, a group of men who met together periodically to read and criticize their own productions.

The outstanding member of Howe's group was Thomas

Chandler Haliburton, author of the famous *Clockmaker* series, which first appeared in the pages of the *Novascotian*. When the sketches were published in book form in 1837, they at once earned for Haliburton an international reputation as a humorist, and he thus became the first Canadian author to be widely known abroad. That a humorist should enjoy this distinction is interesting in view of the frequent allegations that Canadians are a dour and brooding people. It is a charge which receives little support from our literary history. A good case could be made out for the assertion that the freshest and most enduring parts of our literature are primarily or predominantly humorous. Of the stories in this volume, almost a third of the total number are humorous, and in our poetry there is much humour in the work of W. H. Drummond, Tom MacInnes, E. J. Pratt, F. R. Scott, A. M. Klein, Earle Birney, A. J. M. Smith, James Reaney, Irving Layton, and Jay Macpherson. Satire, which is often said to be lacking in our literature, has actually played a large part from the very beginning. The notion of our writers as solemn pedants or canting prophets is a widespread fallacy which has arisen from focusing disproportionate attention upon the romantic Group of the Sixties.

It is in the work of Howe and Haliburton that we find the beginnings of the short story in Canada. Their work was done at a time when the short story had almost disappeared from the literature of the western world, and long before the "art of the short story" had become, in America, France and England, a subject of intense concern. We should not expect in their stories, then, any pronounced technical subtlety, any painstaking care for absolute unity of effect, economy of expression or tightness of plot. Their stories are, however, accurate reflections of the Loyalist culture of which they were representative products. Conservative and correct in temper, concerned to maintain and foster the Imperial connection, they found congenial models in the essays, stories and sketches of the English neo-classicists of the eighteenth century. For all that Haliburton is called, with some justice, the father of

American humour, it is in Addison and Swift, in Johnson and Goldsmith, that we must look for the sources of his art. The epigrammatic flavour, the wit which seizes upon every departure from the reasonable — these qualities of neo-classical satire are the fundamental elements of Haliburton's sketches. It is in the phrasing, in the use of North American idioms and dialect, that we find the new element in his work. In Howe's story the didacticism and sentiment, rather than the satire, of the eighteenth century are most obvious. To preach prudence and industry, to soften and refine the feelings by an appeal to our sense of sympathy with undeserved misfortune—these were obviously Howe's aims in the story, and were it not for the American place-name in its title it would not have seemed out of place in *The Spectator* or *The Rambler*.

Though Haliburton was to influence writers in England and America—Dickens and Mark Twain the most prominent— he had no successors at home, and the short story was not practised with any distinction in the Maritimes again until the late nineteenth century. When the revival did come, in the work of the two Roberts and others, it was romantic rather than neo-classical in mood.

For the next significant turn in the development of the short story in Canada we must look to Montreal, where in 1838 the enterprising John Gibson established the first literary magazine of any permanence in British North America. This was the famous *Literary Garland,* "a monthly repository of Tales, Sketches, Poetry, Music, Engravings", specifically designed to discover and encourage Canadian literary talent. For thirteen years it appeared regularly each month, containing some fifty pages of fine print arranged in two close-set columns. Since ninety per cent of its contents were original productions, its bulk alone is amazing, considering its limited constituency. There is also an astonishing difference in tone and outlook from the work of Howe and Haliburton in the *Novascotian*. Here the models are not Addison and Johnson, but Scott and his progeny of historical romancers: Harrison Ainsworth, Bulwer, G. P. R. James and Lever. "The Jewess of Moscow",

"Monmouth, or The King's Son"—these are sample titles of the long continued stories, their settings remote in time and place, which appeared in issue after issue. Most of the contributions were either anonymous or signed only with initials, and it is now impossible to identify many of their authors; among them, however, were a number who have established lasting if minor reputations: Rosanna Mullins (Mrs. Leprohon), whose novel *Ida Beresford* first appeared serially in *The Garland,* and who later published historical novels such as *Antoinette de Mirecourt* and *The Manor House of de Villerai;* John Richardson, who had already published the first Canadian historical romance, *Wacousta,* and who published sections of its sequel, *The Canadian Brothers,* in the magazine; Susanna Moodie, author of the famous pioneer document, *Roughing it in the Bush,* who contributed not merely pieces later included in that book but also historical novelettes and poems; Mrs. Moodie's almost equally famous sister, Catherine Parr Traill; and Charles Sangster, our chief native poet of the pre-Confederation period.

The output of short stories from this burst of literary activity was much slighter than we might expect. In "Wandering Willie's Tale" Scott had written one of the great short stories in English; but the bulk of his work was done in the novel form, and it was to the writing of novels rather than short stories that most of his followers, both in England and Canada, devoted themselves. Most of the prose fiction published in *The Garland* was in the form of novels or novelettes which extended in serial form through several issues. The idea of the short story as a literary form worthy of special cultivation had apparently not by this time reached the Canadas, although the publication, in one issue of *The Garland,* of Edgar Allen Poe's "The Bells" (it was published anonymously under the title "The Maniac") was an omen of things to come. There were, however, some short stories in *The Garland* by Canadian authors: romantic tales of superstition, horror or adventure; simple stories of pioneer life which centred in such incidents as the acquisition of the first cow; and character studies of strange types among the pioneers.

Of stories of the last variety, Mrs. Susanna Moodie was the foremost exponent. A quick eye for absurdity in conduct and a ready sympathy for misfortune combined to make her an excellent observer of the follies and hardships of pioneer life. In her sketches she was ostensibly concerned to record the events and impressions of her own life as an immigrant suddenly transferred from the comforts of England to the rigours of the undeveloped bush country of Ontario, but in most of them the focus quickly shifts from herself to her neighbours and friends. The result is the finest existent portrait gallery of the early settlers in that area. Unfortunately, her method led her to imbed these character portrayals in the chronological record of her own experiences and it is difficult to detach them from their context for the purposes of an anthology such as this. I trust that readers of "Old Woodruff and His Three Wives", reprinted in this book, will not resent the autobiographical introductory section which does, it must be granted, impair its unity as a short story.

The predominant'y romantic flavour of the contents of *The Garland* was a foretaste of the type of writing which was to dominate the Canadian literary scene for several generations. In the mid-nineteenth century the controversy between realism and romance in fiction was beginning in the three countries most likely to influence Canadian writing habits: England, France and the United States. If this controversy reached Canada it had little discernible effect upon our fiction: romance remained supreme. Closely allied to this controversy over realism, and in a sense a part of it, was the growing insistence upon the "art of fiction". English novelists of the early Victorian period were concerned rather with the content than with the technique of their books; but Poe in the United States, Flaubert, Maupassant and others in France, and Henry James, Moore and Conrad in England, came to lay greater and greater emphasis upon the means by which the writer of fiction achieves his effects. In this respect, too, Canada lagged behind.

With the single exception of Duncan Campbell Scott, no Canadian writer of fiction prior to the twentieth century showed much concern for the finer points of technique which were so avidly discussed in Paris and London.

Had he shared this passion for craftsmanship, the next writer of short stories whom we must consider, Edward William Thomson, might have become a major figure. Thomson had vigour enough, and humour, and a striking gift for character creation, but his work is somewhat crude and unshapely. As it is, his work stands out from that of his Canadian contemporaries in the late nineteenth century by virtue of the realistic observation which it incorporates. An isolated figure in Canada, he had read the work of the foreign realists and sought to apply something of their vision to the Canadian scene.

Thomson was a Torontonian, but a most untypical one who once labelled his native city as an "active Belfast" and who angrily denounced its "narrow, bigoted, canting spirit." A radical journalist on the old Toronto *Globe,* he struck out fearlessly at wickedness in high places, pleaded for free world trade and for Canada's national independence. His short stories were collected in 1895, under the title *Old Man Savarin and Other Stories,* and most of them display his characteristic vitality and unconventionality. Two of them, the title story and "The Privilege of the Limits", are among the most amusing and lively stories ever produced in this country. All of them mingle humour and pathos in the manner of such writers as Dickens, Daudet and Bret Harte, and it seems certain that one or all of these writers exercised a strong influence upon him. Humour and pathos is a hard mixture to control successfully, and it is only in the two stories mentioned that Thomson fully achieved it. In the others, either the pathos slips into bathos or the humour degenerates into burlesque. But Thomson, both as man and writer, deserves more attention than he has received.

In most respects Thomson stands out from the main stream of Canadian fiction, but in one particular he set a precedent which was widely followed. Abandoning the *Globe* in 1891, he moved to the United States and became an editor of the Boston *Youth's Companion*. At about the same time the poet Bliss Carman became associated with the New York *Independent*; in the mid-nineties the Roberts brothers moved to New York, as did Norman Duncan; and they were followed in the next few years by such Canadian writers as W. A. Fraser, Ernest Thompson Seton, Harvey O'Higgins and Arthur Stringer. Varying the pattern slightly, Gilbert Parker went to voluntary exile in England. This exodus, so general that the period might be termed the age of the expatriates, is surely significant. In part no doubt it was a result of the economic depression which gripped Canada in 1874 and continued virtually unabated until the late nineties. Historians testify that pessimism was widespread throughout the newly formed dominion, and the writers must have shared that feeling. At the same time, however, the exodus argues a thinness and poverty in the Canadian cultural atmosphere which contrasts sharply with the relative richness of *The Garland* epoch. So many writers would not have fled the country simply because they could hope for little monetary return: the contributors to the *Garland* made very little material profit from their work, but they remained and continued to write in this country.

The basic fact, I think, is that the degree of public responsiveness had declined in the decades since *The Garland* flourished. The existence of that magazine in the forties proves that there were not only writers ready and able to write but also readers eager to read. By 1895, no magazine of comparable merit existed in Canada: our serious writers could find no suitable medium of publication. Efforts had been made to found similar periodicals, but they had either quietly collapsed through lack of public support or lowered their literary standards in order to catch the popular favour. What outlets for publication existed were for light popular entertainment. In this field, Canadian publishers could not offer rewards comparable with those offered for the same standard of work by English and American magazines. The result was that our potentially serious writers either did not write at all or, if they

were willing to compromise their standards, emigrated to countries where the rewards for compromise made it worth while.

Though written and published abroad, for the most part, the
quantity of fiction produced by this generation of Canadians
was very large. The Roberts brothers, Norman Duncan, Gilbert
Parker, W. A. Fraser, Ernest Thompson Seton and others
turned out a host of short stories and novels, many of which
were published in both magazine and book form. But the
quality was often dubious, the substance and attitude un-
failingly romantic, and the impact upon Canadian cultural
development slight.

It has been claimed for Charles Roberts that he invented
the one original form of fiction which can be credited to a
Canadian writer: the animal story which is neither fable nor
fantasy but a direct transcription of animal behaviour. His
boyhood experiences in the woods of New Brunswick, and
his lifelong interest in all forms of natural life, fitted him to
write this type of story supremely well. It is a very minor
branch of fiction, but Roberts cultivated it to good effect. In
stories like the one reprinted in this book, where he is content
simply to paint the natural environment and to tell some simple
dramatic episode in the life of an animal, he achieves something which is unique and compelling. His powers of observation and description carry him through. Often, however, the
pressure towards a more deliberately romantic mode of treatment was too strong, and he introduced into his animal stories
human adventures of an incredible or artificial sort, or wrote
stories in which human adventures were the centre of interest.
When that happened, his very weak grasp of human char-
acterization reduced the stories to a much lower level of
achievement. Again and again a story of his starts promisingly
with a section of clear descriptive writing and then degenerates
into melodrama when the characters begin to act: "The Black-
water Pot" is a good example.

Theodore Roberts possesses a much firmer grasp of character than his brother, and a keener sense of humour, but he
too was caught up in the vogue for romance and the struggle

for commercial success. A product of the rather nostalgic culture of Fredericton in particular and the Maritimes in general, he has concentrated most of his attention upon the romantic past and the more remote areas of his native province. His stories have a distinction of style and a tincture of irony which often refreshingly modifies their romantic flavour, but the compulsion to make them saleable in the popular magazines has frequently led him to engineer episodes of factitious excitement.

Some of the members of this romantic generation may be more briefly dismissed. Norman Duncan based the bulk of his work in fiction upon the lives of the Newfoundland fishermen. To the portrayal of the hardships of their life he brought intimate knowledge gained by long residence among them, a rapid if somewhat jerky narrative style, obvious sincerity and sympathy, and a peculiarly wry humour. The basic flaw which runs through almost all his work is perhaps best described as artistic irresponsibility: he seems to write carelessly, as if he had insufficiently meditated upon the precise effect he wished to create and the best means of achieving it. W. A. Fraser began his career with stories about the Far East, where he had lived, went on to write animal stories in emulation of Roberts and ended as a writer of stories about horse-racing. Ernest Thompson Seton, a naturalist of distinction, wrote a number of animal stories which had more scientific accuracy than those of Roberts but considerably less literary skill.

Gilbert Parker, by virtue of his once great reputation and the sheer bulk of his output, demands a more extensive notice. Beginning his writing career as a journalist, Parker went to England in his middle twenties, in 1889, and quickly became a disciple of the rising English school of romantic novelists. The first product of his romantic enthusiasm was a volume of short stories dealing with the Canadian North-West frontier, and though he seldom returned to his native country and never for long periods, he frequently embodied a Canadian setting in his subsequent short stories and novels. Canada to him, however, was not a country to interpret seriously to the world, but a remote area whose romantic connotations he could profitably exploit. His best work is only superior journalism, and for all his mastery of the tricks of arousing and maintaining suspense his stories today have a hollow ring. About most of his fiction there is an air of pretentiousness and pomposity; it is only occasionally, when he is content simply to relate a romantic episode and omit his usual attempts at lofty moralizing, that his efforts retain their interest for the modern reader.

Another romanticist of more than average interest from this period was Marjorie Pickthall. She is still widely remembered and well regarded as a poet, but her stories have been largely ignored in recent years. It was by her stories, however, that she first came into wide public notice, and while still in her twenties, in the early years of this century, she had them accepted by such leading magazines as the *Atlantic Monthly*. A highly imitative artist, as she was herself aware, her stories, like her poems, follow closely the work of romantic writers in England. Where Rossetti and the early Yeats were her masters in poetry, Kipling and especially Conrad were her models in prose fiction. At any rate her choice of models showed some discrimination, and her stories as a result have much to commend them: a rich and modulated style, some fairly acute and subtle psychological analysis and a careful portrayal of atmosphere and environment. She had not the breadth of experience enjoyed by her masters, however, and the result is that her portrayals of strange events in far places have not the same degree of authenticity. Occasionally, as in the title story of her volume *Angel's Shoes*, she comes very close indeed to creating the illusion of reality in a remote setting, but her best stories are those in which she writes of the life she knows and exploits her own personal insights. "The Worker in Sandalwood", reprinted here, is such a story: suffused with tenderness and pathos, with simple piety and reverence, it is the sincere and striking impression of a distinctive personality. It is ample proof of the vogue of romance of the adventurous and active sort in this period that Marjorie

Pickthall, so temperamentally alien to it, should have felt obliged to attempt it.

The craftsmanship of Marjorie Pickthall's stories is distinctly more careful than that of most of her Canadian contemporaries, but the finest short story craftsman of this generation, and the one most clearly and decisively influenced by the new interest in the technique of fiction, was Duncan Campbell Scott. E. K. Brown noted that although Scott, as a poet, is considered a member of the Group of the Sixties, he stands apart from that group in many particulars. Much the same is true of his position in fiction. His subject-matter is as romantic as that of his contemporaries, but to its handling he brings a delicacy and subtlety of touch which seriously alters its effect. To set his chief volume of short stories, *In the Village of Viger,* beside Parker's *Pierre and His People,* is to be struck by many sharp contrasts. Where Parker's work is flamboyant and highly coloured, Scott's is quiet, self-effacing and subdued. Overstatement has been replaced by understatement, crude melodrama by refined suggestion and symbolism, Parker's prodigality of words by a deliberate economy of utterance. One feels in Scott's work that every word has been first weighed and considered and finally chosen with a full realization of all its connotations. All parts of the stories have been similarly deliberated upon: characters, setting and events are blended and shaped into a satisfying artistic whole.

Also belonging to this pre-war romantic generation in time but standing apart from it in treatment is Stephen Leacock. Leacock revived and extended the humorous strain in Canadian fiction which had been introduced by Haliburton and carried on with less distinction by E. W. Thomson. Like Haliburton, Leacock was the author of one great or near-great book and of many markedly inferior ones. Haliburton never approached, in his subsequent work, the level of *The Clockmaker,* and *Sunshine Sketches of a Little Town* occupies a similar position in the Leacock canon. Certainly a Canadian, perhaps a world's classic, *Sunshine Sketches* blends irony and sentiment, sympathy and detachment, to form a subtle and distinctive portrait of a typical Canadian small town. There is a fairly close approach to the same mastery in *Arcadian Adventures with the Idle Rich,* but the other books, even the famous *Literary Lapses,* are relatively crude and obvious. Even in *Sunshine Sketches* there is little concern for structure and style, but the humour there is so rich, the characters so vivid, the observation so exact that we willingly overlook its absence.

The years between the two World Wars of 1914 and 1939 did not witness a sharp break with the prevailingly romantic tradition of Canadian fiction. Most members of the generation we have just considered went on writing after the First War, and they were soon joined by other writers of romance: Mazo de la Roche, Alan Sullivan, Frederick Niven, W. G. Hardy, Laura Goodman Salverson, Franklin Davey Macdowell and others too numerous to mention. But in the twenties and thirties a more realistic tradition also began to assert itself, embodied chiefly in the work of Frederick Philip Grove, Raymond Knister, and Morley Callaghan. Other names, of less productive and well-known writers, might be added to this list, but its relative brevity accurately reflects the lack of balance between the two schools. Another feature of the inter-war period was a growing sophistication in technique: there was a perceptible rise in the average level of craftsmanship.

Even the new romance was affected by this increased concern for form and style. Mazo de la Roche, for example, exhibited a deft command of words and a real mastery of narrative structure in *Jalna* and its successors. She had begun, in her first novel, *Possession,* in a way which suggested that she might eventually give us an illuminating account of the real quality of Canadian life; but even here there were strong romantic elements, and the resounding success of *Jalna* confirmed her adherence to the romantic school. She has deliberately refrained from attempting a profound analysis either of society or of personality; but if her writing thus lacks depth, it is abundantly clear and swift. Many of her short stories carry on the tradition of the animal story initiated by Charles Roberts, and they far surpass the work of any other of his followers in that form. Her imagination, like that of Roberts, seems to work with more ease and assurance when it is portraying the sensations of animals or of children rather than those of adult persons. Whatever she writes, however, has grace and *élan,* and in her own way she has given pleasure to thousands.

Of the other romanticists, Alan Sullivan stands out by virtue of his fictional portrayal of the Canadian North. Of his many volumes of novels and short stories the best, in my opinion, are those such as *Under Northern Lights,* which deal with the lives of trappers and Eskimos in our Arctic and sub-Arctic regions. Though journalistic effects are occasionally sought in these stories, they are far less flamboyant and obvious than those in the work of Gilbert Parker. Here again the rise in craftsmanship is patent: Mr. Sullivan was a far more subtle artist than Parker dreamed of being. W. G. Hardy, a professor of classics, has specialized in stories of the ancient world, though occasionally he has written interestingly of contemporary life. All his work has displayed the new spirit of which we are speaking by the careful research which has underlaid it and the vigorous clarity of the style in which it has been expressed. Laura Goodman Salverson, a Canadian of Icelandic descent, has written of the Norse voyages to Canada and of the lives of Icelandic settlers on the prairies, but her novels and especially her vivid and authentic autobiography—*Confessions of an Immigrant's Daughter*—are better known than her short stories.

But these writers, and others like them, though their work marked an advance over the crude melodrama of their immediate predecessors, seldom if ever sought to catch the flavour and texture and rhythm of ordinary Canadian life nor to fashion a new instrument of expression. They went to the remote in time or place for their material or, as in the case of Mazo de la Roche, they cast a glamour of unreality about our present existence; and in technique they followed the traditional paths. Writers were needed who would approach life and language experimentally. This need was to some extent supplied by the writers who, for convenience's sake, I have called realists.

The realistic movement in Canadian fiction was at least a generation later than similar movements elsewhere. When it came, it was the result of many influences, some literary and some social. The literary influences were largely of French and American origin and were, in part at least, accidental. Frederick Philip Grove had spent much of his youth in the Paris of Zola and Maupassant; Morley Callaghan was associated with Ernest Hemingway for a time on the staff of the Toronto *Star*; and Raymond Knister was a student in the American mid-west when the realistic and naturalistic movement in fiction was there at its height.

Thus were the seeds planted; but they could not have taken root in Canada had not the soil been ready. It was prepared largely by two social forces: by the widespread disillusionment which followed the First World War and by the economic depression in 1929. The world of the twenties and thirties was a much less comfortable and complacent place than it had been before the War. For some people, this fact merely increased the need for escape mechanisms of various kinds: hence, the popularity of historical romances. But for others it created a desire for penetrating analyses of the disturbing conditions, for diagnoses which might suggest possible cures: hence the rise of social realism. These factors were, of course, general throughout at least the whole of the Western world. But there was one factor peculiar to Canada which helped to make for more realistic writing in this country. During and after the First War Canada began to be conscious of itself as a separate and independent nation. If the consciousness had existed before, it had certainly never existed in such an acute form. External signs of this—insistence upon our right to an independent place at the Peace Conference, for example—are more important for what they suggest of the national mood than in themselves. And as the nation became more conscious of itself as an entity, it was to be expected that the attitude of our writers and readers would change also. Parker had exploited Canada as a remote and romantic colony; the new writers, though in less strength than we might have hoped, began to probe its life as something worthy of serious study for its own sake.

Of this tendency, the first exponent was Frederick Philip Grove. His first novels and stories were written in the last decade of the nineteenth century, but he must be considered to be a member of this inter-war generation because none of his work was published until 1923. He had arrived in Canada in 1893, a young man of twenty-one fresh from the universities of Paris, Rome and Munich. In Paris he had been on friendly terms with many of the young writers of France, and had been acquainted with most of the established masters. Compelled by his lack of professional training to seek his living by manual labour on the prairies of the mid-west, he came to know thoroughly the lives of the pioneer settlers and conceived the idea of becoming their spokesman. This mission he sought to fulfil in a series of realistic novels and short stories. For thirty years his work was consistently rejected by magazines and publishers, but he persevered in his self-appointed task, refused to compromise his standards, and ultimately gained a belated and somewhat hesitant recognition. Occasionally deficient in mobility and subtlety, marred by touches of awkwardness and angularity, his work has solid strength and power. Taken as a whole, it constitutes the most impressive sustained achievement of all Canadian writers of fiction.

Perhaps his closest rival for the position of eminence is Morley Callaghan. As was mentioned above, Callaghan met Ernest Hemingway shortly after the First War, and through the latter's encouragement became a contributor to the cosmopolitan little magazines of that period, *transition* and *This Quarter*. In the late twenties he spent some time in Paris, and his contacts there, together with his reading of the great masters of French and Russian fiction, influenced him to bring to bear upon the Canadian scene a fresh vision and a new technique. His best stories have something of the economy and irony of Flaubert and Maupassant and of the restrained pathos

of Chekov. But they exhibit at the same time a reliance upon
the Canadian idiom and a personal compassion which makes
them indigenous and distinctive. One feels always in his stories,
even in those which fail, a struggle after truth, an effort to
attain a deeper and fuller awareness of human beings and of
the social forces by which they are directed.

Grove and Callaghan, the two most significant writers of
Canadian fiction in the inter-war period, can be profitably
compared and contrasted, for their work is in several respects
complementary. They have in common a determination to
make their art out of the ordinary processes of contemporary
life, a high conception of the artist's role in society, and a
readiness to make fiction their main life-work. They differ in
that Callaghan has done most of his work, and certainly
achieved his greatest renown, in the short story form, whereas
Grove concentrated upon novels and wrote relatively few and
obscure short stories. Grove's fiction, also, portrayed almost
exclusively the lives of the settlers of the western prairies,
whereas Callaghan concerns himself rather with urban and
suburban life in Ontario. Callaghan is the finer craftsman,
but Grove had a more profound philosophy and a more
movingly tragic vision. Grove achieved his most memorable
effects by the slow and massive accumulation of detail, Callaghan achieves his rather by subtlety and suggestion. Together
they have made an invaluable contribution to our cultural
development.

Raymond Knister's contribution might have equalled or
even exceeded theirs had he lived to develop his talents to the
full. In his brief career—he was drowned at the age of thirty
—Knister laid the foundations of a distinguished reputation
as a poet, novelist, short story writer, editor and critic. His
inspiration seems to have come largely from his contact with
the American mid-western literary movement while a student
at Iowa State in the early twenties. It was the time of Lindsay,
Masters and Sandburg in poetry; of Cather, Dreiser, Anderson
and Lewis in fiction; it was only to be expected that the sensitive and talented young Canadian would be infected with the

prevalent enthusiasm. For a time he was an editor of the literary periodical in which much of the best work of the period appeared—*The Midland*—and when he returned to Canada he set himself to introduce the new outlook to his own countrymen by both practice and precept. He wrote stories and poems in which he sought to hammer out a fresh linguistic instrument and to project his vision of Ontario life. His approach, as will be seen in the story reprinted here, was direct and distinctive, and the result was a fascinating blend of the objective and the subjective, of the observed fact and the personality of the beholder.

These three, then, were the leading practitioners of the new realism in Canadian fiction between the wars. There were others whose work, for various reasons, was slighter in bulk but marked by a similar interest in the contemporary scene and an unhackneyed mode of expression. Leo Kennedy, primarily a poet, wrote a few short stories—about the more sordid districts of our large cities—in which humour, pathos and anger are piquantly mingled. Thomas Murtha, a friend of Raymond Knister, published similar stories of urban disillusionment in both American and Canadian magazines. Robert Ayre wrote a story called "Mr. Sycamore" which was republished in O'Brien's collection and is still remembered by a few discriminating readers. Merrill Denison, best known for his volume of realistic plays, *The Unheroic North* (1923), wrote a few fine stories before leaving for the United States to follow a career in radio and advertising. Will E. Ingersoll wrote realistic stories of Canadian farm life, among them the sardonic tale "The Man Who Slept Till Noon". Professor John D. Robins published several good short stories in the twenties, but is better known to the general public for his humorous *The Incomplete Anglers*. Dorothy Livesay also wrote some short stories of life during the great depression, but has since devoted herself almost exclusively to poetry. Other women writers of short stories that accurately reflected Canadian life in the twenties and thirties were Mary Quayle Innis, who dealt with urban family life, and Luella Bruce Creighton, who chose her themes from rural life. There were also a few efforts to write propagandist stories in the period, but most of these were far too crude in style and form.

The fact that there were so many promising writers whose fictional output remained very small, or who gave up the writing of short stories altogether, is largely the result of the lack of suitable outlets for publication. *The Literary Garland* has not yet had a twentieth-century counterpart which can match its record of thirteen years of continuous publication. *The Canadian Magazine,* founded towards the end of the nineteenth century, continued through several decades and published a good number of stories, but it catered increasingly to the popular taste and provided little room for experimental work. *Saturday Night,* another late nineteenth-century foundation, still survives and has preserved relatively high standards. But it has always been primarily interested in social and political discussion of a factual kind, and although it has printed occasional good short stories, its space for pure literature is very limited. The university quarterlies — *Queen's Quarterly, Dalhousie Review,* and the *University of Toronto Quarterly*—have done much to foster Canadian literature by intelligent, informed reviews and critical articles, but only two of them publish short stories. There have been and are a number of popular magazines, of which *Maclean's* is the best known, but their preference in fiction is for the light romantic type of story which puts little strain upon the reader's intelligence and sensibility. The depression also produced magazines such as *Masses* and *New Frontier,* but they were ready to accept only stories which preached social revolution.

Various efforts were made in the inter-war period to supply this lack of outlets for serious fiction. Little experimental magazines such as *The Rebel* and *The Canadian Mercury* were established in the twenties and published stories by many of the writers we have just discussed, but they quickly collapsed from lack of public response. In 1925 *The Canadian Forum* was established to serve as a vehicle for advanced thought in the fields of politics, social criticism, literature and art. Almost miraculously it has managed to survive, and it has published many of the best poems and stories produced in this country. It has thus provided an audience, but not a living, to our writers, since it has never been able to afford payment for its contributors.

It was the arrival of the Second World War, and its resultant prosperity and sharpened sense of national consciousness, which at least partially solved this problem of a publishing outlet. The years since 1939 have been perhaps the most productive period in the history of Canadian literature, with the possible exception of the years between 1888 and 1893 when the best poetry of Roberts, Carman, Lampman and Scott was making its appearance. In poetry, fiction, literary criticism and history the output of the last decade or so has been large and of relatively high quality.

As I have suggested, the War and its aftermath stimulated the production of Canadian literature in two ways. The high level of employment, wages and profits created a greater potential market for Canadian books and magazines. Publishers brought out volumes which they would formerly have had to reject on grounds of economy, and young writers were able to enlist financial aid for the production of experimental magazines. In the second place, the Second World War did even more than the previous war to bring a new sense of national solidarity to Canada, and Canadians were thus stimulated to write and read about themselves.

Perhaps the most significant development during these years was in the field of poetry, but fiction did not lag far behind. For the first time in the history of Canadian fiction, the dominant position of the historical romance was seriously challenged. Romance continued, of course, and found two new practitioners in Thomas H. Raddall and Will R. Bird, both of whom began to produce novels and short stories in which they exploited the romantic past of the Maritime Provinces. But the younger writers of fiction, almost without exception, strove with varying degrees of success to mirror and interpret the life about them. Sinclair Ross, W. O. Mitchell

and Christine van der Mark wrote novels and short stories in
which the life of the prairies was portrayed accurately and
sensitively, stripped of the false glamour and excitement with
which almost all previous writers except Grove had invested
it. Hugh Maclennan, in novels such as *Two Solitudes* and *The
Precipice*, sought to project in fictional form some of the
fundamental clashes in our culture; it is a matter for regret
that he does not seem to have attempted the short story form.
Ethel Wilson, in *Hetty Dorval* and *The Innocent Traveller*
and various short stories, has written with sophisticated wit and
grace of the middle-class life of Vancouver. Joyce Marshall,
Robertson Davies, Philip Child, Edward McCourt, Mordecai
Richler, Brian Moore, Adele Wiseman and Ernest Buckler
have also written novels which in whole or in part bear witness
to our sharpened sense of the interest and importance of our
own time and place. If from this burst of creative activity no
truly great novel or story has yet emerged, the output is collec-
tively impressive and gives us sound basis for a hopeful view
of the future.

But possibly of even greater long-term significance is the
work which has been appearing, in the last few years, in
various little magazines. Unheralded by the publicity which
has greeted most of the novelists named above, groups of
writers have been perfecting their art and quietly publishing
the results in a series of magazines of small circulation but of
great potential influence. The first of these, *Preview*, made its
unpretentious appearance in 1942 in Montreal. Its founders
—F. R. Scott, P. K. Page, Bruce Ruddick, Neufville Shaw
and Patrick Anderson—were anxious to keep alive creative
and experimental writing in wartime, to fuse the lyric and
didactic elements in modern verse and to make contact with
new writing movements in other parts of the world. They were,
as these aims suggest, mainly interested in poetry, but they
also welcomed experimental short stories and criticism.
Preview was joined, a year or two later, by *First Statement*,
and the two ultimately pooled their resources to found
Northern Review. *Northern Review* ceased publication in

1956, on the untimely death of its editor, John Sutherland, but since that time several literary magazines which print quality short stories have appeared: *The Tamarack Review, Prism, Waterloo Review* and *The Fiddlehead*.

It is perhaps rash to attempt to generalize at such an early date about the products of these new media. The work published in the little magazines has been uneven. Some of it has obviously been written and published in deference to some passing fashion, some of it has sought so crudely to evade the traditional that it has become merely bizarre. There has been at least some trace of a tendency which seems to be inevitable in such ventures—the tendency to cliquishness, to a strange inverted orthodoxy of heresy. The search for the different, the startling image has often gone on to the neglect of the artist's fundamental concerns: clarity, economy, order and decorum. Private and personal jealousies have occasionally obscured and distorted critical judgment. The effort to avoid nationalism and the waving of the maple leaf has led at times to a rootless cosmopolitanism, to an apeing of foreign models which is more slavish in its way than the "imitativeness" which these writers decry in their Canadian predecessors.

But when all this has been said, it remains true that these magazines have been of enormous benefit to this country, and that our future literary success is in large degree dependent upon them and others like them. Even their most freakish products are of infinitely more value than the drearily hackneyed contents of the slick magazines. From their pages a considerable body of really first-class work could be selected, and they have uncovered many fresh and original talents who would otherwise have had no opportunity of getting their writings into print.

Is there any trend discernible in the contents of these magazines which might give us a clue to the probable future course of Canadian letters? The wartime products, as they appeared in both *Preview* and *First Statement*, leaned heavily towards social documentation and social protest, generally along vaguely Marxist lines. More recently, as has also happened in England and the United States, there has been a shift of emphasis towards a more subjective art. Personal reminiscences, especially of childhood, and intensely personal reactions to a world of tension have to some extent replaced the concern with social groups and forces. The best hope for the future, perhaps, lies in a fusion of these two emphases, in stories in which the reaction of the sensitive individual is employed to assess, interpret and illuminate the nature of our corporate life.

III

The foregoing section has been an attempt at a crude first map of Canadian short story writing. To change the metaphor, I have attempted to break a few rough roads and to set up a few preliminary signposts across a territory which has been virtually unexplored before. There are no doubt mistakes of direction. I am especially conscious of having used terms which are far from exact, such as those of realism and romance. In spite of their vagueness, such terms are a necessary convenience, and there is fairly general agreement about their meaning, particularly when applied to the history of fiction. But no work is purely romantic or purely realistic: what we have invariably are mixtures of the two in which one or other predominates (though occasionally, as in much of Conrad and Flaubert's *Salammbô,* the mixture is fairly even). There is a realistic element in the work of Gilbert Parker, just as there are romantic elements in the work of Frederick Philip Grove.

Another danger in such a survey is that the surveyor might mistake his subjective preferences for objective value judgments. My own preference for the more realistic type of fiction will be patently clear to all, and it may have prevented me from doing justice to the authors of romance. It is certainly not true to suggest, as I may unwittingly have done, that the realistic story is by that very fact superior to the romantic story. Realism which is unsupported by imaginative force and vision can be drearily dull and utterly worthless as art. The distinguishing quality of the good story of either type is "aware-ness", the degree to which the artist's sensibility has vibrated in response to its stimulus and the success with which those vibrations have been communicated to the reader. This quality of awareness will, I trust, be found in all the stories which have been selected for this volume.

There is a final danger from which I may not have been immune, and that is of suggesting that chronological order is synonymous with progress. There has certainly been a progress in the quality of fiction produced in Canada in the last century and a quarter, and the more recent writers have had the benefit of the mistakes and discoveries of their predecessors; but it would be rash indeed to suggest that any of our contemporaries surpass Thomas Chandler Haliburton, or even E. W. Thomson at his very best. One thing which I should like to feel this volume will help to prove is that there is a literary tradition of some value in this country, that the names of Haliburton and Howe and *The Literary Garland* could be and should be a far more vital part of our contemporary cultural conscious-ness than they are. We have, in other words, a literary inheri-tance for which to care.

JOSEPH HOWE

ALTHOUGH JOSEPH HOWE is not remembered primarily as a writer of prose fiction—indeed, as far as is known, the story which follows is the only one which he wrote—he was in so many ways a pioneer in the establishment of a distinctive Canadian culture that it is fitting he should be the first author to appear in this anthology. He was born in 1804, eight years after Haliburton, but it was Howe who made Haliburton's literary career possible by printing the Clockmaker sketches in his weekly paper, the *Novascotian*.

Joseph Howe was the son of John Howe, a Boston editor who, from Loyalist principles, emigrated to Halifax at the outbreak of the American Revolutionary War. The son, born in Halifax, was apprenticed to the printing business in his early teens, and in 1828 became owner and editor of the *Novascotian,* a post he continued to hold until 1841. Meanwhile, in 1835, he established the principle of a free press in Canada by eloquently and successfully defending himself against a charge of libel for having dared to criticize the city magistrates. In 1836 he was elected to the Legislative Assembly of Nova Scotia, and held his seat until 1863. He was a leader in the movement for responsible government, but at first opposed Confederation because he feared for the rights of his native province. Won round to the federal proposals, he was a member of Sir John A. Macdonald's first Canadian cabinet but never felt at ease with the arrangement and soon resigned. In 1873 he was honoured by appointment to the Lieutenant-Governorship, but died within a few weeks of taking office.

As a busy man of affairs, Howe had little leisure for the creation of literature. His "literary remains", published posthumously in 1874 as *Poems and Essays,* include some quite interesting poems in the mid eighteenth century manner, a number of essays originally prepared and delivered as speeches, and the one story which follows.

"The Locksmith of Philadelphia", like Howe's poems, is an eighteenth century literary exercise. In its formal, leisurely style, its overt didacticism tinged with sentiment, its strong middle-class feeling, it is such a story as might have graced Johnson's *Rambler*

1

or Washington Irving's *Salmagundi*. Standing at the first of this volume, it is a useful reminder of the fact that Canadian literature did not start from scratch but evolved naturally out of the literature of eighteenth century England.

There are several book-length studies of Howe: *The Tribune of Nova Scotia, a Chronicle of Joseph Howe* by W. L. Grant (Toronto, 1920), and *Joseph Howe; A Study in Achievement and Frustration* by J. A. Roy (Toronto, 1935). A useful magazine article entitled "Joseph Howe as Man of Letters", by David Munroe, appeared in the January, 1941 issue of *The Dalhousie Review*.

The Locksmith of Philadelphia

IN THE SOBER looking city of Philadelphia, there dwelt, some years ago, an ingenious and clever mechanic named Amos Sparks, by trade a locksmith. Nature had blest him with a peculiar turn for the branch of business to which he had been bred. Not only was he skilled in the manufacture and repair of the various articles that in America are usually regarded as "in the locksmith line," but, prompted by a desire to master the more abstruse intricacies of the business, he had studied it so attentively, and with such distinguished success that his proficiency was the theme of admiration, not only with his customers and the neighbourhood, but all who took an interest in mechanical contrivances in the adjoining towns. His counter was generally strewn with all kinds of fastenings for doors, trunks, and desks, which nobody but himself could open; and no lock was ever presented to Amos that he could not pick in a very short time. Like many men of talent in other departments Amos Sparks was poor. Though a very industrious and prudent man, with a small and frugal family, he merely eked out a comfortable existence but never seemed to accumulate property. Whether it was that he was not of the race of money-grubs, whose instinctive desire of accumulation forces them to earn and hoard without a thought beyond the mere means of acquisition, or whether the time occupied by the prosecution of new inquiries into still undiscovered regions of his favourite pursuit, and in conversation with those who came to inspect and admire the fruits of his ingenuity, were the cause of his poverty, we cannot undertake to determine; but perhaps various causes combined to keep his finances low, and it was quite as notorious in the city that Amos Sparks was a poor man, as that he was an ingenious and decent mechanic. But his business was sufficient for the supply of his wants and those of his family, so he studied and worked on and was content.

It happened that in the autumn of 18—, a merchant in the city, whose business was rather extensive, and who had been bustling about the Quay, and on board his vessels all the morning, returned to his counting house to lodge several thousand dollars in the Philadelphia Bank, to retire some paper falling due that day, when to his surprise he found that he had either lost or mislaid the key of his iron chest. After diligent search with no success he was led to conclude that, in drawing out his handkerchief he had dropped the key in the street or perhaps into the dock. What was to be done? It was one o'clock, the Bank closed at three, and there was no time to advertise the key, or to muster so large a sum as that required. In his perplexity the merchant thought of the poor locksmith; he had often heard of Amos Sparks; the case seemed one peculiarly adapted to a trial of his powers, and being a desperate one, if he could not furnish a remedy, where else was there a reasonable expectation of succor? A clerk was hurried off for Amos, and, having explained the difficulty, speedily reappeared, followed by the locksmith with his implements in his hand. A few minutes sufficed to open the chest, and the astonished merchant glanced from the rolls of bank notes and piles of coin strewn along the bottom, to the clock in the corner of his office, which told him that he had still three quarters of an hour, with a feeling of delight and exultation, like one who had escaped from an unexpected dilemma by a lucky thought, and who felt that his credit was secure even from a momentary breath of suspicion. He fancied he felt generous as well as glad, and determined that it should be a cash transaction.

"How much is to pay, Amos?" said he, thrusting his hand into his pocket.

"Five dollars, Sir," said Sparks.

"Five dollars? Why, you are mad, man; you have not been five minutes doing the job. Come." (The genuine spirit of traffic, overcoming the better feelings which had momentary possession of his bosom,) "I'll give you five shillings."

"It is true," replied the locksmith, "that much time has not been employed; but remember how many long years I have been learning to do such a job in five minutes or even to do it at all. A doctor's visit may last but one minute; the service he renders may be but doubtful when all is done, and yet his fee would be as great, if not greater than mine. You should be willing to purchase my skill, humble as it may be, as you would purchase any other commodity in the market, by what it is worth to you."

"Worth to me," said the merchant with a sneer, "well, I think it was worth five shillings. I could have got a new key made for that, or perhaps, might have found the old one."

"But could you have got the one made or found the other, in time to retire your notes at the Bank? Had I been disposed to wrong you, taking advantage of your haste and perplexity I might have bargained for a much larger sum, and as there is not another man in the city who could have opened the chest, you would gladly have given me double the amount I now claim."

"Double the amount! Why, the man's a fool. Here are five shillings," said the merchant, holding them in his hand with the air of a rich man taking advantage of a poor one who could not help himself; "and if you do not choose to take them, why, you may sue as soon as you please, for my time is too precious just now to spend in a matter so trifling."

"I never sued a man in my life," said Sparks, "and I have lost much by my forbearance. But," added he, the trodden worm of a meek spirit beginning to recoil, "you are rich—are able to pay, and although I will not sue you, pay you shall."

The words were scarcely spoken when he dashed down the lid of the chest, and in a moment the strong staples were firmly clasped by the bolts below, and the gold and bank notes were hidden as effectually as though they had vanished like the ill-gotten hoards in the fairy tale.

The merchant stood aghast. He looked at Amos, and then darted a glance at the clock. The hand was within twenty minutes of three, and seemed posting over the figures with the speed of light. What was to be done? At first he tried to bully, but it would not do. Amos told him if he had sustained any injury, "he might sue as soon as he pleased, for his time was too precious just now to be wasted in trifling affairs," and, with a face of unruffled composure, he turned on his heel and was leaving the office.

The merchant called him back: he had no alternative, his credit was at stake, half the city would swear he had lost the key to gain time, and because there was no money in the chest; he was humbled by the necessity of the case, and handing forth the five dollars, "There Sparks," said he, "take your money and let us have no more words."

"I must have ten dollars now," replied the locksmith; "you would have taken advantage of a poor man; and besides opening your strong box there I have a lesson to give you which is well worth a trifling sum. You would not only have deprived me of what had been fairly earned, but have tempted me into a lawsuit which would have ruined my family. You will never in future presume upon your wealth in your dealings with the poor without thinking of the locksmith, and these five dollars may save you much sin and much repentance."

This homily, besides being preached in a tone of calm deliberation, which left no room to hope for any abatement, had exhausted another minute or two of the time already so precious; for the minutes, like the Sibyl's books, increased in value as they diminished in number. The merchant hurriedly counted out the ten dollars, which Amos deliberately inspected to see that they belonged to no broken Bank, and then deposited in his breeches pocket.

"For heaven's sake, be quick man, I would not have the Bank close before this money is paid for fifty dollars," exclaimed the merchant.

"I thought so," was the locksmith's grave reply; but not being a malicious or vindictive man, and satisfied with the punishment already inflicted, he delayed no longer, but opened the chest, giving its owner time to seize the cash and reach the Bank, after a rapid flight, a few minutes before it closed.

About a month after this affair the Philadelphia Bank was robbed of coin and notes to the amount of fifty thousand dollars. The bars of a window had been cut, and the vault entered so ingeniously, that it was evident that the burglar had possessed, besides daring courage, a good deal of mechanical skill. The police scoured the city and country round about, but no clue to the discovery of the robber could be traced. Everybody who had anything to lose, felt that daring and ingenious felons were abroad who might probably pay them a visit; all were therefore interested in their discovery and conviction. Suspicions at length began to settle on Sparks. But yet his poverty and known integrity seemed to give them the lie. The story of the iron chest, which the merchant had hitherto been ashamed, and Amos too forgiving, to tell, for the latter did not care to set the town laughing, even at the man who had wronged him, now began to be noised abroad. The merchant, influenced by a vindictive spirit, had whispered it to the Directors of the Bank, with sundry shrugs and innuendos, and, of course, with all sorts of extravagant variations and additions. Amos thought for several days that some of his neighbours looked and acted rather oddly, and he missed one or two who used to drop in and chat almost every afternoon, but, not suspecting for a moment that there was any cause for altered behaviour, these matters made but a slight impression on his mind. In all such cases the person most interested is the last to hear disagreeable news; and the first hint that the locksmith got of the universal suspicion, was from the officer of police who came with a party of constables to search his premises. Astonishment and grief were of course the portion of Amos and his family for that day. The first shock to a household who had derived, even amidst their humble poverty, much satisfaction from the possession of a good name —a property that they had been taught to value above all earthly treasures—may be easily conceived. To have defrauded a neighbour of sixpence would have been a meanness no one of them would have been guilty of, but fifty thousand dollars, the immensity of the sum seemed to clothe the suspicion with a weight of terror that nearly pressed them to the earth. They clung to each other with bruised and fluttered spirits while the search was proceeding, and it was not until it was completed and the officer declared himself satisfied that there was none of the missing property on the premises, that they began to rally and look calmly at the circumstances which seemed, for the moment, to menace the peace and security they had previously enjoyed.

"Cheer up, my darlings," said Amos, who was the first to recover the sobriety of thought that usually characterized him—"cheer up, all will yet be well; it is impossible that this unjust suspicion can long hover about us. A life of honesty and fair dealing will not be without its reward: there was perhaps something in my trade, and the skill which long practice had given me in it, that naturally enough led the credulous, the thoughtless, and perhaps the mischievous, if any such there be connected with this enquiry, to look towards us. But the real authors of this outrage will probably be discovered soon; for a fraud so extensive will make all parties vigilant, and if not, why then, when our neighbours see us toiling at our usual occupations, with no evidence of increased wealth or lavish expenditures on our persons or at our board, and remember how many years we were so occupied and so attired, without a suspicion of wrong doing, even in small matters, attaching to us, there will be good sense, and good feeling enough in the city to do us justice."

There were sound sense and much consolation in this
reasoning: the obvious probabilities of the case were in favour
of the fulfilment of the locksmith's expectations. But a scene
of trial and excitement, of prolonged agony and hope deferred,
lay before him, the extent of which it would have been
difficult if not impossible for him then to have foreseen.
Foiled in the search, the Directors of the Bank sent one of
their number to negotiate with Amos; to offer him a large sum
of money, and a guarantee from further molestation, if he
would confess, restore the property, and give up his accom-
plices, if any there were. It was in vain that he protested
his innocence, and avowed his abhorrence of the crime;
the Banker rallied him on his assumed composure, and
threatened him with consequences, until the locksmith, who
had been unaccustomed to dialogues founded on the pre-
sumption that he was a villain, ordered his tormentor out of
his shop, with the spirit of a man who, though poor, was
resolved to preserve his self-respect, and protect the sanctity
of his dwelling from impertinent and insulting intrusion.

The Banker retired, baffled and threatening vengeance.
A consultation was held, and it was finally decided to arrest
Sparks, and commit him to prison, in the hope that by shutting him up, and separating him from his family and accom-
plices, he would be less upon his guard against the collection
of evidence necessary to a conviction, and perhaps be
frightened into terms, or induced to make a full confession.
This was a severe blow to the family. They could have borne
much together, for mutual counsel and sympathy can soothe
many of the ills of life; but to be divided—to have the strongest
mind around which the feebler ones had been accustomed to
cling, carried away captive to brood, in solitary confinement,
on an unjust accusation, was almost too much when coupled
with the cloud of suspicion that seemed to gather about their
home and infect the very air they breathed. The privations
forced upon them by the want of the locksmith's earnings
were borne without a murmur, and out of the little that could
be mustered, a portion was always reserved to buy some

trifling but unexpected comfort or luxury to carry to the prison.

Some months having passed without Sparks having made any confession, or the discovery of any new fact whereby his guilt might be established, his persecutors found themselves reluctantly compelled to bring him to trial. They had not a tittle of evidence, except some strange locks and implements found in the shop, and which proved the talent but not the guilt of the mechanic. Yet these were so various, and executed with such elaborate art, and such an evident expenditure of labour that but few, either of the judges, jury, or spectators, could be persuaded that a man so poor would have devoted himself so sedulously to such an employment, unless he had some other object in view than mere instruction or amusement. His friends and neighbours gave him an excellent character; but on their cross-examination all admitted his entire devotion to his favourite pursuit. The counsel for the Bank exerted himself with consummate ability; calculating in some degree on the state of the public mind, and the influence which vague rumours, coupled with the evidence of the mechanic's handicraft exhibited in court, might have on the mind of the jury, he dwelt upon every ward and winding, on the story of the iron chest, on the evident poverty of the locksmith, and yet his apparent waste of time, if all this work were not intended to ensure success in some great design. He believed that a verdict would be immediately followed by a confession, for he thought Amos guilty, and he succeeded in making the belief pretty general among his audience. Some of the jury were half inclined to speculate on the probabilities of a confession, and, swept away by a current of suspicion, were not indisposed to convict without evidence, in order that the result might do credit to their penetration. But this was impossible, even in an American Court in the good old times of which we write. Hanging persons on suspicion, and acquitting felons because the mob think murder no crime, are modern inventions. The charge of the Judge was clear and decisive: he admitted that there were grounds

for suspicion—that there were circumstances connected with
the prisoner's peculiar mode of life that were not reconcilable
with the lowness of his finances; but yet, of direct testimony
there was not a vestige, and of circumstantial evidence there
were not only links wanting in the chain, but in fact there
was not a single link extending beyond the locksmith's
dwelling. Sparks was accordingly acquitted; but as no other
clue was found to direct suspicion, it still lay upon him like
a cloud. The vindictive merchant and the dissatisfied bankers
did not hesitate to declare, that, although the charge could
not be legally brought home, they had no doubt whatever
of his guilt. This opinion was taken up and reiterated, until
thousands who were too careless to investigate the story,
were satisfied that Amos was a rogue. How could the character
of a poor man hold out against the deliberate slanders of so
many rich ones?

Amos rejoiced in his acquittal as one who felt that the
jury had performed a solemn duty faithfully, and who was
glad to find that his personal experience had strengthened,
rather than impaired, his reliance on the tribunals of his
country. He embraced his family, as one snatched from
great responsibility and peril, and his heart overflowed with
thankfulness, when at night they were all once more assembled
round the fireside, the scene of so much happiness and unity
in other days. But yet Amos felt that though acquitted by
the jury he was not by the town. He saw that, in the faces
of some of the jury and most of the audience, which he was
too shrewd an observer to misunderstand. He wished it were
otherwise; but he was contented to take his chance of some
subsequent revelation, and if it came not, of living down the
foul suspicion which Providence had permitted, for some wise
purpose, to hover for a while around his name.

But Amos had never thought of how he was to live. The
cold looks, averted faces, and rude scandal of the neighbourhood, could be borne, because really there was some excuse
to be found in the circumstances, and because he hoped that
there would be a joyful ending of it all at some future day.

But the loss of custom first opened his eyes to his real situation. No work came to his shop. He made articles but could not sell them; and, as the little money he had saved was necessarily exhausted in the unavoidable expenses of the trial, the family found it impossible, with the utmost exertion and economy, to meet their current outlay; one article of furniture after another was reluctantly sacrificed, or some little comfort abridged, until, at the end of months of degradation and absolute distress, their bare board was spread within bare walls, and it became necessary to beg, to starve, or to remove. The latter expedient had often been suggested in family consultations, and it is one that in America is the common remedy for all great calamities. If a man fails in a city on the seaboard, he removes to Ohio; if a clergyman offers violence to a fair parishioner, he removes to Albany, where he soon becomes "very much respected"; if a man in Michigan whips a bowie knife between a neighbour's ribs, he removes to Missouri. So that in fact a removal is "the sovereign'st thing on earth" for all great and otherwise overwhelming evils. The Sparks' would have removed, but they clung to the hope that the real perpetrator would be discovered and the mystery cleared up: and besides, they thought it would be an acknowledgment of the justice of the general suspicion if they turned their backs and fled. They lived upon the expectation of the renewed confidence and companionship of old friends and neighbours, when Providence should deem it right to draw the veil aside. But to live longer in Philadelphia was impossible, and the whole family prepared to depart; their effects were easily transported, and, as they had had no credit since the arrest, there was nobody to prevent them from seeking a livelihood elsewhere.

Embarking in one of the river boats they passed up the Schuylkill and settled at Norristown. The whole family being industrious and obliging, they soon began to gather comforts around them; and as these were not embittered by the cold looks and insulting sneers of the vicinage, they were comparatively happy for a time. But even here there was for them no permanent place of rest. A merchant passing through Norristown on his way from the capital to the Blue Mountains, recognized Sparks and told somebody he knew that he wished the community joy of having added to the number of its inhabitants the notorious locksmith of Philadelphia. The news soon spread, the family found that they were shunned, as they had formerly been by those who had known them longer than the good people of Norristown, and had a fair prospect of starvation opening before them. They removed again. This time there was no inducement to linger, for they had no local attachment to detain them. They crossed the mountains, and descending into the vale of the Susquehanna, pitched their tent at Sunbury. Here the same temporary success excited the same hopes, only to be blighted in the bud by the breath of slander, which seemed so widely circulated as to leave them hardly any asylum within the limits of the State. We need not enumerate the different towns and villages in which they essayed to gain a livelihood, were suspected, shunned and foiled. They had nearly crossed the State in its whole length, been driven from Pittsburgh, were slowly wending their way further west, and were standing on the high ground overlooking Middleton, as though doubtful if there was to be rest for the soles of their feet even there; they hesitated to try a new experiment. Sparks seated himself on a stone beneath a spreading sycamore—his family clustered round him on the grass—they had travelled far and were weary; and without speaking a word, as their eyes met and they thought of their prolonged sufferings and slender hopes, they burst into a flood of tears, in which Sparks, burying his face in the golden locks of the sweet girl who bowed her head upon his knee, joined audibly.

At length, wiping away his tears, and checking the rising sobs that shook his manly bosom, "God's will be done, my children," said the locksmith, "we cannot help weeping, but let us not murmur; our Heavenly Father has tried and is trying us, doubtless for some wise purpose, and if we are still to be wanderers and outcasts on the earth let us never lose sight of his promise, which assures us of an eternal refuge in a place where the wicked cease from troubling and the weary are at rest. I was, perhaps, too proud of that skill of mine; too apt to plume myself upon it above others whose gifts had been less abundant; to take all the credit and give none to Him by whom the human brain is wrought into mysterious adaptation to particular sciences and pursuits. My error has been that of wiser and greater men, who have been made to feel that what we cherish as the richest of earthly blessings sometimes turns out a curse."

To dissipate the gloom which hung over the whole party and beguile the half hour that they intended to rest in that sweet spot, Mrs. Sparks drew out a Philadelphia newspaper, which somebody had given her upon the road, and called their attention to the Deaths and Marriages that they might see what changes were taking place in a city that still interested them though they were banished for ever from its borders. She had hardly opened the paper when her eye glanced at an article which she was too much excited to read. Amos, wondering at the emotion displayed, gently disengaged the paper and read "BANK ROBBERY — SPARKS NOT THE MAN." His own feelings were as powerfully affected as his wife's, but his nerves were stronger, and he read out, to an audience whose ears devoured every syllable of the glad tidings, an account of the conviction and execution of a wretch in Albany, who had confessed among other daring and heinous crimes, the robbery of the Philadelphia Bank, accounting for the dissipation of the property, and entirely exonerating Sparks, whose face he had never seen. These were "glad tidings of great joy" to the weary wayfarers beneath the sycamore, whose hearts overflowed with thankfulness to the Father of Mercies, who had given them strength to bear the burden of affliction, and had lifted it from their spirits ere they had been crushed beneath the weight. Their resolution to return to their native city was formed at once, and before a week had passed they were slowly journeying to the capital of the State.

Meanwhile an extraordinary revulsion of feeling had taken

place at Philadelphia. Newspapers and other periodicals, which had formerly been loud in condemnation of the locksmith, now blazoned abroad the robber's confession, wondered how any man could ever have been for a moment suspected upon such evidence as was adduced at the trial; drew pictures of the domestic felicity once enjoyed by the Sparks, and then painted, partly from what was known of the reality and partly from imagination, their sufferings, privations, and wrongs, in the pilgrimage they had performed in fleeing from an unjust but damnatory accusation. The whole city rang with the story; old friends and neighbours who had been the first to cut them, now became the loud and vehement partisans of the family. Everybody was anxious to know where they were. Some reported that they had perished in the woods; others that they had been burnt on a prairie; while not a few believed that the locksmith, driven to desperation, had first destroyed the family and then himself. All these stories of course created as much excitement as the robbery of the Bank had done before, only that this time the tide set the other way; and by the time the poor locksmith and his family, who had been driven like vagabonds from the city, approached its suburbs, they were met, congratulated and followed by thousands, to whom, from the strange vicissitudes of their lot, they had become objects of interest. In fact, theirs was almost a triumphal entry, and as the public always likes to have a victim, they were advised on all hands to bring action against the Directors of the Bank; large damages would, it was affirmed, be given, and the Bank deserved to suffer for the causeless ruin brought on a poor but industrious family.

Sparks was reluctant to engage in any such proceedings; his character was vindicated, his business restored; he occupied his own shop, and his family were comfortable and content. But the current of public opinion was too strong for him. All Philadelphia had determined that the bankers should pay. An eminent lawyer volunteered to conduct the suit and make no charge if a liberal verdict were not obtained. The locksmith pondered the matter well: his own wrongs he freely forgave; but he thought that there had been a readiness to secure the interests of a wealthy corporation by blasting the prospects of a humble mechanic, which, for the good of society, ought not to pass unrebuked; he felt that the moral effect of such a prosecution would be salutary, teaching the rich not to presume too far upon their affluence, and cheering the heart of the poor while suffering unmerited persecution. The suit was commenced and urged to trial, notwithstanding several attempts at compromise on behalf of the Bank. The pleadings on both sides were able and ingenious; but the counsel for the plaintiff had a theme worthy of the fine powers he possessed; and at the close of a pathetic and eloquent declamation, the audience, which had formerly condemned Amos in their hearts without evidence, were melted to tears by a recital of his sufferings; and when the jury returned with a verdict of Ten Thousand Dollars damages against the Bank, the locksmith was honoured by a ride home on their shoulders, amidst a hurricane of cheers.

THOMAS CHANDLER HALIBURTON

THOMAS CHANDLER HALIBURTON was born at Windsor, Nova Scotia, on December 17, 1796. He was educated at King's College, Windsor, graduating in 1815. After a brief period in England, he was called to the Bar of Nova Scotia in 1820 and opened a law practice in Annapolis Royal. In 1826 he was elected to represent Annapolis in the Legislative Assembly of Nova Scotia, and in 1829 he was appointed a judge of the Court of Common Pleas. His successful career as a jurist was climaxed by his appointment to the Supreme Court of his native province in 1841. The last nine years of his life, from 1856 to 1865, were spent in England, where he was honoured by an Oxford D.C.L. (1858) and by election to the British House of Commons (1859).

Haliburton began his literary career as an historian, publishing the first history of Nova Scotia in 1829, but it is as a humorist, and above all as the creator of Sam Slick, that he is remembered. The Sam Slick papers first appeared in the pages of Joseph Howe's magazine, *The Novascotian,* in 1835 and 1836, and were published in book form in Halifax and London in 1837. They immediately earned for their author an international reputation. He published several sequels to the Sam Slick series, and a number of other books, but none of them reach the level attained by his first effort.

Haliburton is an interesting figure for the literary historian. On the one hand, he points backward to the satirical prose of eighteenth century England: his hatred of sham, spurious enthusiasm and pedantry, and the balanced progression of his neatly turned sentences, remind us of Swift and Addison, Smollett and Johnson. On the other hand, he has been called, and with some justice, the father of American humour, and from this aspect his work points forward to that of Artemus Ward, Mark Twain and Stephen Leacock.

As a writer he is not without faults. There is little care for structure in his work, except the structure of the individual sentence and occasionally of the individual anecdote. He is rather repetitive, harping almost constantly upon two themes: the sloth of his fellow-countrymen and the surpassing boastfulness of Yankees. He has ample gifts to compensate for these deficiencies, however: an apparently inexhaustible fund of anecdotes, a striking gift of thumb-nail portraiture, the capacity to turn a neat phrase, and a vitality which imparts interest even to his less successful productions. The first native Canadian writer to achieve a substantial measure of fame abroad, he remains one of the small number of our writers for whom one feels confident in predicting a permanent, if secondary, place in the history of the literature of the English-speaking world.

The best study of Haliburton is that by V. L. O. Chittick (New York, 1924). The selection which follows consists of the first two chapters of *Sam Slick*.

Sam Slick the Clockmaker

I WAS ALWAYS well mounted: I am fond of a horse, and always piqued myself on having the fastest trotter in the Province. I have made no great progress in the world; I feel doubly, therefore, the pleasure of not being surpassed on the road. I never feel so well or cheerful as on horseback, for there is something exhilarating in quick motion; and, old as I am, I feel a pleasure in making any person whom I meet on the way put his horse to the full gallop, to keep pace with my trotter. Poor Ethiop! you recollect him, how he was wont to lay back his ears on his arched neck, and push away from all competition? He is done, poor fellow! the spavin spoiled his speed, and he now roams at large upon "my farm at Truro." Mohawk never failed me till this summer.

I pride myself—you may laugh at such childish weakness in a man of my age—but still, I pride myself in taking the conceit out of coxcombs I meet on the road, and on the ease with which I can leave a fool behind, whose nonsense disturbs my solitary musings.

On my last journey to Fort Lawrence, as the beautiful view of Colchester had just opened upon me, and as I was contemplating its richness and exquisite scenery, a tall thin man, with hollow cheeks and bright, twinkling black eyes, on a good bay horse, somewhat out of condition, overtook me; and drawing up, said, "I guess you started early this morning, sir?"

"I did, sir," I replied.

"You did not come from Halifax, I presume, sir, did you?" in a dialect too rich to be mistaken as genuine Yankee. "And which way may you be travelling?" asked my inquisitive companion.

"To Fort Lawrence."

"Ah!" said he, "so am I; it is in my circuit."

The word *circuit* sounded so professional, I looked again at him, to ascertain whether I had ever seen him before, or whether I had met with one of those nameless, but innumerable arms of the law, who now flourish in every district of the Province. There was a keenness about his eye, and an acuteness of expression, much in favour of the law; but the dress, and general bearing of the man, made against the supposition. His was not the coat of a man who can afford to wear an old coat, nor was it one of "Tempest and More's," that distinguish country lawyers from country boobies. His clothes were well made, and of good materials, but looked as if their owner had shrunk a little since they were made for him; they hung somewhat loose on him. A large brooch, and some superfluous seals and gold keys, which ornamented his outward man, looked "New England" like. A visit to the States, had perhaps, I thought, turned this Colchester beau into a Yankee fop. Of what consequence was it to me who he was? In either case I had nothing to do with him, and I desired neither his acquaintance nor his company. Still I could not but ask myself, who can this man be?

"I am not aware," said I, "that there is a court sitting at this time at Cumberland."

"Nor am I," said my friend. What, then, could he have to do with the circuit? It occurred to me he must be a Methodist preacher. I looked again, but his appearance again puzzled me. His attire might do, the colour might be suitable, the broad brim not out of place; but there was a want of that staidness of look, that seriousness of countenance, that expression, in short, so characteristic of the clergy.

I could not account for my idle curiosity—a curiosity which, in him, I had the moment before viewed both with suspicion and disgust; but so it was, I felt a desire to know who he could be who was neither lawyer nor preacher, and yet talked of his circuit with the gravity of both. How ridiculous, I thought to myself, is this; I will leave him. Turning towards him, I said I feared I should be late for breakfast, and must therefore bid him good morning. Mohawk felt the pressure of my knees, and away we went at a slapping pace. I congratulated myself on conquering my own curiosity, and on avoiding that of my travelling companion. This, I said to myself, this is the value of a good horse; I patted his neck; I felt proud of him. Presently I heard the steps of the unknown's horse—the clatter increased. Ah, my friend, thought I, it won't do; you should be well mounted if you desire my company. I pushed Mohawk faster, faster, faster—to his best. He outdid himself; he had never trotted so handsomely, so easily, so well.

"I guess that is a pretty considerable smart horse," said the stranger, as he came beside me, and apparently reined in to prevent his horse passing me; "there is not, I reckon, so spry a one on my circuit."

Circuit or no circuit, one thing was settled in my mind—he was a Yankee, and a very impertinent Yankee too. I felt humbled, my pride was hurt, and Mohawk was beaten. To continue this trotting contest was humiliating; I yielded, therefore, before the victory was palpable, and pulled up.

"Yes," continued he, "a horse of pretty considerable good action, and a pretty fair trotter too, I guess." Pride must have a fall; I confess mine was prostrate in the dust. These words cut me to the heart. What! is it come to this, poor Mohawk, that you, the admiration of all but the envious, the great Mohawk, the standard by which all other horses are measured —trots next to Mohawk, only yields to Mohawk, looks like Mohawk—that you are, after all, only a counterfeit, and pronounced by a straggling Yankee to be merely "a pretty fair trotter!"

"If he was trained, I guess that he might be made to do a little more. Excuse me, but if you divide your weight between the knees and the stirrup, rather most on the knee, and rise forward on the saddle, so as to leave a little daylight between you and it, I hope I may never ride this circuit again, if you don't get a mile more an hour out of him."

What! not enough, I mentally groaned, to have my horse beaten, but I must be told that I don't know how to ride him; and that, too, by a Yankee! Aye, there's the rub—a Yankee what? Perhaps a half-bred puppy, half Yankee, half Bluenose. As there is no escape, I'll try to make out my riding master. "Your circuit?" said I, my looks expressing all the surprise they were capable of, "your circuit, pray what may that be?"

"O," said he, "the eastern circuit; I am on the eastern circuit sir."

"I have heard," said I, feeling that I now had a lawyer to deal with, "that there is a great deal of business on this circuit. Pray, are there many cases of importance?"

"There is a pretty fair business to be done, at least there has been, but the cases are of no great value; we do not make much of them, we get them up very easy, but they don't bring much profit." What a beast thought I, is this! and what a curse to the country, to have such an unfeeling, pettifogging rascal practicing in it! a horse jockey, too—what a finished character! I'll try him on that branch of his business.

"That is a superior animal you are mounted on," said I; "I seldom meet one that can travel with mine."

"Yes," said he coolly, "a considerable fair traveller, and most particular good bottom." I hesitated; this man, who talks with such unblushing effrontery of getting up cases, and making profit out of them, cannot be offended at the question —yes, I will put it to him.

"Do you feel an inclination to part with him?"

"I never part with a horse, sir, that suits me," said he. "I am fond of a horse: I don't like to ride in the dust after every

one I meet, and I allow no man to pass me but when I choose."
Is it possible, I thought, that he can know me—that he has
heard of my foible, and is quizzing me? or have I this feeling
in common with him?

"But," continued I, "you might supply yourself again."

"Not on this circuit, I guess," said he, "nor yet in Campbell's circuit."

"Campbell's circuit—pray, sir, what is that?"

"That," said he, "is the western; and Lampton rides the
shore circuit; and as for the people on the shore, they know
so little of horses that, Lampton tells me, a man from Ayles-
ford once sold a hornless ox there, whose tail he had cut and
nicked, for a horse of the Goliath breed."

"I should think," said I, "that Mr. Lampton must have no
lack of cases among such enlightened clients."

"Clients, sir!" said my friend, "Mr. Lampton is not a
lawyer."

"I beg pardon, I thought you said he rode the circuit."

"We call it a circuit," said the stranger, who seemed by no
means flattered by the mistake; "we divide the Province, as in
the almanac, into circuits, in each of which we separately carry
on our business of manufacturing and selling clocks. There
are few, I guess," said the Clockmaker, "who go upon *tick* as
much as we do, who have so little use for lawyers; if attorneys
could wind a man up again, after he has been fairly run down,
I guess they'd be a pretty harmless sort of folks."

This explanation restored my good humour, and as I could
not quit my companion, and he did not feel disposed to leave
me, I made up my mind to travel with him to Fort Lawrence,
the limit of his circuit. I had heard of Yankee clock peddlers,
tin peddlers, and Bible peddlers, especially of him who sold
Polyglot Bibles (*all in English*) to the amount of sixteen
thousand pounds. The house of every substantial farmer had
three substantial ornaments: a wooden clock, a tin reflector,
and a Polyglot Bible. How is it that an American can sell his
wares, at whatever price he pleases, where a Bluenose would

fail to make a sale at all? I will enquire of the Clockmaker the secret of his success.

"What a pity it is, Mr. Slick"—for such was his name—"what a pity it is," said I, "that you, who are so successful in teaching these people the value of clocks, could not also teach them the value of time."

"I guess," said he, "they have got that ring to grow on their horns yet, which every four-year-old has in our country. We reckon hours and minutes to be dollars and cents. They do nothing in these parts but eat, drink, smoke, sleep, ride about, lounge at taverns, make speeches at temperance meetings, and talk about 'House of Assembly.' If a man don't hoe his corn, and he don't get a crop, he says it is owing to the bank; and if he runs into debt and is sued, why, he says the lawyers are a curse to the country. They are a most idle set of folks, I tell you."

"But how is it," said I, "that you manage to sell such an immense number of clocks, which certainly cannot be called necessary articles, among a people with whom there seems to be so great a scarcity of money?" Mr. Slick paused, as if considering the propriety of answering the question, and looking me in the face, said in a confidential tone—

"Why, I don't care if I do tell you, for the market is glutted, and I shall quit this circuit. It is done by a knowledge of *soft sawder* and *human natur'*. But here is Deacon Flint's," said he; "I have but one clock left, and I guess I will sell it to him."

At the gate of a most comfortable looking farm-house stood Deacon Flint, a respectable old man, who had understood the value of time better than most of his neighbours, if one might judge from the appearance of everything about him. After the usual salutation, an invitation to "alight" was accepted by Mr. Slick, who said he wished to take leave of Mrs. Flint before he left Colchester.

We had hardly entered the house, before the Clockmaker pointed to the view from the window, and, addressing himself to me, said, "If I was to tell them in Connecticut there was such a farm as this away down East here in Nova Scotia, they wouldn't believe me. Why, there ain't such a location in all New England. The Deacon has a hundred acres of dyke"—

"Seventy," said the Deacon, "only seventy."

"Well, seventy; but then there is your fine deep bottom, why I could run a ramrod into it"—

"Interval, we call it," said the Deacon, who though evidently pleased at this eulogium, seemed to wish the experiment of the ramrod to be tried in the right place.

"Well, interval, if you please—though Professor Eleazer Cumstock, in his work on Ohio, calls them bottoms—is just as good as dyke. Then there is that water privilege, worth three or four thousand dollars, twice as good as what Governor Cass paid fifteen thousand dollars for. I wonder, Deacon, you don't put up a carding mill on it; the same works would carry a turning lathe, a shingle machine, a circular saw, grind bark, and"—

"Too old," said the Deacon, "too old for all those speculations"—

"Old!" repeated the Clockmaker, "not you; why you are worth half a dozen of the young men we see, nowadays; you are young enough to have"—here he said something in a lower tone of voice, which I did not distinctly hear; but whatever it was, the Deacon was pleased; he smiled, and said he did not think of such things now.

"But your beasts, dear me, your beasts must be put in and have a feed;" saying which, he went out to order them to be taken to the stable.

As the old gentleman closed the door after him, Mr. Slick drew near to me, and said in an undertone, "That is what I call 'soft sawder.' An Englishman would pass that man as a sheep passes a hog in a pasture, without looking at him; or," said he, looking rather archly, "if he was mounted on a pretty smart horse, I guess he'd trot away, if he could. Now I find"— Here his lecture on "soft sawder" was cut short by the entrance of Mrs. Flint.

"Jist come to say good-bye, Mrs. Flint."

"What, have you sold all your clocks?"

"Yes, and very low too, for money is scarce, and I wish to close the consarn; no, I am wrong in saying all, for I have just one left. Neighbour Steel's wife asked to have the refusal of it, but I guess I won't sell it; I had but two of them, this one and the feller of it, that I sold Governor Lincoln. General Green, the Secretary of State for Maine, said he'd give me fifty dollars for this here one—it has composition wheels and patent axles, is a beautiful article, a real first chop, no mistake, genuine superfine—but I guess I'll take it back; and besides, Squire Hawk might think kinder hard, that I did not give him the offer."

"Dear me!" said Mrs. Flint, "I should like to see it; where is it?"

"It is in a chest of mine over the way, at Tom Tape's store. I guess he can ship it on to Eastport."

"That's a good man," said Mrs. Flint, "jist let's look at it."

Mr. Slick, willing to oblige, yielded to these entreaties, and soon produced the clock—a gaudy, highly varnished, trumpery looking affair. He placed it on the chimney-piece, where its beauties were pointed out and duly appreciated by Mrs. Flint, whose admiration was about ending in a proposal, when Mr. Flint returned from giving his directions about the care of the horses. The Deacon praised the clock; he too thought it a handsome one; but the Deacon was a prudent man; he had a watch; he was sorry, but he had no occasion for a clock.

"I guess you're in the wrong furrow this time, Deacon, it ain't for sale," said Mr. Slick; "and if it was, I reckon neighbour Steel's wife would have it, for she gave me no peace about it." Mrs. Flint said that Mr. Steel had enough to do, poor man, to pay his interest, without buying clocks for his wife.

"It is no consarn of mine," said Mr. Slick, "as long as he pays me, what he has to do; but I guess I don't want to sell it, and besides, it comes too high; that clock can't be made at Rhode Island under forty dollars. Why, it ain't possible," said the Clockmaker, in apparent surprise, looking at his watch, "why as I'm alive it is four o'clock, and if I haven't been two hours here. How on airth shall I reach River Philip tonight? I'll tell you what, Mrs. Flint, I'll leave the clock in your care till I return, on my way to the States. I'll set it a going, and put it to the right time."

As soon as this operation was performed, he delivered the key to the Deacon with a sort of serio-comic injunction to wind up the clock every Saturday night, which Mrs. Flint said she would take care should be done, and promised to remind her husband of it, in case he should chance to forget it.

"That," said the Clockmaker, as soon as we were mounted, "that I call 'human natur'!' Now that clock is sold for forty dollars; it cost me just six dollars and fifty cents. Mrs. Flint will never let Mrs. Steel have the refusal, nor will the Deacon learn until I call for the clock, that having once indulged in the use of a superfluity, how difficult it is to give it up. We can do without any article of luxury we have never had, but when once obtained, it is not in 'human natur'' to surrender it voluntarily. Of fifteen thousand sold by myself and partners in this province, twelve thousand were left in this manner, and only ten clocks were ever returned; when we called for them they invariably kept them. We trust to 'soft sawder' to get them into the house, and to 'human natur',' that they never come out of it."

SUSANNA MOODIE

MRS. SUSANNA MOODIE (née Strickland) was a cultured English-woman who emigrated to Canada with her husband, a British army officer, in 1831. Born at Reydon Hall, Suffolk, England, in 1803, she read widely as a girl in the literature of the eighteenth century, and on her arrival in Canada was quick to see that the new country offered a wealth of material for the exercise of her literary inclinations. After a brief stay on a farm near Port Hope, she and her husband settled in the backwoods of Ontario, in the region north of Peterborough, where they spent several strenuous years clearing a homestead. Their pioneering hardships and adventures Mrs. Moodie recorded accurately and wittily in her masterpiece of documentary prose, *Roughing It in the Bush* (1853). Many of the sketches which eventually appeared in this book were first printed in *The Literary Garland,* the first literary periodical to have a prolonged life in Canada, and to which Mrs. Moodie was one of the first and most consistent contributors. Her husband played a prominent part in suppressing the Rebellion of 1837—interesting references to this uprising may be found in her book, notably in the sketch entitled "A Walk to Dummer"—and was shortly afterwards appointed sheriff of Hastings County. This appointment brought an end to their life in the backwoods, and the Moodies settled in Belleville. It is this move which is referred to in the sketch reprinted below. Mrs. Moodie died in 1885.

Mrs. Moodie was a versatile writer, and her contributions to *The Literary Garland* included contemplative nature lyrics, historical romances, sketches and stories of pioneer life. It is in the last category that her best work is to be found. A keen eye for physical detail, an unfailing perception of and interest in eccentricities of character, a sympathy for misfortune which her sturdy common-sense holds back from sentimentality, and a lean, idiomatic prose style—these gifts ideally fit her for the role of chronicler of the early pioneer days. Judged strictly as short stories, her sketches are somewhat rambling and discursive, but her work was done before the late nineteenth century revival of interest in the short story as a special art form. Like those of Haliburton, her narrative sketches are anecdotes rather than stories in the modern sense of the word, but they are so rich in observation that it would be pedantic to omit them from an anthology of this sort. A useful article on Mrs. Moodie, entitled "Roughing It with the Moodies", was written by Professor E. A. McCourt, and published in the *Queen's Quarterly* in 1945. The sketch which follows appeared originally in *The Literary Garland* in 1847.

Old Woodruff and His Three Wives

THIS must have been an adventurous old man. Three wives! Yes; and he was actually thinking of a fourth when we became acquainted with him. There are no histories so graphic as those which people tell of themselves, for self-love is sure to embellish the most common-place occurrences with a tinge of the marvellous, and everyday events become quite romantic in the mouths of some narrators. Our biographer was not one of these flighty historians. There was not a dash of romance in his composition. Had a phrenologist examined his head, I verily believe that no bump of ideality could have been discovered in the mountain range of skull-land—all about that wondrous region, being a dead flat—the aspect of his head giving you the idea of a copper pot with head closely screwed down. He was a shrewd, humorous looking Yorkshire man, with a sharp red weather-beaten face, a pair of small keen grey eyes, glancing knowingly towards his ridgy nose, or looking obliquely back upon his high cheek bones. A large coarse goodnatured mouth in a great measure relieved the upper portion of his face from the sinister expression which had been acquired by long dealing with the world, and in overcoming the knavery of his species; for Woodruff was not a rogue himself, though very expert in detecting roguery in others. His tall athletic figure, bent as it was with hard labour, gave indication of great personal strength; and his appearance altogether was rather pleasing than otherwise. His manners were frank and easy; and the old man was such an hospitable entertainer that you felt at home with him in a minute.

But to begin at the beginning, for I have a little outrun my story, the picture of the old yeoman coming so forcibly before me that I could not forbear sketching it, prior to introducing the owner to my readers. A bad precedent—but I have not time to step back and go over the ground again.

In the year 1840, a change in my husband's circumstances removed him from a long residence in the back woods, to fill a public situation in a populous town. He went down to B---, some months previous to the removal of his family, to enter upon his new office, and prepare things comfortably for their reception.

He left his forest home in October, and we were to follow with the household wares, and five little children, the first of sleighing. Never did eager British children look for the first violets and primroses of spring with more impatience than my baby boys and girls watched, day after day, for the first snow-flakes that were to form the road to convey them to their absent father and their new home.

"Winter never means to come this year. It will never snow again!" exclaimed my eldest boy, turning from the window on Christmas Day, with the most rueful aspect that ever greeted the broad gay beams of the glorious sun.

It was like a spring day. The little lake in front of the window glittered like a mirror of silver, set in its dark frame of pine woods.

I, too, was wearying for the snow; and was tempted to think that it did not come as early as usual in order to disappoint us. But I kept this to myself, and comforted the expecting child with the oft-repeated assertion, "that it would certainly snow upon the morrow."

But the morrow came and passed away, and many other morrows; and the same mild open weather prevailed. The last night of the old year was ushered in with furious storms of wind and snow. The rafters of our log cabin shook beneath the violence of the gale, which swept up from the lake like a lion roaring for its prey, driving the snow-flakes through every open crevice, of which there were not a few, and powdering the floor till it was as white as the ground without.

"Oh! what a dreadful night," we cried, as we all huddled shivering around the stove. "A person abroad in the woods tonight would be frozen."

"Thank God," I said, "we are not travelling this night to B---."

"But, tomorrow!" said my eldest boy, lifting up his curly head from my lap. "It will be fine tomorrow, and we shall see dear papa again."

In this hope he lay down with the rest, in his little bed upon the floor, and was soon fast asleep. The tempest raged so furiously without that I was fearful that the house would be unroofed; and the night was far advanced when my faithful old Irish servant, Jenny, and myself, retired to bed.

My boy's words were prophetic. That was the last night I ever spent in the bush—in the dear forest home, which I had loved in spite of all the hardships which I had endured since we pitched our tent in the back woods. It was the birthplace of my three boys; the school of high resolve and energetic action, in which we had learned to meet calmly and battle successfully with the ills of life. I did not leave it without many regretful tears, to mingle once more with a world to whose usages, in my long solitude, I had become almost a stranger, and to whose praise or blame I felt alike indifferent.

When the day dawned the whole forest scenery lay glittering in a mantle of dazzling white. The sun shone brightly, the heavens were intensely blue, but the cold was so severe that every article of food had to be thawed before we could get our breakfast. The very blankets that covered us during the night were stiff with our frozen breath.

"I hope the people won't come to take away the furniture today," I cried. "We should be frozen on the long journey."

About noon two sleighs with fine spans of horses made their appearance at the head of the clearing. The snow had been two days in advance of us at B---, and my husband had

sent up the teams to remove us. The children jumped about
and laughed aloud for joy—while old Jenny and myself commenced packing up trunks and boxes as fast as our cold hands
would permit us. In the midst of our muddles, my brother
arrived, like a good genius, to our assistance, declaring his
determination of taking us down to B--- himself, in his large
lumber sleigh. This was indeed joyful news—and in three
hours he had dispatched the two sleighs and their loads, and
we all stood together in the empty house, striving to warm ourselves over the embers of the expiring fire.

How cold and desolate every object appeared! The small
windows half blocked up with snow scarcely allowed a glimpse
of the declining sun to cheer us with his serene aspect. In
spite of the cold, several kind friends had waded through the
deep snow to say "God bless you—Good-bye!" while a group
of silent Indians stood together, gazing upon our proceedings
with an earnestness which showed that they were not un-
interested in the scene. As the children and I passed out to
the sleigh, each one pressed forward and silently held out a
hand, while the poor squaws kissed me with tearful eyes. They
had been true friends to us in our dire necessity, and I returned
their mute farewell from my very heart.

Mr. S--- sprang into his sleigh. One of our party was wanting. "Jenny!" shouted my brother at the top of his voice, "it
is too cold to keep your mistress and the little children waiting
here."

"Och! sure then, I'm after coming," returned the old body,
as she issued from the house.

Shouts of laughter greeted her appearance. The figure she
cut on that memorable day I shall never forget. My brother
dropped the reins upon the horses' necks and fairly roared.
Jenny was about to commence her journey in three hats. Was
it to protect her from the cold? Oh! no—Jenny was not afraid
of the cold. She could have eaten her breakfast on the north
side of an iceberg, and always dispensed with shoes during
the most severe of our Canadian winters. It was to protect
those precious articles from injury. Our good neighbour, Mrs.

W---, had presented her with an old sky-blue drawn silk bonnet, as a parting benediction. This, by way of distinction, as she had never possessed such an article of luxury as a silk bonnet in her life, Jenny had placed over the coarse calico cap with its full yellow furbelow of the same homely material, next her head. Over this, as next in degree, a sunburnt straw hat, with faded pink ribbons, a bequest from Miss A---, just showed its brown brim and tawdry trimmings; and, to crown all, and serve as a guard to the rest—a really serviceable grey beaver bonnet of mine towered up as high as the celebrated crown in which Brother Peter figures in the Tale of the Tub.

"Mercy, Jenny! You don't mean to go with us that figure?"

"Och! my dear heart—I have no bandbox that will keep out the cold from my illigant bonnets," returned the old woman, laying her hand upon the sleigh.

"Go back, Jenny! Go back"—cried my brother between suffocating peals of mirth. "For God's sake take that tom-foolery from off your head. We shall be the laughing stock of every village we pass through."

"Och! sure now, Mr. S---, who wo'd think of looking at an ould crathur like me? It's only yerself that wo'd notice the like."

"All the world. Everybody would look at you. I believe you put those hats on to be stared at by all the young fellows we meet. Ha, Jenny?"

With offended dignity the old woman retired to re-arrange her toilet, and provide for the safety of her "illigant bonnets," one of which she suspended to the strings of her cloak; and no persuasion of mine could induce her to put it out of sight.

Many painful and conflicting emotions rose up in my heart, but found no utterance in words, as we entered the forest path, and I looked my last upon that humble home of many sorrows. Every object had become familiar during my long exile from civilized life. I loved the lonely lake with its magnificent belt "of dark pines sighing in the breeze"; the cedar swamp—the summer home of my dark Indian friends; my own dear little garden with its rugged fence, cultivated by my own

hands, in which I had so often braved the tormenting mosquitoes, black-flies, and intense heat, to provide vegetables and
melons for the use of the family. Even the cows, which had
given a breakfast for the last time to my little ones, were
regarded with mournful affection. A poor labourer stood at
the deserted door, holding my noble water-dog, Rover, in a
string. The poor fellow gave a joyous bark as my eyes fell
upon him, and struggled to get free.

"James J---," I said, "take care of my dog."

"Never fear, ma'am! he shall bide with me as long as he
lives."

"He and the poor Indians, at least, feel grief for our
departure," I thought. "Love is so scarce in this world that
we ought to prize it, however lowly the source from which it
glows."

We accomplished only twelve miles of our journey that
night, which lay through the bush along the banks of the
grand, rushing, foaming Octonabee River—the wildest and
most beautiful of forest streams. We slept at the house of
kind friends, and in the morning resumed our long journey.
Winter had now set in fairly. The children were glad to
huddle together in the bottom of the sleigh, under the buffaloes
and blankets; all but my eldest boy, a child of four years old,
who, enchanted by all he saw, continued to stand up and gaze
around him.

Born in the forest which he had never quitted before, the
sight of a town was such a novelty that he could find no words
wherewith to express his astonishment.

"Are the houses come to see one another?" he asked. "How
did they all meet here?"

The question greatly amused his uncle, who took some pains
to explain to him the difference between town and country.
On putting up for the night, we rejoiced to find that truly the
long distance which separated us from the husband and father
was nearly accomplished. During our ride we had got rid of
old Jenny and her bonnets, whom we found a very refractory
travelling companion. Fortunately, we overtook the sleighs

with the furniture, and Mr. S--- had transferred Jenny to the care of the driver; an arrangement which proved satisfactory to all parties but little Donald, her darling pet, who was fast asleep in my lap when Jenny and her bonnets made their exit. At supper he asked for his old nurse, and his uncle, to tease him, told him that Jenny was dead and that we were going to have some of her fried for supper.

When the beef steaks were brought to table, in spite of his long day's fast Donald cried piteously and refused to touch a bit of them; until some fried chickens making their appearance, one of the children cried out—"See, Donald! here is more of Jenny."

"No, no," said the sobbing child, wiping his eyes and laughing once more. "Ninny is not dead, for I know she had not wings."

The next morning was so intensely cold that out of tender consideration for our noses, Mr. S--- would not resume the journey until past ten o'clock; and even then it was a desperate experiment. We had not proceeded four miles before the horses were covered with icicles. Our hair was frozen as white as Time's solitary forelock, and our eyelids were stiff, and every limb aching with cold.

"This will never do," said my brother, turning to me. "The children will freeze. We must put up somewhere. I never felt the cold so severe as this."

"Where can we stop?" said I. "We are miles from any inn, and I see no prospect of the weather becoming milder."

"Yes, yes, I know by the very intensity of the cold that a change is at hand. At all events, it is much warmer at night in this country than during the day. The wind falls off, and the frost is more bearable. I know a worthy farmer who lives about a mile ahead. He will give us houseroom for a few hours, and we will resume our journey in the evening."

My teeth were chattering with cold. The children were crying in the bottom of the sleigh, and I gladly consented to his proposal.

A few minutes' ride brought us to a large frame house,

surrounded by commodious sheds and barns. A fine orchard opposite, and a yard well stocked with fat cattle and sheep, sleek geese and plethoric looking swine, gave promise of a land of abundance and comfort. My brother ran into the house to see if the owner was at home, and presently returned with the gentleman whose portrait we have already drawn, followed by two fine young women, his daughters, who gave us a truly warm welcome and assisted in removing the children from the sleigh, to the cheerful fire that made all bright and easy within.

"Well! how are you, Mr. S---?" cried the farmer, shaking my brother heartily by the hand. "Toiling in the bush still, eh?"

"Just in the same place."

"And the wife and children?"

"Hearty. Some half dozen have been added since you were in our parts, Woodruff."

"So much the better. The more the merrier, Mr. S---. Children are riches in this country."

"I know not how that may be. I find it deuced hard to feed and clothe mine."

"Wait until they grow up. They will be brave helps to you then. The price of labour—the price of labour, Mr. S---, is the destruction of the farmer."

"It does not seem to trouble you much," said my brother, glancing around the well furnished, comfortable apartment.

"My son and I do it all," cried the old man. "Of course the girls help in busy times, and take care of the dairy, and we hire occasionally. But small as the sum is which is expended in hiring during seed time and harvest, I feel it, I can tell you."

"You are not married again, Woodruff?"

"No Sir," said the old man with a peculiar smile, which did not entirely preclude the possibility of such an event.

"That tall girl with the fair hair is my eldest daughter. She manages the house, and an excellent housekeeper she is. But I cannot keep her forever," continued he with a knowing wink. "Girls will think of getting married, and seldom consult the wishes of their parents on the subject. But it is natural, Mr. S---; it is natural."

My brother looked laughingly towards the fine handsome young woman, as she placed upon the table hot water, whisky, and a huge plate of plum cake, which did not lack a companion stored with the finest specimens which the orchard could produce.

The young girl looked down and blushed.

"Ah! I see how it is, Woodruff—you will soon lose your daughter. I wonder that you have kept her so long. But who are these young ladies?" said my brother, as the three fine girls very demurely entered the room.

"The two shortest are my galls, by my last wife," replied Woodruff "who, I fear, mean soon to follow the bad example of their sister. The other lady," said the old man, with a reverential air, "is a *particular* friend of my eldest daughter."

My brother laughed slyly, and the old man's cheek took a deeper glow, as he stooped forward to mix the punch.

"You said these two ladies were by your last wife, Woodruff. How many wives have you had?"

"Only three, Mr. S---. It is impossible, they say in my country, to have too much of a good thing."

"So I suppose you think," said my brother, again glancing towards the comely Miss Smith. "Three wives! You have been a fortunate man to survive them all."

"Aye! Have I not? But I have been both lucky and unlucky in the wife way, Mr. S---. I was quite a youngster when I married my first woman. My father died when I was quite a child, and I was brought up by an uncle who rented one of those small snug farms in the North Riding, which are now so rarely to be met with in the Old Country. He had saved a little money, and his whole family consisted of one gall and me. She was not very pretty, but she was good and industrious; and would have at his death all the old man had to bestow. She was fond of me, and I thought I could not do better than make her my wife. It is all very well to marry for love, Mr. S---, if a fellow can afford it; but a little money is not to be despised; it goes a great way towards making the home comfortable. Uncle had no great objections, and so we were married. She managed the dairy and I helped upon the farm. We lived very happily together until my poor Betsy died in her confinement with that gall. Yes, Miss—you cost me a good wife, and should not be so anxious to run away and leave me in the lurch."

"Dear father," commenced the young woman.

"There, hold your tongue, Miss. The least said the soonest mended," continued the old man, smiling good-humouredly—for it was not only evident that he was extremely proud of his eldest daughter, but proud of her being the affianced wife of a gentleman in the neighbourhood.

"Well, Mr. S---, I felt very lonely after Betsy died; and I had been so comfortable as a married man, that I thought the best compliment I could pay to her memory was to take another wife."

"Perhaps she would not have thought it one," said I.

"Why, to be sure, women are often a leetle unreasonable," returned Woodruff. "But as she was not there to consult upon the subject, I took the liberty to please myself. Well, Mr. S---, I was always a great admirer of beauty, and so I thought I would try my luck this time with a handsome wife. There was a devilish fine gall in our village, only she was a leetle flighty, or so. The lads said to me, when they saw what I was arter—'Sam, you had better carry your pigs to another market. The lass is not right in the upper works.' 'I'll take the chance of that,' says I. 'There is not a prettier gall atween this and York.' Well, my uncle did not like the match by no manner of means.

" 'If you put that madcap,' says he, 'in my poor Betsy's place, I will never leave you a shilling.'

" 'You may do as you please,' returned I, for you must know, Mr. S---, that I was desperately in love, which I had never been before in my life, 'for I mean to marry the girl right off.'

"I kept my word, and we were married."

The narrator made a long and, I thought, rather ominous

pause, and took a deep draught from a fresh brewage of hot punch.

"Well," said I, rather impatiently, "and how did this second marriage turn out?"

"Bad enough for me," said he, with the most comical expression on his hard countenance, as he turned towards my brother.

Whether he was inclined to laugh or to cry was no easy matter to determine; but it is certain that neither my brother nor myself could well maintain our gravity, as he exclaimed:

"Well, Mr. S---, would you believe it? She thought fit to cut her throat only three days arter the wedding. What put such a thing in her head, I never could find out, but you may depend upon it, I never felt so uncomfortable in all my life."

The idea of a man telling such a dreadful circumstance in such a calm, matter of fact manner, and declaring with the greatest philosophy that it only made him feel uncomfortable, had in it something so irresistibly comic, that I was forced to hasten to the window to ascertain the state of the weather, in order to conceal the laugh which would come to my lips in spite of every effort to restrain it.

"No wonder that it made you feel uncomfortable, Woodruff," said my brother, casting a wicked look at me, which made me turn again to the window. "It would have been the death of some people. But you are a remarkably strong minded man, or you could not take it so coolly."

"I flatter myself I am," returned the farmer, who did not perceive that my brother was quizzing him. "What was the use of making a fuss? She preferred killing herself to living comfortably with me, and I was not going to play the fool with her. But the worst of it was, that all the galls looked suspiciously at me; and I found that I must go farther a-field, for a third wife. My uncle had a drove of cattle for the London market—I undertook the charge of them—sold the beasts advantageously for him, and returned with the money and a wife. My uncle was glad enough to get the money, but he made a sour face at the wife. She was not to his taste, but she

exactly suited mine. We had a bit of a quarrel about my hasty
marriage, as he called it. I got mad at the rude things he said,
and we parted. I thought that he was too fond of little Betsy
to do an ill-natured thing; but I was mistaken. In order to
revenge himself on me, he married his housekeeper, by whom
he had soon a large young family.

"All my hopes in that quarter were now at an end. Says I to
my wife, 'My dear, we can no longer depend upon my uncle—
we must learn to shift for ourselves.'

"With the little property I got with my third wife, I opened
a butcher's shop; and we got on comfortably enough for a few
years. She was a good woman, and made me an excellent
wife. She was the mother of my son and the two youngest of
my galls. Suddenly our luck took a turn. My partner (for I
had been fool enough to take one) ran off, and took along
with him all my little savings, leaving me to pay his debts and
my own. This was a hard blow. I felt it more than the death
of either of my wives.

"To repine was useless, so I sold all my cattle and furniture,
paid my creditors the last farthing, and then wrote to my uncle
requesting him to lend me fifty pounds to transport myself
and family to Canada. The old man knew me to be an honest,
hardworking fellow, and for little Betsy's sake, for so ran the
letter, he sent me a draft upon his banker for fifty pounds,
with a gentle hint that it would be the last I must expect from
him, as children were nearer to him than grandchildren. This
was true enough, but I still thought that those children had
no right to stand between little Betsy and him. I was very glad
of the money, and I wrote him a letter of thanks, promising
to repay it if ever I was able. This, with the blessing of God,
I did two years ago; and the money found him in a worse
state than I was when I left England; and I have his letter full
of gratitude for the same.

"But to return to the wife. She and the children reached
these shores in perfect health. It was in 1832, the year of
the great cholera; and I never once imagined that it would
attack us who were strangers in the country. A friend whom

I had known in England, hearing of my arrival, wrote to me from Bytown, to come up and look at a farm near him which he wished me to hire.

"Not caring to drag my wife and children up the country, until I had seen the place myself and prepared all things for their reception, I left them in lodgings at Quebec and proceeded up the country. I had not been two days at my friend's, and was still undecided about the farm, when I got a letter, written by my eldest gall, which informed me that my poor wife lay bad of the cholera; and if I wished to see her alive, I must start immediately.

"Off I went that very day, vexed to my heart at this untoward accident. Still, Mr. S---, I had left her so well, that I did not think it possible that she could die so soon. While stopping for the boat at Montreal, to proceed on my journey, I met an old schoolfellow whom I had not seen for many years, and did not know what had become of him. He had been settled for twenty years in the country, and was now a wealthy merchant in the city.

" 'Oh! Sam Woodruff,' says he; 'who would have thought of meeting with you in Canada. You must come home and dine with me, and talk over old times.'

" 'With all my heart,' says I—'but my wife is sick of the cholera at Quebec, and I am waiting for the next boat, to go down and see her.'

" 'That is bad,' says he; 'But a few hours cannot make much difference; there is another, and a far better and more commodious boat, starts at six in the evening. Come, don't say no. I long to have a friendly chat over a bottle of good wine.'

"Well, Mr. S---, I did not think it could make much difference. It was only three hours. I should certainly be in time to see my wife—besides I felt sure that she was already better.

"I went to my friend's. We had an excellent dinner, and some of the best wine to relish I ever tasted. And what with hearing his adventures and telling my own, and comparing the merits of the two countries, the time slipped away very fast.

"I heard the clock strike six. 'My wife,' says I, springing to my feet. 'Depend upon it, Woodruff,' says my friend, 'that you will find her quite well, and don't forget to bring her to see me, as you pass up.'

"I was only just in time for the boat, and I reached Quebec late the next evening."

"And your wife?" said I.

"Was just dead when I arrived. If I had not gone to dine with my friend, I should have seen her alive. But who would have thought that the trifling delay could have made such a difference?"

My brother looked again at me. "What an unfeeling wretch!" thought I. "This man looks upon his wives much in the same light that he would upon a horse. His grief for their death only amounts to the inconvenience which it occasions. Heaven defend me from such a husband!"

"I wonder," said my brother, "that you could live so long without a fourth."

The old man's heart now began to warm with the punch which he had been drinking—and nodding facetiously towards Miss Smith, he said:

"All in good time, Mr. S---. I am not so old that a wife would come amiss. When my girls are married, I must get a woman to take care of the house, and make and mend my clothes. Besides, these long winter nights are cruelly cold, and blankets are very dear; depend upon it, the very best thing an old man can do, to keep himself warm and comfortable, and to prolong his days upon the earth, is to take a young wife."

The old man was as good as his word. The next time I passed through ----, I found the pretty young wife in the chimney corner, and the old man as hearty and hale as ever.

EDWARD W. THOMSON

EDWARD WILLIAM THOMSON was born in York Township, Upper Canada, on February 12, 1849. He was educated at the Brantford Grammar School and at Trinity College School, Weston. In 1865, when only a boy of sixteen, he saw service in the American Civil War, and two years later he helped repel the Fenian Raids. He first chose the profession of civil engineering, but abandoned it in late 1878 to become an editorial writer on the Toronto *Globe*. This position he held until 1891, when he joined the staff of the *Youth's Companion,* in Boston, as revising editor. From 1902 to 1922 Thomson was Canadian correspondent for the Boston *Transcript*. He died in Boston in 1924. He had been elected a Fellow of the Royal Society of Literature in 1909, and of the Royal Society of Canada in 1910.

Thomson had a striking personality. As a journalist, he was an ardent controversialist who espoused fearlessly the radical causes of the day: free trade, Canadian nationalism, and the end of the spoils system. A friend of Bourassa and Laurier, he wrote, in one of his letters, of Toronto as "that active Belfast" whose "narrow, bigoted, canting spirit" he had always detested.

He was widely read in the modern literature of America, France, and England, as well as of his native Canada, and made some very shrewd comments upon his literary contemporaries. His taste inclined towards the realistic treatment of common life, and Zola, Howells and Whitman were among his favourite authors. His own literary output consisted of a volume of short stories, *Old Man Savarin and Other Stories* (1895), and a volume of poems, *The Many Mansioned House and Other Poems* (1909). His stories, which are his best work, deal for the most part with the life he knew in his early manhood as a surveyor along the lower Ottawa Valley, and have as their protagonists lumbermen, farmers, and habitants. In their constant mingling of humour and pathos, and in their grotesquerie of character and situation, they remind us of Dickens and Daudet. The best of them are those in which humour predominates: when Thomson becomes too concerned with the pathetic he usually slips over into the ludicrous.

41

Brief treatments of Thomson's life and work will be found in most of the handbooks of Canadian literature, but there is no extended critical analysis available. "The Privilege of the Limits" is reprinted from *Old Man Savarin and Other Stories*.

The Privilege of the Limits

"YES, indeed, my grandfather wass once in jail," said old Mrs. McTavish, of the county of Glengarry, in Ontario, Canada; "but that wass for debt, and he wass a ferry honest man whateffer, and he would not broke his promise—no, not for all the money in Canada. If you will listen to me, I will tell chust exactly the true story about that debt, to show you what an honest man my grandfather wass.

"One time Tougal Stewart, him that wass the poy's grandfather that keeps the same store in Cornwall to this day, sold a plough to my grandfather, and my grandfather said he would pay half the plough in October, and the other half whateffer time he felt able to pay the money. Yes, indeed, that was the very promise my grandfather gave.

"So he was at Tougal Stewart's store on the first of October early in the morning before the shutters wass taken off, and he paid half chust exactly to keep his word. Then the crop wass ferry bad next year, and the year after that one of his horses was killed by lightning, and the next year his brother, that wass not rich and had a big family, died, and do you think wass my grandfather to let the family be disgraced without a big funeral? No, indeed. So my grandfather paid for the funeral, and there wass at it plenty of meat and drink for everybody, as wass the right Hielan' custom those days; and after the funeral my grandfather did not feel chust exactly able to pay the other half for the plough that year either.

"So, then, Tougal Stewart met my grandfather in Cornwall next day after the funeral, and asked him if he had some money to spare.

" 'Wass you in need of help, Mr. Stewart?' says my grandfather, kindly. 'For if it's in any want you are, Tugal,' says my grandfather, 'I will sell the coat off my back, if there is no other way to lend you a loan'; for that wass always the way of my grandfather with all his friends, and a bigger-hearted man there never wass in all Glengarry, or in Stormont, or in Dundas, moreofer.

" 'In want!' says Tougal—'in want, Mr. McTavish!' says he, very high. 'Would you wish to insult a gentleman, and him of the name of Stewart, that's the name of princes of the world?' he said, so he did.

"Seeing Tougal had his temper up, my grandfather spoke softly, being a quiet, peaceable man, and in wonder what he said to offend Tougal.

" 'Mr. Stewart,' says my grandfather, 'it wass not in my mind to anger you whatefer. Only I thought, from your asking me if I had some money, that you might be looking fir a wee bit of a loan, as many a gentleman has to do at times, and no shame to him at all,' said my grandfather.

" 'A loan?' says Tougal, sneering. 'A loan, is it? Where's your memory, Mr. McTavish! Are you not owing me half the price of the plough you've had these three years?'

" 'And wass you asking me for money for the other half of the plough?' says my grandfather, very astonished.

" 'Just that,' says Tougal.

" 'Have you no shame or honour in you?' says my grandfather, firing up. 'How could I feel able to pay that now, and me chust yesterday been giving my poor brother a funeral fit for the McTavishes' own grandnephew, that wass as good chentleman's plood as any Stewart in Glengarry. You saw the expense I wass at, for there you wass, and I thank you for the politeness of coming, Mr. Stewart,' says my grandfather, ending mild, for the anger would never stay in him more than a minute, so kind was the nature he had.

" 'If you can spend money on a funeral like that, you can pay me for my plough,' says Stewart; for with buying and selling he wass become a poor creature, and the heart of a

Hielan'man wass half gone out of him, for all he wass so proud of his name of monarchs and kings.

" 'My grandfather had a mind to strike him down on the spot, so he often said; but he thought of the time when he hit Hamish Cochrane in anger, and he minded the penances the priest put on him for breaking the silly man's jaw with that blow, so he smothered the heat that wass in him, and turned away in scorn. With that Tougal went to court, and sued my grandfather, puir mean creature.

"You might think that Judge Jones—him that wass judge in Cornwall before Judge Jarvis that's dead—would do justice. But no, he made it the law that my grandfather must pay at once, though Tougal Stewart could not deny what the bargain wass.

" 'Your Honour,' says my grandfather, 'I said I'd pay when I felt able. And do I feel able now? No, I do not,' says he. 'It's a disgrace to Tougal Stewart to ask me, and himself telling you what the bargain wass,' said my grandfather. But Judge Jones said that he must pay, for all that he did not feel able.

" 'I will nefer pay one copper till I feel able,' says my grandfather; 'but I'll keep my Hielan' promise to my dying day, as I always done,' says he.

"And with that the old judge laughed, and said he would have to give judgment. And so he did; and after that Tougal Stewart got out an execution. But not the worth of a handful of oatmeal could the bailiff lay hands on, because my grandfather had chust exactly taken the precaution to give a bill of sale on his gear to his neighbour, Alexander Frazer, that could be trusted to do what was right after the law play was over.

"The whole settlement had great contempt for Tougal Stewart's conduct; but he wass a headstrong body, and once he begun to do wrong against my grandfather, he held on, for all that his trade fell away; and finally he had my grandfather arrested for debt, though you'll understand, sir, that he was owing Stewart nothing that he ought to pay when he didn't feel able.

"In those times prisoners for debt wass taken to jail in Cornwall, and if they had friends to give bail that they would not go beyond the posts that wass around the sixteen acres nearest the jail walls, the prisoners could go where they liked on that ground. This was called 'the privilege of the limits.' The limits, you'll understand, was marked by cedar posts painted white about the size of hitching-posts.

"The whole settlement was ready to go bail for my grandfather if he wanted it, and for the health of him he needed to be in the open air, and so he gave Tuncan Macdonnell of the Greenfields, and Aeneas Macdonald of the Sandfields, for his bail, and he promised, on his Hielan' word of honour, not to go beyond the posts. With that he went where he pleased, only taking care that he never put even the toe of his foot beyond a post, for all that some prisoners of the limits would chump ofer them and back again, or maybe swing round them, holding by their hands.

"Efery day the neighbours would go into Cornwall to give my grandfather the good word, and they would offer to pay Tougal Stewart for the other half of the plough, only that vexed my grandfather, for he wass too proud to borrow, and, of course, every day he felt less and less able to pay on account of him having to hire a man to be doing the spring ploughing and seeding and making the kale-yard.

"All this time, you'll mind, Tougal Stewart had to pay five shillings a week for my grandfather's keep, the law being so that if the debtor swore he had not five pounds' worth of property to his name, then the creditor had to pay the five shillings, and, of course, my grandfather had nothing to his name after he gave the bill of sale to Alexander Frazer. A great diversion it was to my grandfather to be reckoning up that if he lived as long as his father, that was hale and strong at ninety-six, Tougal would need to pay five or six hundred pounds for him, and there was only two pounds ten shillings to be paid on the plough.

"So it was like that all summer, my grandfather keeping heartsome, with the neighbours coming in so steady to bring him the news of the settlement. There he would sit, just inside one of the posts, for to pass his jokes, and tell what he wished the family to be doing next. This way it might have kept going on for forty years, only it came about that my grandfather's youngest child—him that was my father—fell sick, and seemed like to die.

"Well, when my grandfather heard that bad news, he wass in a terrible way, to be sure, for he would be longing to hold the child in his arms, so that his heart was sore and like to break. Eat he could not, sleep he could not: all night he would be groaning, and all day he would be walking around by the posts, wishing that he had not passed his Hielan' word of honour not to go beyond a post; for he thought how he could have broken out like a chentleman, and gone to see his sick child, if he had stayed inside the jail wall. So it went on three days and three nights pefore the wise thought came into my grandfather's head to show him how he need not go beyond the posts to see his little sick boy. With that he went straight to one of the white cedar posts, and pulled it up out of the hole, and started for home, taking great care to carry it in his hands pefore him, so he would not be beyond it one bit.

"My grandfather wass not half a mile out of Cornwall, which was only a little place in those days, when two of the turnkeys came after him.

" 'Stop, Mr. McTavish,' says the turnkeys.

" 'What for would I stop?' says my grandfather.

" 'You have broke your bail,' says they.

" 'It's a lie for you,' says my grandfather, for his temper flared up for anybody to say he would broke his bail. 'Am I beyond the post?' says my grandfather.

"With that they run in on him, only that he knocked the two of them over with the post, and went on rejoicing, like an honest man should, at keeping his word and overcoming them that would slander his good name. The only thing besides thoughts of the child that troubled him was questioning whether he had been strictly right in turning round for to use the post to defend himself in such a way that it was nearer the jail than he wass. But he remembered how the jailer never complained of prisoners of the limits chumping ofer the posts, if so they chumped back again in a moment, the trouble went out of his mind.

"Pretty soon after that he met Tuncan Macdonnell of Greenfields, coming into Cornwall with the wagon.

" 'And how is this Glengatchie?' says Tuncan. 'For you were never the man to broke your bail.'

"Glengatchie, you'll understand, sir, is the name of my grandfather's farm.

" 'Never fear, Greenfields,' says my grandfather, 'for I'm not beyond the post.'

"So Greenfields looked at the post, and he looked at my grandfather, and he scratched his head a wee, and he seen it was so; and then he fell into a great admiration entirely.

" 'Get in with me, Glengatchie—it's proud I'll be to carry you home'; and he turned his team around. My grandfather did so, taking great care to keep the post in front of him all the time; and that way he reached home. Out comes my grandmother running to embrace him; but she had to throw her arms around the post and my grandfather's neck at the same time, he was that strict to be within his promise. Pefore going ben the house, he went to the back end of the kale-yard which was farthest from the jail, and there he stuck the post; and then he went back to see his sick child, while all the neighbours that came round was glad to see what a wise thought the saints had put into his mind to save his bail and his promise.

"So there he stayed a week till my father got well. Of course the constables came after my grandfather, but the settlement would not let the creatures come within a mile of Glengatchie. You might think, sir, that my grandfather would have stayed with his wife and weans, seeing the post was all the time in the kale-yard, and him careful not to go beyond it; but he was putting the settlement to a great deal of trouble day and night to keep the constables off, and he was fearful that they might take the post away, if ever they got to Glengatchie, and give him the name of false, which no McTavish ever had. So Tuncan Greenfields and Aeneas Sandfield drove

my grandfather back to the jail, him with the post behind him
in the wagon, so as he would be between it and the jail. Of
course Tougal Stewart tried his best to have the bail declared
forfeited; but old Judge Jones only laughed, and said my
grandfather was a Hielan' gentleman, with a very nice sense
of honour, and that was chust exactly the truth.

"How did my grandfather get free in the end? Oh, then,
that was because of Tougal Stewart being careless—him that
thought he knew so much of the law. The law was, you will
mind, that Tougal had to pay five shillings a week for keeping
my grandfather in the limits. The money was to be paid efery
Monday, and it was to be paid in lawful money of Canada,
too. Well, would you belief that Tougal paid in four shillings
in silver one Monday, and one shilling in coppers, for he took
up the collection in church the day pefore, and it wass not
till Tougal had gone away that the jailer saw that one of the
coppers was a Brock copper—a medal, you will understand,
made at General Brock's death, and not lawful money of
Canada at all. With that the jailer came out to my grandfather.

" 'Mr. McTavish,' says he, taking off his hat, 'you are a
free man, and I'm glad of it.' Then he told him what Tougal
had done.

" 'I hope you will not have any hard feelings toward me,
Mr. McTavish,' said the jailer; and a decent man he wass, for
all that there wass not a drop of Hielan' blood in him. 'I hope
you will not think hard of me for not being hospitable to you,
sir,' he says; 'but it's against the rules and regulations for the
jailer to be offering the best he can command to the prisoners.
Now that you are free, Mr. McTavish,' says the jailer, 'I would
be a proud man if Mr. McTavish of Glengatchie would do me
the honour of taking supper with me this night. I will be
asking your leave to invite some of the gentlemen of the place,
if you will say the word, Mr. McTavish,' says he.

"Well, my grandfather could never bear malice, the kind
man he wass, and he seen how bad the jailer felt, so he consented, and a great company came in, to be sure, to celebrate
the occasion.

"Did my grandfather pay the balance on the plough? What for should you suspicion, sir, that my grandfather would refuse his honest debt? Of course he paid for the plough, for the crop was good that fall.

" 'I would be paying you the other half of the plough now, Mr. Stewart,' says my grandfather, comin' in when the store was full.

" 'Hoich, but YOU are the honest McTavish,' says Tougal, sneering.

"But my grandfather made no answer to the creature, for he thought it would be unkind to mention how Tougal had paid out six pounds four shillings and eleven pence to keep him in on account of a debt of two pound ten that never was due till it was paid."

CHARLES G. D. ROBERTS

SIR CHARLES G. D. ROBERTS was born near Fredericton, New Brunswick, on January 10, 1860. He was educated at the Fredericton Collegiate School and the University of New Brunswick, from which he graduated in 1879 with honours in philosophy and political economy. After graduation he taught school, first in Chatham, New Brunswick, and then in Fredericton, but gave it up to become, for a short period in 1883, editor of Goldwin Smith's magazine, *The Week*. From 1885-1895 Roberts was professor of English and French at King's College, Windsor, Nova Scotia, but from 1896 onward he devoted all his time to literature, spending most of the time prior to the First World War in New York City. At the outbreak of the war, he enlisted in the Canadian Army as a private. He soon rose to the rank of major, and was one of the official Canadian war historians. He lived in England for a few years after the Armistice, but returned to Canada in 1925. He was knighted for his services to Canadian letters in 1935, and died on November 26, 1943.

Roberts began his literary career within a few months of graduation with the publication, in 1880, of *Orion and Other Poems,* a book which is a landmark in the history of Canadian poetry. There followed several other volumes of poetry, some novels and many volumes of short stories concerned chiefly with animal life. Of these volumes of short stories, the best are *The Kindred of the Wild, Earth's Enigmas* and *Watchers of the Trail.*

Critics of Roberts' poetry are, for the most part, agreed that his best work is done when he is content to describe the surface of nature and the homely details of common life. Much the same is true of his fiction except that, unfortunately, he is less frequently content with such a limited aim in his prose. In most of his stories he chooses melodramatic incidents which so offend modern taste that the genuinely fresh and creative part of his work—his talent for the observation and description of nature and for the imaginative re-creation of animal life—tends to be lost sight of. The story which follows, taken from *Earth's Enigmas,* is one of the few in which his best qualities are found undiluted.

There are several book-length studies of Roberts, the best of which are *Roberts and the Influences of His Time* (Toronto, 1905), by James Cappon, and the same author's volume on Roberts in the "Makers of Canadian Literature" series (Toronto, 1925). An exhaustive biography by Elsie Pomeroy was published in 1943. Desmond Pacey's *Ten Canadian Poets* (Toronto, 1958) contains a chapter on Roberts.

"The Young Ravens that Call Upon Him"

IT WAS JUST before dawn, and a greyness was beginning to trouble the dark about the top of the mountain.

Even at that cold height there was no wind. The veil of cloud that hid the stars hung but a hand-breadth above the naked summit. To eastward the peak broke away sheer, beetling in a perpetual menace to the valleys and the lower hills. Just under the brow, on a splintered and creviced ledge, was the nest of the eagles.

As the thick dark shrank down the steep like a receding tide, and the greyness reached the ragged heap of branches forming the nest, the young eagles stirred uneasily under the loose droop of the mother's wings. She raised her head and peered about her, slightly lifting her wings as she did so; and the nestlings, complaining at the chill air that came in upon their unfledged bodies, thrust themselves up amid the warm feathers of her thighs. The male bird, perched on a jutting fragment beside the nest, did not move. But he was awake. His white, narrow, flat-crowned head was turned to one side, and his yellow eye, under its straight, fierce lid, watched the pale streak that was growing along the distant eastern sea-line.

The great birds were racked with hunger. Even the nestlings, to meet the petitions of whose gaping beaks they stinted themselves without mercy, felt meagre and uncomforted. Day after day the parent birds had fished almost in vain; day after day their wide and tireless hunting had brought them scant reward. The schools of alewives, mackerel, and herring seemed to shun their shores that spring. The rabbits seemed to have fled from all the coverts about their mountain.

The mother eagle, larger and of mightier wing than her mate, looked as if she had met with misadventure. Her plumage was disordered. Her eyes, fiercely and restlessly anxious, at moments grew dull as if with exhaustion. On the day before, while circling at her viewless height above a lake far inland, she had marked a huge lake-trout, basking near the surface of the water. Dropping upon it with half-closed, hissing wings, she had fixed her talons in its back. But the fish had proved too powerful for her. Again and again it had dragged her under water, and she had almost been drowned before she could unloose the terrible grip of her claws. Hardly, and late, had she beaten her way back to the mountain-top.

And now the pale streak in the east grew ruddy. Rust-red stains and purple, crawling fissures began to show on the rocky face of the peak. A piece of scarlet cloth, woven among the faggots of the nest, glowed like new blood in the increasing light. And presently a wave of rose appeared to break and wash down over the summit, as the rim of the sun came above the horizon.

The male eagle stretched his head far out over the depth, lifted his wings and screamed harshly, as if in greeting of the day. He paused a moment in that position, rolling his eye upon the nest. Then his head went lower, his wings spread wider, and he launched himself swiftly and smoothly into the abyss of air as a swimmer glides into the sea. The female watched him, a faint wraith of a bird darting through the gloom, till presently, completing his mighty arc, he rose again into the full light of the morning. Then on level, all but moveless wing, he sailed away toward the horizon.

As the sun rose higher and higher, the darkness began to melt on the tops of the lower hills and to diminish on the slopes of the upland pastures, lingering in the valleys as the snow delays there in spring. As point by point the landscape uncovered itself to his view, the eagle shaped his flight into a vast circle, or rather into a series of stupendous loops. His neck was stretched toward the earth, in the intensity of his search for something to ease the bitter hunger of his nestlings and his mate.

Not far from the sea, and still in darkness, stood a low, round hill, or swelling upland. Bleak and shelterless, whipped by every wind that the heavens could let loose, it bore no bush but an occasional juniper scrub. It was covered with mossy hillocks, and with a short grass, meagre but sweet. There in the chilly gloom, straining her ears to catch the lightest footfall of approaching peril, but hearing only the hushed thunder of the surf, stood a lonely ewe over the lamb to which she had given birth in the night.

Having lost the flock when the pangs of travail came upon her, the unwonted solitude filled her with apprehension. But as soon as the first feeble bleating of the lamb fell upon her ear, everything was changed. Her terrors all at once increased ten-fold—but they were for her young, not for herself; and with them came a strange boldness such as her heart had never known before. As the little weakling shivered against her side, she uttered low, short bleats and murmurs of tenderness. When an owl hooted in the woods across the valley, she raised her head angrily and faced the sound, suspecting a menace to her young. When a mouse scurried past her, with a small, rustling noise amid the withered mosses of the hillock, she stamped fiercely, and would have charged had the intruder been a lion.

When the first grey of dawn descended over the pasture, the ewe feasted her eyes with the sight of the trembling little creature, as it lay on the wet grass. With gentle nose she coaxed it and caressed it, till presently it struggled to its feet, and, with its pathetically awkward legs spread wide apart to preserve its balance, it began to nurse. Turning her head as far around as she could, the ewe watched its every motion with soft murmurings of delight.

And now that wave of rose, which had long ago washed the mountain and waked the eagles, spread tenderly across the open pasture. The lamb stopped nursing; and the ewe, moving forward two or three steps, tried to persuade it to follow her. She was anxious that it should as soon as possible learn to walk freely, so they might together rejoin the flock. She felt that the open pasture was full of dangers.

The lamb seemed afraid to take so many steps. It shook its ears and bleated piteously. The mother returned to its side, caressed it anew, pushed it with her nose, and again moved away a few feet, urging it to go with her. Again the feeble little creature refused, bleating loudly. At this moment there came a terrible hissing rush out of the sky, and a great form fell upon the lamb. The ewe wheeled and charged madly; but at the same instant the eagle, with two mighty buffetings of his wings, rose beyond her reach and soared away toward the mountain. The lamb hung limp from his talons; and with piteous cries the ewe ran beneath, gazing upward, and stumbling over the hillocks and juniper bushes.

In the nest of the eagles there was content. The pain of their hunger appeased, the nestlings lay dozing in the sun, the neck of one resting across the back of the other. The triumphant male sat erect upon his perch, staring out over the splendid world that displayed itself beneath him. Now and again he half lifted his wings and screamed joyously at the sun. The mother bird, perched upon a limb on the edge of the nest, busily rearranged her plumage. At times she stooped her head into the nest to utter over her sleeping eaglets a soft chuckling noise, which seemed to come from the bottom of her throat.

But hither and thither over the round bleak hill wandered the ewe, calling for her lamb, unmindful of the flock, which had been moved to other pastures.

DUNCAN CAMPBELL SCOTT

DUNCAN CAMPBELL SCOTT is unique among Canadian writers in that he has produced equally distinguished work in poetry and prose fiction. In both media he was one of our most accomplished craftsmen.

There are few striking events to record of Scott's life: it was the long, quiet and unspectacular career of an artist and civil servant. Born in Ottawa in 1862, he was educated there and at Stanstead College, and spent almost all of his life in the capital city. When he was eighteen he entered the Department of Indian Affairs, and remained in that department until his retirement. He died on December 19, 1947. It was his friend, Archibald Lampman, who encouraged him to write, and Scott repaid the debt by editing Lampman's collected poems after the latter's death and by contributing a critical and biographical introduction to a later volume of selections.

Scott's first volume of poetry, *The Magic House and Other Poems*, was published in 1893, and it was followed by eight other volumes. There were also two volumes of short stories—*In the Village of Viger* (1896, 1945) and *The Witching of Elspie* (1923) —and a final volume which included stories, poems and essays: *The Circle of Affection* (1947).

Professor E. K. Brown has said of Scott's poetry that its emotional centre is "a search for the adequate theme and the adequate form in which restrained intensity may express itself." This seems to me to apply to his short stories also. His stories, like his poems, take as their usual subject matter rather sinister themes: death, insanity, frustration, loneliness. But he treats these themes, at his best, not in a crudely melodramatic fashion, but with fine restraint, so that the effects are, in a fascinating way, muted and muffled. A haunting suggestiveness, achieved by the use of a quiet but luminous style and of symbolism, is the distinctive quality of his work.

There are other parallels between Scott's poetry and his stories. The most obvious of these is the distinguished description of nature which is common to both. And in both prose and poetry, the descriptive passages are employed always to create the mood or, by their overtones of symbolism, to reinforce the theme. Another similarity is the richly sensuous quality of his work in both media: ear and eye especially, but all the senses to some extent, are constantly appealed to. Finally, in all that Scott wrote, there is evident his deep sympathy for his fellowman, his quick response to all forms of human suffering.

There is no book on Scott. There are critical articles by Pelham Edgar (*The Dalhousie Review,* 1927-1928), E. K. Brown (*Manitoba Arts Review,* Spring, 1941), W. J. Sykes (*Queen's Quarterly,* Spring, 1939), A. J. M. Smith (*The Dalhousie Review,* April, 1948) and Desmond Pacey (*The Canadian Forum,* August, 1948). Dr. Brown has devoted a chapter to Scott in his monograph *On Canadian Poetry,* and there is a chapter on his work as a poet in Desmond Pacey's *Ten Canadian Poets* (Toronto, 1958). The story which follows is taken from *In the Village of Viger.*

Paul Farlotte

NEAR THE OUTSKIRTS of Viger, to the west, far away from the Blanche, but having a country outlook of their own, and a glimpse of a shadowy range of hills, stood two houses which would have attracted attention by their contrast, if for no other reason. One was a low cottage, surrounded by a garden, and covered with roses, which formed jalousies for the encircling veranda. The garden was laid out with the care and completeness that told of a master hand. The cottage itself had the air of having been secured from the inroads of time as thoroughly as paint and a nail in the right place at the right time could effect that end. The other was a large gaunt-looking house, narrow and high, with many windows, some of which were boarded up, as if there was no further use for the chambers into which they had once admitted light. Standing on a rough piece of ground it seemed given over to the rudeness of decay. It appeared to have been the intention of its builder to veneer it with brick; but it stood there a wooden shell,

discoloured by the weather, disjointed by the frost, and with
the wind fluttering the rags of tar-paper which had been
intended as a protection against the cold, but which now hung
in patches and ribbons. But despite this dilapidation it had a
sort of martial air about it, and seemed to watch over its
embowered companion, warding off tempests and gradually
falling to pieces on guard, like a faithful soldier who suffers
at his post. In the road, just between the two, stood a beautiful
Lombardy poplar. Its shadow fell upon the little cottage in the
morning, and travelled across the garden, and in the evening
touched the corner of the tall house, and faded out with the
sun, only to float there again in the moonlight, or to commence the journey next morning with the dawn. This shadow
seemed, with its constant movement, to figure the connection
that existed between the two houses.

The garden of the cottage was a marvel; there the finest
roses in the parish grew, roses which people came miles to see,
and parterres of old-fashioned flowers, the seed of which came
from France, and which in consequence seemed to blow with
a rarer colour and more delicate perfume. This garden was a
striking contrast to the stony ground about the neighbouring
house, where only the commonest weeds grew unregarded;
but its master had been born a gardener, just as another man
is born a musician or a poet. There was a superstition in the
village that all he had to do was to put anything, even a dry
stick, into the ground, and it would grow. He was the village
schoolmaster, and Madame Laroque would remark spitefully
enough that if Monsieur Paul Farlotte had been as successful
in planting knowledge in the heads of his scholars as he was
in planting roses in his garden Viger would have been celebrated the world over. But he was born a gardener, not a
teacher; and he made the best of the fate which compelled
him to depend for his living on something he disliked. He
looked almost as dry as one of his own hyacinth bulbs; but
like it he had life at his heart. He was a very small man, and
frail, and looked older than he was. It was strange, but you
rarely seemed to see his face; for he was bent with weeding

and digging, and it seemed an effort for him to raise his head
and look at you with the full glance of his eye. But when he
did, you saw the eye was honest and full of light. He was not
careful of his personal appearance, clinging to his old garments with a fondness which often laid him open to ridicule,
which he was willing to bear for the sake of the comfort of an
old pair of shoes, or a hat which had accommodated itself to
the irregularities of his head. On the street he wore a curious
skirt-coat that seemed to be made of some indestructible
material, for he had worn it for years, and might be buried
in it. It received an extra brush for Sundays and holidays, and
always looked as good as new. He made a quaint picture, as
he came down the road from school. He had a hesitating walk,
and constantly stopped and looked behind him; for he always
fancied he heard a voice calling him by his name. He would
be working in his flower-beds when he would hear it over his
shoulder, "Paul"; or when he went to draw water from his
well, "Paul"; or when he was reading by his fire, someone
calling him softly, "Paul, Paul"; or in the dead of night, when
nothing moved in his cottage, he would hear it out of the
dark, "Paul." So it came to be a sort of companionship for
him, this haunting voice; and sometimes one could have seen
him in his garden stretch out his hand and smile, as if he
were welcoming an invisible guest. Sometimes the guest was
not invisible, but took body and shape, and was a real presence; and often Paul was greeted with visions of things that
had been, or that would be, and saw figures where, for other
eyes, hung only the impalpable air.

He had one other passion besides his garden, and that was
Montaigne. He delved in one in the summer, in the other in
the winter. With his feet on his stove he would become so
absorbed with his author that he would burn his slippers and
come to himself disturbed by the smell of the singed leather.
He had only one great ambition, that was to return to France
to see his mother before she died; and he had for years been
trying to save enough money to take the journey. People who
did not know him called him stingy, and said the saving for

his journey was only a pretext to cover his miserly habits. It was strange, he had been saving for years, and yet he had not saved enough. Whenever anyone would ask him, "Well, Monsieur Farlotte, when do you go to France?" he would answer, "Next year—next year." So when he announced one spring that he was actually going, and when people saw that he was not making his garden with his accustomed care, it became the talk of the village: "Monsieur Farlotte is going to France"; "Monsieur Farlotte has saved enough money, true, true, he is going to France."

His proposed visit gave no one so much pleasure as it gave his neighbours in the gaunt, unkempt house which seemed to watch over his own; and no one would have imagined what a joy it was to Marie St. Denis, the tall girl who was mother to her orphan brothers and sisters, to hear Monsieur Farlotte say, "When I am in France"; for she knew what none of the villagers knew, that if it had not been for her and her troubles, Monsieur Farlotte would have seen France many years before. How often she would recall the time when her father, who was in the employ of the great match factory near Viger, used to drive about collecting the little paper match-boxes which were made by hundreds of women in the village and the country around; how he had conceived the idea of making a machine in which a strip of paper would go in at one end, and the completed match-boxes would fall out at the other; how he had given up his situation and devoted his whole time and energy to the invention of this machine; how he had failed time and again, but continued with a perseverance which at last became a frantic passion; and how, to keep the family together, her mother, herself, and the children joined that army of workers which was making the match-boxes by hand. She would think of what would have happened to them then if Monsieur Farlotte had not been there with his help, or what would have happened when her mother died, worn out, and her father, overcome with disappointment, gave up his life and his task together, in despair. But whenever she would try to speak of these things Monsieur Farlotte would prevent her with a gesture, "Well, but what would you have me do—besides, I will go some day—now who knows, next year, perhaps." So here was "next year," which she had so longed to see, and Monsieur Farlotte was giving her a daily lecture on how to treat the tulips after they had done flowering, preluding everything he had to say with, "When I am in France," for his heart was already there.

He had two places to visit, one was his old home, the other was the birthplace of his beloved Montaigne. He had often described to Marie the little cottage where he was born, with the vine arbours and the long garden walks, the lilac-bushes, with their cool dark-green leaves, the white eaves where the swallows nested, and the poplar, sentinel over all. "You see," he would say, "I have tried to make this little place like it; and my memory may have played me a trick, but I often fancy myself at home. That poplar and this long walk and the vines on the arbour—sometimes when I see the tulips by the border I fancy it is all in France."

Marie was going over his scant wardrobe, mending with her skilful fingers, putting a stitch in the trusty old coat, and securing its buttons. She was anxious that Monsieur Farlotte should get a new suit before he went on his journey; but he would not hear of it. "Not a bit of it," he would say, "if I made my appearance in a new suit, they would think I had been making money; and when they would find out that I had not enough to buy cabbage for the soup there would be disappointment." She could not get him to write that he was coming. "No, no," he would say, "if I do that they will expect me." "Well, and why not—why not?" "Well, they would think about it—in ten days Paul comes home, then in five days Paul comes home, and then when I came they would set the dogs on me. No, I will just walk in—so—and when they are staring at my old coat I will sit down in a corner, and my old mother will commence to cry. Oh, I have it all arranged."

So Marie let him have his own way; but she was fixed on having her way in some things. To save Monsieur Farlotte the heavier work, and allow him to keep his strength for the journey, she would make her brother Guy do the spading in the garden, much to his disgust, and that of Monsieur Farlotte, who would stand by and interfere, taking the spade into his own hands with infinite satisfaction. "See," he would say, "go deeper and turn it over so." And when Guy would dig in his own clumsy way, he would go off in despair, with the words, "God help us, nothing will grow there."

When Monsieur Farlotte insisted on taking his clothes in an old box covered with raw-hide, with his initials in brass tacks on the cover, Marie would not consent to it, and made Guy carry off the box without his knowledge and hide it. She had a good tin trunk which had belonged to her mother, which she knew where to find in the attic, and which would contain everything Monsieur Farlotte had to carry. Poor Marie never went into this attic without a shudder, for occupying most of the space was her father's work bench, and that complicated wheel, the model of his invention, which he had tried so hard to perfect, and which stood there like a monument to his failure. She had made Guy promise never to move it, fearing lest he might be tempted to finish what his father had begun—a fear that was almost an apprehension, so like him was he growing. He was tall and large-boned, with a dark restless eye, set under an overhanging forehead. He had long arms, out of proportion to his height, and he hung his head when he walked. His likeness to his father made him seem a man before his time. He felt himself a man; for he had a good position in the match factory, and was like a father to his little brothers and sisters.

Although the model had always had a strange fascination for him, the lad had kept his promise to his sister, and had never touched the mechanism which had literally taken his father's life. Often when he went into the attic he would stand and gaze at the model and wonder why it had not succeeded, and recall his father bending over his work, with his compass and pencil. But he had a dread of it, too, and sometimes would hurry away, afraid lest its fascination would conquer him.

Monsieur Farlotte was to leave as soon as his school closed, but weeks before that he had everything ready, and could enjoy his roses in peace. After school hours he would walk in his garden, to and fro, to and fro, with his hands behind his back, and his eyes upon the ground, meditating; and once in a while he would pause and smile, or look over his shoulder when the haunting voice would call his name. His scholars had commenced to view him with additional interest, now that he was going to take such a prodigious journey; and two or three of them could always be seen peering through the palings, watching him as he walked up and down the path; and Marie would watch him too, and wonder what he would say when he found that his trunk had disappeared. He missed it fully a month before he could expect to start; but he had resolved to pack that very evening.

"But there is plenty of time," remonstrated Marie.

"That's always the way," he answered. "Would you expect me to leave everything until the last moment?"

"But, Monsieur Farlotte, in ten minutes everything goes into the trunk."

"So, and in the same ten minutes something is left out of the trunk, and I am in France, and my shoes are in Viger, that will be the end of it."

So, to pacify him, she had to ask Guy to bring down the trunk from the attic. It was not yet dark there; the sunset threw a great colour into the room, touching all the familiar objects with transfiguring light, and giving the shadows a rich depth. Guy saw the model glowing like some magic golden wheel, the metal points upon it gleaming like jewels in the light. As he passed he touched it, and with a musical click something dropped from it. He picked it up: it was one of the little paper match-boxes, but the defect that he remembered to have heard talked of was there. He held it in his hand and examined it; then he pulled it apart and spread it out. "Ah," he said to himself, "the fault was in the cutting." Then he turned the wheel, and one by one the imperfect boxes dropped out, until the strip of paper was exhausted. "But why,"—the question rose in his mind—"why could not that little difficulty be overcome?"

He took the trunk down to Marie, who at last persuaded Monsieur Farlotte to let her pack his clothes in it. He did so with a protestation, "Well, I know how it will be with a fine box like that, some fellow will whip it off when I am looking the other way, and that will be the end of it."

As soon as he could do so without attracting Marie's attention Guy returned to the attic with a lamp. When Marie had finished packing Monsieur Farlotte's wardrobe, she went home to put her children to bed; but when she saw that light in the attic window she nearly fainted from apprehension. When she pushed open the door of that room which she had entered so often with the scant meals she used to bring her father, she saw Guy bending over the model, examining every part of it. "Guy," she said, trying to command her voice, "you have broken your promise." He looked up quickly. "Marie, I am going to find it out—I can understand it—there is just one thing, if I can get that we will make a fortune out of it."

"Guy, don't delude yourself; those were father's words, and day after day I brought him his meals here, when he was too busy even to come downstairs; but nothing came of it, and while he was trying to make a machine for the boxes, we were making them with our fingers. O Guy," she cried, with her voice rising into a sob, "remember those days, remember what Monsieur Farlotte did for us, and what he would have to do again if you lost your place!"

"That's all nonsense, Marie. Two weeks will do it, and after that I could send Monsieur Farlotte home with a pocket full of gold."

"Guy, you are making a terrible mistake. That wheel was our curse, and it will follow us if you don't leave it alone. And think of Monsieur Farlotte; if he finds out what you are working at he will not go to France—I know him; he will believe it his duty to stay here and help us, as he did when father was alive. Guy, Guy, listen to me!"

But Guy was bending over the model, absorbed in its labyrinths. In vain did Marie argue with him, try to persuade him, and threaten him; she attempted to lock the attic door and keep him out, but he twisted the lock off, and after that the door was always open. Then she resolved to break the wheel into a thousand pieces; but when she went upstairs, when Guy was away, she could not strike it with the axe she held. It seemed like a human thing that cried out with a hundred tongues against the murder she would do; and she could only sink down sobbing, and pray. Then failing everything else she simulated an interest in the thing, and tried to lead Guy to work at it moderately, and not to give up his whole time to it.

But he seemed to take up his father's passion where he had laid it down. Marie could do nothing with him; and the younger children, at first hanging around the attic door, as if he were their father come back again, gradually ventured into the room, and whispered together as they watched their rapt and unobservant brother working at his task. Marie's one thought was to devise a means of keeping the fact from Monsieur Farlotte; and she told him blankly that Guy had been sent away on business, and would not be back for six weeks. She hoped that by that time Monsieur Farlotte would be safely started on his journey. But night after night he saw a light in the attic window. In the past years it had been a constant there, and he could only connect it with one cause. But he could get no answer from Marie when he asked her the reason; and the next night the distracted girl draped the window so that no ray of light could find its way out into the night. But Monsieur Farlotte was not satisfied; and a few evenings afterwards, as it was growing dusk, he went quietly into the house, and upstairs into the attic. There he saw Guy stretched along the work bench, his head in his hands, using the last light to ponder over the sketch he was making, and beside him, figured very clearly in the thick gold air of the sunset, the form of his father, bending over him, with the old eager, haggard look in his eyes. Monsieur Farlotte watched the two figures for a moment as they glowed in their rich atmosphere; then the apparition turned his head slowly, and warned him away with a motion of his hand.

All night long Monsieur Farlotte walked in his garden, patient and undisturbed, fixing his duty so that nothing could root it out. He found the comfort that comes to those who give up some exceeding deep desire of the heart, and when next morning the market-gardener from St. Valerie, driving by as the matin bell was clanging from St. Joseph's, and seeing the old teacher as if he were taking an early look at his growing roses, asked him, "Well, Monsieur Farlotte, when do you go to France?" he was able to answer cheerfully, "Next year—next year."

Marie could not unfix his determination. "No," he said, "they do not expect me. No one will be disappointed. I am too old to travel. I might be lost in the sea. Until Guy makes his invention we must not be apart."

At first the villagers thought that he was only joking, and that they would some morning wake up and find him gone; but when the holidays came, and when enough time had elapsed for him to make his journey twice over they began to think he was in earnest. When they knew that Guy St. Denis was chained to his father's invention, and when they saw that Marie and the children had commenced to make match-boxes again, they shook their heads. Some of them at least seemed to understand why Monsieur Farlotte had not gone to France.

But he never repined. He took up his garden again, was as contented as ever, and comforted himself with the wisdom of Montaigne. The people dropped the old question, "When are you going to France?" Only his companion voice called him more loudly, and more often he saw figures in the air that no one else could see.

Early one morning, as he was working in his garden around a growing pear tree, he fell into a sort of stupor, and sinking down quietly on his knees he leaned against the slender stem for support. He saw a garden much like his own, flooded with the clear sunlight; in the shade of an arbour an old woman in a white cap was leaning back in a wheeled chair; her eyes were closed, she seemed asleep. A young woman was beside her, holding her hand. Suddenly the old woman smiled, a childish smile, as if she were well pleased. "Paul," she murmured, "Paul, Paul." A moment later her companion started up with a cry; but she did not move, she was silent and tranquil. Then the young woman fell on her knees and wept, hiding her face. But the aged face was inexpressibly calm in the shadow, with the smile lingering upon it, fixed by the deeper sleep into which she had fallen.

Gradually the vision faded away, and Paul Farlotte found himself leaning against his pear-tree, which was almost too young as yet to support his weight. The bell was ringing from St. Joseph's, and had shaken the swallows from their nests in the steeple into the clear air. He heard their cries as they flew into his garden, and he heard the voices of his neighbour children as they played around the house.

Later in the day he told Marie that his mother had died that morning, and she wondered how he knew.

STEPHEN LEACOCK

STEPHEN LEACOCK was born at Swanmoor, Hants, England, on December 30, 1869, and came to Canada with his parents when he was a boy of seven. He was educated at Upper Canada College, Toronto, and at the University of Toronto, graduating in 1891. For the next eight years he was a master at Upper Canada College, but gave up school teaching in 1899 to study economics and political science at the University of Chicago. He received the degree of Doctor of Philosophy from Chicago in 1903; meanwhile he had been appointed to the staff of McGill University in Montreal, and ultimately became Head of the Department of Economics and Political Science. He died in 1944.

Leacock began his writing career relatively late in life: he was thirty-seven when his first book, *Elements of Political Science*, was published, and it was not until 1910 that he found his true métier as a humorist with the publication of *Literary Lapses*. There followed some sixty books, some of them scholarly studies in history, economics and politics, the bulk of them humorous and satirical. Outstanding among the latter are *Sunshine Sketches of a Little Town* (1912) and *Arcadian Adventures with the Idle Rich* (1914).

It is too early to forecast with confidence the permanent status of Leacock as a humourist. He has been called the greatest humourist of his age, and he has certainly been almost universally read and enjoyed. Dr. E. K. Brown has noted the appreciation of his humour by students at the Sorbonne; his books are among the most popular in the library of the Cambridge Union; in the United States he has been generally regarded as the contemporary heir of Mark Twain's mantle. One of his books, *Sunshine Sketches*, is so redolent of the most amusing features of Canadian small-town life that it seems certain that his countrymen will always cherish it. But on re-reading the bulk of his work, one is struck by its unevenness and by the quantity of it which does not withstand re-reading. *Nonsense Novels*, for instance, was undoubtedly funny once, but most of its humour has met the same fate as the novels it set out to parody; and much the same is true of *Moonbeams from the Larger*

Lunacy and even of most of *Literary Lapses*. But this, after all, is true of Haliburton and Twain and even, to a lesser extent, of Dickens; and it is certainly churlish to cavil at one who has so richly delighted at least two generations already and will undoubtedly delight many more.

There is a study of Leacock by Peter McArthur in the "Makers of Canadian Literature" series. Professor Ralph L. Curry's *Stephen Leacock, Humorist and Humanist* appeared in 1959. An excellent critical article is that by Professor G. G. Sedgwick in the *University of Toronto Quarterly* XV: 17-26 (October, 1945). The selection which follows is taken from *Sunshine Sketches of a Little Town*.

The Speculations of Jefferson Thorpe

IT WAS NOT until the mining boom, at the time when everybody went simply crazy over the Cobalt and Porcupine mines of the new silver country near the Hudson Bay, that Jefferson Thorpe reached what you might call public importance in Mariposa.

Of course everybody knew Jeff and his little barber shop that stood just across the street from Smith's Hotel. Everybody knew him and everybody got shaved there. From early morning, when the commercial travellers off the 6.30 express got shaved into the resemblance of human beings, there were always people going in and out of the barber shop.

Mullins, the manager of the Exchange Bank, took his morning shave from Jeff as a form of resuscitation, with enough wet towels laid on his face to stew him and with Jeff moving about in the steam, razor in hand, as grave as an operating surgeon.

Then, as I think I said, Mr. Smith came in every morning and there was a tremendous outpouring of Florida water and rums, essences and revivers and renovators, regardless of expense. What with Jeff's white coat and Mr. Smith's flowered waistcoat and the red geranium in the window and the Florida water and the double extract of hyacinth, the little shop seemed multi-coloured and luxurious enough for the annex of a Sultan's harem.

But what I mean is that, till the mining boom, Jefferson Thorpe never occupied a position of real prominence in Mariposa. You couldn't, for example, have compared him with a man like Golgotha Gingham, who, as undertaker, stood in a direct relation to life and death, or to Trelawney, the postmaster, who drew money from the Federal Government of Canada, and was regarded as virtually a member of the Dominion Cabinet.

Everybody knew Jeff and liked him, but the odd thing was that till he made money nobody took any stock in his ideas at all. It was only after he made the "clean up" that they came to see what a splendid fellow he was. "Level-headed" I think was the term; indeed in the speech of Mariposa, the highest form of endowment was to have the head set on horizontally as with a theodolite.

As I say, it was when Jeff made money that they saw how gifted he was, and when he lost it—but still, there's no need to go into that. I believe it's something the same in other places, too.

The barber shop, you will remember, stands across the street from Smith's Hotel, and stares at it face to face.

It is one of those wooden structures—I don't know whether you know them—with a false front that sticks up above its real height and gives it an air at once rectangular and imposing. It is a form of architecture much used in Mariposa and understood to be in keeping with the pretentious and artificial character of modern business. There is a red, white and blue post in front of the shop and the shop itself has a large square window out of proportion to its little flat face.

Painted on the panes of the window is the remains of a legend that once spelt BARBER SHOP, executed with the flourishes that prevailed in the golden age of sign painting in Mariposa. Through the window you can see the geraniums in the window shelf and behind them Jeff Thorpe with his little black skull cap on and his spectacles drooped upon his nose as he bends forward in the absorption of shaving.

As you open the door, it sets in violent agitation a coiled spring up above and a bell that almost rings. Inside, there are two shaving chairs of the heavier, or electrocution pattern, with mirrors in front of them and pigeon holes with individual shaving mugs. There must be ever so many of them, fifteen or sixteen. It is the current supposition of each of Jeff's customers that everyone else but himself uses a separate mug. One corner of the shop is partitioned off and bears the sign: HOT AND COLD BATHS, 50 CENTS. There has been no bath inside the partition for twenty years—only old newspapers and a mop. Still, it lends distinction somehow, just as do the faded cardboard signs that hang against the mirror with the legends: TURKISH SHAMPOO, 75 CENTS, and ROMAN MASSAGE, $1.00.

They said commonly in Mariposa that Jeff made money out of the barber shop. He may have, and it may have been that that turned his mind to investment. But it's hard to see how he could. A shave cost five cents, and a haircut fifteen (or the two, if you liked, for a quarter), and at that it is hard to see how he could make money, even when he had both chairs going and shaved first in one and then in the other.

You see, in Mariposa, shaving isn't the hurried, perfunctory thing that it is in the city. A shave is looked upon as a form of physical pleasure and lasts anywhere from twenty-five minutes to three-quarters of an hour.

In the morning hours, perhaps, there was a semblance of haste about it, but in the long quiet of the afternoon, as Jeff leaned forward towards the customer and talked to him in a soft confidential monotone, like a portrait painter, the razor would go slower and slower, and pause and stop, move and pause again, till the shave died away into the mere drowse of conversation.

At such hours, the Mariposa barber shop would become a very Palace of Slumber, and as you waited your turn in one of the wooden arm-chairs beside the wall, what with the quiet of the hour, and the low drone of Jeff's conversation, the buzzing of the flies against the window pane and the measured tick of the clock above the mirror, your head sank dreaming on your breast, and the Mariposa *Newspacket* rustled unheeded on the floor. It makes one drowsy just to think of it!

The conversation, of course, was the real charm of the place. You see, Jefferson's forte, or specialty, was information. He could tell you more things within the compass of a half-hour's shave than you get in days of laborious research in an encyclopædia. Where he got it all, I don't know, but I am inclined to think it came more or less out of the newspapers.

In the city, people never read the newspapers, not really, only little bits and scraps of them. But in Mariposa it's different. There they read the whole thing from cover to cover, and they build up on it, in the course of years, a range of acquirement that would put a college president to the blush. Anybody who has ever heard Henry Mullins and Peter Glover talk about the future of China will know just what I mean.

And, of course, the peculiarity of Jeff's conversation was that he could suit it to his man every time. He had a kind of divination about it. There was a certain kind of man that Jeff would size up sideways as he stropped the razor, and in whose ear he would whisper: "I see where Saint Louis has took four straight games off Chicago"—and so hold him fascinated to the end.

In the same way he would say to Mr. Smith: "I see where it says that this 'Flying Squirl' run a dead heat for the King's Plate."

To a humble intellect like mine he would explain in full the relations of the Keesar to the German Rich Dog.

But first and foremost, Jeff's specialty in the way of conversation was finance and the money market, the huge fortunes that a man with the right kind of head could make.

I've known Jefferson to pause in his shaving with the razor suspended in the air as long as five minutes while he described, with his eye half closed, exactly the kind of a head a man needed in order to make a "haul" or a "clean up." It was evidently simply a matter of the head, and as far as one could judge, Jeff's own was the very type required.

I don't know just at what time or how Jefferson first began his speculative enterprises. It was probably in him from the start. There is no doubt that the very idea of such things as Traction Stock and Amalgamated Asbestos went to his head: and whenever he spoke of Mr. Carnegie and Mr. Rockefeller, the yearning tone of his voice made it as soft as lathered soap.

I suppose the most rudimentary form of his speculation was the hens. That was years ago. He kept them out at the back of his house—which itself stood up a grass plot behind and beyond the barber shop—and in the old days Jeff would say, with a certain note of pride in his voice, that The Woman had sold as many as two dozen eggs in a day to the summer visitors.

But what with reading about Amalgamated Asbestos and Consolidated Copper and all that, the hens began to seem pretty small business, and, in any case, the idea of two dozen eggs at a cent apiece almost makes one blush. I suppose a good many of us have felt just as Jeff did about our poor little earnings. Anyway, I remember Jeff telling me one day that he could take the whole lot of the hens and sell them off and crack the money into Chicago wheat on margin and turn it over in twenty-four hours. He did it, too. Only somehow when it was turned over it came upside down on top of the hens.

After that the hen house stood empty and The Woman had to throw away chicken feed every day, at a dead loss of perhaps a shave and a half. But it made no difference to Jeff, for his mind had floated away already on the possibilities of what he called "displacement" mining on the Yukon.

So you can understand that when the mining boom struck Mariposa, Jefferson Thorpe was in it right from the very start. Why, no wonder; it seemed like the finger of providence. Here was this great silver country spread out to north of us, where people had thought there was only a wilderness. And right at our very doors! You could see, as I saw, the night express going north every evening; for all one knew Rockefeller or

Carnegie or anyone might be on it! Here was the wealth of Calcutta, as the Mariposa *Newspacket* put it, poured out at our very feet.

So no wonder the town went wild! All day in the street you could hear men talking of veins, and smelters and dips and deposits and faults—the town hummed with it like a geology class on examination day. And there were men about the hotels with mining outfits and theodolites and dunnage bags, and at Smith's bar they would hand chunks of rock up and down, some of which would run as high as ten drinks to the pound.

The fever just caught the town and ran through it! Within a fortnight they put a partition down Robertson's Coal and Wood Office and opened the Mariposa Mining Exchange, and just about every man on the Main Street started buying scrip. Then presently young Fizzlechip, who had been teller in Mullins's Bank and that everybody had thought a worthless jackass before, came back from the Cobalt country with a fortune, and loafed around in the Mariposa House in English khaki and a horizontal hat, drunk all the time, and everybody holding him up as an example of what it was possible to do if you tried.

They all went in. Jim Eliot mortgaged the inside of the drug store and jammed it into Twin Tamagami. Pete Glover at the hardware store bought Nippewa stock at thirteen cents and sold it to his brother at seventeen and bought it back in less than a week at nineteen. They didn't care! They took a chance. Judge Pepperleigh put the rest of his wife's money into Temiskaming Common, and Lawyer Macartney got the fever, too, and put every cent that his sister possessed into Tulip Preferred.

And even when young Fizzlechip shot himself in the back room of the Mariposa House, Mr. Gingham buried him in a casket with silver handles and it was felt that there was a Monte Carlo touch about the whole thing.

They all went in—or all except Mr. Smith. You see, Mr. Smith had come from down there, and he knew all about rocks and mining and canoes and the north country. He knew what it was to eat flour-baked dampers under the lee side of a canoe propped among the underbrush, and to drink the last drop of whisky within fifty miles. Mr. Smith had mighty little use for the North. But what he did do, was to buy up enough early potatoes to send fifteen carload lots into Cobalt at a profit of five dollars a bag.

Mr. Smith, I say, hung back. But Jeff Thorpe was in the mining boom right from the start. He bought in on the Nippewa mine even before the interim prospectus was out. He took a "block" of one hundred shares of Abitibi Development at fourteen cents, and he and Johnson, the livery stable keeper next door, formed a syndicate and got a thousand shares of Metagami Lake at three and a quarter cents and then "unloaded" them on one of the sausage men at Netley's butcher shop at a clear cent per cent. advance.

Jeff would open the little drawer below the mirror in the barber shop and show you all kinds and sorts of Cobalt country mining certificates—blue ones, pink ones, green ones, with outlandish and fascinating names on them that ran clear from Mattawa to the Hudson Bay.

And right from the start he was confident of winning.

"There ain't no difficulty to it," he said, "there's lots of silver up there in that country and if you buy some here and some there you can't fail to come out somewhere. I don't say," he used to continue with the scissors open and ready to cut, "that some of the greenhorns won't get bit. But if a feller knows the country and keeps his head level, he can't lose."

Jefferson had looked at so many prospectuses and so many pictures of mines and pine trees and smelters, that I think he'd forgotten that he'd never been in the country. Anyway, what's two hundred miles!

To an onlooker it certainly didn't seem so simple. I never knew the meanness, the trickery, of the mining business, the sheer obstinate determination of the bigger capitalists not to make money when they might, till I heard the accounts of Jeff's different mines. Take the case of the Corona Jewel.

There was a good mine, simply going to ruin for lack of common sense.

"She ain't been developed," Jeff would say. "There's silver enough in her so you could dig it out with a shovel. She's full of it. But they won't get at her and work her."

Then he'd take a look at the pink and blue certificates of the Corona Jewel and slam the drawer on them in disgust.

Worse than that was the Silent Pine—a clear case of *stupid incompetence!* Utter lack of engineering skill was all that was keeping the Silent Pine from making a fortune for its holders.

"The only trouble with that mine," said Jeff, "is they won't go deep enough. They followed the vein down to where it kind o' thinned out and then they quit. If they'd just go right into her good, they'd get it again. She's down there all right."

But perhaps the meanest case of all was the Northern Star. That always seemed to me, every time I heard of it, a straight case for the criminal law. The thing was so evidently a conspiracy.

"I bought her," said Jeff, "at thirty-two, and she stayed right there tight, like she was stuck. Then a bunch of these fellers in the city started to drive her down and they got her pushed down to twenty-four, and I held on to her and they shoved her down to twenty-one. This morning they've got her down to sixteen, but I don't mean to let go. No, sir."

In another fortnight they shoved her, the same unscrupulous crowd, down to nine cents, and Jefferson still held on.

"They're working her down," he admitted, "but I'm holding her."

No conflict between vice and virtue was ever grimmer.

"She's at six," said Jeff, "but I've got her. They can't squeeze me."

A few days after that, the same criminal gang had her down further than ever.

"They've got her down to three cents," said Jeff, "but I'm with her. Yes, sir, they think they can shove her clean off the market, but they can't do it. I've boughten in Johnson's shares, and the whole of Netley's, and I'll stay with her till she breaks."

So they shoved and pushed and clawed her down — that unseen nefarious crowd in the city — and Jeff held on to her and they writhed and twisted at his grip, and then—

And then—well, that's just the queer thing about the mining business. Why, sudden as a flash of lightning, it seemed, the news came over the wire to the Mariposa *Newspacket,* that they had struck a vein of silver in the Northern Star as thick as a sidewalk, and that the stock had jumped to seventeen dollars a share, and even at that you couldn't get it! And Jeff stood there flushed and half-staggered against the mirror of the little shop, with a bunch of mining scrip in his hand that was worth forty thousand dollars!

Excitement! It was all over the town in a minute. They ran off a news extra at the Mariposa *Newspacket,* and in less than no time there wasn't standing room in the barber shop, and over in Smith's Hotel they had three extra bar-keepers working on the lager beer pumps.

They were selling mining shares on the Main Street in Mariposa that afternoon and people were just clutching for them. Then at night there was a big oyster supper in Smith's caff, with speeches and the Mariposa band outside.

And the queer thing was that the very next afternoon was the funeral of young Fizzlechip, and Dean Drone had to change the whole text of his Sunday sermon at two days' notice for fear of offending public sentiment.

But I think what Jeff liked best of it all was the sort of public recognition that it meant. He'd stand there in the shop, hardly bothering to shave, and explain to the men in the arm-chairs how he held her, and they shoved her, and he clung to her, and what he'd said to himself—a perfect Iliad—while he was clinging to her.

The whole thing was in the city papers a few days after with a photograph of Jeff, taken specially at Ed. Moore's studio (upstairs over Netley's). It showed Jeff sitting among palm trees, as all mining men do, with one hand on his knee, and a dog, one of those regular mining dogs, at his feet, and a look of piercing intelligence in his face that would easily account for forty thousand dollars.

I say that the recognition meant a lot to Jeff for its own sake. But no doubt the fortune meant quite a bit to him, too, on account of Myra.

Did I mention Myra, Jeff's daughter? Perhaps not. That's the trouble with the people in Mariposa; they're all so separate and so different—not a bit like the people in the cities—that unless you hear about them separately and one by one you can't for a moment understand what they're like.

Myra had golden hair and a Greek face and would come bursting through the barber shop in a hat at least six inches wider than what they wear in Paris. As you saw her swinging up the street to the Telephone Exchange in a suit that was straight out of the *Delineator* and brown American boots, there was style written all over her—the kind of thing that Mariposa recognized and did homage to. And to see her in the Exchange—she was one of the four girls that I spoke of— on her high stool with a steel cap on—jabbing the connecting plugs in and out as if electricity cost nothing—well, all I mean is that you could understand why it was that the commercial travellers would stand round in the Exchange calling up all sorts of impossible villages, and waiting about so pleasant and genial!—it made one realize how naturally good-tempered men are. And then when Myra would go off duty and Miss Cleghorn, who was sallow, would come on, the commercial men would be off again like autumn leaves.

It just shows the difference between people. There was Myra who treated lovers like dogs and would slap them across the face with a banana skin to show her utter independence. And there was Miss Cleghorn, who was sallow, and who bought a forty-cent Ancient History to improve herself: and yet if she'd hit any man in Mariposa with a banana skin, he'd have had her arrested for assault.

Mind you, I don't mean that Myra was merely flippant and worthless. Not at all. She was a girl with any amount of talent. You should have heard her recite "The Raven" at the

Methodist Social! Simply genius! And when she acted Portia in the Trial Scene of *The Merchant of Venice* at the High School concert, everybody in Mariposa admitted that you couldn't have told it from the original.

So, of course, as soon as Jeff made the fortune, Myra had her resignation in next morning and everybody knew that she was to go to a dramatic school for three months in the fall and become a leading actress.

But, as I said, the public recognition counted a lot for Jeff. The moment you begin to get that sort of thing it comes in quickly enough. Brains, you know, are recognized right away. That was why, of course, within a week from this Jeff received the first big packet of stuff from the Cuban Land Development Company, with coloured pictures of Cuba, and fields of bananas, and haciendas and insurrectos with machetes and Heaven knows what. They heard of him, somehow—it wasn't for a modest man like Jefferson to say how. After all, the capitalists of the world are just one and the same crowd. If you're in it, you're in it, that's all! Jeff realized why it is that of course men like Carnegie or Rockefeller and Morgan all know one another. They have to.

For all I know, this Cuban stuff may have been sent from Morgan himself. Some of the people in Mariposa said yes, others said no. There was no certainty.

Anyway, they were fair and straight, this Cuban crowd that wrote to Jeff. They offered him to come right in and be one of themselves. If a man's got the brains, you may as well recognize it right away. Just as well write him to be a director now as wait and hesitate till he forces his way into it.

Anyhow, they didn't hesitate, these Cuban people that wrote to Jeff from Cuba—or from a post-office box in New York—it's all the same thing because Cuba being so near to New York the mail is all distributed from there. I suppose in some financial circles they might have been slower, wanted guarantees of some sort, and so on, but these Cubans, you know, have got a sort of Spanish warmth of heart, that you don't see in business men in America, and that touches you.

No, they asked no guarantee. Just send the money—whether by express order or by bank draft or cheque, they left that entirely to oneself, as a matter between Cuban gentlemen.

And they were quite frank about their enterprise—bananas and tobacco in the plantation district reclaimed from the insurrectos. You could see it all there in the pictures—the tobacco plants and the insurrectos—everything. They made no rash promises, just admitted straight out that the enterprise might realize four hundred per cent. or might conceivably make less. There was no hint of more.

So within a month, everybody in Mariposa knew that Jeff Thorpe was "in Cuban lands" and would probably clean up half a million by New Year's. You couldn't have failed to know it. All round the little shop there were pictures of banana groves and the harbour of Havana, and Cubans in white suits and scarlet sashes, smoking cigarettes in the sun and too ignorant to know that you can make four hundred per cent. by planting a banana tree.

I liked it about Jeff that he didn't stop shaving. He went on just the same. Even when Johnson, the livery stable man, came in with five hundred dollars and asked him to see if the Cuban Board of Directors would let him put it in, Jeff laid it in the drawer and then shaved him for five cents, in the same old way. Of course, he must have felt proud when, a few days later, he got a letter from the Cuban people, from New York, accepting the money straight off without a single question, and without knowing anything more of Johnson except that he was a friend of Jeff's. They wrote most handsomely. Any friends of Jeff's were friends of Cuba. All money they might send would be treated just as Jeff's would be treated.

One reason, perhaps, why Jeff didn't give up shaving was because it allowed him to talk about Cuba. You see, everybody knew in Mariposa that Jeff Thorpe had sold out of Cobalts and had gone into Cuban Renovated Lands — and that spread round him a kind of halo of wealth and mystery and outlandishness — oh, something Spanish. Perhaps you've felt it about people that you know. Anyhow, they asked him about the climate, and yellow fever and what the Negroes were like and all that sort of thing.

"This Cubey, it appears, is an island," Jeff would explain. Of course, everybody knows how easily islands lend themselves to making money—"and for fruit, they say it comes up so fast you can't stop it." And then he would pass into details about the Hash-enders and the resurrectos and technical things like that till it was thought a wonder how he could know it. Still, it was realized that a man with money has got to know these things. Look at Morgan and Rockefeller and all the men that make a pile. They know just as much as Jeff did about the countries where they make it. It stands to reason.

Did I say that Jeff shaved in the same old way? Not quite. There was something even dreamier about it now, and a sort of new element in the way Jeff fell out of his monotone into lapses of thought that I, for one, misunderstood. I thought that perhaps getting so much money—well, you know the way it acts on people in the larger cities. It seemed to spoil one's idea of Jeff that copper and asbestos and banana lands should form the goal of his thought when, if he knew it, the little shop and the sunlight of Mariposa was so much better.

In fact, I had perhaps borne him a grudge for what seemed to me his perpetual interest in the great capitalists. He always had some item out of the paper about them.

"I see where this here Carnegie has give fifty thousand dollars for one of them observatories," he would say.

And another day he would pause in the course of shaving, and almost whisper: "Did you ever *see* this Rockefeller?"

It was only by a sort of accident that I came to know that there was another side to Jefferson's speculation that no one in Mariposa ever knew, or will ever know now.

I knew it because I went in to see Jeff in his house one night. The house—I think I said it—stood out behind the barber shop. You went out of the back door of the shop, and through a grass plot with petunias beside it and the house stood at the end. You could see the light of the lamp behind the blind and through the screen door as you came along. And it was here that Jefferson used to sit in the evenings when the shop got empty.

There was a round table that The Woman used to lay for supper, and after supper there used to be a chequered cloth on it and a lamp with a shade. And beside it Jeff would sit, with his spectacles on and the paper spread out, reading about Carnegie and Rockefeller. Near him, but away from the table was The Woman doing needlework, and Myra, when she wasn't working in the Telephone Exchange, was there, too, with her elbows on the table reading Marie Corelli—only now, of course, after the fortune, she was reading the prospectuses of Dramatic Schools.

So this night—I don't know just what it was in the paper that caused it—Jeff laid down what he was reading and started to talk about Carnegie.

"This Carnegie, I bet you, would be worth," said Jeff, closing up his eyes in calculation, "as much as perhaps two million dollars, if you was to sell him up. And this Rockefeller and this Morgan, either of them to sell them up clean, would be worth another couple of million—"

I may say in parenthesis that it was a favourite method in Mariposa if you wanted to get at the real worth of a man, to imagine him clean sold up, put up for auction, as it were. It was the only way to test him.

"And now look at 'em," Jeff went on. "They make their money and what do they do with it? They give it away. And who do they give it to? Why, to those as don't want it, every time. They give it to these professors and to this research and that, and do the poor get any of it? Not a cent and never will."

"I tell you, boys," continued Jeff (there were no boys present, but in Mariposa all really important speeches are addressed to an imaginary audience of boys)—"I tell you if I was to make a million out of this Cubey, I'd give it straight to the poor, yes, sir—divide it up into a hundred lots of a thousand dollars each and give it to the people that hadn't nothing."

So always after that I knew just what those bananas were being grown for.

Indeed, after that, though Jefferson never spoke of his intentions directly, he said a number of things that seemed to bear on them. He asked me, for instance, one day, how many blind people it would take to fill one of these blind homes and how a feller could get ahold of them. And at another time he asked whether if a feller advertised for some of these incurables a feller could get enough of them to make a showing. I know for a fact that he got Nivens, the lawyer, to draw ιp a document that was to give an acre of banana land in Cuba to every idiot in Missinaba county.

But still—what's the use of talking of what Jeff meant to do? Nobody knows or cares about it now.

The end of it was bound to come. Even in Mariposa some of the people must have thought so. Else how was it that Henry Mullins made such a fuss about selling a draft for forty thousand on New York? And why was it that Mr. Smith wouldn't pay Billy, the desk clerk, his back wages when he wanted to put it into Cuba?

Oh, yes; some of them must have seen it. And yet when it came, it seemed so quiet—ever so quiet—not a bit like the Northern Star mine and the oyster supper and the Mariposa band. It is strange how quiet these things look, the other way round.

You remember the Cuban Land frauds in New York—and Porforio Gomez shooting the detective, and him and Maximo Morez getting clear away with two hundred thousand? No, of course you don't; why, even in the city papers it only filled an inch or two of type and anyway the names were hard to remember. That was Jeff's money—part of it. Mullins got the telegram, from a broker or someone, and he showed it to Jeff just as he was going up the street with an estate agent to look at a big empty lot on the hill behind the town—the very place for these incurables.

And Jeff went back to the shop so quiet—have you ever

seen an animal that is stricken through, how quiet it seems to move?

Well, that's how he walked.

And since that, though it's quite a little while ago, the shop's open till eleven every night now, and Jeff is shaving away to pay back that five hundred that Johnson, the livery man, sent to the Cubans, and—

Pathetic? tut! tut! You don't know Mariposa. Jeff has to work pretty late, but that's nothing—nothing at all, if you've worked hard all your lifetime. And Myra is back at the Telephone Exchange—they were glad enough to get her, and she says now that if there's one thing she hates, it's the stage, and she can't see how the actresses put up with it.

Anyway, things are not so bad. You see, it was just at this time that Mr. Smith's caff opened, and Mr. Smith came to Jeff's Woman and said he wanted seven dozen eggs a day, and wanted them handy, and so the hens are back, and more of them, and they exult so every morning over the eggs they lay that if you wanted to talk of Rockefeller in the barber shop you couldn't hear his name for the cackling.

NORMAN DUNCAN

NORMAN DUNCAN was born at Brantford, Ontario, on July 2, 1871. After a boyhood spent in various Ontario towns, he entered the University of Toronto in 1891. At the university he took an active part in all forms of social and literary activity. From 1895 to 1897 he was a reporter for the *Auburn* (N.Y.) *Bulletin,* and from 1897 to 1900 was on the staff of the *New York Evening Post.* His life in New York City provided the material for his first book, a collection of short stories of life in the Syrian quarter of that city which was published in 1900 under the title *The Soul of the Street.* These stories have been described by T. G. Marquis as "a series of sketches which for insight into life and for character drawing are as fine as anything done in the short story in America"; and although the praise is too extravagant, they are far above the level of ordinary journalism. Duncan found his most congenial subject matter, however, in 1900 when he went to Newfoundland as a correspondent for *McClure's Magazine.* He was so interested in the life of the fishing villages that he returned to it at every opportunity during the remainder of his life. His best books and stories deal with fishermen and the sea: *The Way of the Sea* (1903), *Doctor Luke of the Labrador* (1904), *The Cruise of the Shining Light* (1907), *Harbour Tales Down North* (1918).

From 1901 to 1906 Duncan was on the staff of Washington and Jefferson College as professor of rhetoric, and from 1909 to 1911 served as adjunct professor of English at the University of Kansas. In the intervals of his academic experience he was a foreign correspondent for *Harper's Magazine,* first in Palestine, Arabia and Egypt, and later in Australia, New Guinea and Malaya. He died on October 18, 1916.

Duncan was an extremely prolific writer, publishing in his rather short lifetime no fewer than sixteen books. As we might expect, in view of his productivity and his journalistic proclivities, his work is markedly uneven in quality. Unfortunately, this unevenness extends to every one of his stories, so that not one of them is flawless. One's final impression of him is of a writer of considerable power, capable of surprisingly good things on occasion, who never became sufficiently self-critical to make his writing genuinely and permanently significant. Like that of most Canadian writers of fiction in the nineteenth and early twentieth centuries, his work is marred by sudden lapses into melodrama and sentimentality, by deviations from good literary taste. His literary affiliations are obviously with Dickens and Bret Harte, and he shares, in a measure, both their strength and weakness. His best qualities have thus been neatly summarized by Dr. Grenfell: "Variety and colour in characters and situations, vividness of descriptions—especially in those of the stormy sea—rapidity of movement and dramatic intensity in narratives, genuine sentiment and real tenderness, humour, and pathos. . . ." The story which follows is taken from *The Way of the Sea.*

The Fruits of Toil

NOW the wilderness, savage and remote, yields to the strength of men. A generation strips it of tree and rock, a generation tames it and tills it, a generation passes into the evening shadows as into rest in a garden, and thereafter the children of that place possess it in peace and plenty, through succeeding generations, without end, and shall to the end of the world. But the sea is tameless: as it was in the beginning, it is now, and shall ever be—mighty, savage, dread, infinitely treacherous and hateful, yielding only that which is wrested from it, snarling, raging, snatching lives, spoiling souls of their graces. The tiller of the soil sows in peace, and in a yellow, hazy peace he reaps; he passes his hand over a field, and, lo, in good season he gathers a harvest, for the earth rejoices to serve him. The deep is not thus subdued; the toiler of the sea—the Newfoundlander of the upper shore—is born to conflict, ceaseless and deadly, and, in the dawn of all the days, he puts forth anew to wage it, as his father did, and his father's father, and as his children must, and his children's children, to the last of them; nor from day to day can he foresee the issue, nor from season to season foretell the worth of the spoil, which is what chance allows. Thus laboriously, precariously, he slips through life: he follows hope through the toilsome years; and past summers are a black regret and bitterness to him, but summers to come are all rosy with new promise.

Long ago, when young Luke Dart, the Boot Bay trader, was ambitious for Shore patronage, he said to Solomon Stride, of Ragged Harbour, a punt fisherman: "Solomon, b'y, an you be willin', I'll trust you with twine for a cod-trap. An you trade with me, b'y, I'll trade with you, come good times or bad." Solomon was young and lusty, a mighty youth in bone and seasoned muscle, lunged like a blast furnace, courageous and finely sanguine. Said he: "An you trust me with twine for a trap, skipper, I'll deal fair by you, come good times or bad. I'll pay for un, skipper, with the first fish I cotches." Said Luke Dart: "When I trust, b'y, I trust. You pays for un when you can." It was a compact, so, at the end of the season, Solomon builded a cottage under the Man-o'-War, Broad Cove way, and married a maid of the place. In five months of that winter he made the trap, every net of it, leader and all, with his own hands, that he might know that the work was good, to the last knot and splice. In the spring, he put up the stage and the flake, and made the skiff; which done, he waited for a sign of fish. When the tempered days came, he hung the net on a horse, where it could be seen from the threshold of the cottage. In the evenings he sat with Priscilla on the bench at the door, and dreamed great dreams, while the red sun went down in the sea, and the shadows crept out of the wilderness.

"Woman, dear," said this young Solomon Stride, with a slap of his great thigh, " 'twill be a gran' season for fish this year."

"Sure, b'y," said Priscilla, tenderly; " 'twill be a gran' season for fish."

"Ay," Solomon sighed, " 'twill that—this year."

The gloaming shadows gathered over the harbour water, and hung, sullenly, between the great rocks, rising all round about.

" 'Tis handy t' three hundred and fifty dollars I owes Luke Dart for the twine," mused Solomon.

" 'Tis a hape of money t'owe," said Priscilla.

"Hut!" growled Solomon, deep in his chest, "'Tis like nothin'."

" 'Tis not much," said Priscilla, smiling, "when you has a trap."

Dusk and a clammy mist chased the glory from the hills; the rocks turned black, and a wind, black and cold, swept out of the wilderness and ran to sea.

"Is'll pay un all up this year," said Solomon. "Oh," he added loftily, " 'twill be easy. 'Tis to be a gran' season!"

"Sure," said she, echoing his confidence.

Night filled the cloudy heavens overhead. It drove the flush of pink in upon the sun, and, following fast and overwhelmingly, thrust the flaring red and gold over the rim of the sea; and it was dark.

"Us'll pay un for a trap, dear," chuckled Solomon, "an' have enough left over t' buy a—"

"Oh," she cried with an ecstatic gasp, "a sewin' machine!"

"Iss," he roared. "Sure, girl!"

But, in the beginning of that season, when the first fish ran in for the caplin and the nets were set out, the ice was still hanging off shore, drifting vagrantly with the wind; and there came a gale in the night, springing from the northeast—a great, vicious wind, which gathered the ice in a pack and drove it swiftly in upon the land. Solomon Stride put off in a punt, in a sea tossing and white, to loose the trap from its moorings. Three times, while the pack swept nearer, crunching and horribly groaning, as though lashed to cruel speed by the gale, the wind beat him back through the tickle;[1] and, upon the fourth essay, when his strength was breaking, the ice ran over the place where the trap was, and chased the punt into the harbour, frothing upon its flank. When, three days thereafter, a west wind carried the ice to sea, Solomon dragged the trap from the

---

[1] A narrow passage between two islands or to a harbour.

bottom. Great holes were bruised in the nets, head rope and span line were ground to pulp, the anchors were lost. Thirty-seven days and nights it took to make the nets whole again, and in that time the great spring run of cod passed by. So, in the next spring, Solomon was deeper in the debt of sympathetic Luke Dart—for the new twine and for the winter's food he had eaten; but, of an evening, when he sat on the bench with Priscilla, he looked through the gloaming shadows gathered over the harbour water and hanging between the great rocks, to the golden summer approaching, and dreamed gloriously of the fish he would catch in his trap.

"Priscilla, dear," said Solomon Stride, slapping his iron thigh, "they be a fine sign of fish down the coast. 'Twill be a gran' season, I'm thinkin'."

"Sure, b'y," Priscilla agreed; " 'twill be a gran' cotch o' fish you'll have this year."

Dusk and the mist touched the hills, and, in the dreamful silence, their glory faded; the rocks turned black, and the wind from the wilderness ruffled the water beyond the flake.

"Us'll pay Luke Dart this year, I tells you," said Solomon, like a boastful boy. "Us'll pay un twice over."

" 'Twill be fine to have the machane," said she, with shining eyes.

"An' the calico t'use un on," said he.

And so, while the night spread overhead, these two simple folk feasted upon all the sweets of life; and all that they desired they possessed, as fast as fancy could form wishes, just as though the bench were a bit of magic furniture, to bring dreams true—until the night, advancing, thrust the red and gold of the sunset clouds over the rim of the sea, and it was dark.

"Leave us goa in," said Priscilla.

"This year," said Solomon, rising, "I be goaing to cotch three hundred quintals of fish. Sure, I be—this year."

"'Twill be fine," said she.

It chanced in that year that the fish failed utterly; hence, in the winter following, Ragged Harbour fell upon days of distress; and three women and one old man starved to death—and five children, of whom one was the infant son of Solomon Stride. Neither in that season, nor in any one of the thirteen years coming after, did this man catch three hundred quintals of cod in his trap. In pure might of body—in plenitude and quality of strength—in the full, eager power of brawn—he was great as the men of any time, a towering glory to the whole race, here hidden; but he could not catch three hundred quintals of cod. In spirit—in patience, hope, courage, and the fine will for toil—he was great; but, good season or bad, he could not catch three hundred quintals of cod. He met night, cold, fog, wind, and the fury of waves, in their craft, in their swift assault, in their slow, crushing descent; but all the cod he could wrest from the sea, being given into the hands of Luke Dart, an honest man, yielded only sufficient provision for food and clothing for himself and Priscilla—only enough to keep their bodies warm and still the crying of their stomachs. Thus, while the nets of the trap rotted, and Solomon came near to middle age, the debt swung from seven hundred dollars to seven, and back to seventy-three, which it was in an evening in spring, when he sat with Priscilla on the sunken bench at the door, and dreamed great dreams as he watched the shadows gather over the harbour water and sullenly hang between the great rocks, rising all round about.

"I wonder, b'y," said Priscilla, "if 'twill be a good season—this year."

"Oh, sure!" exclaimed Solomon. "Sure!"

"D'ye think it, b'y?" wistfully.

"Woman," said he impressively, "us'll cotch a hape o' fish in the trap this year. They be millions o' fish t' the say," he went on excitedly; "millions o' fish t' the say. They be there, woman. 'Tis oan'y for us t' take un out. I be goain' t' wark hard this year."

"You be a great warker, Solomon," said she; "my, but you be!"

Priscilla smiled, and Solomon smiled; and it was as though all the labour and peril of the season were past, and the stage was full to the roof with salt cod. In the happiness of this dream they smiled again, and turned their eyes to the hills, from which the glory of purple and yellow was departing to make way for the misty dusk.

"Skipper Luke Dart says t' me," said Solomon, "that 'tis the luxuries that keep folks poor."

Priscilla said nothing at all.

"They be nine dollars agin me in seven years for crame o' tartar," said Solomon. "Think o' that!"

"My," said she, "but 'tis a lot! But we be used to un now, Solomon, and we can't get along without un."

"Sure," said he, " 'tis good we're not poor like some folk."

Night drove the flush of pink in upon the rim and followed the red and gold of the horizon over the rim of the sea.

" 'Tis growing cold," said she.

"Leave us goa in," said he.

In thirty years after that time, Solomon Stride put to sea ten thousand times. Ten thousand times he passed through the tickle rocks to the free, heaving deep for salmon and cod, thereto compelled by the inland waste, which contributes nothing to the sustenance of the men of that coast. Hunger, lurking in the shadows of days to come, inexorably drove him into the chances of the conflict. Perforce he matched himself ten thousand times against the restless might of the sea, immeasurable and unrestrained, surviving the gamut of its moods, because he was great in strength, fearlessness, and cunning. He weathered four hundred gales, from the grey gusts which come down between Quid Nunc and the Man-o'-War, leaping upon the fleet, to the summer tempests, swift and black, and the first blizzards of winter. He was wrecked off the Mull, off the Three Poor Sisters, on the Pancake Rock, and again off the Mull. Seven times he was swept to sea by the off-shore wind. Eighteen times he was frozen to the seat of his punt; and of these, eight times his feet were frozen, and thrice his festered right hand. All this he suffered, and more, of which I may set down six separate periods of starvation, in which thirty-eight men, women, and children died—all this, with all the toil, cold, despair, loneliness, hunger, peril, and disappointment therein contained. And so he came down to old age—with a bent back, shrunken arms, and filmy eyes—old Solomon Stride, now prey for the young sea. But, of an evening in spring, he sat with Priscilla on the sunken bench at the door, and talked hopefully of the fish he would catch from his punt.

"Priscilla, dear," said he, rubbing his hand over his weazened thigh, "I be thinkin' us punt fishermen'll have a—"

Priscilla was not attending; she was looking into the shadows above the harbour water, dreaming deeply of a mystery of the Book, which had long puzzled her; so, in silence, Solomon, too, watched the shadows rise and sullenly hang between the great rocks.

"Solomon, b'y," she whispered, "I wonder what the seven thunders uttered?"

" 'Tis quare, that—what the seven thunders uttered," said Solomon. "My, woman, but 'tis!"

" 'An' he set his right foot upon the sea,' " she repeated, staring over the greying water to the clouds which flamed gloriously at the edge of the world, " 'an' his left foot on the earth—' "

" 'An' cried with a loud voice,' " said he, whispering in awe, " 'as when a lion roareth; an' when he had cried, *seven thunders uttered their voices*.' "

" 'Seven thunders uttered their voices,' " said she; " 'an' when the seven thunders had uttered their voices, I was about to write, an' I heard a voice from heaven sayin' unto me, Seal up those things which the seven thunders uttered, and write them not.' "

The wind from the wilderness, cold and black, covered the hills with mist; the dusk fell, and the glory faded from the heights.

"Oh, Solomon," she said, clasping her hands, "I wonder what the seven thunders uttered! Think you, b'y, 'twas the kind o' sins that can't be forgiven?"

" 'Tis the seven mysteries!"

"I wonder what they be," said she.

"Sh-h-, dear," he said, patting her grey head; "thinkin' on they things'll capsize you an' you don't look out."

The night had driven all the colour from the sky; it had descended upon the red and gold of the cloudy west, and covered them. It was cold and dark.

" 'An' seven thunders uttered their voices,' " she said, dreamily.

"Sh-h-h-h, dear!" said he. "Leave us goa in."

Twenty-one years longer old Solomon Stride fished out of Ragged Harbour. He put to sea five thousand times more, weathered two hundred more gales, survived five more famines —all in the toil for salmon and cod. He was a punt fisherman again, was old Solomon; for the nets of the trap had rotted, had been renewed six times, strand by strand, and had rotted at last beyond repair. What with the weather he dared not pit his failing strength against, the return of fish to Luke Dart fell off from year to year; but, as Solomon said to Luke, "livin' expenses kep' up wonderful," notwithstanding.

"I be so used t' luxuries," he went on, running his hand through his long grey hair, "that 'twould be hard t' come down t' common livin'. Sure, 'tis sugar I wants t' me tea—not black-strap. 'Tis what I l'arned," he added proudly, "when I were a trap fisherman."

" 'Tis all right, Solomon," said Luke. "Many's the quintal o' fish you traded with me."

"Sure," Solomon chuckled, " 'twould take a year t' count un."

In course of time it came to the end of Solomon's last season—those days of it when, as the folk of the coast say, the sea is hungry for lives—and the man was eighty-one years old, and the debt to Luke Dart had crept up to $230.80. The off-shore wind, rising suddenly, with a blizzard in its train, caught him alone on the Grappling Hook grounds. He was old, very old—old and feeble and dull: the cold numbed him; the snow blinded him; the wind made sport of the strength of his arms. He was carried out to sea, rowing doggedly, thinking all the time that he was drawing near the harbour tickle; for it did not occur to him then that the last of eight hundred gales could be too great for him. He was carried out from the sea, where the strength of his youth had been spent, to the Deep, which had been a mystery to him all his days. That night he passed on a pan of ice, where he burned his boat, splinter by splinter, to keep warm. At dawn he lay down to die. The snow ceased, the wind changed; the ice was carried to Ragged Harbour. Eleazar Manuel spied the body of Solomon from the lookout, and put out and brought him in—revived him and took him home to Priscilla. Through the winter the old man doddered about the Harbour, dying of consumption. When the tempered days came—the days of balmy sunshine and cold evening winds—he came quickly to the pass of glittering visions, which, for such as die of the lung trouble, come at the end of life.

In the spring, when the *Lucky Star,* three days out from Boot Bay, put into Ragged Harbour to trade for the first catch, old Skipper Luke Dart was aboard, making his last voyage to the Shore; for he was very old, and longed once more to see the rocks of all that coast before he made ready to die. When he came ashore, Eleazar Manuel told him that Solomon Stride lay dying at home; so the skipper went to the cottage under the Man-o'-War to say good-bye to his old customer and friend —and there found him, propped up in bed, staring at the sea.

"Skipper Luke," Solomon quavered, in deep excitement, "be you just come in, b'y?"

"Iss—but an hour gone."

"What be the big craft hangin' off shoare? Eh—what be she, b'y?"

There had been no craft in sight when the *Lucky Star* beat in. "Were she a fore-an'-after, Solomon?" said Luke, evasively.

"Sure, noa, b'y!" cried Solomon. "She were a square-rigged craft, with all sail set—a great, gran' craft—a quare craft, b'y —like she were made o' glass, canvas an' hull an' all; an' she had shinin' ropes, an' she were shinin' all over. Sure, they be a star t' the tip o' her bowsprit, b'y, an' a star t' the peak o' her mainmast—seven stars they be, in all. Oh, she were a gran' sight!"

"Hem-m!" said Luke, stroking his beard. "She've not come in yet."

"A gran' craft!" said Solomon.

" 'Tis according," said Luke, "t' whether you be sot on oak bottoms or glass ones."

"She were bound down north t' the Labrador," Solomon went on quickly, "an' when she made the Grapplin' Hook grounds she come about an' headed for the tickle, with her sails squared. Sure she ran right over the Pancake, b'y, like he weren't there at all, an'——How's the wind, b'y?"

"Dead off shore from the tickle."

Solomon stared at Luke. "She were comin' straight in agin the wind," he said, hoarsely. "Maybe, skipper," he went on, with a little laugh, "she do be the ship for souls. They be many things strong men knows nothin' about. What think you?"

"Ay—maybe; maybe she be."

"Maybe—maybe—she do be invisible t' mortal eyes. Maybe, skipper, you hasn't seed her; maybe 'tis that my eyes do be opened t' such sights. Maybe she've turned in—for me."

The men turned their faces to the window again, and gazed long and intently at the sea, which a storm cloud had turned black. Solomon dozed for a moment, and when he awoke, Luke Dart was still staring dreamily out to sea.

"Skipper Luke," said Solomon, with a smile as of one in an enviable situation, " 'tis fine t' have nothin' agin you on the books when you comes t' die."

"Sure, b'y," said Luke, hesitating not at all, though he knew to a cent what was on the books against Solomon's name, " 'tis fine to be free o' debt."

"Ah," said Solomon, the smile broadening gloriously, " 'tis fine, I tells you! 'Twas the three hundred quintal I cotched last season that paid un all up. 'Twas a gran' cotch—last year. Ah," he sighed, " 'twas a gran' cotch o' fish."

"Iss—you be free o' debt now, b'y."

"What be the balance t' my credit, skipper? Sure I forget."

"Hem-m," the skipper coughed, pausing to form a guess

which might be within Solomon's dream; then he ventured: "Fifty dollars?"

"Iss," said Solomon, "fifty an' moare, skipper. Sure, you has forgot the eighty cents."

"Fifty-eighty," said the skipper, positively. " 'Tis that. I call un t' mind now. 'Tis fifty-eighty—iss, sure. Did you get a receipt for un' Solomon?"

"I doan't mind me now."

"Um-m-m—well," said the skipper, "I'll send un t' the woman the night—an order on the *Lucky Star*."

"Fifty-eighty for the woman!" said Solomon. " 'Twill kape her off the Gov'ment for three years, an she be savin'. 'Tis fine—that!"

When the skipper had gone, Priscilla crept in, and sat at the head of the bed, holding Solomon's hand; and they were silent for a long time, while the evening approached.

"I be goain' t' die the night, dear," said Solomon at last.

"Iss, b'y," she answered; "you be goain' t' die."

Solomon was feverish now; and, thereafter, when he talked, his utterance was thick and fast.

" 'Tis not hard," said Solomon. "Sh-h-h," he whispered, as though about to impart a secret. "The ship that's hangin' off shoare, waitin' for me soul, do be a fine craft—with shinin' canvas an' ropes. Sh-h! She do be t'other side o' Mad Mull now—waitin'."

Priscilla trembled, for Solomon had come to the time of visions—when the words of the dying are the words of prophets, and contain revelations. What of the utterings of the seven thunders?

"Sure the Lard he've blessed us, Priscilla," said Solomon, rational again. "Goodness an' marcy has followed us all the days o' our lives. Our cup runneth over."

"Praise the Lard," said Priscilla.

"Sure," Solomon went on, smiling like a little child, "We've had but eleven famines, an' we've had the means o' grace pretty reg'lar, which is what they hastn't t' Round 'Arbour. We've had one little baby for a little while. Iss—one

de-ear little baby, Priscilla; an' there's them that's had none
o' their own, at all. Sure we've had enough t' eat when there
wasn't a famine—an' baking powder, an' raisins, an' all they
things, an' sugar, an' rale good tea. An' you had a merino
dress, an' I had a suit o' rale tweed—come straight from
England. We hasn't seed a railroad train, dear, but we've
seed a steamer, an' we've heard tell o' the quare things they
be t' St. John's. Ah, the Lard he've favoured us above our
deserts. He've been good t' us, Priscilla. But, oh, you hasn't
had the sewin' machane, an' you hasn't had the peach-stone
t' plant in the garden. 'Tis my fault, dear—'tis not the Lard's.
I should 'a' got you the peach-stone from St. John's, you did
want un so much—oh, so much! 'Tis that I be sorry for, now,
dear; but 'tis all over, an' I can't help it. It wouldn't 'a' growed
anyway, I know it wouldn't; but you thought it would, an' I
wisht I'd got un for you."

" 'Tis nothin', Solomon," she sobbed. "Sure, I was joakin' all
the time. 'Twouldn't 'a' growed."

"Ah," he cried, radiant, "was you joakin'?"

"Sure," she said.

"We've not been poor, Priscilla," said he, continuing, "an'
they be many folk that's poor. I be past me labour now," he
went on, talking with rising effort, for it was at the sinking of
the sun, "An' 'tis time for me t' die. 'Tis time—for I be past me
labour."

Priscilla held his hand a long time after that—a long, silent
time, in which the soul of the man struggled to release itself,
until it was held but by a thread.

"Solomon!"

The old man seemed not to hear.

"Solomon, b'y!" she cried.

"Iss?" faintly.

She leaned over him to whisper in his ear, "Does you see
the gates o' heaven?" she said. "Oh, does you?"

"Sure, dear; heaven do be—

Solomon had not strength enough to complete the sentence.

"B'y! B'y!"

He opened his eyes and turned them to her face. There was the gleam of a tender smile in them.

"The seven thunders," she said. "The utterin's of the seven thunders—what was they, b'y?"

" 'An' the seven thunders uttered their voices,' " he mumbled, " 'an'—' "

She waited, rigid, listening, to hear the rest; but no words came to her ears.

"Does you hear me, b'y?" she said.

" 'An' seven—thunders—uttered their voices,' " he gasped, " 'an' the seven thunders—said—said—' "

The light failed; all the light and golden glory went out of the sky, for the first cloud of a tempest had curtained the sun.

" 'An' said—' " she prompted.

" 'an' uttered—an' said—an' said—' "

"Oh, what?" she moaned.

Now, in that night, when the body of old Solomon Stride, a worn-out hulk, aged and wrecked in the toil of the deep, fell into the hands of Death, the sea, like a lusty youth, raged furiously in those parts. The ribs of many schooners, slimy and rotten, and the white bones of men in the off-shore depths, know of its strength in that hour—of its black, hard wrath, in gust and wave and breaker. Eternal in might and malignance is the sea; It groweth not old with the men who toil from its coasts. Generation upon the heels of generations, infinitely arising, go forth in hope against it, continuing for a space, and returning spent to the dust. They age and crumble and vanish, each in its turn, and the wretchedness of the first is the wretchedness of the last. Ay, the sea has measured the strength of the dust in old graves, and, in this day, contends with the sons of dust, whose sons will follow to the fight for an hundred generations, and thereafter, until harvests may be gathered from rocks. As it is written, the life of a man is a shadow, swiftly passing, and the days of his strength are less; but the sea shall endure in the might of youth to the wreck of the world.

FREDERICK PHILIP GROVE

FREDERICK PHILIP GROVE was born of wealthy Anglo-Swedish parents in Sweden in 1871. His childhood and early youth were spent wandering among the capital cities of Europe with his mother, and from her constant association with writers and artists came Grove's desire to write. In 1887 his mother died, and in 1888 he made a journey across northern Russia and thence to the Far East. From 1889 to 1892 he was in attendance at the universities of Paris, Rome and Munich, majoring in archæology. A pleasure tour of North America in 1892 was cut short by news of his father's death and bankruptcy. The result was that the penniless young man was forced to seek employment in Toronto, where he was stranded. After various unsatisfactory jobs, he settled down to the life of a hobo for twenty years, following the harvests from Kansas to Alberta. During these twenty years he wrote a dozen realistic novels of the Canadian West, but none were published until 1927. In 1912 he became a school teacher in Manitoba, where he lived until 1929. In that year he came to Ontario, and after a year or two in Ottawa with a publishing firm settled on a farm near Simcoe, where he lived until his death on August 19, 1948.

Grove is considered by some critics to be the greatest Canadian novelist yet to emerge. In Paris he was friendly with most of the young writers of the day, and in his novels he embodies the features of French realism and, to a lesser extent, of French naturalism. He published eight novels in all: *Settlers of the Marsh* (1925); *A Search for America* (1927); *Our Daily Bread* (1928); *The Yoke of Life* (1930); *Fruits of the Earth* (1933); *Two Generations* (1939); *The Master of the Mill* (1944); and *Consider Her Ways* (1947). He also published three volumes of essays *(Over Prairie Trails. The Turn of the Year* and *It Needs to be Said)*, his autobiography *In Search of Myself* and, in the periodicals, a number of short stories and critical essays. His short stories are not, in my opinion, the equal of his novels, for his art is of the sort which depends for its greatest effect upon the slow accumulation of detail and the gradual unfolding of tragic circumstance. In the following story several of his strongest qualities are evident: his accurate observation of natural phenomena, his painstaking transcription of every significant detail and his refusal to compromise with the temptation to contrive a comforting conclusion.

Frederick Philip Grove, a biographical and critical study by Desmond Pacey, was published in 1945. There are articles by Isabel Skelton (*The Dalhousie Review,* July, 1939), Robert Ayre (*The Canadian Forum,* 1932), G. H. Clarke (*Queen's Quarterly,* Autumn, 1946), Carleton Stanley (*The Dalhousie Review,* January, 1946) and Desmond Pacey (*Manitoba Arts Review,* Spring, 1943). E. A. McCourt's *The Canadian West in Fiction* (1949) includes a chapter on Grove. See also Kay M. Rowe (*Manitoba Arts Review,* Spring, 1949). "Snow" was the first short story to appear in the pages of *Queen's Quarterly.*

Snow

TOWARDS MORNING the blizzard had died down, though it was still far from daylight. Stars without number blazed in the dark-blue sky which presented that brilliant and uncompromising appearance always characterizing, on the northern plains of America, those nights in the dead of winter when the thermometer dips to its lowest levels.

In the west, Orion was sinking to the horizon. It was between five and six o'clock.

In the bush-fringe of the Big Marsh, sheltered by thick but bare bluffs of aspens, stood a large house, built of logs, whitewashed, solid—such as a settler who is still single would put up only when he thinks of getting married. It, too, looked ice-cold, frozen in the night. Not a breath stirred where it stood; a thin thread of whitish smoke, reaching up to the level of the tree-tops, seemed to be suspended into the chimney rather than to issue from it.

Through the deep snow of the yard, newly packed, a man was fighting his way to the door. Arrived there, he knocked and knocked, first tapping with his knuckles, then hammering with his fists.

Two, three minutes passed. Then a sound awoke in the house, as of somebody stirring, getting out of bed.

The figure on the door-slab—a medium-sized, slim man in sheepskin and high rubber boots into which his trousers were tucked, with the ear-flaps of his cap pulled down—stood and waited, bent over, hands thrust into the pockets of the short coat, as if he wished to shrink into the smallest possible space so as to offer the smallest possible surface to the attack of the cold. In order to get rid of the dry, powdery snow which filled every crease of his foot-gear and trousers, he stamped his feet. His chin was drawn deep into the turned-up collar on whose points his breath had settled in the form of a thick layer of hoarfrost.

At last a bolt was withdrawn inside.

The face of a man peered out, just discernible in the starlight.

Then the door was opened; in ominous silence the figure from the outside entered, still stamping its feet.

Not a word was spoken till the door had been closed. Then a voice sounded through the cold and dreary darkness of the room.

"Redcliff hasn't come home. He went to town about noon and expected to get back by midnight. We're afraid he's lost."

The other man, quite invisible in the dark, had listened, his teeth chattering with the cold. "Are you sure he started out from town?"

"Well," the newcomer answered hesitatingly, "one of the horses came to the yard."

"One of his horses?"

"Yes. One of those he drove. The woman worked her way to my place to get help."

The owner of the house did not speak again. He went, in the dark, to the door in the rear and opened it. There, he groped about for matches and, finding them, lighted a lamp. In the room stood a big stove, a coal-stove of the self-feeder type; but the fuel used was wood. He opened the drafts and shook the grate clear of ashes; there were two big blocks of spruce in the fire-box, smouldering away for the night. In less than a minute they blazed up.

The newcomer entered, blinking in the light of the lamp, and looked on. Before many minutes the heat from the stove began to tell.

"I'll call Bill," the owner of the house said. He was himself of medium height or only slightly above it, but of enormous breadth of shoulder: a figure built for lifting loads. By his side the other man looked small, weakly, dwarfed.

He left the room and, returning through the cold, bare hall in front, went upstairs.

A few minutes later a tall, slender, well-built youth bolted into the room where the newcomer was waiting. Bill, Carroll's hired man, was in his underwear and carried his clothes, thrown in a heap over his arm. Without loss of time, but jumping, stamping, swinging his arms, he began at once to dress.

He greeted the visitor. "Hello, Mike! What's that Abe tells me? Redcliff got lost?"

"Seems that way," said Mike listlessly.

"By gringo," Bill went on, "I shouldn't wonder. In that storm! I'd have waited in town! Wouldn't catch me going out in that kind of weather!"

"Didn't start till late in the afternoon," Mike Sobotski said in his shivering way.

"No. And didn't last long, either," Bill agreed while he shouldered into his overalls. "But while she lasted. . . ."

At this moment Abe Carroll, the owner of the farm, re-entered, with sheepskin, fur cap, and long woollen scarf on his arm. His deeply lined, striking, square face bore a settled frown while he held the inside of his sheepskin to the stove, to warm it up. Then, without saying a word, he got deliberately into it.

Mike Sobotski still stood bent over, shivering, though he had opened his coat and, on his side of the stove, was catching all the heat it afforded.

Abe, with the least motion needed to complete dressing, made for the door. In passing Bill, he flung out an elbow which touched the young man's arm. "Come on," he said; and to the other, pointing to the stove, "Close the drafts."

A few minutes later a noise as of rearing and snorting horses in front of the house. . . .

Mike, buttoning up his coat and pulling his mitts over his hands, went out.

They mounted three unsaddled horses. Abe leading, they dashed through the new drifts in the yard and out through the gate to the road. Here, where the shelter of the bluffs screening the house was no longer effective, a light but freshening breeze from the north-west made itself felt as if fine little knives were cutting into the flesh of their faces.

Abe dug his heels into the flank of his rearing mount. The horse was unwilling to obey his guidance, for Abe wanted to leave the road and to cut across wild land to the south-west.

The darkness was still inky black, though here and there, where the slope of the drifts slanted in the right direction, starlight was dimly reflected from the snow. The drifts were six, eight, in places ten feet high; and the snow was once more crawling up their flanks, it was so light and fine. It would fill the tracks in half an hour. As the horses plunged through, the crystals dusted up in clouds, flying aloft over horses and riders.

In less than half an hour they came to a group of two little buildings, of logs, that seemed to squat on their haunches in the snow. Having entered the yard through a gate, they passed one of the buildings and made for the other, a little stable; their horses snorting, they stopped in its lee.

Mike dismounted, throwing the halter-shank of his horse to Bill. He went to the house, which stood a hundred feet or so away. The shack was even smaller than the stable, twelve by fifteen feet perhaps. From its flue-pipe a thick, white plume of smoke blew to the south-east.

Mike returned with a lantern; the other two sprang to the ground; and they opened the door to examine the horse which the woman had allowed to enter.

The horse was there, still excited, snorting at the leaping

light and shadows from the lantern, its eyes wild, its nostrils dilated. It was covered with white frost and fully harnessed, though its traces were tied up to the back-band.

"He let him go," said Mike, taking in these signs. "Must have stopped and unhitched him."

"Must have been stuck in a drift," Bill said, assenting.

"And tried to walk it," Abe added.

For a minute or so they stood silent, each following his own gloomy thoughts. Weird, luminous little clouds issued fitfully from the nostrils of the horse inside.

"I'll get the cutter," Abe said at last.

"I'll get it," Bill volunteered. "I'll take the drivers along. We'll leave the filly here in the stable."

"All right."

Bill remounted, leading Abe's horse. He disappeared into the night.

Abe and Mike, having tied the filly and the other horse in their stalls, went out, closed the door, and turned to the house.

There, by the light of a little coal-oil lamp, they saw the woman sitting at the stove, pale, shivering, her teeth achatter, trying to warm her hands which were cold with fever, and looking with lack-lustre eyes at the men as they entered.

The children were sleeping; the oldest, a girl, on the floor, wrapped in a blanket and curled up like a dog; four others in one narrow bed, with hay for a mattress, two at the head, two at the foot; the baby on, rather than in, a sort of cradle made of a wide board slung by thin ropes to the pole-roof of the shack.

The other bed was empty and unmade. The air was stifling from a night of exhalations.

"We're going to hunt for him," Mike said quietly. "We've sent for a cutter. He must have tried to walk."

The woman did not answer. She sat and shivered.

"We'll take some blankets," Mike went on. "And some whisky if you've got any in the house."

He and Abe were standing by the stove, opposite the

woman, and warming their hands, their mitts held under their armpits.

The woman pointed with a look to a home-made little cupboard nailed to the wall and apathetically turned back to the stove. Mike went, opened the door of the cupboard, took a bottle from it, and slipped it into the pocket of his sheepskin. Then he raised the blankets from the empty bed, rolled them roughly into a bundle, dropped it, and returned to the stove where, with stiff fingers, he fell to rolling a cigarette.

Thus they stood for an hour or so.

Abe's eye was fastened on the woman. He would have liked to say a word of comfort, of hope. What was there to be said?

She was the daughter of a German settler in the bush, some six or seven miles north-east of Abe's place. Her father, an oldish, unctuous, bearded man, had, some ten years ago, got tired of the hard life in the bush where work meant clearing, picking stones, and digging stumps. He had sold his homestead and bought a prairie-farm, half a section, on crop-payments, giving notes for the equipment which he needed to handle the place. He had not been able to make it a "go." His bush farm had fallen back on his hands; he had lost his all and returned to the place. He had been counting on the help of his two boys—big, strapping young fellows—who were to clear much land and to raise crops which would lift the debt. But the boys had refused to go back to the bush; they could get easy work in town. Ready money would help. But the ready money had melted away in their hands. Redcliff, the old people's son-in-law, had been their last hope. They were on the point of losing even their bush farm. Here they might perhaps still have found a refuge for their old age—though Redcliff's homestead lay on the sand-flats bordering on the marsh where the soil was thin, dreadfully thin; it drifted when the scrub-brush was cleared off. Still, with Redcliff living, this place had been a hope. What were they to do if he was gone? And this woman, hardly more than a girl, in spite of her six children!

The two tiny, square windows of the shack began to turn grey.

At last Abe, thinking he heard a sound, went to the door and stepped out. Bill was there; the horses were shaking the snow out of their pelts; one of them was pawing the ground.

Once more Abe opened the door and gave Mike a look for a signal. Mike gathered the bundle of blankets into his arms, pulled on his mitts, and came out.

Abe reached for the lines, but Bill objected.

"No. Let me drive. I found something."

And as soon as the two older men had climbed in, squeezing into the scant space on the seat, he clicked his tongue.

"Get up there!" he shouted, hitting the horses' backs with his lines. And with a leap they darted away.

Bill turned, heading back to the Carroll farm. The horses plunged, reared, snorted, and then, throwing their heads, shot along in a gallop, scattering snow-slabs right and left and throwing wing-waves of the fresh, powdery snow, especially on the lee side. Repeatedly they tried to turn into the wind, which they were cutting at right angles. But Bill plied the whip and guided them expertly.

Nothing was visible anywhere; nothing but the snow in the first grey of dawn. Then, like enormous ghosts, or like evanescent apparitions, the trees of the bluff were adumbrated behind the lingering veils of the night.

Bill turned to the south, along the straight trail which bordered Abe Carroll's farm. He kept looking out sharply to right and left. But after awhile he drew his galloping horses in.

"Whoa!" he shouted, tearing at the lines in seesaw fashion. And when the rearing horses came to a stop, excited and breathless, he added, "I've missed it." He turned.

"What is it?" Abe asked.

"The other horse," Bill answered. "It must have had the scent of our yard. It's dead . . . frozen stiff."

A few minutes later he pointed to a huge white mound on top of a drift to the left. "That's it," he said, turned the horses into the wind, and stopped.

To the right, the bluffs of the farm slowly outlined themselves in the morning greyness.

The two older men alighted and, with their hands, shovelled the snow away. There lay the horse, stiff and cold, frozen into a rock-like mass.

"Must have been here a long while," Abe said.

Mike nodded. "Five, six hours." Then he added, "Couldn't have had the smell of the yard. Unless the wind has turned."

"It has," Abe answered and pointed to a fold in the flank of the snow-drift which indicated that the present drift had been superimposed on a lower one whose longitudinal axis ran to the north-east.

For a moment longer they stood and pondered.

Then Abe went back to the cutter and reached for the lines. "I'll drive," he said.

Mike climbed in.

Abe took his bearings, looking for landmarks. They were only two or three hundred feet from his fence. That enabled him to estimate the exact direction of the breeze. He clicked his tongue. "Get up!"

And the horses, catching the infection of a dull excitement, shot away. They went straight into the desert of drifts to the west, plunging ahead without any trail, without any landmark in front to guide them.

They went for half an hour, an hour, and longer.

None of the three men said a word. Abe knew the sandflats better than any other; Abe reasoned better than they. If anyone could find the missing man, it was Abe.

Abe's thought ran thus. The horse had gone against the wind. It would never have done so without good reason; that reason could have been no other than a scent to follow. If that was so, however, it would have gone in as straight a line as it could. The sand-flats stretched away to the south-west for sixteen miles with not a settlement, not a farm but Redcliff's. If Abe managed to strike that line of scent, it must take him to the point whence the horses had started.

Clear and glaring, with an almost indifferent air, the sun rose to their left.

And suddenly they saw the wagon-box of the sleigh sticking out of the snow ahead of them.

Abe stopped, handed Bill the lines, and got out. Mike followed. Nobody said a word.

The two men dug the tongue of the vehicle out of the snow and tried it. This was part of the old, burnt-over bush land south of the sand-flats. The sleigh was tightly wedged in between several charred stumps which stuck up through the snow. That was the reason why the man had unhitched the horses and turned them loose. What else, indeed, could he have done?

The box was filled with a drift which, toward the tail-gate, was piled high, for there three bags of flour were standing on end and leaning against a barrel half-filled with small parcels the interstices between which were packed with mealy snow.

Abe waded all around the sleigh, reconnoitring; and as he did so, wading at the height of the upper-edge of the wagon-box, the snow suddenly gave way beneath him; he broke in; the drift was hollow.

A suspicion took hold of him; with a few quick reaches of his arm he demolished the roof of the drift all about.

And there, in the hollow, lay the man's body as if he were sleeping, a quiet expression, as of painless rest, on his face. His eyes were closed; a couple of bags were wrapped about his shoulders. Apparently he had not even tried to walk! Already chilled to the bone, he had given in to that desire for rest, for shelter at any price, which overcomes him who is doomed to freeze.

Without a word the two men carried him to the cutter and laid him down on the snow.

Bill, meanwhile, had unhitched the horses and was hooking them to the tongue of the sleigh. The two others looked on in silence. Four times the horses sprang, excited because Bill tried to make them pull with a sudden twist. The sleigh did not stir.

"Need an axe," Mike said at last, "to cut the stumps. We'll get the sleigh later."

Mike hitched up again and turned the cutter. The broken snow-drifts through which they had come gave the direction.

Then they laid the stiff, dead body across the floor of their vehicle, leaving the side-doors open, for it protruded both ways. They themselves climbed up on the seat and crouched down, so as not to put their feet on the corpse.

Thus they returned to Abe Carroll's farm where, still in silence, they deposited the body in the granary.

Thus done, they stood for a moment as if in doubt. Then Bill unhitched the horses and took them to the stable to feed.

"I'll tell the woman," said Mike. "Will you go tell her father?"

Abe nodded. "Wait for breakfast," he added.

It was ten o'clock; and none of them had eaten since the previous night.

On the way to Altmann's place in the bush, drifts were no obstacles to driving. Drifts lay on the marsh, on the open sand-flats.

Every minute of the time Abe, as he drove along, thought of that woman in the shack: the woman, alone, with six children, and with the knowledge that her man was dead.

Altmann's place in the bush looked the picture of peace and comfort: a large log-house of two rooms. Window-frames and doors were painted green. A place to stay with, not to leave. . . .

When Abe knocked, the woman, whom he had seen but once in his life, at the sale where they had lost their possessions, opened the door—an enormously fat woman, overflowing her clothes. The man, tall, broad, with a long, rolling beard, now grey, stood behind her, peering over her shoulder. A visit is an event in the bush!

"Come in," he said cheerfully when he saw Abe. "What a storm that was!"

Abe entered the kitchen which was also dining- and living-room. He sat down on the chair which was pushed forward for him and looked at the two old people, who remained standing.

Suddenly, from the expression of his face, they anticipated something of his message. No use dissembling.

"Redcliff is dead," he said. "He was frozen to death last night on his way home from town."

The two old people also sat down; it looked as if their knees had given way beneath them. They stared at him, dumbly, a sudden expression of panic fright in their eyes.

"I thought you might want to go to your daughter," Abe added sympathetically.

The man's big frame seemed to shrink as he sat there. All the unctuousness and the conceit of the handsome man dwindled out of his bearing. The woman's eyes had already filled with tears.

Thus they remained for two, three minutes.

Then the woman folded her fat, pudgy hands; her head sank low on her breast; and she sobbed, "God's will be done!"

MARJORIE PICKTHALL

MARJORIE PICKTHALL was born in Middlesex, England, in 1883, but she came to Canada with her parents as a child of six. Her childhood and youth were spent in Toronto, where she attended the Bishop Strachan School for Girls. A delicate child, she spent much time reading romantic novels and poetry, the Bible and other religious literature, and writing stories and poems of her own. In 1898 she sold her first story to the Toronto *Globe,* and within a decade, while still in her early twenties, she had become an established contributor to most of the leading literary periodicals of Canada, the United States and England, and had published three novels for juveniles. Her first volume of poems, *A Drift of Pinions,* was published in 1913, shortly after she had returned to England, and it was followed two years later by her first adult novel, *Little Hearts.* A second volume of poems, *The Lamp of Poor Souls,* appeared in 1916. She returned to Canada in 1920, choosing to live in Vancouver and Victoria for the sake of her delicate health. In 1921 a second novel, *The Bridge*, was published; in 1922 another volume of verse, *The Wood Carver's Wife and Other Poems*; and in 1923 a volume of short stories, *Angel's Shoes.* She died on April 19, 1922.

The exuberant praise which greeted Miss Pickthall's verse has now matured to a more sober estimate, but its undeniable merits—verbal melody, colourful description, sincere religious emotion—continue to give pleasure. To the admirer of her poetry, her stories come as something of a shock; for the quiet lyricism of the former is substituted a violence, at times a crudeness, of tone and theme. Most of them deal with melodramatic situations in exotic or remote settings, and even the best of these, such as "Luck" or "The Desert Road", lack the solidity, the authenticity and realism which result from direct observation.

Her chief weakness as an artist—she herself was conscious of it and fought against it—was a tendency to fall under the spell of other writers and produce mere pastiches. Her novel, *The Bridge,* is in many respects an echo of *Lord Jim,* and a story such as "Angel's Shoes" might easily be mistaken by a casual reader for

110

one of Conrad's. The story printed here, which first appeared in *The Atlantic Monthly*, is more in the manner of her poetry and, in my opinion, much better than her more pretentious stories of violent adventure.

Marjorie Pickthall: A Book of Remembrance by Lorne Pierce was published in 1925. It contains many illuminating excerpts from her journals and letters. *Marjorie Pickthall,* a memorial address by the same author, given at Victoria College, 1943, was privately printed. A valuable critical article was written by E. J. Pratt for *The Canadian Forum,* June, 1933.

The Worker in Sandalwood

I LIKE TO THINK of this as a true story, but you who read may please yourselves, siding either with the curé, who says Hyacinthe dreamed it all, and did the carving himself in his sleep, or with Madame. I am sure that Hyacinthe thinks it true, and so does Madame, but then she has the cabinet, with the little birds and the lilies carved at the corners. Monsieur le curé shrugs his patient shoulders; but then he is tainted with the infidelities of cities, good man, having been three times to Montreal, and once, in an electric car, to Saint Anne. He and Madame still talk it over whenever they meet, though it happened so many years ago, and each leaves the other forever unconvinced. Meanwhile the dust gathers in the infinite fine lines of the little birds' feathers, and softens the lily stamens where Madame's duster may not go; and the wood, ageing, takes on a golden gleam as of immemorial sunsets: that pale red wood, heavy with the scent of the ancient East; the wood that Hyacinthe loved.

It was the only wood of that kind which had ever been seen in Terminaison. Pierre L'Oreillard brought it into the workshop one morning; a small heavy bundle wrapped in sacking, and then in burlap, and then in fine soft cloths. He laid it on a pile of shavings, and unwrapped it carefully and a dim sweetness filled the dark shed and hung heavily in the thin winter sunbeams.

Pierre L'Oreillard rubbed the wood respectfully with his knobby fingers. "It is sandalwood," he explained to Hyacinthe, pride of knowledge making him expansive; "a most precious wood that grows in warm countries, thou great goblin. Smell it, *imbécile*. It is sweeter than cedar. It is to make a cabinet for the old Madame at the big house. Thy great hands shall smooth the wood, *nigaud,* and I—I, Pierre the cabinet-maker, shall render it beautiful." Then he went out, locking the door behind him.

When he was gone, Hyacinthe laid down his plane, blew on his stiff fingers, and shambled slowly over to the wood. He was a great clumsy boy of fourteen, dark-faced, very slow of speech, dull-eyed and uncared for. He was clumsy because it is impossible to move gracefully when you are growing very big and fast on quite insufficient food. He was dull-eyed because all eyes met his unlovingly; uncared for, because none knew the beauty of his soul. But his heavy young hands could carve simple things, like flowers and birds and beasts, to perfection, as the curé pointed out. Simon has a tobacco-jar, carved with pine-cones and squirrels, and the curé has a pipe whose bowl is the bloom of a moccasin-flower, that I have seen. But it is all very long ago. And facts, in these lonely villages, easily become transfigured, touched upon their gray with a golden gleam.

"Thy hands shall smooth the wood, *nigaud,* and I shall render it beautiful," said Pierre L'Oreillard, and went off to drink brandy at the Cinq Chateaux.

Hyacinthe knew that the making of the cabinet would fall to him, as most of the other work did. He also touched the strange sweet wood, and at last laid his cheek against it, while the fragrance caught his breath. "How beautiful it is," said Hyacinthe, and for a moment his eyes glowed and he was happy. Then the light passed, and with bent head he shuffled back to his bench through a foam of white shavings curling almost to his knees.

"Madame perhaps will want the cabinet next week, for that is Christmas," said Hyacinthe, and fell to work harder than ever, though it was so cold in the shed that his breath hung like a little silver cloud and the steel stung his hands. There was a tiny window to his right, through which, when it was clear of frost, one looked on Terminaison, and that was cheerful and made one whistle. But to the left, through the chink of the ill-fitting door, there was nothing but the forest and the road dying away in it, and the trees moving heavily under the snow. Yet, from there came all Hyacinthe's dumb dreams and slow reluctant fancies, which he sometimes found himself able to tell—in wood, not in words.

Brandy was good at the Cinq Chateaux, and Pierre L'Oriellard gave Hyacinthe plenty of directions, but no further help with the cabinet.

"That is to be finished for Madame on the festival, *gros escargot!*" said he, cuffing Hyacinthe's ears furiously, "finished, and with a prettiness about the corners, hearest thou, *ourson*? I suffer from a delicacy of the constitution and a little feebleness in the legs on these days, so that I cannot handle the tools. I must leave this work to thee, *gacheur*. See it is done properly, and stand up and touch a hand to thy cap when I address thee, *orvet*, great slow-worm."

"Yes, monsieur," said Hyacinthe, wearily.

It is hard, when you do all the work, to be cuffed into the bargain, and fourteen is not very old. He went to work on the cabinet with slow, exquisite skill, but on the eve of Noel, he was still at work, and the cabinet unfinished. It meant a thrashing from Pierre if the morrow came and found it still unfinished, and Pierre's thrashings were cruel. But it was growing into a thing of perfection under his slow hands, and Hyacinthe would not hurry over it.

"Then work on it all night, and show it to me all completed in the morning, or thy bones shall mourn thy idleness," said Pierre with a flicker of his little eyes. And he shut Hyacinthe into the workshop with a smoky lamp, his tools, and the sandalwood cabinet.

It was nothing unusual. The boy had often been left before to finish a piece of work overnight while Pierre went off to his brandies. But this was Christmas Eve, and he was very tired. The cold crept into the shed until the scent of the sandalwood could not make him dream himself warm, and the roof cracked sullenly in the forest. There came upon Hyacinthe one of those awful, hopeless despairs that children know. It seemed to be a living presence that caught up his soul and crushed it in black hands. "In all the world, nothing!" said he, staring at the dull flame; "no place, no heart, no love! O kind God, is there a place, a love for me in another world?"

I cannot endure to think of Hyacinthe, poor lad, shut up despairing in the workshop with his loneliness, his cold, and his hunger, on the eve of Christmas. He was but an overgrown, unhappy child, and for unhappy children no aid, at this season, seems too divine for faith. So Madame says, and she is very old and very wise. Hyacinthe even looked at the chisel in his hand, and thought that by a touch of that he might lose it all, all, and be at peace, somewhere not far from God; only it was forbidden. Then came the tears, and great sobs that sickened and deafened him, so that he scarcely heard the gentle rattling of the latch.

At least, I suppose it came then, but it may have been later. The story is all so vague here, so confused with fancies that have spoiled the first simplicity. I think that Hyacinthe must have gone to the door, opening it upon the still woods and the frosty stars, and the lad who stood outside must have said: "I see you are working late, comrade. May I come in?" or something like it.

Hyacinthe brushed his ragged sleeve across his eyes, and opened the door wider with a little nod to the other to enter. Those little lonely villages strung along the great river see strange wayfarers adrift inland from the sea. Hyacinthe said to himself that surely here was such a one.

Afterwards he told the curé that for a moment he had been bewildered. Dully blinking into the stranger's eyes, he lost for a flash the first impression of youth and received one of some

incredible age or sadness. But this also passed and he knew
that the wanderer's eyes were only quiet, very quiet, like the
little pools in the wood where the wild does went to drink. As
he turned within the door, smiling at Hyacinthe and shaking
some snow from his fur cap, he did not seem more than sixteen
or so.

"It is very cold outside," he said. "There is a big oak tree
on the edge of the fields that has split in the frost and frightened
all the little squirrels asleep there. Next year it will make an
even better home for them. And see what I found close by!"
He opened his fingers, and showed Hyacinthe a little sparrow
lying unruffled in his palm.

"*Pauvrette!*" said the dull Hyacinthe.

"*Pauvrette!* Is it then dead?" He touched it with a gentle
forefinger.

"No," answered the strange boy, "it is not dead. We'll put
it here among the shavings, not far from the lamp, and it will
be well by morning."

He smiled at Hyacinthe again, and the shambling lad felt
dimly as if the scent of sandalwood had deepened and the
lamp-flame burned clearer. But the stranger's eyes were only
quiet, quiet.

"Have you come far?" asked Hyacinthe. "It is a bad season
for travelling, and the wolves are out in the woods."

"A long way," said the other; "a long, long way. I heard a
child cry. . . ."

"There is no child here," answered Hyacinthe, shaking his
head. "Monsieur L'Oreillard is not fond of children, he says
they cost too much money. But if you have come far, you must
be cold and hungry, and I have no food or fire. At the Cinq
Chateaux you will find both!"

The stranger looked at him again with those quiet eyes, and
Hyacinthe fancied his face was familiar. "I will stay here," he
said, "you are very late at work and you are unhappy."

"Why, as to that," answered Hyacinthe, rubbing again at
his cheeks and ashamed of his tears, "most of us are sad at
one time or another, the good God knows. Stay here and

welcome if it pleases you, and you may take a share of my bed, though it is no more than a pile of balsam boughs and an old blanket, in the loft. But I must work at this cabinet, for the drawer must be finished and the handles put on and these corners carved, all by the holy morning; or my wages will be paid with a stick."

"You have a hard master," put in the other boy, "if he would pay you with blows upon the feast of Noel."

"He is hard enough," said Hyacinthe; "but once he gave me a dinner of sausages and white wine, and once, in the summer, melons. If my eyes will stay open, I will finish this by morning, but indeed I am sleepy. Stay with me an hour or so, comrade, and talk to me of your wanderings, so that the time may pass more quickly."

"I will tell you of the country where I was a child," answered the stranger.

And while Hyacinthe worked, he told — of sunshine and dust; of the shadows of vine-leaves on the flat white walls of a house; of rosy doves on the flat roof; of the flowers that come in the spring, crimson and blue, and the white cyclamen in the shadow of the rocks; of the olive, the myrtle and almond; until Hyacinthe's slow fingers ceased working, and his sleepy eyes blinked wonderingly.

"See what you have done, comrade," he said at last; "you have told of such pretty things that I have done no work for an hour. And now the cabinet will never be finished, and I shall be beaten."

"Let me help you," smiled the other; "I also was bred a carpenter."

At first Hyacinthe would not, fearing to trust the sweet wood out of his own hands, but at length he allowed the stranger to fit in one of the little drawers, and so deftly was the work done, that Hyacinthe pounded his fists on the bench in admiration. "You have a pretty knack," he cried; "it seemed as if you did but hold the drawer in your hands a moment, and hey! ho! it jumped into its place!"

"Let me fit in the other little drawers, while you go and rest

a while," said the wanderer. So Hyacinthe curled up among
the shavings, and the stranger fell to work upon the little
cabinet of sandalwood.

Here begins what the curé will have it is a dream within a
dream. Sweetest of dreams was ever dreamed, if that is so.
Sometimes I am forced to think with him, but again I see as
clearly as with old Madame's eyes, that have not seen the
earthly light for twenty years, and with her and Hyacinthe, I
say "Credo."

Hyacinthe said that he lay upon the shavings in the sweetness of the sandalwood, and was very tired. He thought of the
country where the stranger had been a boy; of the flowers on
the hills; of the laughing leaves of aspen, and poplar; of the
golden flowering anise and the golden sun upon the dusty
roads, until he was warm. All the time through these pictures,
as through a painted veil, he was aware of that other boy with
the quiet eyes, at work upon the cabinet, smoothing, fitting,
polishing. "He does better work than I," thought Hyacinthe,
but he was not jealous. And again he thought, "It is growing
towards morning. In a little while I will get up and help him."
But he did not, for the dream of warmth and the smell of the
sandalwood held him in a sweet drowse. Also he said that he
thought the stranger was singing as he worked, for there
seemed to be a sense of some music in the shed, though he
could not tell whether it came from the other boy's lips, or
from the shabby old tools as he used them, or from the stars.
"The stars are much paler," thought Hyacinthe, "and soon it
will be morning, and the corners are not carved yet. I must
get up and help this kind one in a little moment. Only I am so
tired, and the music and the sweetness seem to wrap me and
fold me close, so that I may not move."

He lay without moving, and behind the forest there shone
a pale glow of some indescribable colour that was neither
green nor blue, while in Terminaison the church bells began to
ring. "Day will soon be here!" thought Hyacinthe, immovable
in that deep dream of his, "and with day will come Monsieur

L'Oreillard and his stick. I must get up and help, for even yet the corners are not carved."

But he did not get up. Instead, he saw the stranger look at him again, smiling as if he loved him, and lay his brown finger lightly upon the four empty corners of the cabinet. And Hyacinthe saw the little squares of reddish wood ripple and heave and break, as little clouds when the wind goes through the sky. And out of them thrust forth little birds, and after them the lilies, for a moment living, but even while Hyacinthe looked, growing hard and reddish-brown and settling back into the sweet wood. Then the stranger smiled again, and laid all the tools neatly in order, and, opening the door quietly, went away into the woods.

Hyacinthe lay still among the shavings for a long time, and then he crept slowly to the door. The sun, not yet risen, set its first beams upon the delicate mist of frost afloat beneath the trees, and so all the world was aflame with splendid gold. Far away down the road a dim figure seemed to move amid the glory, but the glow and the splendour were such that Hyacinthe was blinded. His breath came sharply as the glow beat in great waves on the wretched shed; on the foam of shavings; on the cabinet with the little birds and the lilies carved at the corners.

He was too pure of heart to feel afraid. But, "Blessed be the Lord," whispered Hyacinthe, clasping his slow hands, "for He hath visited and redeemed His people. But who will believe?"

Then the sun of Christ's day rose gloriously, and the little sparrow came from his nest among the shavings and shook his wings to the light.

MAZO de la ROCHE

MAZO DE LA ROCHE was born in 1885 in Toronto, an only child, of French, English and Irish descent. Brought up with her, as a sister, was her cousin, Caroline Clement. Some of her earliest attempts at writing were short plays which the two acted for friends in their own home. The greater part of her education was private. She intended to become an illustrator and for a time studied art. Soon she realized, however, that her real bent was toward imaginative writing and, before she was twenty, she had her short stories published. She spent some years of her girlhood on a fruit and stock farm on the shore of Lake Ontario, where she developed a love of country life, of animals and birds. This love has had a great influence upon her writing: it is evident in all her novels and stories and her *Portrait of a Dog* is among her best-known works. For many years Miss de la Roche lived in England, and spent several winters in Italy. More recently she lived in a country house at York Mills, Ontario, where she kept a bird sanctuary. She died in Toronto in June of 1961.

By 1926 Mazo de la Roche had produced three novels, no one of which had brought her great success though the English critics praised them. In 1927, however, her novel *Jalna* won *The Atlantic Monthly* Prize of ten thousand dollars as the "most interesting novel of any description submitted by any writer whether born in London or Indianapolis". There were almost twelve thousand entries in the competition. The book was enthusiastically received and the public demanded to hear further news of the Whiteoaks. Twelve novels, following the fortunes of the family, have since appeared, as well as four other novels with a different setting: *Lark Ascending, Growth of a Man, The Two Saplings,* and *A Boy in the House.* In addition, she has written two books about children: *Beside a Norman Tower* and *The Very House*; a collection of short stories about animals entitled *The Sacred Bullock*; and the biography of her Scottish terrier, *Portrait of a Dog.* She has also published a history of the port of Quebec and her autobiography, *Ringing the Changes.* The above books have been supplemented by dozens of short stories in the leading magazines of England, the United States and Canada, by her well-known one-act play, *Low Life,* and by her own dramatization of her novel, *Whiteoaks.* This latter play was produced in a London West End

119

theatre in 1936 and ran for more than two years. It still is frequently revived in England and has been produced in Budapest
and Dublin. It had a successful run in New York with Ethel
Barrymore in the principal role.

The immense popular following which Miss de la Roche has
built up is testimony to the charm and interest of her work. Though
critics may deplore the fact that she has devoted so much of her
time and energy to the Whiteoak chronicles, to the exclusion of
more solid and penetrating analyses of contemporary life, the fact
remains that she has brought pleasure to millions. She is perhaps
the most deft of all our prose writers, writing always with ease
and grace. She is at her best in the portrayal of the whims and
eccentricities of the very old and the very young, and in the
imaginative re-creation of the lives of animals and birds. The story
which follows appeared originally in *The Atlantic Monthly*.

Come Fly with Me

HE HAD HAD HIS EYE on her for some time. Each time he looked
at her something deep inside him thrilled in sudden joy. There
was that about her which made her unlike all other young
females. An observer might have discovered nothing different
in her. Nothing to cause that vibration through his nerves. But
even in the far South, where they had wintered, she had had
an attraction for him and in some subtle way he had been able
to communicate this to her. So now after the long flight north-
ward, during which he had had only occasional glimpses of
her, he awaited her coming with confidence. He and a group
of other swallows had sought out the breeding place of last
year, a country home in the southern part of Ontario.

He had been hatched in one of the tall chimneys of this
stone house on the hill and he now circled with unerring
instinct about it. If any of the other swallows were his kin, he
was unaware of the fact. His vibrant little being was held by
only one bond, the bond between him and the one whom he
awaited. For three days he awaited her.

Then suddenly he saw her.

There was no mistaking her! The instinct that had guided

him to this home of his desire had guided her to him. Between them there passed a joyous tremor of recognition.

But she did not fly to his side. Instead she alighted on a gable of the house. She was tired after her long and hazardous journey, during which she had encountered gales and driving rain. Now in the warm spring sunshine she shook out her plumage and sank contentedly to her breast. She left the next move in their courtship to him.

He had but one thought, to delight her by the marvel of his flight and by his beauty. Back and forth he darted in front of her, his forked tail, his long, pointed wings etched in myriad gestures against the sky. He circled, he wheeled, he soared, he turned from side to side so that she might be dazzled by the beauty of his throat and the underside of his wings. She did not move. She looked almost indifferent and began to preen the feathers of her breast which she had neglected on the journey.

His new spring plumage, glittering with health, shone in the sunshine. Now he swam close above her. He picked up an imaginary straw and flew into the chimney with it, in a symbolic gesture of nest-building. When at last he alighted not far from her she remained motionless, accepting his nearness.

Other birds were circling skyward, delighting in the warmth and the ardour of the mating season. The gardener was digging in the perennial border and several full-breasted robins were drawing sleek worms from the freshly turned soil. Beyond a lattice fence the lawn fell steeply down to a stream. On this lower level there was a great elm tree where a pair of orioles were already building their nest. Like a small flame miraculously detached from a heavenly conflagration, the male darted in and out of the elm's foliage, beating the air with his bright wings in the haste of construction.

The two on the gable of the house sat motionless, held by the fragile but exquisite bond of this new experience. They were so young, yet nature's ritual lay open before them. Another male swallow approached them. In graceful swoops and glides he displayed his power and beauty. She looked not ill-pleased but presently, as though to show her unconcern, she spread her own wings and flew over the roof and beyond, into the wood. The newcomer was disconcerted but he who had awaited her coming flew close behind her, and, when she alighted on the branch of a wild cherry tree, he dropped there beside her.

In the small wood they spent the night perched quite near each other. At sunrise he again wooed her with all the ardour that was in him.

Away she flew and he after her! But in her flight she uttered a sharp, clear note. They sped above the dark pines, above the house-top and, when she sank to the lawn, the mating rite took place.

In wild delight he now led, now pursued her, through the sunny air, but always his flight drew them toward the chimney. He would dart into it, making the symbolic gestures of nest-building, then up again to her side, fluttering about her, urging her to the descent. At last she flew down into the chimney with him.

Together they perched on the very smoke-blackened ledge where he had been hatched. Remnants of the nest still clung to it though the chimney had been cleaned. She looked about her and was satisfied.

Now began their joyful work of building a home. In and out of the chimney they sped carrying morsels of clay or strands of dry grass in their beaks. Squatting in it they smoothed and rounded it with their breasts. She was the more expert at this. Indeed she now became the leader. Like the wind she sped from field or stream's edge to nest, never tiring of her task. But at times he led her to fly with him for the mere pleasure of flying. Then, in an abandon of delight they soared upward till they were no more than two shimmering specks against the blue, or skimmed low to the stream and without resting sipped to quench their thirst, or even ruffled the surface of the water with their wings and sped on, bathed and refreshed.

Then she would bethink herself of her unlaid eggs and how she must conserve her vitality for them. More than once the marital rite had been accomplished while in full flight.

The nest was lined with feathers and down and there rested finally in it seven white eggs flecked with brown.

All this had not been completed without interference. During the time of nest-building her other suitor had followed them enviously, sometimes darting between them. The mated birds had borne this tolerantly but, when another female had approached and even entered the chimney, she had been driven off in a frenzy of anger by the little wife. Beneath the eave the sparrows were already feeding their young.

Now the oriole's nest was complete and hung with its hidden treasures high in the elm. All day the oriole sent forth his challenging song. At eventide his voice was the last to be heard, in a grave sweet cadence. The stream rustled on among its reeds. The dim shape of an owl drifted across the fields. In the nest in the chimney the little wife felt the eggs quicken beneath her breast.

2

At the bottom of the chimney there was a deep fireplace in a long, dark-panelled study. This room was cool, though outdoors the weather was very hot. The little girl came in quietly, not quite knowing what to do with herself. She came softly in her sandals, making no noise.

Then she saw that she was not alone. A young bird, fully fledged but still not able to fly, sat on the hearth. When he saw her he spread his pointed wings and hopped toward her. He did not seem to be afraid but came as though he sought her help.

She gave a little cry of delight and caught him up in her hands. She ran with him to her aunt who was dying rose petals for *pot-pourri*.

"Look!" she cried. "A fledgling! He has fallen from the nest in the chimney."

They had known from the twittering of the young that there was a nest in the chimney. For that reason they had not been able to have a fire in the study all that summer.

"Poor little thing," said the aunt, dropping a handful of rose petals. "If only we could put him back!"

Now the child's mother appeared and, holding the fledgling to her breast, mourned over him. She ran with him to the fireplace and, crouching in the aperture, held him as far up as she could, urging his parents to notice him. But they were intent on feeding those which were left in the nest. Excited twitterings came from the young ones and when the one in her hands heard this he strained upward with his beak wide open.

"There is nothing for it," said the child's mother, "but to bring him up by hand."

"We have tried that before," said the aunt, laying some bright blue larkspur flowerettes among the rose petals, "and failed."

"But they were miserable little fledglings!" cried the mother. "See how strong and beautiful he is! See how long his wings and his forked tail! He's sure to live if we feed him properly."

"He is a pet," said the little girl. "Shall we name him Arthur?"

"Why Arthur?"

"Oh, I don't know, but it seems to suit him."

Arthur very much wanted to live. Whatever they brought him he eagerly swallowed. But now came the difficulty. Of a sudden flies and moths had almost disappeared from the scene. There had been a long drought. The dry earth refused to give up more than an occasional worm. The little girl had to abandon her play, the mother her work, the aunt her *potpourri,* in order to find food for Arthur.

He knew no fear. He fluttered to them with little cries of joy when they came to him. The next day he was stronger. He spread his long pointed wings and sought to raise himself from the floor. He looked from face to face without fear. The great thing was to find food for him. He was always hungry. They searched the lawn, the shrubbery, the orchard, and whenever they found insect or worm they flew with it to Arthur.

On the third day they went out to lunch, though with misgivings.

"I should not go," said the mother. "I should stay at home and feed Arthur."

"We must give him a good meal before we leave," said the aunt, "and come home early."

The little girl, all in white and wearing her best gloves, hung over Arthur in his nest of cotton wool, promised to return soon. But they went off with anxious hearts.

They could scarcely enjoy the luncheon party for their anxiety over Arthur, and hastened home. They hurried out of the car and into the house.

A change had come over the fledgling. He was ravenous but he was weak. He no longer fluttered or tried to fly but sat quite still.

"There now!" cried the mother. "What did I tell you? I should not have gone out to lunch. I have killed him."

"No, no," said the aunt. "He is just hungry. We must give him warm milk." She hurried to inspect her rose petals which she had left in a copper kettle on the terrace to dry. "Oh, my *pot-pourri*!" she said distractedly. "The wind has blown half of it away."

The child and she set about picking up the innumerable petals while the mother warmed milk.

Arthur took it eagerly. They began then to search for food for him. But no insects were to be found. They heaved up heavy stones to see what might be beneath but those wriggling hairy worms were too repulsive to offer Arthur.

"At the bottom of the ravine," said the little girl, "the earth is damp. We might find worms."

They scrambled through the undergrowth down beneath the bridge. They had brought a trowel but the earth, though damp, was hard. They had a time of it to dig up half a dozen thin worms. Arthur ate them as though famished. Then, with his tiny crop distended he slept. They had not realized that, being a swallow, insects and not worms should be his only food. But there were no insects.

The next morning the little girl hurried to peep into Arthur's box. She saw at once that he was dead. She said nothing but ran to the swing and swung as hard as she could.

After a while she decided to give Arthur a beautiful funeral.

She lined a small box with rose petals and gently laid him on them. Then she made a little coverlet of pansies. He looked sweet and peaceful in there.

She took a sheet of her best drawing paper, cut a square from it and carefully inscribed his memorial notice.

In Memory of

ARTHUR

A little fledgling which
fell down the Chimney

on

August the 7th, 1940

On the oak chest in the hall she set his bier with the notice above it. All day he lay in state. Everyone who passed through the hall stopped to look.

In the evening she buried him in the flower border. She placed forget-me-nots in a little jar on the grave and the memorial at its head. A gentle rain began to fall.

3

Now the nest was empty. The young birds had been taught to fly. Now in the evening they circled and swooped with their parents in search of insects. At night all perched in a row on a secluded branch of one of the pines. Once more the mates were free to care. Still they were held in the bond of their love. Sometimes they forgot the young ones and rode the summer breeze together as in the first rapture of their mating. They had seen the orchard bloom. Now they looked down on the golden fields of the harvest. The orioles too had reared their young and the song of the male rang out bold and free. The sparrows beneath the eave were rearing a second brood. As the swallows darted past they could hear the cheeping of the young ones.

Perhaps it was this that gave her the idea. Certainly it was no wish of his. When he peered down into the chimney and saw her on the nest he was astonished. When she uttered her sharp love cry and swept before him above the lawn he followed, almost reluctant. But she had her will.

The first time she had laid seven eggs. This time she laid five. She showed almost fierce absorption in the brooding over them. Storms came and the sparrows' fledglings were swept from their nest and washed in a torrent of rain down the verandah roof. Their naked blue bodies lay scattered in the morning sun. But her nest was safe. In due time she hatched out five lusty ones.

He did his share of the feeding without enthusiasm. Often he was restive and longed to fly, with her winging at his side. But he was loyal. The fledglings throve and began to grow their feathers. This was well because a chill was now in the air. At night they were thankful to snuggle beneath her comforting breast.

One morning when the reeds by the river were whispering and a golden mist hung on the horizon, he fed the young ones with no help from her. She did not come. He flew in wide circles above the housetop and the trees, looking for her.

Suddenly he saw her perched on the chimney. He flew joyfully to her side. She darted away and he after her. They flew for a space, then he sought to turn her back. In cajoling circles she led him on. But the thought of the fledglings held him. He pressed back to them with strong strokes of his wings. On the way he captured a plump moth and flew with it down to the nest. Five upward straining beaks greeted him. He thrust the moth into the throat of the nearest and flew up and looked anxiously about for his mate.

What he saw was his grown-up brood, perched with two score of other swallows on the telegraph wire. There they sat, like beads on a necklace, and she was fluttering above! She was urging him to join them!

He tried to drive her, to harry her back to the fledglings, but she would have none of them. The flock rose and moved swiftly southward, their forked tails etched against the sky. He hesitated, torn between love and fatherhood, then spread his wings and flew away with her.

ETHEL WILSON

MRS. WILSON was born in Port Elizabeth, South Africa, in 1890, of English parents. She lived in England until the age of eight when, upon the death of both her parents, she came to Vancouver to live with her grandmother and other relatives. She attended private schools in Vancouver and England, and after graduating from the Provincial Normal School in Vancouver taught in that city's public schools for some years. In 1920 she married Dr. Wallace Wilson, who is a past president of the Canadian Medical Association, and they have made their home in Vancouver. Dr. and Mrs. Wilson have travelled widely throughout Canada, the United States, the Mediterranean, the Levant, Southern Europe, Scandinavia and the United Kingdom.

Short stories by Ethel Wilson have appeared in *The New Statesman and Nation, Orion 4,* a miscellany edited by C. Day Lewis, *Here and Now* and *The Canadian Forum.* One of her stories was included in O'Brien's *Best British Short Stories of 1938.* She has also published four novels: *Hetty Dorval* (1947), *The Innocent Traveller* (1949), *Swamp Angel* (1954), *Love and Salt Water* (1956); and two novelettes: "Lilly's Story" and "Tuesday and Wednesday" under the joint title of *Equations of Love* (1952). Ethel Wilson has contributed some charming essays to such magazines as *Canadian Literature* and *The Tamarack Review,* and *Mr. Golightly and other stories* appeared in 1961.

There is in all of Mrs. Wilson's work a deceptive simplicity: she writes with an apparent ease, casualness and artlessness which masks an intense concern with the subtler details of craftsmanship. Her work is quiet and unassuming, but it gradually takes on a compelling intensity. Whether she is dealing with persons, animals or places, she treats them with great honesty and imaginative sympathy. The story which follows was first printed in *The New Statesman and Nation.*

Hurry, Hurry!

WHEN THE MOUNTAINS beyond the city are covered with snow to their base, the late afternoon light falling obliquely from the west upon the long slopes discloses new contours. For a few moments of time the austerity vanishes, and the mountains appear innocently folded in furry white. Their daily look has gone. For these few moments the slanting rays curiously discover each separate tree behind each separate tree in the infinite white forests. Then the light fades, and the familiar mountains resume their daily look again. The light has gone, but those who have seen it will remember.

As Miriam stood at the far point of Sea Island, with the wind blowing in from the west, she looked back towards the city. There was a high ground fog at the base of the mountains, and so the white flanks and peaks seemed to lie unsupported in the clear spring sky. They seemed to be unattached to the earth. She wished that Harry were with her to see this sight of beauty which passed even as she looked upon it. But Harry was away, and she had come for a walk upon the dyke alone with her dogs.

It was the very day in spring that the soldier blackbirds had returned from Mexico to the marshes of the delta. Just a few had come, but in the stubble fields behind the high dyke, and in the salt marshes seawards from the dyke, and on the shallow sea, and over the sea there were thousands of other birds. No people anywhere. Just birds. The salt wind blew softly from the sea, and the two terrier dogs ran this way and that, with and against the wind. A multitude of little sandpipers ran along the wet sands as if they were on wheels. They whispered and whimpered together as they ran, stabbing with their long bills into the wet sand and running on. There was a continuous small noise of birds in the air. The terriers bore down upon the little sandpipers. The terriers ran clumsily, sinking in the marshy blackish sand, encumbered as they ran. And the little sandpipers rose and flew low together to a safer sandbank. They whispered and wept together as they fled in a cloud, animated by one enfolding spirit of motion. They settled on their sandbank, running and jabbing the wet sand with their bills. The terriers like little earnest monsters bore down upon them again in futile chase, and again the whispering cloud of birds arose. Miriam laughed at the silly hopeful dogs.

Farther out to sea were the duck and the brant and the seagulls. These strutted on the marsh-like sands, or lay upon the shallow water or flew idly above the water. Sometimes a great solitary crane arose from nowhere and flapped across the wet shore. The melancholy crane settled itself in a motionless hump, and again took its place in obscurity among stakes and rushes.

Behind the dyke where Miriam stood looking out to sea was a steep bank sloping to a shallow salt water ditch, and beyond that again, inland, lay the stubble fields of Sea Island, crossed by rough hedges. From the fields arose the first song of the meadow lark, just one lark, how curious after winter to hear its authentic song again. Thousands of ducks disclosed themselves from the stubble fields, rising and flying without haste or fear to the sea.

Miriam called to the dogs and walked on along the narrow clay path at the top of the dyke. She delighted in the birds and the breeze and the featureless ocean. The dogs raced after her.

Clumps of bare twisted bushes were scattered along the edge of the path, sometimes obscuring the curving line of the dyke ahead. In a bush a few early soldier blackbirds talked to each other. Miriam stood still to listen. "Oh-kee-*ree*," called a blackbird. "Oh-kee-*ree*," answered his mate. "Oh-kee-*ree*," he said. "Oh-kee-*ree*," she answered. Then the male bird flew. His red epaulettes shone finely. What a strange note, thought Miriam, there's something sweet and something very ugly. The soldier blackbird's cry began on a clear flute's note and ended in piercing sweetness. The middle sound grated like a rusty lock. As Miriam walked on between the twisted black bushes more soldier blackbirds called and flew. Oh-kee-*ree*! Oh-kee-*ree*! Sweet and very ugly.

Suddenly she saw a strange object. Below her on the left, at the edge of the salt water ditch, there was an unlikely heap of something. Miriam stopped and looked. This thing was about the size of a tremendous hunched cat, amorphous, of a rich reddish brown. It was a rich brown of a lump of rotted wood. Although it did not move, Miriam had instant warning that this creature was alive and had some meaning for her. She called the dogs, who came wagging. She leashed them and they went forward together. The dogs tugged and tugged. Soon they, too, looked down the bank at the strange object. In the brown mass something now moved. Miriam saw that the brown object was a large wounded hawk. The hawk was intensely aware of the woman and the dogs. As they paused, and then as they passed along the high dyke path, the hawk's head turned slowly, very slowly, to observe them. Its body was motionless. Its eyes were bright with comprehension. Miriam was glad that she had leashed the dogs. In another minute they would have descended on the hawk. One brown wing lay trailed behind the big bird, but with its sharp beak and tearing claws it would have mauled the terriers, and they would have tormented it. Miriam looked at the hawk and the hawk stared brightly at her. She wished that she could save the hawk from its lingering death on the marshes, but there was nothing she could do. Motionless, save for the slowly turning head, the great hawk followed them with intent gaze. Its eyes were bright with comprehension, but no fear. It was ready. The hawk made Miriam feel uneasy. She walked on faster, keeping the dogs still on the leash. She looked back. The hawk steadily watched her. She turned and walked on still faster.

One of the dogs suddenly growled and then both barked loudly. Round a thorn bush, hurrying towards her, came a man. In all their walks upon the dyke, Harry and she had never met another human being. Miriam was startled. She was almost afraid. The strange hawk. The strange man. The man

stopped. He was startled, too. Then he hurried again toward
her. Crowded on the narrow clayey path of the dyke stood
Miriam and the two dogs, uncertain. The man came close to
her and stopped.

"Don't go on," he said urgently, "don't go on. It isn't safe.
There's a cougar. I'm going to a farmhouse. To warn them.
Perhaps I can get a gun. Turn back. And keep your dogs on
the leash," he said sharply.

"Oh," said Miriam, "you must be mistaken. There's never
been a cougar on these islands. No, of course, I won't go on,
though. I'll turn back at once. But you *must* be mistaken. A
dog or even a coyote, but not a cougar!"

"It *is* a cougar," said the man vehemently, "did you never
hear of the cougar that swam across from the North Shore last
year? Well—I can't stop to argue—there *is* a cougar, I saw it.
Beside the dyke. It's driven in by hunger, starving, I expect.
Well?"

He looked at her. He held her eyes with his eyes.

"Oh," said Miriam, "of course, I won't go on. I should never
have come! I'm so glad I met you. But it's extraordinary!"
and she turned in haste.

The man paid her no further attention. He stepped down
a bit from the path on to the steep grassy side of the dyke, and
pushed past her and the restless dogs. He walked on very fast
without another word. Miriam hurried after him along the
narrow dyke path, the dogs impeding her as she hurried. This
was like a bad dream. Hurry, hurry! I can't hurry.

She nearly ran along the slippery bumpy dyke path, past
the brown heap of the wounded hawk whose bright eyes
watched her, and past the straggly bushes where the soldier
blackbirds flew from tree to tree and sang. She hurried along
until she turned the curve of the dyke and saw again the
mountains behind the city. The peaks now hung pink and gold
in the cold spring sky. To the farthest range of the Golden
Ears the sunset caught them. Miriam fled on. The leashed dogs
ran, too, bounding and hindering her as she ran. She crossed
the little footbridge that led to the lane that led to her car.

She had lost sight of the man a long time ago. He had hurried on to give the alarm. She had seen him stumbling down the steep dyke side and splashing across the salt water ditch to the stubble fields.

. . . Far behind them along the dyke the body of the young woman who had just been murdered lay humped beside the salt water ditch.

The man who had killed her reached the cover of the hedge, out of sight of that woman with the dogs. When he reached the cover of the hedge he began to run across the tussocky field, stumbling, half blind, sobbing, crying out loud.

WILL R. BIRD

WILL R. BIRD was born at East Mapleton, Nova Scotia, on May 11, 1891, and was educated at the Cumberland County Academy, in Amherst, Nova Scotia. From 1916 to 1919 he served as battalion scout with the Royal Canadian Highlanders, and was awarded the Military Medal. He married Ethel May Sutton on June 18, 1919, and they had two children, a daughter who survives and a son who was killed in action in the recent war. Mr. Bird has served for many years on the staff of the Nova Scotia Bureau of Information and Publicity, and makes his home in Halifax. He has taken a prominent part in the affairs of the Canadian Authors Association, and was elected to the presidency of that body in 1948.

Mr. Bird has published almost a score of books and hundreds of stories and articles. Among his best known novels are *Here Stays Good Yorkshire* (1945), *Judgment Glen* (1947), *The Passionate Pilgrim* (1949), and *Tristram's Salvation* (1957).

Most of Mr. Bird's stories have as their settings either the war of 1914–1918 or the life of the Maritime Provinces, and are concerned with the heroism of simple people under stress. They are seldom profound in meaning or brilliant in technique, but they have an unassuming sincerity, regional authenticity and a refreshing tincture of sly humour. They have appeared in most of the leading popular magazines, *Maclean's*, *Collier's* and *The Family Herald*, and in one collected volume, *Sunrise for Peter and Other Stories* (1946). The story which follows is taken from *Sunrise for Peter*.

The Movies Come to Gull Point

FOUR MEN were mending nets in a shack behind the fish wharf at Granny Cove. Spring had come grudgingly, but now the warm sun was melting the ice and sending steamy

134

vapours from tarred roofs. The Cove front murmured with activity as all its men prepared for the sea.

The four worked in silence, seated on benches, half-hidden by the drab folds that hung from the cross-beams overhead, their hands flicking in and out among the meshes, tying, knotting, threading. All at once they paused and listened. There were new voices outside.

"Them's the two back from pulp-cuttin'," said Simon Holder. He was a small lean man.

"Wonder if they got their pay," said Dick Berry, a red-faced man with big bony shoulders.

The two working in the rear were young, and brothers, Ben and Matthew Crowdy, proud of being hired with Simon. Ben was only seventeen, and slim, but he carried himself as seriously as the other three.

"Ho, Willyum," shouted Berry as a man passed the open door. "Don't rush yourself. What's the word down along?"

The man came back and peered in at them. "Not much new," he said. "They're havin' movin' pictures. . . ."

"Movin'!" Berry's mouth fell open. "How?"

"The man's got a machine'n engine to drive her. He's over't Gull Point tonight givin' a showin'."

"Over't Gull Point!" Berry rose from his bench, his red face glowing. "Simon, let's go over?"

"What's he chargin'?" asked Simon.

"Twenty-five cents, but he's got good pictures. There's one. . . ."

"Don't tell us," blurted Matthew. "That would spoil it. What say we go, Simon?" He had a solemn face, like Ben, but his eyes were bright.

Simon left his bench and went outside. The others followed him and they stood, gazing at the sea.

The ice was breaking up. The warm sun had been aided by a strong wind off land and a lane of black water was steadily widening along the foot of the cliffs, while smaller leads angled in all directions, opening as the pack surged and

loosened. Southward, toward Gull Point, there seemed plenty
of open sea.

"Risky," pronounced Simon.

"Chancy," agreed Berry, "but not too much."

"Wind's favourin', too," added Matthew.

There was a slow shrill screaming of the ice. Floes and pans
were grinding together; the harsh noises never stilled.

Ben looked up. There were no clouds and the sky was a
blue that seemed to reflect the endless ice.

"Looks fairish weather," he said, "but it's comin' tonight."

"You boys got money?" asked Simon.

They shook their heads and Berry grinned.

"That's makes a dollar," Simon said gravely. "That's a lot
of money."

"There ain't never been," said Ben, "movin' pictures up
here. I never seen any in my life."

"Bet she's open to the Point," said Berry. "We'd do fine
with a lugsail."

Simon rubbed his salt-bitten chin. They four were the best
in the Cove. "Git geared," he said suddenly.

"It's six mile," Simon said an hour later. They had launched
their dory and were well into the wide lead but the lug-sail was
proving a menace. A stiffer breeze caught them and tipped the
boat. He pulled the canvas in. "Mebbe we're fools."

They had lost much time. Matthew had broken a thole pin
in his eagerness and they had not turned back to repair it.
They had trusted in the sail, and his oars were idle.

"The wind'll be strong outside," said Berry. He was rowing
and he grunted his words.

They were true enough. Once away from the shelter of the
high black cliffs, the wind caught the dory and they swung
along sharply. There were many wide lanes and the sea
was running higher than it had seemed, and spray flung
over them.

Simon steered with a long sweep and Matthew was seated
next him, squatted low but ready to lend a hand. As they

swayed with the dory all four seemed a jumble of sou-westers and oilskins.

They did not attempt conversation. The shrieking, jarring crashes of the ice mingled with the whistling of the breeze and drowned all lesser sounds. The rapidly-widening lane they were in became a sea of racing, tumbling water that spewed spray as it struck the dory. Simon's oilskins dripped and his cheeks were wet but his expression never changed. He was gauging every wave with the instinct of one born to the sea.

Suddenly each man braced himself for action. A loose floe hove in their path and the waves pitched it about dangerously. Simon and Berry used all their strength and skill as they managed to avoid it, but neither man spoke. Matthew was bailing instantly and they moved slowly until he had scooped from the dory the gallons of water shipped during the swinging manoeuvre. It seemed, in that short time, to become night.

The rocky point behind them had cut off the sun as it sank rapidly, and with its going the wind keened to a penetrating chill. The darkness added greatly to their risks and Matthew peered ahead.

"She started to fog," he shouted. "She's a bank now."

The shore, hazy before, had become mist-drowned, shrouded with a thick white creeping veil. It seemed to permeate the air.

"She's come behind the same," yelled Ben.

They were half their journey and a swirling blanket of gray vapours closed about them. They would have to chance their passage ahead where the contour of the coast veered so that the slow-moving field of ice might bar their way.

It was Matthew who first saw that they had entered a wide lane and were between shifting ice. He peered again.

"Keep straight on!" he cried.

Short waves were deluging the boat with freezing spray. Berry rowed with quick strokes, and the roar of wind and grinding ice filled the night.

The water became smoother. Matthew reached and touched Berry on the back and at the signal the bigger man changed places with him. They were tense and watchful; only men of their experience could know the risk of a channel between rafted ice. Deep booming sounds seemed to pass over them as though they had sunk in a trough of the sea, and it grew darker.

"Look!" yelled Ben. "She's closin' in."

There was a muttered undertone beneath the booming and their lane of open water had narrowed to feet in width.

They slipped awkwardly in their sealskin boots as each man scrambled onto the floe, but they secured footing and with desperate hurried strength dragged the heavy dory from the water. It taxed them to their utmost and no one spoke. The ice was an uneven surging field and a blurred grayness covered everything.

"She's bad," said Berry. "We should have. . . ."

He did not finish. There was a crash of giant floes colliding and they were sprawled beside the dory. In an instant the night was a wilder chaos of wind and clamour.

"Watch out!" Simon's voice rose above the tumult like a cracking whip. "She's breakin'."

The floe buckled. It rose and lowered under them. There were sudden surgings that pitched them about. They seized the dory sides and pushed landward. The roaring of surf at the face of the floe came clearly.

"Watch her!" It was a scream more than a shout. The ice was parting.

The floe rocked and settled. Water sloshed over the ice, reached them. There was another settling.

"There!" yelled Ben.

The field had opened and the sea drove into the vent with foaming fury. It poured over the ice to meet them. Then, its weight, and the driving surf, heaved the floe.

They slid backward in the wash. Ben, caught by the dory, fell, and water washed over him. He rose, sobbing with his immersion, clinging to the dory, and, as if a signal were given, they rushed the boat toward the open water. The lane had widened into a broad lead.

Again the floe surged, and the dory slid into the water.

Ben leaped into it, tilting it dangerously. Matthew sprang in beside him, rocking it to a safer keel. Berry had given a great thrust forward to clear them from the ice and as he sprang he lunged against Simon, knocking him backward.

For a heartbeat it seemed they must capsize. The churning water had caught them as the dory took its plunge. Berry grasped his oars and threw his weight against the surge. Behind them, in the screaming murk, Simon was lost to view.

Ben had seized Simon's sweep and they toiled to bring the dory about. The lane was a smother of surf. Danger hovered over every move and the water boiled with changing currents.

They drove back alongside, catching, with perfect co-ordination, a minute lull at the ice edge, and Simon, gauging their move, joined them. It was a risky plunge, challenging all their chances, but once more Berry's strength saved the dory and then they had swung away and Ben was bailing.

In the thick darkness the surf seemed wilder than before but the worst was soon behind them. Then, just ahead, a pin-point of light shone steadily.

Within ten minutes they were in calmer waters, and lamp glows began to pierce the gloom. They landed and hurried Ben, shaking and almost numbed with cold, to the nearest house.

"Us is from Granny Cove," announced Simon, "Ben were wet on the ice. Could us dry him here?"

"Sure, the stove's red-hot." A woman wrapped in a thick jacket and ready to leave for the hall where the movies were to be shown, answered them. "I'll git a rig for him to put on and his'll dry while we're gone."

Ben was shaking as with ague and tiny pools formed on the floor beside him as the warmth of the stove softened his frozen clothing. He drank a scalding mixture the woman provided and his trembling ceased. He stripped his sodden clothing and Matthew ranged it on a chair back alongside the stove. Then Ben dressed in a makeshift outfit and they followed the path the woman had taken.

The building where the movies were being shown was

packed with people. It was a low-roofed structure and heated by a huge box stove. There were high odours of perspiration and many faces were beaded with moisture. Children were sandwiched among their elders and every seat was taken. Simon led the way along one wall and they stood against it, tightly wedged by others who crowded after. Ben struggled from the borrowed reefer that blanketed him.

"We're lucky," he gasped. "She's jist startin'."

There were gasps and murmurings as the lamps were extinguished and the hum of a motor began. Headings appeared on the screen and a dozen voices tried to read them.

"Let teacher read 'em," bellowed a husky voice at the rear.

" 'She Knew She Was Wrong'," a high pitched voice shrilled in the darkness as "teacher" assumed her task. "Pretty Virginia. . . ."

The audience had stilled. It was seeing the incredible . . . mirrored eating places . . . ladies with bare backs and cigarettes . . . bewildering dances . . . racing cars . . . a bathing beach teeming with thousands. And one face dominated.

"See that one!" said Berry hoarsely. "Her's. . . ."

"Keep shut," ordered Simon in a sibilant whisper.

They watched the heroine driving in city traffic and there were cries of admiration.

"Ho!" shouted Berry. "Look at she." He clapped his hands.

"She's won'erful sharp in steerin'," responded Simon, "but . . . ." He couldn't express himself.

"Her smokes," objected Ben.

Another picture began and all voices stilled. It was a story of rival airmen, and the planes in action did marvellous stunting. A flight of machines gave a thrilling performance, all manner of stunt flying.

Berry tensed, his big hands gripping a seat back. Simon breathed with sharp little intakes. Ben and Matthew gave shrill exclamations, unable to restrain themselves.

"They're hittin'!"

"No—yes—there!"

"Lookit—lookit—*lookit!*"

A dozen voices yelled with him. The airmen were shooting earthward at dizzy speed, headed toward each other.

There was a dull grinding sound and the screen went blank.

A lamp was lighted and the operator of the movie machine worked desperately with various tools. Then he came forward.

"Sorry, folks," he said, "but the machine's broke and I've got to send the piece away. I can't show any more."

There were sighs of disappointment but no one gave criticism. They began filing from the building and the night was filled with excited voices.

Ben went to change his clothes again and the woman insisted on them stopping to drink scalding tea and to eat slices of hard bread.

"Stay the night," she urged. "I've blankets enough to fix you up on the kitchen floor."

"No," refused Simon. "The fog's cleared and she's light as day. We've got a mortal sight of work to do, gettin' ready to fish."

Berry ate and drank hugely but said nothing. The unexpected ending of the show had given him vast disappointment.

It was breaking day as the dory swung to the wharf at Granny's Cove. The sea had been much rougher than they anticipated and they had been forced to keep near the shore line all the way. For hours there had been but the creak of boat timbers and the slap of heavy water; each was silent, and dull-minded.

A slight breeze stirred the morning. It was from the west and warm. There would be a perfect day. The sunrise began in a fire of orange and crimson that merged into soft pinks and changing blues. The heavens were a mass of colour.

The light spread over the hills and reached the sleeping houses. It found iced places in the hollows and they glittered like jewels.

They dragged the dory to its landing and stood away from it. Ben was bruised and stiff. Matthew had lost a mitten and each was conscious of clothing damp with spray.

"We're back," said Simon tersely, "but it were worth it."

"Sure," agreed Berry, yawning mightily. "That girl were a prime one."

"It must be great," said Matthew, "to live where you kin see won'erful sights all the time."

The light strengthened and the sea was blue as sapphire where the sun rays reached it slantingly. Still they stood, as if each were labouring with thoughts they could not put into words. Then Simon spat and faced them.

"I don't know what youse think," he said, "but takin' all them risks to make a picture don't seem right to me."

Matthew nodded gravely. "Us been thinkin' just that," he said. "It's for nothin' but pleasurin' and it's queer they ain't laws to stop it."

"Sure," added Ben, "there should be a law ag'in it. They might have been killed."

There was no further comment. Smoke began to curl from a chimney. Ben yawned again. They had expressed that which stirred them most, so they turned and filed soberly to their homes.

RAYMOND KNISTER

RAYMOND KNISTER was born in 1900 at Blenheim, Ontario, and spent most of his life working on an Ontario farm. He was a graduate of the University of Toronto and of Iowa State University, and for a period of less than two years in the early twenties was Associate Editor of *The Midland,* a literary monthly published in Iowa City through which such mid-western writers as Ruth Suckow made their debut. He met a tragic and premature death by drowning in 1932, at the time when his work as a poet, short story writer and critic was coming into general recognition. He was undoubtedly one of the most promising young writers whom Canada has yet produced.

Knister's work, in both poetry and prose, was concerned for the most part with the rural life of Ontario. His stories and poems appeared in such magazines as *The Canadian Forum, The Midland, Poetry, Voices, transition* and *This Quarter.* In addition to his contributions to these magazines, he published three books: two novels, *White Narcissus* and *My Star Predominant*; and *Canadian Short Stories,* an anthology.

The most striking features of his short stories are his unerring sense of atmosphere and his fresh use of language. He establishes the atmosphere or tone of his stories from the first lines, and maintains it to the end by the choice of expressive and harmonious words, images and backgrounds. To Knister words were not mere counters to be handled casually, but vivid signs of concrete things. Occasionally his determination not to be content with the conventional cliché leads him him into tortuosity and quaintness, but even then our attitude is one of alertness and eagerness. His work, of course, was not entirely uninfluenced: the sombreness of his outlook, the rather drab realism of his subject matter, have obvious kinships with the work of the American mid-western school of the twenties; but the directness with which he applied himself to the Canadian scene, and the stubborn independence of his wrestle with language, mark him as genuinely creative.

A critical article on Knister by Leo Kennedy was published in *The Canadian Forum*, September, 1932. Dorothy Livesay prepared, in 1949, a collected edition of Knister's poetry, to which she prefaced a study of his life and work. "The Strawstack" appeared first in *The Canadian Forum*.

The Strawstack

HE HAD WALKED ten hours before he came to it. Usually he did not walk so many hours in one stretch. He was able to wander far enough, he had found, walking three or four of a day, when he went at all. In the years since he had left the place, far enough.

He could not understand fully yet what brought him back now. All the years which might have done so had failed. His first homesickness had been a sandbar only from which he soon floated away not free, and distantly.

The place was the same, with the sorrowful sameness he found in the chances of life, in its monotonous recurrence, inescapable; the horrible rise and sinking of the sun, moons. And tiny beyond his toughened expectation. Only a few minutes' walking, the passing of a few sombre reflections which did not save themselves from the monotony, was the meaning of that lane to the back of the farm which had appeared so unending to the boy going back in the dark for the cattle after the day in the harvest-field.

The trees were shrunken, grizzled, and unkempt, stood vagabonds, in an air of desperately-attempted sturdy carelessness. The fields, worse; tiny closed places, which his unthinking toil had made into sky-seeking deserts of plowed land or unfathomable mazes of corn.

As he looked, the wind shook dirty stubble that was a great brush waiting for the fur of some monstrous wallowing animal; shook weeds by the fence-corner, which, brittle, he marvelled did not shatter — who had broken them with difficulty in childish hands and, stripping leaves and branches, used them for goads to drive the beasts.

The tininess of everything large in his memory drew a terror about him which, too searching, he could not try to understand. He had not known his memory demanded so much from the place, had created so much of it.

Through the fields he came from the road caved with woods at the back of the farm, seeing little and experiencing a sadness which crushed him closer and closer and made him wonder, when if the pain had been physical he should have cried out, why he could have thought to find surcease here, and why his mind had not shied back from the contemplation of return, knowing its own danger.

The sun had set when he came forth from the woods, and the incomparable quiet was there which comes before the moon rises or the greater dark begins. He found himself asking, "I wonder if there will be a moon tonight," before his memory told him of last night's dark as he tramped the endless bald road.

Dark splotches in one little field were peacefully still, and the cool munching of cows had something obscene about it, like the ravening of wolves at the finding of a dead hunter: the field, dead, was not the less silently complaining, he saw.

He came nearer, and they woofed and scampered leadenly away, turning about to face him at a distance. He went on without seeing them.

The wind lifted again, and he stopped with a jerk which drew his head back, stiffened as before a brink. His face was compressed in a colour of terror which made his unshaven features frightful. Then he stepped on again after an instant, with limp strides as before. It was only a few days, one day ago, that he began to hear a soft crackling, a tearing in one side of his brain answering to the tenseness of his moods. And still it was hard to forget, to remember the tiny flapping of the ripped silk band about his felt hat.

It was the house which shocked his numbness most, which filled him with a sorrowful terror of all new revelations he should have learned before, if this was yet the place of all his furbished memories. It was so ugly, with its tatter of clapboards and peeled paint, two boards torn off at the ground, showing black underneath. Verandah posts hung baseless, steps were not there. One ridge of the roof as he looked at it against the red sky was bent, the spine of some old animal worn down with burdens.

He had gone nearly all the way around before he became conscious that no life was in it, and realized that he had not expected any, though someone must be caring for the farm. Years since his mother and father had died — while he was serving his first term.

He stepped back from the house to the barn, desperately recalling that the yard had seemed as wide as a field when he ran out in the night for an armful of wood to put in the stove.

The tiny stable which had seemed so long when you stood behind the row of stalls and looked across the hips of horses between them! The roof which it had seemed such an Alpine labour to mount and affix a little wooden windmill. He turned away quickly, fearing that someone might be within, passed the corn-crib, the pig-pen, and came back of the barn.

A strawstack was there, sprawling dark-brown over a great area of soil, unbuilt, but taking what shape it might as it was spewed forth from the thresher. It must have lain there three or four years. Hummocks and holes were about its edges, made by time and the burrowing of animals.

He crept among these for a place which would shelter him for the night, recalling how his father had disapproved the sprawled carelessness of such stacks, and the prudence with which his own were built, before the boy's eyes, looking on with a curiosity which made all things pertinent.

He searched out a place, a hole in the side, pulled handfuls of straw and enlarged it, and at last leaned back looking out from where he sat beneath the edge of the cupola roof towards the back of the farm.

He sat, burrowing and making the most of the warmth and trying to refuse his thoughts. Many a farmer's barn or strawstack had made his bed for the night in the course of his wanderings without his dreaming of coming so to the old place.

He took out of a package some cheese and bread with bologna and hard cakes. The dark had come on, and a musty smell from the old straw he had moved spread around him. It brought back in a whelming wave the nights on which he had gone to sparrow hunts. The parties made up, they took different ways and went loudly talking by dark roads to neighbours' barns and stacks, carrying lanterns. Reaching their hands into holes about the eaves of the stack, they seized the birds, or held a net before it and beat upon the straw beside the hole. The birds flew out with squeaking chirps. They twisted off the heads to take for proof when the bodies became too bulky. The greatest number won the catchers an oyster-supper, which the losing side bought and helped to eat. The oblivion!

But sometimes stepping up to the stack, a bird would fly out, blindly in the dark, wind of its wings velvet against his cheek, and be free. . . . The smell was about him yet, making more keen a sense of the years since those times.

They had not seemed such unforgiven years as they went. It was when he looked at them all from one point that he loathed them suddenly, their whirling inconsequence swinging to crime that lent nothing to hope, until he could blot them away with diversions to give memory worse stings for the future.

The years muffled him as he went through them, persuaded him that they were brief, that they would change, deliver to his hands chance. But, waiting, the wanderings, the wanderings they had led him.

Because of the witless inanity of a moment.

He was only a boy when it happened, fifteen years old. His parents had gone to the village that afternoon, and left him to do the chores about the house and barn when he returned from school. His sister, younger than himself, came home together with him, running after when she had left the other girls at their gates. They set about their tasks.

Presently he came to that of filling the woodbox, empty from the day's burning. A huge woodpile stood in the back yard, the outcome of a day and a half of buzzing. At the bottom, where he had been pulling out the wood, the sticks had become bound in, for the pile had been thrown together into whatever shape it might take as the cutting went on, and was not yet piled in tiers. So he climbed to the top and began pulling the sticks out and tossing them down below.

The little sister came out of the house to help him, for she was lonely in the house; and stooped down to the ground to pick up the sticks as they tumbled and dropped to the bottom.

Faster and faster the sticks twirled down to one side of him, the boy stooping over all the time and not looking where they fell.

Then he did look around, under a sudden impulsion, and seemed to hear a low moan broken. One of the sticks had been lighter than most and flew to strike the little girl on the forehead.

He jumped down the pile without consciousness of doing so until he stumbled on a projecting piece and nearly fell headlong on the thickset stubs.

She was lying on the ground, with a bruise above her temple. He could not waken her. He pulled at her shoulder, called her name in tones that fought with fear and could not rise to loudness.

He lifted her and carried her into the house, with unwitting dragging steps, such a breaking heart as he had never known before. Dusk was closing about the flat country. In the vivid wind the leafless trees howled madly in sorrow, and from the barnyard came cattle's lowing.

Inside it was darker, as he moved to a couch and placed his burden upon it. He looked at the little form for a moment, unable to think. Then he called her name again, and went to get cold water.

There was no sign. The child was still as before. Still he looked at the glimmering form in the dark, the furniture crowding about him, with such a heart within as he thought must at any moment bring his death. He called her name and with fear-sped legs fled from the house.

The dark was there, holding back like an ambush of armed ruffians. They boy ran the gauntlet of it to the road, and stood waiting, listening and peering. There was not a sound, and as he watched, the thought came on wings of a different terror that perhaps it was better so. He made a movement to set off in the direction opposite that from which he expected his father's and his mother's coming. The world was suddenly so big. . . . He must stay a little yet. He must return to the house and get his overcoat and mittens.

He entered again and secured them and went to the side of his sister. With a great effort he again shaped her name with his lips, but he dare not feel her wrist or her forehead.

As he left the place he felt that he could not go far. He himself would die under the weight.

In the darkness of early morning he got aboard a freight train. Six months later he heard that his sister had recovered and come to no further harm, but those ten or fifteen minutes never were to be less in his memory than the years which they had become.

There was no need for his continued wanderings, except in himself. He might have returned at any time after he had learned, but those few months, few instants, had shaped the rest of his life. From town to city he went, falling in with groups ever more questionable. He was surprised mightily after his first serious crime and began then to wonder whither he was tending. After prison he thought that he would make another start, and all would be well. But he had merely a steeper slope down which to glide.

Prison meant little to him. The change in the routine of his days hid no other change. Life was the same and left him with the same feeling after a few weeks behind the high iron fences and walls as it had outside. In spite of his conviction that he should think of nothing else. Some perversity in him kept his thoughts from wandering there. People were outside, people were there, inside. He was able to find as much and little in one place as in another.

It was not altogether indifference. Other men who seemed to be of his calibre knew him from meagre intercourse to be a pal. Without more than a few words, or probably, he felt, the capability to any extent of understanding him. That was his defence in all his wanderings, the reason for his escape from many a dubious situation, and it was his bane. People of the class he came sometimes to frequent in the way of affairs couldn't think badly of him, and they could not understand him. When they began to trust him he could not resist showing them in error, and he constantly thrust himself back beyond beginnings.

While imprisonment meant little, freedom for a time did live with him. He was surprised with his own pleasure in all the manifestations of a trivial life around him. His record at the prison had been good, and with the encouragement of that he went to a ranch far off in the hills and got a job which in time was changed to a responsible one. But it was the same there. He began to realize that he was trusted, even to things beyond his normal activities. The upshot was prison again, and came near being lynching, but he left the stolen horses in time and managed to be caught by a brace of police.

Prison again, and he could not mind it this time either. It occurred to him one day that it was wrong, that he should be ashamed and repentant. The idea clung with him and bothered him the remainder of his term. He fancied that if he could not come to care there could be no hope for him. He wondered why something within him refused to care, and he asked the chaplain. The worthy man, puzzled, in ten minutes gave him enough reasons to make him more uncertainly dumbfounded than ever.

Freedom never came to him afterward. He rustled now in the straw. How could it after those years. . . . Yes, they were years; the old place made him realize. Drifting about from city to country he could not try to find himself again. And now he had made the final break with, pitiful to call it, his destiny.—

With himself, which could not spare him again. The crime he had committed he had always looked on as the last in the world for him. He would have, in its revelation, prepared for the last. Now it was done. At once, when he had hidden the traces, he had made for the old place, passing through that part of the country to another city, begging and tramping, careless of discovery, splitting a pile of wood now and then for a bowl of bread and milk. He walked all the first night, rested, and came on again through the day, desperately certain that if he could be once more there, all would be well.

Now he had come. He looked out of the hole in the straw at the long fence which stretched from alongside the stack and shot, long and arrowy, to the back of the farm. When he had been a boy the fence was a rail one, crawling snakily, in the corners of which the cattle nibbled the ground bare of grass, and where may-apples sometimes grew. Despair burst through his soul at the thought that he even now refused to care, that his crime, his crimes, refused to present themselves to his mind in the colours in which they existed in the daylight of other men's sight.

His sight was never daylit. His trouble. Something dark and all-shrouding must be holding the light within him. If he might only search even over the world and find something, some sharp beauty he had never known, which would tear apart the curtain that stood, elastically resisting prisoners' blows, between himself and life! The search alone would steady him, set him again upon his feet.

He was leaning backward, the brim of his felt hat resting against the solid straw. He rolled his head from side to side wearily as he lay staring at the old pictures from his life which filled the entrance of the hole, against the bare dusty sky.

The nights he had lain so, or in the dark of a barn, his eyes seeking slits to light night skies. Or in the filtering dusk rose and went on as the stars thinned. A November morning, when crows had cawed with restricted throats, susurrant and shrill. The roads, though; they were what he remembered, not one by one, but as a great stretch before him containing all the different sorts he had come upon, waves of dust or of mire. But rarely he really saw other things. The limp crows flopping by. . . .

He had never had great faith in the evil of men. In spite of his farings among them he had still somehow blinded himself to much of the worst in them. And now he began to see the worst, and at once to know that the worst was in all. The faces came before him, in animal-like roundness or animal-like sharpness of feature, half a dozen, more, or the men he had thought to know, until they had shown themselves. Now he looked at them and knew that *they* knew, they understood, and defied or conciliated remorse. Theirs was not his numbness to conscience.

Something pricking was against his neck and he sat up, and half turning round, felt in the straw until his fingers came on the end of a piece of string. He drew it forth, the stiff-fibred binder-twine, used to bind the sheaves, and blown out with the straw. He probed about in the straw again, to get any others that might irritate; and pulled out three or four, which he threw down beside him.

He leaned forward and looked out. It seemed to have become a little lighter. Fields, fences, and trees stood and lay in a pale and black dust. Then at one side he saw the moon, slight, sabre-thin, with the round penumbra. Below stood trees, short thin branches reaching up like baby fingers toward a mother's face.

A new moon! Why new? How could one call anything new? People must have thought sometime that when they became gross and replete with light the moons died. Or their souls appeared again on the other side of death. Then it could be right to call it new.

He drew back into the straw cave on his hands and knees, and felt the bunch of twine. (The dread moon, and the frost!) The coarseness of it beneath his hands brought back a vision of an old rope swing dangling in the wind, seatless, from a maple bough opposite the back door as he left the house forever. He had taken the rope long before from about a bag of binder-twine and climbed with twisting, stubby, bare toes, to tie it to the limb. Many an afternoon the two children had swung on it, while the leaves of the maple limb shivered with the shock. One day he sat on the seat idly after twisting the ropes together and then letting them whirl him around, and looked up along it to see that it was only twine after all like the twine in the balls, that was used in the binder. Some day he would twist some together and make a rope of his own.

His fingers still held the bits of twine in the straw. Then he took them up and tied them together. He stopped. Why was he doing that? He threw them aside as though in sudden fright.

Yet why should he be afraid—of himself? His weakness had been not being afraid perhaps. He could not pick on that part of him which should be blamed. He leaned back again and a straw brushed the band of his hat. His heart leaped before he could remember once more the cause of that half-noise, half-feeling. It reminded him that he was in a strange condition when he could imagine the crackling within his head. Yet not when the knife fell did his heart feel, and he was quiet as he put away the corpse. A strange condition, truly, he scoffed, having committed that crime, not to care to think about it, about punishment or danger.

He shivered.

Then the old despair filled him once more. He could never care. Were all these years an effort, a seeking to care about life, about sin? His mind pictured the shrinking and remorse which he ought to experience at the very thought of his deed, and strangely for an instant it began to come, in something of the way which another must feel it. Then he groaned. It would only be the same years over again, the same walkings, cold alley-brawls, debauch, the years alike and he limping over them as a dog on a treadmill; to learn and discover nothing but death and sorrow. The strange things men made of themselves in the course of years, and the terrible part of it: that they never knew, until moments such as this. All; if it were only such as he!

He found himself on his hands and knees tearing the straw

out in handfuls, sifting it, searching out the lengths of binder-twine. Then he stopped in sudden fright and made to leave the place. He tried to think: the posse; they knew his record, might seek him here. But it was not that. . . . He looked about the dark ground and sleeping trees that held so much of his real life. Then he came within again. His movements stirred up the sharp musty smell of mouldy straw.

He tied the strings together, sought more and more of them, frenziedly began braiding them. "I can't think," his mind warned him, "I must not think." Soon he could be heard saying it aloud, rhythmically "I can't think, I'll not think. . . . I'll not think, I can't think."

And soon the thin moon would come and peer in short-sightedly, and see nothing there.

THOMAS H. RADDALL

THOMAS H. RADDALL was born in England in 1903 and came to Canada as a young boy. His parents settled in Halifax, and he was educated there in the Chebucto School and the Halifax Academy. His first occupation was that of wireless operator on ships and shore stations along the Nova Scotia coast, and he served in this capacity during and after the First World War. He was also for a time an accountant in a Nova Scotia pulp mill, a position which enabled him to become acquainted with the ways of lumberjacks, millhands, hunters, trappers and Micmac Indians. His knowledge of the sea and of the groups just enumerated he has put to good use in his novels and stories. Since 1938 he has devoted all his time to writing, but he had previously begun to contribute stories to such periodicals as *Blackwood's, Maclean's* and *The Saturday Evening Post.*

Mr. Raddall has published several novels, including *His Majesty's Yankees* (1942), *The Nymph and the Lamp* (1950) and *Tidefall* (1953), plus three volumes of short stories, *The Pied Piper of Dipper Creek* (1939), *Tambour* (1945) and *The Wedding Gift* (1947). He has also produced a history of Halifax entitled *Halifax, Warden of the North* (1949).

Raddall is the leading present-day exponent of the romantic tradition in Canadian fiction, a tradition which goes back to John Richardson and Rosanna Leprohon in the early nineteenth century and was carried on by William Kirby, Gilbert Parker, the two Roberts, and others. It is probable, however, that the chief influence upon his work was the romantic school of fiction which developed in England in the last decades of the nineteenth century as a reaction against realism: a school which, at its higher level, contained Stevenson and, in a sense, Conrad and, at its lower level "Ouida", Haggard and Hall Caine. Raddall has neither the psychological subtlety nor the rich style of Conrad and Stevenson, but he has his share of vividness and vigour. Perhaps his chief strength is a painstaking concern for factual detail, which gives to his work a certain documentary interest. He knows how to tell a story in such a way as to create and maintain suspense, and his work is always rich in local colour. "The Amulet" is taken from *Tambour and Other Stories.*

The Amulet

THE REVEREND PHILIP MUIR had chosen a pleasant spot for his retirement. The old colonial farmhouse stood on a green bluff by the river. Its clapboards were painted white, its doors and shutters green, its roof a cheerful red. It had been built in early times by an aesthete among pioneers who turned his back on the wandering dirt road and faced his abode towards the river for the view, the broad shining stream, the island tufted with swamp maples and fringed with reeds, the rolling pine woods on the other side. It was a place for meditation.

The young licentiate from River Gap, a mile or two down river, liked to walk there on sunny afternoons to discuss theology and its place in the lives of his fishermen. His name was Carson and he was city-bred, an earnest young man rather flabbergasted to find himself in a community that measured the world by a literal interpretation of the scriptures — and demanded that its minister do the same.

"I've given my views on Jonah and the whale, the Creation, the Flood," he said whimsically, "and yesterday a patriarch fixed me with a bright blue eye and demanded to know how I stood on Methuselah."

"What did you say?" asked the Reverend Philip.

"Oh, the usual things. Giants in the earth in those days, and all that. It seemed dangerous to suggest that the scriptures, being human works, were subject to human misinterpretations. They regard the Bible as the absolute word of God."

"Then you don't believe, yourself, that man could live for centuries?"

"Frankly, no."

The Reverend Philip smiled.

"Do you believe in metempsychosis?"

"The transmigration of souls? Of course not. That's purely pagan."

The little grey man leaned back in the deep verandah chair and closed his eyes.

"I'm going to tell you something that may shake your ideas. It's not something I read or heard. It's something I saw with my own eyes.

"Just after the first German war I had a church in Alding, fifteen miles up the river. There's a Micmac community in the outskirts, a few little huts, half a dozen families, the usual thing. They weren't my parishioners—they were Catholics as a matter of fact, although my good friend Father Egan could never get them near his church except to bury them. Now and again you find groups like that, professing Christianity as a sort of fire insurance but secretly confirmed in the vague nature worship of their ancestors.

"Sometimes I went fishing with an Indian named Paul Luksi, a big fine-looking man with a broad dark face and sombre black eyes and the light husky voice that always makes you wonder how they managed a war-whoop. I should say Paul was forty at the time, his wife perhaps thirty-five— Indians are hard to judge after thirty—and they had a son and daughter grown up and gone away. There was another member of the household, and the first time I was invited inside the little two-room shack I got a shock.

"I suppose I'd been in there a full minute before I looked in a corner and met the eyes of an extraordinary creature sitting on the floor. By the dress, it was a woman, a little old squaw with almost no hair, a few straggling wisps, and a face fallen in upon itself like a brown withered apple, a living skull.

"I can't describe the skin of her face. It sagged against the bones in a confusion of lifeless wrinkles. Her lips were thin lines of violet, tucked back into the toothless jaws. Her eyes were black and so glazed with age that in some lights they looked blue, a horrible unearthly blue, and they were set very deep in those wrinkled sockets. She was like an unwrapped mummy.

"I spoke to her but beyond a flicker of the eyes she gave no sign of having heard. Her dress was of heavy black cloth in voluminous folds, the sort women wore everywhere forty or fifty years ago. It was patched in many places. Her one ornament was a curious amulet of putty-coloured stone. I'd no chance to examine it closely but I saw it was a crude representation of a turtle and that it had been broken and a lower portion detached. It hung from her skinny neck by a thong.

"I saw her a number of times after that, usually squatting in the corner or crawling like some incredible beast about the floor. I decided she was semi-paralytic, but one day I saw her splitting wood in the door-yard, standing up and swinging the axe vigorously, an amazing sight . . . as if you saw me, for instance, get up at this moment and turn handsprings the length of the verandah.

"Once or twice I heard her speak, a strange mewing that Paul and his wife seemed to understand quite readily. I could never get them to say what relation she was to them. They spoke of her reluctantly and in a queer disinterested way, as if she were a keepsake passed down to them through so many generations that her origin had been forgotten. They held her in great respect, though. I fancied she was a great-grandmother on one side or the other, and the air of mystery they hung about her was just one of those inexplicable Indian whims.

"One day she disappeared. Completely. The Indians had spent the day in Alding, dipping alewives out of the brook that flowed past my church, and when they returned to their shacks in the evening with their dip-nets and their sacks of fish the old crone was missing. Paul was in a fearful state. None of the traditional Indian calm. He and his wife were weeping loudly on their doorstep when Bailey, the Alding constable — we hadn't the Mounted Police in Nova Scotia then — came to organize a search party.

"They found nothing except that someone had stolen Paul's canoe from the river bank. For three days they hunted the woods and dragged the river without success. On the fourth day the old squaw was found at Anse Blanche, a small uninhabited inlet down the coast, twenty miles by river and sea from Alding. A fisherman discovered her while hunting for sapling oaks to make bows for his lobster traps. The missing canoe was drawn up on the banks of a small brook flowing into Anse Blanche. The squaw was dead.

"I came down from Alding with Father Egan and the constable and one or two others, and we went to Anse Blanche in a motor boat from River Gap. The place was five miles along the coast from the mouth of the river. The body was lying curled up on a low mound in the bush about a hundred yards from the shore. There was a similar mound a few steps away. The small stream flowed between. We searched the spot thoroughly, probing amongst the ferns with sticks, and somebody turned up a bit of turf at the side of the mound, and revealed a mass of crumbled clam shells.

"We widened the hole a bit and found that the shells went down a foot or more, with little pockets of decayed bird and fish and animal bones. An old camp site, evidently. Among the shells was a piece of crude pottery such as I'd seen in the Micmac section of the Halifax museum, thick drab-coloured stuff made of clay and tempered with fragments of shell, and decorated with marks like basket-work, and fired at low temperatures. That clinched the matter. That poor old thing had gone back to some long-remembered scene of her youth. It was spring, the season of the ancient migration to the coast, and somewhere in the back of that senile skull there had flickered a memory, an instinct, an animal stirring that made her go down to the canoes and start for the sea. The river carried her fifteen miles to the tide, but she must have paddled the whole five miles along the coast to that lonely spot.

"We took that little rigid wisp back to Alding, and the inquest was short. Death was due to natural causes . . . in fact, young Doctor Ridgeway said she'd lived a long time in defiance of all natural causes. He told the coroner, 'She's like something out of a tomb in Egypt.' We all smiled, of course. Ridgeway was given to picturesque phrases. Nothing was gained from the testimony of the Indians. They were ill at ease in the midst of this solemnity, and when questioned they blurted out a few absurd statements and relapsed into a glum

silence that nothing could shake. They had some sort of
tradition about an annual migration to the seashore, but
nothing in their own time or the time of their fathers and
grandfathers.

"The Micmacs gave up their seasonal movements when
civilization compelled them to squat on any land they wished
to keep. Of seventeen Indian adults in Alding, only three had
ever seen the sea, just fifteen miles away.

"There was some difficulty over the old woman's name.
At first Paul insisted he didn't know her name. That seemed
absurd. Braxton, the Alding coroner, a fussy little man full
of his momentary importance, snapped, 'Come now, Paul!
Answer the questions properly or there will be trouble. You'll
be liable for contempt if you keep this up. Who did she belong
to, you or your wife?'

"Now the modern Micmac speaks English quite well, but
within the family he sticks to his own tongue; it's the language
of the household, the peg he hangs his private life on; he thinks
in it even when he's talking English. I could see him struggling
with a phrase that would not flow in English. At last he blurted
out, '*Sa-ak-a-wach-kik!*'

"Braxton *was* annoyed. 'How many times, Paul, must I tell
you to speak English at this inquest? You know English. You
must speak English. Let's have no more of this nonsense.
Come now, her name was Luksi, wasn't it?'

"Paul's face settled in that frozen look an Indian puts on
when he doesn't want to talk. 'Yes,' he said sullenly.

" 'And her Christian name?'

" 'No Christian name.'

" 'Nonsense! She *must* have a Christian name.'

"Paul shrugged, and grunted, 'Molly.'

"Braxton told the clerk to write it down, and I remember
he turned to us quite pleased with himself and delivered a little
homily on the virtue of perseverance in dealing with cases of
this kind. As if he or anyone else in MacDougal's mortuary
had ever seen a case of this kind! It seemed to me that Paul
said 'Molly' just as you or I would have said Tom, Dick

or Harry if somebody demanded—in plain English and no quibbling—the Christian name of the Piltdown Man. Molly's a very common name amongst Micmac women.

"So Father Egan conducted the funeral of 'Molly Luksi' and consigned her to a Christian grave in the churchyard of Saint Gregory's, a lovely little church that you must see if you want to appreciate all that is simple and beautiful in wooden architecture. Most of the Indians were there, standing well back, as if the old lady might jump out of the coffin any minute, and crossing themselves vigorously.

"After the service Father Egan presented me with the little stone necklet. 'Here,' he said, 'you're interested in these things. I wouldn't bury the woman with that pagan symbol about her neck; I made the undertaker take it off.' It wasn't much of a trinket; just a crude little turtle cut out of some fairly hard stone and polished a bit. On the top the stone went upwards in a V-shape like the tip of a Maltese cross, and there was a hole bored for the thong. The lower side of the turtle extended in the same fashion, but what might have been another V was broken off. I looked at the thing and threw it in a drawer.

"A year or two later an archæologist came to see me. I'd never seen one before. I'd pictured them as a breed apart, thin men with sun helmets and grey torpedo beards, and associated always with pyramids and Mongol ponies and mysterious ruins in the Central American jungle. Beckles didn't fit the picture. A thick-set, powerful man with a bald, sloping brow, a humorous mouth and a nose like a potato. Said he was making a study of the prehistoric Micmacs, one of the least-known tribes in North America, and he understood I knew of a kitchen midden somewhere in this vicinity. Middens are fairly common in some parts of Nova Scotia but they've been ruined by souvenir hunters. Beckles wanted one absolutely untouched.

"He explained to me, 'These prehistoric Micmacs went inland in winter and lived in communities for mutual warmth and protection. By doing so they avoided the bitter coastal storms and got the best of the caribou hunting. But it must have been a miserable existence in those bark huts in the cold, and the fortunes of hunting meant famine more often than feast. So in spring they were very glad to go down the river in canoes as soon as the ice was out. They scattered in small groups along the coast, setting up a few wigwams whenever there was a clam flat, a trickle of fresh water, and a chance to fish. There were sea fish of all kinds, especially alewives and salmon and shad crowding into the rivers to spawn. There were seals and probably walrus. Wild-fowl were in multitude, migrating from the south. And in the woods there was always a chance of meeting anything from a squirrel to a bull moose. For the Micmacs summer was the good time, the warm time, the easy time. When all else failed, the squaw could go out on the clam flat at low tide and dig up a dinner with a stick. These coastal middens contain all we'll ever know of Micmac life at its best.'

"I told him, 'Well, I could show you such a midden but it's not the thing you want. I mean it's been occupied within the lifetime of a squaw I knew.' He looked surprised at that, for he thought — what we all thought — that the Micmacs had given up their coastal camps at least a century before. I told him the story of Molly Luksi and he was impressed, but, he said, 'Say she was a hundred years old; that puts the mound well into historic times, of course. It's relatively modern when you remember that European influence in Nova Scotia began before the Spanish Armada. I'd like to have a dig at it, though. The mound may go back to antiquity, in which case we'd be able to trace the culture right into modern times. That would be simply marvellous.'

"Off he went, and came back in a week's time with a small party—his son, Bob, a student at McGill; Doctor Daly, who was osteologist at the Werning Museum of Natural History; and a cook-handyman. They had two cars piled with tents and equipment and groceries and baggage.

"I went out with them in a small fishing schooner from River Gap. The coast is a saw-edge of narrow bays and coves, and those that run far back into the land are almost dry at low tide. Anse Blanche is like that. The ebb-tide leaves a long, shining basin of sand speckled with fragments of clam shell. You have to come and go at high tide. It's a desolate place. The surrounding ridges were burned to the granite rock by a bad forest fire about 1919; the woods were very dry that year and the soil burned like peat; then the rains came and washed all the residue into the lower levels. At Anse Blanche now the bald rocks occupy most of the landscape, with thickets of wire birch and scrub maples in the hollows. It's a miracle how that old Indian woman recognized the place at all, for when she was young the whole place was covered in virgin timber.

"Those bygone Indians had chosen the site with care, well back from the shore and around a bend in the little stream, so that nothing was visible from the sea. The brook is now a miserable trickle seeping down from the barren ridges, but it must have been a good trout stream in the days of the green forest. I waited over between tides and watched the party set up their tents. They pitched them by the shore for the benefit of the sea breeze, for it was hot in Anse Blanche, especially with the tide out and the sun beating on the flats. They did some exploring but found no more than two low mounds beside the brook.

" 'Two wigwams,' Daly said. 'Generation after generation, gradually building up those middens. What happened to their natural increase, I wonder? Disease? War? The perils of a hunting life? Or did they rule that the place could support two wigwams and no more? It almost suggests a system of seasonal land tenure.' The mounds were about four feet above the general level at the foot of the ridge, and spread in irregular circles perhaps forty feet across, rising gradually to the flat wigwam site at the top. You could picture those ancient savages roasting meat over the fire, or baking clams in a wrapping of seaweed, or boiling fish in their brittle pots, and tossing the shells and bones right and left.

"There was now a stout growth of ferns and wire birch, nourished in the rich humus of the heaps and the lime in the shells. Where we'd turned up the turf in 1920 the exposed clam shells, washed clean by the rains, were shining white, marking the spot where we'd found the old squaw like the X in a news photograph. Beckles and the others were enthusiastic. I went away promising to visit them soon; but church affairs came in a swarm, as they always do, and it was three weeks before I returned to Anse Blanche. Just before I left the parsonage I slipped the little pagan necklace into my pocket. It might be of some value to Beckles. It was wasted in my drawer.

"I found the whole party taking advantage of the tide, enjoying a swim. They must have lived in their bathing trunks, for they were wonderfully sunburned and, as I told them, a fine-looking lot of savages. They all came splattering out of the water and dragged me off to see their operations. They'd worn a path through the bush to the mounds, probably on the site of the original Indian track. The first mound—the mound of the dead squaw—had been sifted and shovelled aside, a great heap of broken shells and black dust. At the bottom they'd found two inches of black humus containing a few scraps of charcoal, and then the hard yellow subsoil.

"The second mound had been cleared of the flourishing birches and a working face dug at one side. The whole thing was marked off in small squares by stakes driven right through the mound, and the stakes were lettered and numbered so that every find could be recorded in its exact position. The working face was a story in itself, a close-knit mass of clam shells with pockets of bird, fish and animal bones, occasional layers of grey ash, and the whole sifted through with black dust. They showed me how they took off layer after layer with trowels, sifting everything. It was marvellous, you know. So painstaking. I could understand Beckles' scorn of 'pick-and-shovel amateurs.'

"And with great pride they showed me what young Bob called the loot. The site had proved rich. There were arrowheads in all stages of manufacture, of chipped quartz and flint, of bone, and two made very simply and effectively from sharks' teeth. Several harpoon points of bone and walrus ivory—made with a toggle, mind you, and a hole bored for the line, just like the lily-irons our fishermen use today for sword-fish. Knives and cutting tools made of split beaver teeth and the teeth of porcupine and woodchuck, fitted in wooden handles originally, no doubt, and the wood gone to dust long since. Bear teeth and wolf teeth bored to hang as pendants or part of a necklace; bone awls and needles of all sizes; a few celts of hard stone, battered from use; a lot of fan-shaped tools of chipped quartz, probably used by the squaw for scraping skins; and several hundred shards of pottery, all decorated with milled impressions like basket-work, some pieces containing the hole for the pot-bail, and two bearing the clear imprints of the potter's finger nails. And there were two large packing-cases full of bones and teeth, representing, Daly said, everything from eider duck to moose. It was enormously interesting. I could have stayed for hours just picking the things over and trying to imagine them in use.

"Beckles said, 'I'm afraid you'll have to put the old squaw's visit down to sheer coincidence. Everything here is prehistoric. The Micmacs stopped making pottery and stone arrow-heads soon after the Europeans came with metal to trade, and we haven't found so much as a nail.'

" 'Coincidence?' I said. 'That's not possible. Look here, that woman came fifteen miles down the river and then paddled five miles along the shore, passing a number of inlets exactly like this, until she came to Anse Blanche, to this little stream. After all that exertion she had to struggle through a hundred yards of thicket to reach the mound. No, no! It's impossible that it was chance. She knew exactly where she was going and she spent her last breath getting here.'

"Beckles looked at Daly and they smiled broadly.

" 'The last wolf recorded in Nova Scotia,' Beckles said, 'was killed in the late 1790's, more than a hundred and twenty years ago. We've found bones and teeth of the wolf all through this mound, a whole jaw-bone within two inches of the top—in other words, towards the end of the life of this camp.'

" 'But that's not proof enough,' I protested. 'After all, the woman may have been well over a hundred when she died in 1920. Centenarians aren't rare.'

" 'Right,' agreed Daly. 'We also found bones of an extinct native dog. But let that go. Here's something that shoots your theory to pieces. We found bones of the white-tailed deer— *odocoileus virginianus*—all through the mound. Need I tell you that the deer was extinct in Nova Scotia when the Europeans came? It was reintroduced by sportsmen in 1888, and the deer now in this province are sprung from that stock. Now surely, Mr. Muir, you'll admit these mounds are prehistoric.'

" 'Besides,' Beckles said, 'we found the charred stump of an oak, killed obviously in the fire of 1910. Its roots were all through Mound Two. We counted 120 rings on that stump, which takes you back to 1790 at the very least. And remember, please, it would take years after the camp was abandoned before enough forest humus gathered on the heap to support tree growth. Why, the proofs are overwhelming!'

"Well, they were. The old squaw's choice of a place to die was simply a curious accident. It couldn't possibly have meant anything in her lifetime. I put my hand in pocket absently and my fingers encountered the little stone amulet. I'd forgotten the thing. It had never seemed more than a worthless bit of Indian trumpery, crude in design and workmanship, not even intact. I passed it over to Beckles diffidently and said something about it, about the squaw wearing it about her neck— I don't remember now—but I remember how they all gasped. They stared at the thing as if it were poisonous. I felt abashed. Then with a most unscientific violence they rummaged in their 'unclassified' boxes and—you've guessed, haven't you— brought out the missing fragment.

"The ragged edges fitted perfectly. The part they'd found was in the shape of a beaver, the same queer putty-coloured stone, the same sort of design and workmanship, and they'd found it — they searched their records feverishly — thirteen inches below the surface of Mound One. 'In an undisturbed stratum of fish and bird bones, with some humus and shell, and in proximity to a nugget of hematite showing signs of grinding, possibly used in the making of war-paint.'

"There it was. The incontrovertible fact. I was just as stupefied as they were. I even went so far as to question Daly's identification of the deer bones, which to the osteologist of a famous natural history museum must have seemed downright heresy. He was polite, as well as positive, and pointed out that *odocoileus virginianus* had been identified in other Nova Scotia middens by authorities beyond question.

"I stayed that night with them and we talked into the small hours trying to make some sense of it. They cross-examined me severely about the old squaw and all the circumstances that led up to the finding of the body. They'd ask me suddenly, without warning, in the midst of something else, when I saw the amulet on the old squaw's neck. Things like that, brusquely —like policemen, you know. Well, I didn't blame them. When you tread on the corns of science you can't expect science to be polite about it.

"We sat over a folding canvas table in the larger of the tents, in the violet glare of a patent gasoline lamp, staring at those inscrutable pieces of stone and at each other. And before we stumbled off to bed I could see their minds uniting in a single accusation. They didn't make it aloud, of course, out of respect for the cloth, I suppose. But they went away ten days later firmly convinced that I'd found the gorget — Beckles' word — when we scratched the heap in 1920, and that for some senile reason I was giving their legs a terrific pull.

"At any rate, when Beckles sent me a copy of his report— an inch thick, illustrated with photographs and a map, a brilliant piece of work — I couldn't find the stone beaver fragment anywhere on the list of 'artifacts.' A pity, you know. Finds like that are rare. Any sort of sculpture was rare amongst the Micmacs, and such an amulet would be worn only by a person of importance, a chief perhaps, or more likely a medicine-man."

Young Carson stirred in his chair. "What do you make of it, yourself?"

"To my mind," the Reverend Philip said, "the old squaw knew exactly where she was going. The place was familiar to her by actual association. The significance of the broken amulet, of course, we shall never know. That goes back to a remote age when the Micmacs took birds and beasts and fish for their totems and believed that man could transfer his life-spirit into the body of his totem-beast at will. Why were the Beaver and the Turtle joined in stone, in a single imperishable totem, and then broken asunder? A tribal alliance, perhaps, ended by a symbolic sundering and war. The Micmacs and the other Algonkin tribes never had that instinct for confederacy which made the Iroquois the Romans of their world."

"But the woman!" Carson said impatiently.

"Ah, the woman, to be sure. You've got a choice of two things. You've got to believe in the transmigration of souls and say that 'Molly Luksi' was the essence—I don't know what else to call it — of an Indian who lived on that shell-mound and that the broken amulet had passed from hand to hand in a direct line of descent following exactly the descent of the spirit. In that you'd be voicing the tenets of ancient savages, which, as a minister of the Christian faith, you must reject. Or you've to believe—you have no other choice—that old age, or rather senility, is pathological and preventable, and assume that now and again an individual may escape the various toxins that give rise to it and live to a tremendous age.

"The distinction between senescence and senility may be as wide as the sea, as wide as the division of medical opinion on the subject. Of course, I'm well aware that Indians—like some white people—have a tendency to exaggerate their age after passing four-score. At ninety they're calling it a hundred, and at a hundred they may say anything, depending on the credulity of the listener.

"But the woman Father Egan buried as Molly Luksi had no age. None of the Indians at the inquest would hazard a guess. One after another they said she had 'always been there,' and would say no more. And there was the strange word Paul used.

"Afterwards, after that amazing discovery of the missing

fragment, the word came back to me with the force of a blow. For *Sa-ak-a-wach-kik* means literally 'The Folk of Old,' or, getting down to the root of it, 'The Primitives.'

"Of course, Paul and the others stood in great awe of the coroner. They thought they were being held responsible for the old lady's escapade. There was a tendency—very natural if you know Indians—to dissociate themselves from her as much as possible."

The young licentiate sat up very straight. "Do you know what you're suggesting? You're suggesting that this Micmac woman lived well over three hundred years ago, before Demonts and Champlain came to Nova Scotia!"

The small grey man nodded absently. "Exactly. That old woman might have told us all we want to know about the Micmacs. Where did they come from and why? What people did they find here? Was it the Eskimo? If not, what's the explanation of those typical Eskimo harpoon points in the same heap with Micmac pottery?

"What happened to the white-tailed deer? What's the meaning of the picture-carving on the rocks at Kejumkujik? Of the curious milled pottery decoration, always the same? What was the use of those stone tools we call 'gouges,' of the slim and brittle slate blades we call 'bayonets,' and why do we find them in the sites of winter camps and never in the shell mounds on the coast? How did they make those arrowheads of the hardest quartz, without steel tools and a jeweller's vise? A thousand things. All lost now."

"It's incredible!" young Carson cried. "Incredible!"

"So," murmured the Reverend Philip, "is Methuselah."

MORLEY CALLAGHAN

MORLEY CALLAGHAN was born in Toronto in 1903, and is a graduate of St. Michael's College in the University of Toronto and of the Osgoode Hall Law School. After graduation he became a reporter for *The Toronto Star*. It happened that Ernest Hemingway was on the staff of the *Star* at the same time, and he encouraged Callaghan to try his hand at short stories and to submit them to the editors of the experimental magazines, *transition* and *This Quarter*. Several of the stories were accepted and Max Perkins of Scribner's was favourably impressed with them. He accordingly invited Callaghan to submit a novel, and Scribner's published it, *Strange Fugitive,* in 1928. The novel received a warm welcome from both critics and public, and its success enabled Callaghan to visit Paris and establish direct contact with the lively group of experimental writers which included, among others, James Joyce, Gertrude Stein, Scott Fitzgerald and Ernest Hemingway. In 1929 Callaghan married Loretto Dee, and since that time has spent most of his life in his native city of Toronto.

Callaghan has published nine novels since *Strange Fugitive*. They are, in the order of their appearance, *It's Never Over* (1930), *A Broken Journey* (1932), *Such Is My Beloved* (1934), *They Shall Inherit the Earth* (1935), *More Joy in Heaven* (1937), *The Varsity Story* (1948), *The Loved and the Lost* (1950), *The Many Coloured Coat* (1960) and *A Passion in Rome* (1961). His short stories have appeared in all the leading American magazines, in many anthologies, and in four volumes of his own: *A Native Argosy* (1929), *No Man's Meat* (1931), *Now That April's Here* (1936) and *Morley Callaghan's Stories* (1959).

Of all Canadian writers of the short story, Callaghan is most obviously in the great modern tradition which includes such writers as Flaubert, Maupassant, Chekov, Mansfield, Anderson and Hemingway. Familiarity with their work has bred in him an interest in language as an instrument of precision and beauty, a determination to find his material in the unostentatious events of everyday life, a preoccupation with the subtleties of individual psychology and a deliberate effort to avoid the rhetorical and the melodramatic by the use of understatement and a uniformly quiet tone.

These similarities between his work and that of others should not blind us to the fact that Callaghan has a distinctive literary personality of his own. The tincture of cynicism, the slightly brittle irony which we find in the work of Maupassant and Hemingway is absent in Callaghan; in its place there is a profoundly Christian sensibility which finds expression in a rich compassion and a sincere idealism. The story which follows is taken from *Now That April's Here*.

The Blue Kimono

IT WAS HARDLY more than dawn when George woke up so suddenly. He lay wide awake listening to a heavy truck moving slowly on the street below; he heard one truck-driver shout angrily to another; he heard a hundred small street sounds multiplying and rolling with the motion of the city awakening.

For many mornings in the last six months George had lain awake waiting to hear all the noises of people preparing to go to work, the noises of doors slamming, of women taking in the milk, of cars starting, and sometimes, later on in the morning, he had wondered where all these people went when they hurried out briskly with so much assurance.

Each morning he awakened a little earlier and was wide awake at once. But this time he was more restless than ever and he thought with despair, "We're unlucky, that's it. We've never had any luck since we've come here. There's something you can't put your hands on working to destroy us. Everything goes steadily against us from bad to worse. We'll never have any luck. I can feel it. We'll starve before I get a job."

Then he realized that his wife, Marthe, was no longer in the bed beside him. He looked around the room that seemed so much larger and so much emptier in that light and he thought. "What's the matter with Marthe? Is it getting that she can't sleep?" Sitting up, he peered uneasily into the room's dark corners. There was a light coming from the kitchenette. As he got out of bed slowly, with his thick hair standing up straight all over his head, and reached for his slippers and dressing-gown, the notion that something mysterious and inexorable was working to destroy them was so strong in him that he suddenly wanted to stand in front of his wife and shout in anger, "What can I do? You tell me something to do. What's the use of me going out to the streets today? I'm going to sit down here and wait, day after day." That time when they had first got married and were secure now seemed such a little far-away forgotten time.

In his eagerness to make his wife feel the bad luck he felt within him, he went striding across the room, his old, shapeless slippers flapping on the floor, his dressing-gown only half pulled on, looking in that dim light like someone huge, reckless, and full of sudden savage impulse, who wanted to pound a table, and shout. "Marthe, Marthe," he called, "what's the matter with you? Why are you up at this time?"

She came into the room carrying their two-year-old boy. "There's nothing the matter with me," she said. "I got up when I heard Walter crying." She was a small, slim, dark woman with black hair hanging on her shoulders, a thin eager face, and large soft eyes, and as she walked over to the window with the boy she swayed her body as though she were humming to him. The light from the window was now a little stronger. She sat there in her old blue kimono holding the boy tight and feeling his head with her hand.

"What's the matter with him?" George said.

"I don't know, I heard him whimpering, so I got up. His head felt so hot."

"Is there anything I can do?" he said.

"I don't think so."

She seemed so puzzled, so worried and aloof from even the deepest bitterness within him, that George felt impatient, as if it were her fault that the child was sick. For a while he watched her rocking back and forth, making always the same faint humming sound, with the stronger light showing the deep frown on her face, and he couldn't seem to think of the child at all. He wanted to speak with sympathy, but he burst out, "I had to get up because I couldn't go on with my own thoughts. We're unlucky, Marthe. We haven't had a day's luck since we've come to this city. How much longer can this go on before they throw us out on the street? I tell you we never should have come here."

She looked up at him indignantly. He couldn't see the fierceness in her face because her head was against the window light. Twice he walked the length of the room, then he stood beside her, looking down at the street. There was now traffic and an increasing steady hum of motion. He felt chilled and his fingers grasped at the collar of his dressing-gown, pulling it across his chest. "It's cold here, and you can imagine what it'll be like in the winter," he said. And when Marthe again did not answer, he said sullenly, "You wanted us to come here. You wanted us to give up what we had and come to a bigger city where there were bigger things ahead. Where we might amount to something because of my fine education and your charming manner. You thought we didn't have enough ambition, didn't you?"

"Why talk about it now, George?"

"I want you to see what's happened to us."

"Say I'm responsible. Say anything you wish."

"All right. I'll tell you what I feel in my bones. Luck is against us. Something far stronger than our two lives is working against us. I was thinking about it when I woke up. I must have been thinking about it all through my sleep."

"We've been unlucky, but we've often had a good time, haven't we?" she said.

"Tell me honestly, have we had a day's luck since we got married?" he said brutally.

"I don't know," she said with her head down. Then she looked up suddenly, almost pleading, but afraid to speak.

The little boy started to whimper and then sat up straight, pushing away the blanket his mother tried to keep around him. When she insisted on covering him, he began to fight and she had a hard time holding him till suddenly he was limp in her arms, looking around the darkened room with the bright wonder that comes in a child's fevered eyes.

George watched Marthe trying to soothe the child. The morning light began to fall on her face, making it seem a little leaner, a little narrower and so dreadfully worried. A few years ago everybody used to speak about her extraordinary smile, about the way the lines around her mouth were shaped for laughter, and they used to say, too, that she had a mysterious, tapering, Florentine face. Once a man had said to George, "I remember clearly the first time I met your wife. I said to myself, 'Who is the lady with that marvelous smile?' "

George was now looking at this face as though it belonged to a stranger. He could think of nothing but the shape of it. There were so many angles in that light; it seemed so narrow. "I used to think it was beautiful. It doesn't look beautiful. Would anybody say it was beautiful?" he thought, and yet these thoughts had nothing to do with his love for her.

In some intuitive way she knew that he was no longer thinking of his bad luck, but was thinking of her, so she said patiently, "Walter seems to have quite a fever, George." Then he stopped walking and touched Walter's head, which was very hot.

"Here, let me hold him a while and you get something," he said. "Get him some aspirin."

"I'll put it in orange juice, if he'll take it," she said.

"For God's sake, turn on the light, Marthe," he called. "This ghastly light is getting on my nerves."

He tried talking to his son while Marthe was away. "Hello, Walter, old boy, what's the matter with you? Look at me, big boy, say something bright to your old man." But the little boy shook his head violently, stared vacantly at the wall a moment, and then tried to bury his face in his father's shoulder. So George, looking disconsolately around the cold room, felt that it was more barren than ever.

Marthe returned with the orange juice and the aspirin. They both began to coax Walter to take it. They pretended to be drinking it themselves, made ecstatic noises with their tongues as though it were delicious and kept it up till the boy cried, "Orange, orange, me too," with an unnatural animation. His eyes were brilliant. Then he swayed as if his spine were made of putty and fell back in his mother's arms.

"We'd better get a doctor in a hurry, George," Marthe said.

"Do you think it's that bad?"

"Look at him," she said, laying him on the bed. "I'm sure he's very sick. You don't want to lose him, do you?" and she stared at Walter, who had closed his eyes and was sleeping.

As Marthe in her fear kept looking up at George, she was fingering her old blue kimono, drawing it tighter around her to keep her warm. The kimono had been of a Japanese pattern adorned with clusters of brilliant flowers sewn in silk. George had given it to her at the time of their marriage; now he stared at it, torn as it was at the arms, with pieces of old padding hanging out at the hem, with the lighter-colored lining showing through in many places, and he remembered how, when the kimono was new, Marthe used to make the dark hair across her forehead into bangs, fold her arms across her breasts, with her wrists and hands concealed in the sleeve folds, and go around the room in the bright kimono, taking short, prancing steps, pretending she was a Japanese girl.

The kimono now was ragged and gone; it was gone, he thought, like so many bright dreams and aspirations they had once had in the beginning, like so many fine resolutions he had sworn to accomplish, like so many plans they had made and hopes they had cherished.

"Marthe, in God's name," he said suddenly, "the very first money we get, even if we just have enough to put a little down, you'll have to get a decent dressing-gown. Do you hear?"

She was startled. Looking up at him in bewilderment, she swallowed hard, then turned her eyes down again.

"It's terrible to have to look at you in that thing," he muttered.

After he had spoken in this way he was ashamed, and he

was able to see for the first time the wild terrified look on her face as she bent over Walter.

"Why do you look like that?" he asked. "Hasn't he just got a little fever?"

"Did you see the way he held the glass when he took the orange juice?"

"No. I didn't notice."

"His hand trembled. Earlier, when I first went to him, and gave him a drink I noticed the strange trembling in his hand."

"What does it mean?" he said, awed by the fearful way she was whispering.

"His body seemed limp and he could not sit up either. Last night I was reading about such symptoms in the medical column in the paper. Symptoms like that with a fever are symptoms of infantile paralysis."

"Where's the paper?"

"Over there on the table."

George sat down and began to read the bit of newspaper medical advice very calmly; over and over he read it, very calmly. Marthe had described the symptoms accurately; but in a stupid way he could not get used to the notion that his son might have such a dreadful disease. He remained there calmly for a long time.

And then he suddenly realized how they had been dogged by bad luck; he realized how surely everything they loved was being destroyed day by day and he jumped up and cried out, "We'll have to get a doctor." And as if he realized to the full what was inevitably impending, he cried out, "You're right, Marthe, he'll die. That child will die. It's the luck that's following us. Then it's over. Everything's over. I tell you I'll curse the day I ever saw the light of the world. I'll curse the day we ever met and ever married. I'll smash everything I can put my hands on in this world."

"George, don't go on like that. You'll bring something dreadful down on us," she whispered in terror.

"What else can happen? What else can happen to us worse than this?"

"Nothing, nothing, but please don't go on saying it, George."

Then they both bent down over Walter and they took turns putting their hands on his head. "What doctor will come to us at this hour when we have no money?" he kept muttering. "We'll have to take him to a hospital." They remained kneeling together, silent for a long time, almost afraid to speak.

Marthe said suddenly, "Feel, feel his head. Isn't it a little cooler?"

"What could that be?"

"It might be the aspirin working on him."

So they watched, breathing steadily together while the child's head gradually got cooler. Their breathing and their silence seemed to waken the child, for he opened his eyes and stared at them vaguely. "He must be feeling better," George said. "See the way he's looking at us."

"His head does feel a lot cooler."

"What could have been the matter with him, Marthe?"

"Look at him, if you please. Watch me make the rascal laugh."

With desperate eagerness George rushed over to the table, tore off a sheet of newspaper, folded it into a thin strip about eight inches long and twisted it like a cord. Then he knelt down in front of Walter and cried, "See, see," and thrust the twisted paper under his own nose and held it with his upper lip while he wiggled it up and down. He screwed up his eyes diabolically. He pressed his face against the boy's.

Laughing, Walter put out his hand. "Let me," he said. So George tried to hold the paper mustache against Walter's lip. But that was no good. Walter pushed the paper away and said, "You, you."

"I think his head is cool now," Marthe said. "Maybe he'll be all right."

She got up and walked away from the bed, over to the window with her head down. Standing up, George went to follow her, but his son shouted tyrannically so he had to kneel down and hold the paper mustache under his nose and say, "Look here, look, Walter."

Marthe was trying to smile as she watched them. She took one deep breath after another, as though she would never succeed in filling her lungs with air. But even while she stood there, she grew troubled. She hesitated, she lowered her head and wanted to say, "One of us will find work of some kind, George," but she was afraid.

"I'll get dressed now," she said quietly, and she started to take off her kimono.

As she took off the kimono and was holding it on her arm, her face grew full of deep concern. She held the kimono up so the light shone on the gay silken flowers. Sitting down in the chair, she spread the faded silk on her knee and looked across the room at her sewing basket which was on the dresser by the mirror. She fumbled patiently with the lining, patting the places that were worn; and suddenly she was sure she could draw the torn parts tight together and make it look bright and new.

"I think I can fix it up so it'll look fine, George," she said.

"Eh," he said. "What are you bothering with that for?" Then he ducked down to the floor again and wiggled his paper mustache fiercely at the child.

SINCLAIR ROSS

SINCLAIR ROSS was born on a homestead in the northern part of Saskatchewan, near Prince Albert, in 1908. His father died in 1920, and as a result the boy was unable to look forward to a university education. Instead, in 1924, he became a bank clerk, serving in the small Saskatchewan towns of Abbey, Lancer and Arcola before being transferred to Winnipeg. In 1942 Mr. Ross joined the Royal Canadian Ordnance Corps, and served overseas for a considerable period with that unit. He is at present with the Royal Bank in Montreal.

Ross made his literary debut by winning a short story contest sponsored by an English magazine, but most of his stories have appeared in *Queen's Quarterly*. One of his stories was included in the Penguin anthology of Canadian prose and verse, *Canadian Accent*, edited by Ralph Gustafson. His first novel, *As For Me and My House*, was published in 1941, and his second, *The Well*, in 1958.

All of Mr. Ross's work deals with life on the farms and in the small towns of Saskatchewan. The distinguishing note of his art is a controlled intensity which, at his best, is strangely powerful. Isolating a fragment of experience, he explores its psychological ramifications with clinical seriousness. The intense sincerity of the writer is always evident, and his stories have a ring of authenticity and truth. The story included here, which first appeared in *Queen's Quarterly*, is the finest prose expression I know of the plight of the Saskatchewan farmer under the scourge of dust and drought in the thirties. There is a brief but interesting appreciation of Ross's work in E. A. McCourt's *The Canadian West in Fiction* (1949).

The Lamp at Noon

A LITTLE BEFORE NOON she lit the lamp. Demented wind fled keening past the house: a wail through the eaves that died every minute or two. Three days now without respite it had held. The dust was thickening to an impenetrable fog.

She lit the lamp, then for a long time stood at the window motionless. In dim, fitful outline the stable and oat granary still were visible; beyond, obscuring fields and landmarks, the lower of dust clouds made the farmyard seem an isolated acre, poised aloft above a sombre void. At each blast of wind it shook, as if to topple and spin hurtling with the dust-reel into space.

From the window she went to the door, opening it a little, and peering towards the stable again. He was not coming yet. As she watched there was a sudden rift overhead, and for a moment through the tattered clouds the sun raced like a wizened orange. It shed a soft, diffused light, dim and yellow as if it were the light from the lamp reaching out through the open door.

She closed the door, and going to the stove tried the potatoes with a fork. Her eyes all the while were fixed and wide with a curious immobility. It was the window. Standing at it, she had let her forehead press against the pane until the eyes were strained apart and rigid. Wide like that they had looked out to the deepening ruin of the storm. Now she could not close them.

The baby started to cry. He was lying in a home-made crib over which she had arranged a tent of muslin. Careful not to disturb the folds of it, she knelt and tried to still him, whispering huskily in a singsong voice that he must hush and go to sleep again. She would have liked to rock him, to feel the comfort of his little body in her arms, but a fear had obsessed her that in the dust-filled air he might contract pneumonia. There was dust sifting everywhere. Her own throat was parched with it. The table had been set less than ten minutes, and already a film was gathering on the dishes. The little cry continued, and with wincing, frightened lips she glanced around as if to find a corner where the air was less oppressive. But while the lips winced the eyes maintained their wide, immobile stare. "Sleep," she whispered again. "It's too soon for you to be hungry. Daddy's coming for his dinner."

He seemed a long time. Even the clock, still a few minutes

off noon, could not dispel a foreboding sense that he was longer than he should be. She went to the door again—and then recoiled slowly to stand white and breathless in the middle of the room. She mustn't. He would only despise her if she ran to the stable looking for him. There was too much grim endurance in his nature ever to let him understand the fear and weakness of a woman. She must stay quiet and wait. Nothing was wrong. At noon he would come—and perhaps after dinner stay with her awhile.

Yesterday, and again at breakfast this morning, they had quarrelled bitterly. She wanted him now, the assurance of his strength and nearness, but he would stand aloof, wary, remembering the words she had flung at him in her anger, unable to understand it was only the dust and wind that had driven her.

Tense, she fixed her eyes upon the clock, listening. There were two winds: the wind in flight, and the wind that pursued. The one sought refuge in the eaves, whimpering, in fear; the other assailed it there, and shook the eaves apart to make it flee again. Once as she listened this first wind sprang into the room, distraught like a bird that has felt the graze of talons on its wing; while furious the other wind shook the walls, and thudded tumbleweeds against the window till its quarry glanced away again in fright. But only to return—to return and quake among the feeble eaves, as if in all this dust-mad wilderness it knew no other sanctuary.

Then Paul came. At his step she hurried to the stove intent upon the pots and frying-pan. "The worst wind yet," he ventured, hanging up his cap and smock. "I had to light the lantern in the tool shed, too."

They looked at each other, then away. She wanted to go to him, to feel his arms supporting her, to cry a little just that he might soothe her, but because his presence made the menace of the wind seem less, she gripped herself and thought, "I'm in the right. I won't give in. For his sake, too, I won't."

He washed, hurriedly, so that a few dark welts of dust remained to indent upon his face a haggard strength. It was all she could see as she wiped the dishes and set the food before him: the strength, the grimness, the young Paul growing old and hard, buckled against a desert even grimmer than his will. "Hungry?" she asked, touched to a twinge of pity she had not intended. "There's dust in everything. It keeps coming faster than I can clean it up."

He nodded. "Tonight, though, you'll see it go down. This is the third day."

She looked at him in silence a moment, and then as if to herself muttered broodingly, "Until the next time. Until it starts again."

There was a dark timbre of resentment in her voice now that boded another quarrel. He waited, his eyes on her dubiously as she mashed a potato with her fork. The lamp between them threw strong lights and shadows on their faces. Dust and drought, earth that betrayed alike his labour and his faith, to him the struggle had given sternness, an impassive courage. Beneath the whip of sand his youth had been effaced. Youth, zest, exuberance—there remained only a harsh and clenched virility that yet became him, that seemed at the cost of more engaging qualities to be fulfilment of his inmost and essential nature. Whereas to her the same debts and poverty had brought a plaintive indignation, a nervous dread of what was still to come. The eyes were hollowed, the lips pinched dry and colourless. It was the face of a woman that had aged without maturing, that had loved the little vanities of life, and lost them wistfully.

"I'm afraid, Paul," she said suddenly. "I can't stand it any longer. He cries all the time. You will go, Paul—say you will. We aren't living here—not really living—"

The pleading in her voice now, after its shrill bitterness yesterday, made him think that this was only another way to persuade him. Evenly he answered, "I told you this morning, Ellen; we keep on right where we are. At least I do. It's yourself you're thinking about, not the baby."

This morning, such an accusation would have stung her to rage; now, her voice swift and panting, she pressed on,

"Listen, Paul—I'm thinking of all of us—you, too. Look at the sky—and your fields. Are you blind? Thistles and tumbleweeds—it's a desert, Paul. You won't have a straw this fall. You won't be able to feed a cow or a chicken. Please, Paul, say that we'll go away—"

"No, Ellen—" His voice as he answered was still remote and even, inflexibly in unison with the narrowed eyes, and the great hunch of muscle-knotted shoulder. "Even as a desert it's better than sweeping out your father's store and running his errands. That's all I've got ahead of me if I do what you want."

"And here—" she faltered. "What's ahead of you here? At least we'll get enough to eat and wear when you're sweeping out his store. Look at it—look at it, you fool. Desert—the lamp lit at noon—"

"You'll see it come back," he said quietly. "There's good wheat in it yet."

"But in the meantime—year after year—can't you understand, Paul? We'll never get them back—"

He put down his knife and fork and leaned towards her across the table. "I can't go, Ellen. Living off your people—charity—stop and think of it. This is where I belong. I've no trade or education. I can't do anything else."

"Charity!" she repeated him, letting her voice rise in derision. "And this—you call this independence! Borrowed money you can't even pay the interest on, seed from the government—grocery bills—doctor bills—"

"We'll have crops again," he persisted. "Good crops—the land will come back. It's worth waiting for."

"And while we're waiting, Paul!" It was not anger now, but a kind of sob. "Think of me—and him. It's not fair. We have our lives, too, to live."

"And you think that going home to your family—taking your husband with you—"

"I don't care—anything would be better than this. Look at the air he's breathing. He cries all the time. For his sake, Paul. What's ahead of him here, even if you do get crops?"

He clenched his lips a minute, then with his eyes hard and

contemptuous, struck back. "As much as in town, growing up
a pauper. You're the one who wants to go, Ellen—it's not for
his sake. You think that in town you'd have a better time—
not so much work—more clothes—"

"Maybe—" She dropped her head defencelessly. "I'm young
still. I like pretty things."

There was silence now—a deep fastness of it enclosed by
rushing wind and creaking walls. It seemed the yellow lamp-
light cast a hush upon them. Through the haze of dusty air
the walls receded, dimmed, and came again. Listlessly at last
she said, "Go on—your dinner's getting cold. Don't sit and
stare at me. I've said it all."

The spent quietness in her voice was harder even than her
anger to endure. It reproached him, against his will insisted
that he see and understand her lot. To justify himself he tried,
"I was a poor man when you married me. You said you didn't
mind. Farming's never been easy, and never will be."

"I wouldn't mind the work or the skimping if there was
something to look forward to. It's the hopelessness—going on
—watching the land blow away."

"The land's all right," he repeated. "The dry years won't
last for ever."

"But it's not just dry years, Paul!" The little sob in her voice
gave way suddenly to a ring of exasperation. "Will you never
see? It's the land itself—the soil. You've plowed and harrowed
it until there's not a root or fibre left to hold it down. That's
why the soil drifts—that's why in a year or two there'll be
nothing left but the bare clay. If in the first place you farmers
had taken care of your land—if you hadn't been so greedy
for wheat every year—"

She had taught school before she married him, and of late
in her anger there had been a kind of disdain, an attitude
almost of condescension, as if she no longer looked upon the
farmers as equals. He sat still, his eyes fixed on the yellow
lamp-flame, and seeming to know how her words had hurt
him, she went on softly, "I want to help you, Paul. That's
why I won't sit quiet while you go on wasting your life. You're

only thirty—you owe it to yourself as well as me."

Still he sat, with his lips drawn and white and his eyes on the lamp-flame. It seemed indifference now, as if he were ignoring her, and stung to anger again she cried, "Do you ever think what my life is? Two rooms to live in—once a month to town, and nothing to spend when I get there. I'm still young —I wasn't brought up this way."

Stolidly he answered, "You're a farmer's wife now. It doesn't matter what you used to be, or how you were brought up. You can get enough to eat and wear. Just now that's all that I can do. I'm not to blame that we've been dried out five years."

"Enough to eat!" she laughed back shrilly, her eyes all the while fixed expressionless and wide. "Enough salt pork— enough potatoes and eggs. And look—" Springing to the middle of the room she thrust out a foot for him to see the scuffed old slipper. "When they're completely gone I suppose you'll tell me I can go barefoot—that I'm a farmer's wife— that it's not your fault we're dried out—"

"And look at these—" He pushed his chair away from the table now to let her see what he was wearing. "Cowhide— hard as boards—but my feet are so calloused I don't feel them any more."

Then hurriedly he stood up, ashamed of having tried to match her hardships with his own. But frightened now as he reached for his smock she pressed close to him. "Don't go yet. I brood and worry when I'm left alone. Please, Paul— you can't work on the land anyway."

"And keep on like this?" Grimly he buttoned his smock right up to his throat. "You start before I'm through the door. Week in and week out—I've troubles enough of my own."

"Paul—please stay—" The eyes were glazed now, distended a little as if with the intensity of her dread and pleading. "We won't quarrel any more. Hear it! I can't work—I just stand still and listen—"

The eyes frightened him, but responding to a kind of instinct that he must withstand her, that it was his self-respect and manhood against the fretful weakness of a woman, he answered unfeelingly, "In here safe and quiet — you don't know how well off you are. If you were out in it — fighting it—swallowing it—"

"Sometimes, Paul, I wish I were. I'm so caged—if I could only break away and run. See—I stand like this all day. I can't relax. My throat's so tight it aches—"

Firmly he loosened his smock from the clutch of her hands. "If I stay we'll only keep on like this all afternoon. Tomorrow when the wind's down we can talk over things quietly."

Then without meeting her eyes again he swung outside, and doubled low against the buffets of the wind, fought his way slowly towards the stable. There was a deep hollow calm within, a vast darkness engulfed beneath the tides of moaning wind. He stood breathless a moment, hushed almost to a stupor by the sudden extinction of the storm and the incredible stillness that enfolded him. It was a long, far-reaching stillness. The first dim stalls and rafters led the way into cavern-like obscurity, into vaults and recesses that extended far beyond the stable walls. Nor in these first quiet moments did he forbid the illusion, the sense of release from a harsh, familiar world into one of immeasurable peace and darkness. The contentious mood that his stand against Ellen had roused him to, his tenacity and clenched despair before the ravages of wind, it was ebbing now, losing itself in the hover of darkness. Ellen and the wheat seemed remote, unimportant. At a whinny from the bay mare, Bess, he went forward and into her stall. She seemed grateful for his presence, and thrust her nose deep between his arm and body. They stood a long time thus, comforting and assuring each other.

For soon again the first deep sense of quiet and peace was shrunken to the battered shelter of the stable. Instead of release or escape from the assaulting wind, the walls were but a feeble stand against it. They creaked and sawed as if the fingers of a giant hand were tightening to collapse them; the empty loft sustained a pipe-like cry that rose and fell but never ended.

He saw the dust-black sky again, and his fields blown smooth with drifted soil.

But always, even while listening to the storm outside, he could feel the tense and apprehensive stillness of the stable. There was not a hoof that clumped or shifted, not a rub of halter against manger. And yet, though it had been a strange stable, he would have known, despite the darkness, that every stall was filled. They, too, were all listening.

From Bess he went to the big grey gelding, Prince. Prince was twenty years old, with rib-grooved sides, and high, protruding hip-bones. Paul ran his hand over the ribs, and felt a sudden shame, a sting of fear that Ellen might be right in what she said. For wasn't it true—nine years a farmer now on his own land, and still he couldn't even feed his horses? What, then, could he hope to do for his wife and son?

There was much he planned. And so vivid was the future of his planning, so real and constant, that often the actual present was but half-felt, but half-endured. Its difficulties were lessened by a confidence in what lay beyond them. A new house for Ellen, new furniture, new clothes. Land for the boy —land and still more land—or education, whatever he might want.

But all the time was he only a blind and stubborn fool? Was Ellen right? Was he trampling on her life, and throwing away his own? The five years since he married her, were they to go on repeating themselves, five, ten, twenty, until all the brave future he looked forward to was but a stark and futile past?

She looked forward to no future. She had no faith or dream with which to make the dust and poverty less real. He understood suddenly. He saw her face again as only a few minutes ago it had begged him not to leave her. The darkness round him now was as a slate on which her lonely terror limned itself. He went from Prince to the other horses, combing their manes and forelocks with his fingers, but always still it was her face he saw, its staring eyes and twisted suffering. "See, Paul—I stand like this all day. I just stand still—My throat's so tight it aches—"

And always the wind, the creak of walls, the wild lipless wailing through the loft. Until at last as he stood there, staring into the livid face before him, it seemed that this scream of wind was a cry from her parched and frantic lips. He knew it couldn't be, he knew that she was safe within the house, but still the wind persisted as a woman's cry. The cry of a woman with eyes like those that watched him through the dark. Eyes that were mad now—lips that even as they cried still pleaded, "See, Paul — I stand like this all day. I just stand still — so caged! If I could only run!"

He saw her running, pulled and driven headlong by the wind, but when at last he returned to the house, compelled by his anxiety, she was walking quietly back and forth with the baby in her arms. Careful, despite his concern, not to reveal a fear or weakness that she might think capitulation to her wishes, he watched a moment through the window, and then went off to the tool shed to mend harness. All afternoon he stitched and rivetted. It was easier with the lantern lit and his hands occupied. There was a wind whining high past the tool shed too, but it was only wind. He remembered the arguments with which Ellen had tried to persuade him away from the farm, and one by one he defeated them. There would be rain again—next year or the next. Maybe in his ignorance he had farmed his land the wrong way, seeding wheat every year, working the soil till it was lifeless dust—but he would do better now. He would plant clover and alfalfa, breed cattle, acre by acre and year by year restore to his land its fibre and fertility. That was something to work for, a way to prove himself. It was ruthless wind, blackening the sky with his earth, but it was not his master. Out of his land it had made a wilderness. He now, out of the wilderness, would make a farm and home again.

Tonight he must talk with Ellen. Patiently, when the wind was down, and they were both quiet again. It was she who had told him to grow fibrous crops, who had called him an ignorant fool because he kept on with summer fallow and wheat. Now she might be gratified to find him acknowledging her wisdom. Perhaps she would begin to feel the power and steadfastness of the land, to take a pride in it, to understand that he was not a fool, but working for her future and their son's.

And already the wind was slackening. At four o'clock he could sense a lull. At five, straining his eyes from the tool shed doorway, he could make out a neighbour's buildings half a mile away. It was over—three days of blight and havoc like a scourge—three days so bitter and so long that for a moment he stood still, unseeing, his senses idle with a numbness of relief.

But only for a moment. Suddenly he emerged from the numbness; suddenly the fields before him struck his eyes to comprehension. They lay black, naked. Beaten and mounded smooth with dust as if a sea in gentle swell had turned to stone. And though he had tried to prepare himself for such a scene, though he had known since yesterday that not a blade would last the storm, still now, before the utter waste confronting him, he sickened and stood cold. Suddenly like the fields he was naked. Everything that had sheathed him a little from the realities of existence: vision and purpose, faith in the land, in the future, in himself—it was all rent now, all stripped away. "Desert," he heard her voice begin to sob. "Desert, you fool —the lamp lit at noon!"

In the stable again, measuring out their feed to the horses, he wondered what he would say to her tonight. For so deep were his instincts of loyalty to the land that still, even with the images of his betrayal stark upon his mind, his concern was how to withstand her, how to go again and justify himself. It had not occurred to him yet that he might or should abandon the land. He had lived with it too long. Rather was his impulse to defend it still—as a man defends against the scorn of strangers even his most worthless kin.

He fed his horses, then waited. She too would be waiting, ready to cry at him, "Look now—that crop was to feed and clothe us! And you'll still keep on! You'll still say Next year —there'll be rain next year'!"

But she was gone when he reached the house. The door was open, the lamp blown out, the crib empty. The dishes from their meal at noon were still on the table. She had perhaps begun to sweep, for the broom was lying in the middle of the floor. He tried to call, but a terror clamped upon his throat. In the wan, returning light it seemed that even the deserted kitchen was straining to whisper what it had seen. The tatters of the storm still whimpered through the eaves, and in their moaning told the desolation of the miles they had traversed. On tiptoe at last he crossed to the adjoining room; then at the threshold, without even a glance inside to satisfy himself that she was really gone, he wheeled again and plunged outside.

He ran a long time—distraught and headlong as a few hours ago he had seemed to watch her run—around the farmyard, a little distance into the pasture, back again blindly to the house to see whether she had returned—and then at a stumble down the road for help.

They joined him in the search, rode away for others, spread calling across the fields in the direction she might have been carried by the wind—but nearly two hours later it was himself who came upon her. Crouched down against a drift of sand as if for shelter, her hair in matted strands around her neck and face, the child clasped tightly in her arms.

The child was quite cold. It had been her arms, perhaps, too frantic to protect him, or the smother of dust upon his throat and lungs. "Hold him," she said as he knelt beside her. "So—with his face away from the wind. Hold him until I tidy my hair."

Her eyes were still wide in an immobile stare, but with her lips she smiled at him. For a long time he knelt transfixed, trying to speak to her, touching fearfully with his finger-tips the dust-grimed cheeks and eyelids of the child. At last she said, "I'll take him again. Such clumsy hands—you don't know how to hold a baby yet. See how his head falls forward on your arm."

Yet it all seemed familiar—a confirmation of what he had known since noon. He gave her the child, then, gathering them both up in his arms, struggled to his feet, and turned towards home.

It was evening now. Across the fields a few spent clouds of dust still shook and fled. Beyond, as if through smoke, the sunset smouldered like a distant fire.

He walked with a long dull stride, his eyes before him, heedless of her weight. Once he glanced down and with her eyes she still was smiling. "Such strong arms, Paul — and I was so tired with carrying just him. . . ."

He tried to answer, but it seemed that now the dusk was drawn apart in breathless waiting, a finger on its lips until they passed. "You were right, Paul. . . ." Her voice came whispering, as if she too could feel the hush. "You said tonight we'd see the storm go down. So still now, and the sky burning —it means tomorrow will be fine."

ERNEST BUCKLER

ERNEST BUCKLER was born at Dalhousie West, Nova Scotia, in 1908, and he received his B.A. from Dalhousie University in Halifax and his M.A. in Philosophy from the University of Toronto. He did actuarial work in Toronto for five years after leaving university, and has since operated a small farm near Bridgetown, Nova Scotia.

Mr. Buckler's first successful writing was a prize-winning article in *Coronet*. Since then he has published short stories and articles in many magazines in Canada and the United States, including *Esquire, Collier's, The Atlantic Monthly, Maclean's, Chatelaine, Saturday Night, Atlantic Advocate* and others. He has also broadcast talks and book reviews over the CBC, and had several radio plays produced by the Corporation. One of his stories won the first prize of $1,000 in the *Maclean's* fiction contest of 1948, and two others have won the President's Medal as the best Canadian short story of the year.

Ernest Buckler's first novel, into which the story below was incorporated, was *The Mountain and the Valley,* published in New York and in the New American Library. Excerpts from the novel have been reprinted in *Atlantic Anthology* and *Christmas in Canada*, and have been read over the air on "CBC Wednesday Night". He is now at work on a second novel.

Buckler is in a sense a regional writer, who seeks to recreate in fiction the life of his native Nova Scotia. His treatment of his region, however, has none of that saccharine sweetness that we associate with the regional idyll. He looks fearlessly at the full range of provincial life, and penetrates deeply into the consciousness of his characters. Like Sinclair Ross and Ralph Gustafson, he is particularly interested in the tensions that arise within a family group. The story which follows appeared first in *Esquire*.

The First Born Son

THE PALE CAST of fatigue smudged Martin's skin and little grooves of it emptied into the corners of his mouth. But this land was his own, and a son of his own flesh was holding the plow that broke it. His thoughts were tired half-thoughts but they did not ache.

He felt the wine of the fall day and for a minute his feet wandered, inattentive, from the furrow. The dogged, slow-eyed oxen followed him, straining nose-down at his heels. The plow ran out wide in the sod. David tried to flip over the furrow with a sudden wrench of the handles, but the chocolate-curling lip of earth broke and the share came clear.

"Whoa!" David yelled.

"Whoa!" Martin roared at the oxen.

"For God's sake, Dad, can't you watch where you're going? It's hard enough to hold this damn thing when you keep 'em straight."

"Now don't get high," Martin said. But there was no echo of David's temper in his voice. He knew David was tired. And David could not learn to handle his weariness. He fought it. It was no use to do that. If you let it come and go, quietly, after supper it made a lazy song in your muscles and was good to think about. Martin remembered the night David was born. They had thought Ellen would die. It was Christmas Eve. There was not a breath of wind in the moonlit, Christmas-kindled air. Snow lay in kind folds on the ground, shadowed in the dead-still moonlight like the wrinkles of a white cloak. On the brook Martin could watch the gay, meaningless movements of the children skating. And sometimes a fragment of their heartless laughter would break away and fall inside the room. Ellen's pain-tight face stared at her pale hands outside the quilt. The kind-smelling Christmas tree was a cruel mockery. Now and then Martin would go outside and listen, bare-headed, for the doctor's sleighbells, trying to separate their faint, far-off tinkle from the frost-crackle of the spruces. He would think he heard them. Then there would be nothing. Runner tracks shone like ising-glass in the moonlight. He heard nothing but the heartless laughter of the children.

It seemed hours later, when he was not listening at all, that he looked out and all at once the dark body of the horse turned in the gate, by the corner of the house. His heart gave a great leap. The helplessness left him. This man could hold Ellen back from death. The moonlight seemed to turn warm. After the doctor went in with Ellen the laughing of the children did not seem so far-off and strange.

The quick white grip of fear came again when he heard the doctor's hand on the door again . . . but Martin looked up and the doctor was *smiling*. Suddenly the whole night was a great, neighbourly, tear-starting friend. He had a son now. He knew it would be a son.

Martin felt shy to kiss Ellen in front of the doctor, but there was a new peace and a strange swagger in his soul. When he got the doctor's horse for him, it seemed like the best horse in all the world; and half-ashamed and half-afraid not to, but somehow wanting desperately to thank *someone,* he knelt down for a minute on the hay and prayed. Outside the barn, the voices of the children laughing were a glad song in his ears, now In the bedroom, Ellen murmured "My own little Jesus" . . . and the thick spruce-cosy smell of the Christmas tree and the shining moonlight outside and the soft peace after danger past clothed the minutes in a sweet armour . . . A son . . . A son . . . And Ellen well . . . Martin couldn't believe how good it was. He would never die now. He had a son, now . . . when he was too old to break up the land he loved, any more, this son would come in at night and they would plan together, just the same. This son's sons . . . .

"Well, maybe you think it's *easy* to hold this damn thing," David said. It *must* be that he's tired, Martin thought. He can't mean that . . . this same David . . . my own son cannot find it hard to plow this land of our own. I never found it so, when I was young. Plowed land was always the prettiest sight in the world to me. It was always good at the end of the day, to stand and look over the brown waves of earth and know that I had opened my land to the sun and the air and the rain. I don't like to hear this son of mine talk that way. He says too many things like that. I don't like to hear my son talk that way. The plowed land was here before us and it will last after us and our hands should be proud to work in it.

"Haw," Martin called, and the lip of the earth curled back and buried the grass again.

In the city, David thought, their bodies are not dead-tired now. They have not walked all day in their own tracks . . . back and forth, back and forth, in their own damn tracks. There is movement and lights and laughing. Every day there is something *new* . . . something to keep alive for. The same people here . . . the same talk . . . the same eternal drudgery . . . your nose in the ground all day long, from morning till night, like a damned ox . . . cooped up in that damned circle of trees.

The last brown beech leaves on the hardwood hill drifted down to the ground, dreamily, a little sad to die. A flock of partridges made their heavy headlong flight into an apple tree and began to bud. In the fields, the potato stalks lay in blackened heaps. The earth was grey and brown. All the colour was in the sky or hung in the thin air. Only the stray pumpkins, left to ripen on the withered vines, gave back any of it. They were like bubbles of the sad October sunshine. Martin loved these quick chill dusks, and then later the kind eye of lamp-light in the window, and the friendly, wood-warmed, table-set kitchen.

They came to the end of the furrow. Martin split the rest of the acre with his eye.

"Will we finish her before supper, son?" he asked.

"Do you want to work all night too!"

Martin stopped the oxen.

"What's wrong with you today, Dave?" he said. "If you planned to go after the partridges . . . ."

"Partridges, hell!"

"Well then, what's . . . . ."

David hesitated.

"I'm so damn sick of this place I . . . ."

"Is *that* so!" Martin said slowly. "What's wrong with this place?" He kicked over a sod with the toe of his shabby boot. An old man looked out of his face for the first time. It was true, then . . . It had never been because David was tired or lonely or weak or young . . . It was because David had always *hated* this land . . . the land that would be his own some day. A sick little cloud settled on his heart. He *had* no son, then.

"What's *wrong* with it?" David said. "The same damn thing over and over from morning till night . . . every day and every day . . . what future is there for anyone here?" David kept his back bent to the plow handles. He felt a little mean and ashamed when he heard the sound of his own words.

"What future is there here?" The question sounded meaningless to Martin. He had the truth, to contradict it. There is the first day in April when the fields stir again and it is good all day just to feel your breathing . . . There is the sky-blue August day when the whole green wind is full of leaves and growing, and Sunday morning you walk in the waving growth-full garden rows and wish you could keep this day forever, hold it back from going . . . It is good, too, when the snow whistles cold and mournful because it can never get inside the pane to warm itself . . . It is *all* good, all of it . . . Men live here as long as their sons live, to see the clearings their axes have made and the living grass that sprang from their tracks in the first furrow and the green things their hands gave life to . . . "The same thing over and over . . ." Martin did not speak. Only his sick thoughts pleaded, patiently, silently, incredulously. We did not plough yesterday, David. We took the day off and last night this time we sat at the edge of the woods and waited for the shy-eyed deer to come out into the old back field.

I thought it was good to sit there and smoke with my son after we boiled the supper kettle, not talking much but not feeling the silence either, and watch the dead leaves drifting down past the rocks in the cool-talking brook. The fire itself felt good, in spite of the sun, and it was good to hear the nervous twitter of the partridges in the apple trees just before it got too dark to pick out their heads along the sights of the gun . . . Or is this like the day last spring we nodded at each other across the pool with the foam on it each time we held a broken-neck trout throbbing in the tight of our palms? Or the day we cursed the heat in the alder-circled meadow and our shirts stuck to our backs like broken blisters? The hay smelt good that night, just the same, and it was good to hear the wagon wheels groan on the sill just before the dark thunder-frown of the sky burst and the barn roof beat back the rain. I remember the night we ate our first supper in the house I had built with my own hands. That night the neighbours came in, and we danced half the night to the fiddles. It was easy with everyone, like with brothers, and we loved them all . . . and it was good that night to lie in bed and let sleep's drowsy wind blow out the candles of thought. The day they brought your brother Peter home loose in their arms before it was dinner time, his dead body so broken your mother could not hold it, that day was different . . . And the next day . . . And the next day . . . .

"Well what kind of a place suits *you*?" Martin said at last. David straightened.

"The city, of course! Who'd want to live in this God-for-saken hole when you can get a job in the city?"

"Did you say the *city*?"

"Yeah. The city," he said laconically.

Martin listened with sick wonder to this stranger who had been his son. The city . . . It's *there* the days are the same. I thought it was very lonely in the city, the time I was there. The stone things move, but they do not change. My feet were always on stone. I could not walk on the ground and look over it and know it was my own. They never looked at the sky there, or listened for the rain.

When I looked at the sky there, the sun I saw was a strange one . . . it did not make friends with the stone. The stone houses were alike, and the days were alike, and never till they died could the people lie in bed at night and listen to rain on the corn after a long heat. They had nothing to breathe but their own tired breaths. I remember their faces. There was stone in them, too. They were all alike. They looked as if they never awoke from their tired dreams of the night. Their minds kept turning in their own tracks, like the weary wheels that could find no rest on the pavements. The soft-fingered women-

faced men lived in houses, and the house-smell clung to everything they said or did when they went outside. When they
talked, it was empty, because their eyes saw nothing but the
stone things that their hands had not built . . . and none of
them had anything to say that could not be said with words.
It was very lonely there. They laughed too much. But not even
love or death could melt their aloneness. Even when they
laughed, their eyes did not change. And when they died, no
one remembered, and there was nothing left of them.

I liked it in the city, now, this time, David thought. The
street lights began to come on, a little before it was dark, and
excitement seemed to stir in the busy pavements. The wind
was not strong enough to lift itself above the street, but the
women's skirts clung to their bodies as they passed. So many
different women's bodies! What if they *didn't* speak? The
bright, metallic faces of always-rich women seemed to shine
in the shop-window light, and you knew you would feel clumsy
and ashamed with them, but it was good to think of having
their soft flesh alone somewhere in the dark. There was so
much light there, then . . . and life. Like when you took off
your work-clothes and shaved and felt smoother and brighter
and ready for things. There was life, not death, at the end of
the day. Here, my God . . . the same old bare maples weaving
back and forth against a sky that made your lips blue just to
look at it, and never the sound of a strange voice, and later
the snow sifting lonely through the spokes of the wagon
wheels . . . What a God-forsaken place to be *young* in. Maybe
his father didn't mind, they didn't seem to mind *missing* things
when they got old. Old people didn't seem to dread being quiet
and letting things slip like this. They thought it was because
they were wise . . . it was because they were half-dead already.
If he thought he'd ever get like that about things when he got
old . . . He'd never get old. He swore a desperate promise to
himself that he'd never, never, never get that awful patience
like his father . . . standing there now, with that stupid look
on his face, like one of the oxen . . . .

"But Dave," Martin said slowly, "this place will be *yours* some day, you know that."

"What do *I* want of this old *place*?"

A whiteness came into Martin's face that was different from the whiteness of the cold or the weariness. He remembered the day his father had said the same thing to him. They had both felt shy and awkward, and he could say nothing, but as soon as he was alone, he had looked over this land, the tight tears of pride came warm into his eyes. He had kept this place, the best thing he had, till he could give it to his own son, and now when he offered it to David he saw it meant nothing. That he despised it. He had known through and through how his own father felt.

"It was always good enough here for *me*," Martin said.

"All right, but what did you ever *amount* to?"

Martin was stung into a sudden anger. "As much as *you* ever will, you . . . ."

Then he looked over the fields, slowly, and a break came into his anger. Why today, only a few hours ago, starting to plow, it had been, without a thought, so sweet, so safe, so sure . . . he and his son plowing and him trying to show David how to turn the furrow better and David trying his best. Things just didn't come handy for David, it must be that. He had half felt Ellen working quiet and happy in the house and the smoke went straight from the chimney into the clear, sun-filled air and there had been no hurry or fret in the fields or the slow oxen or his thoughts. Now . . . it could never be the same again between him and David, now. Every time they said a sharp word to each other now, these sick things would all come back . . . What if David was right? What *had* he ever amounted to? Well, he had been young here, and youth was very fresh and full here in the fields and the sun and very long, some of it never died, it grew green again with each April sun. He had had a wife of his own kind, and everything they had, they had got with their own hands, his hands and hers. There had been a lot of tiredness but there was always the quiet night afterwards and the slow kindly talk. There had never been an end of work, but you could always stop to talk across the fields to your neighbour, and you got along just the same. There had not been much money, but there had always been the sweet smell of bread in the kitchen and the soft song of wood in the kitchen stove. There had been no strangers among them, and when you died these men you had lived your whole life with would not work that day, even if there was clover to be hauled in and rain in the wind . . . and you would lie in the land that your hands and your feet knew best, and the same breezes you had breathed would always blow over you. Surely that was enough for a man. If your son . . . If David . . . It was hard to believe that your own son stayed on . . . It was hard to believe that your own son was not like you wanted him to be. But, Martin thought sadly, you couldn't make him see, if he didn't feel that way. You wished . . . but if he felt that way, there was no way to make him see.

"Well Dave," Martin said slowly, "if you're *bound* to go away, I suppose . . . ."

"Oh," David said impatiently, "let it go, let it go . . . I'll stay," he added sullenly.

He is almost afraid of me, Martin thought. He won't even talk it over with me. He has no use for my talk. He wants to keep me away from him. He don't think I can understand him at all. I try . . . .

He walked around to the oxen's heads and picked up the whip.

"Haw," he said quietly. "Just cut her light here, son."

David put his hands back on the handles but he didn't speak. He threw the plow around when they turned the furrows, so the chain jerked taut in the yoke. "Easy now, boys," Martin cajoled the oxen.

A bare little wind started in the bare maples. The sun burned cold and lonesome in the blind windows of the church across the road and the long withered grass bent over the cold grey sand in the middle of the built-up graves. Peter's grave . . . Peter would coax to hold the whip. He could hardly make his small voice loud enough to stir the oxen, but they obeyed him.

Martin could see the crazy nostrils of the running horses and then Peter's small crumpled body on the rock heap where the wheel had struck . . . .

The cows came up from the pasture, calling hollowly to be let in. The sky looked away from its own darkening face in the mud-bottomed puddles of the road. The blood in Martin's face came blue to the skin, and his blue eyes, a little faded with weariness, looked like frozen spots holding up the weight of his face. He walked back-to, guiding the oxen by the horns to help David keep the furrow straight, but David did not straighten his back, even when Martin stopped for a rock. Martin would come around and kick out the rock himself.

Martin blew on his hands and tried to start a smile in the corners of his tired, cold-thin, lips.

"Time for mittens, I guess. *Your* hands cold?"

"No," David said.

A shaft of the sun broke for a minute through the blue, wind-cold clouds. Long bands of it searchlit the grey rocks, without warming them.

"Snow comin'," Martin said.

The sun went down, and the sky made a few cold-pink patterns at the horizon. It would not be as sad again until April.

Martin turned the oxen for one more furrow. He could not stop, until he was *sure* how David . . . Maybe if he kept on, David would say something himself about stopping, and he could show him then how ready he was to listen to him and take the oxen off the tongue.

"*I'll* never ask him to stop if he plows all night . . ." David was so tired the muscles in his legs felt like a frayed rope and a tight cord drew his temples together. The blood seemed to drain from his face and throb heavy in his neck. The ashes of weariness sifted through the bright surface of his thoughts. The oxen lifted their heavy feet and deposited them carefully on the ground. The plow dug its slow way through the earth.

"I guess we're just gettin' her done in time," Martin said.

David said nothing.

"I guess this clears things up, about, for winter. You'll have a little more time to hunt, now, Dave."

Ellen came to the corner of the house, holding down her apron with one hand against the tug of the wind, and called supper.

"All right," Martin called back.

"Hungry, Dave?" he said.

"No."

David glanced at his father's face. For the first time he noticed how tired it looked. He felt sorry for his father, for a minute, and a little ashamed. He'd *have* to stay as long as his father was alive, he supposed.

They came to the end of the furrow. Martin hesitated.

"Well, I guess we'll let her go at that for tonight," he said. "We can wind her up in the morning, easy." He hesitated again.

"Dave," he said, "if you really *want* to go away. . . ."

David's impatience flared again. He forgot his father's face.

"Oh, for God's sake," he said, "can't you let that *drop*? I said I'd stay, didn't I? What more do you want? I'll stay here as long as *you're* here, anyway. So you need not worry."

So it is that way. A small coal touched suddenly against Martin's heart. He will wait, but he will be glad . . . so he can go away. If he was waiting for it, so the place would be all his own then, it would be . . . but he will be waiting, so he can go away. There will be a stranger here, and nothing will be done the same. There will be a strange name in my house, and maybe they will let the alders creep back over the acre field because they did not clear it for the first time and plow it with their own hands . . . and the grass will grow tall and strange over the graves.

He pulled the bolt from the tongue. It was true. It was true, then. He *had* no son. David took his hands from the plow. Martin waited for a minute to see if he would line the plow up for the next furrow in the morning. David did not move. Martin walked around to the plow. David went to the oxen's head, took up the whip and started with them to the barn.

Martin pulled the plow around and lay the chain straight out along the next furrow. Ellen came to the corner of the house and called supper again, but Martin did not answer. He watched David take the oxen past the house. He saw Ellen say something to him, but David did not reply.

He bent down and dug the mud from the plowshare. It shone underneath, where the earth had polished it, like a sword. The earth smelled cold and silent. He moved a few stones, absently, with his foot and stood for a minute with his eyes on the ground. Like the night they buried Peter. He felt lost in the long, dead day.

In the porch, he listened to see if David might be talking to the oxen. There was no sound but the bells, as David jerked the yoke-straps. Martin caught his breath quickly. He *had* no son. Peter was dead. He *had* no son, now. He scraped the dirt from his heels with a stick from the chipyard and went inside the house.

"Well, what in the *world* have you two been doing?" Ellen said, moving across the scrubbed soft-wood floor from the stove to the table. The warm breath of food rose sweet in the oil-lamplight. She held the dipper of water for Martin's hands over the basin in the sink. "Are you goin' to do a coupla more acres after supper?" she joked.

"Yeah, I was kinda thinkin' we might," Martin laughed.

But his laughter was heavy and grey, like a hawk rising.

RALPH GUSTAFSON

RALPH GUSTAFSON was born in 1909 near Sherbrooke, Quebec, and graduated from Bishop's University as gold medallist in 1930. For the next three years he pursued his studies at Oxford, and then returned to Canada to teach in a boys' school in Ontario. He did not remain long in his native country, however. After another brief stay in England he settled in the United States. During the war he was attached to the British Information Services in New York City, where he still lives. He remains strongly Canadian in his interests: he makes frequent visits here, follows Canadian literary developments closely and has been a valuable publicist for Canadian writing abroad.

Mr. Gustafson has published several books of poetry and edited various anthologies of Canadian poetry and prose. His anthologies have included three Penguin selections of Canadian writing— *Anthology of Canadian Poetry* (1942), *Canadian Accent* (1944), *The Penguin Anthology of Canadian Verse* (1958)—and a volume published by New Directions in 1943 under the title *A Little Anthology of Canadian Poets*. His own books of verse include, among others, the early *Golden Chalice* (1935), *Flight Into Darkness* (1944), *Rocky Mountain Poems* (1960) and *Rivers Among Rocks* (1960).

Mr. Gustafson's stories have appeared in such leading literary magazines as *Story, Atlantic Monthly, Here and Now, Epoch, Tomorrow, Northern Review, New Mexico Quarterly Review* and *Argosy* (London). These stories are distinguished by their psychological insight and their emotional intensity. In particular, Gustafson seems to be fascinated by the stresses and strains which arise between members of a family. The story which follows was first published in *Northern Review* and reprinted in *The Best American Short Stories,* 1950, edited by Martha Foley.

The Pigeon

DEBORAH huddled terrified in her little upholstered armchair, listening. It had been her "pouting" chair and although she was now ten years old and the chair's silly meaning outgrown, it

204

still intimately held her small unfulfilled figure. She sat by the open window of her bedroom overlooking the front lawn.

She was alone in the large wooden house which stood on the brow of the hill outside the town—where the river plunges fearfully between the cliffs of the Magog Gorge. Her father and mother had gone out in the car shortly after supper, leaving Deborah with the usual instruction that she be in bed by eight o'clock. But it was late spring when the long daylight lingers, the air rich with lilac and the wings of swallows, and Deborah had sat quietly through the twilight, filled with the wonder of existence and the loneliness in which it seemed only to be.

Then the sound had come, alien, sudden, shattering the familiar silence into quick fragments of terror. Deborah's heart leaped. For minutes she waited, scarce daring to breathe. Again it came—violent, broken, above her head almost. Then the silence swept back over her.

It was in the attic. Deborah sat rigid, her hands clasping each other tightly, her eyes wide.

She pleaded that her mother come—but her father hardly ever brought her mother home from being out before Deborah was long in bed. She told when they were coming by the swath of light her father's car made on the ceiling as it turned from the hill into the driveway.

The darkness of the hallway behind her bedroom door grew enormous, crushing to get in. At the hallway's far end were the stairs of the attic where her father had forbidden her to play. But she had memorized every one of the floorboards which creaked in the hallway for the times when she stole up into the attic without them knowing. She would know now when what was in the attic was coming. Deborah listened with her whole body, her eyes on the back of the closed door.

Vehemently, she wished she was a boy. She could kill it with a gun. Her father had a gun but you had to be a boy to shoot a gun. Her father wished she was a boy, she knew he did by the disgust he made sometimes on his face. He had put his gun, one day, against her shoulder under her chin but her finger wouldn't pull the trigger no matter how hard she wanted not to be afraid. With his finger he made hers press it. Nothing happened to her from the explosion but he told her for God's sake why weren't you a boy, Deborah?

She was afraid, even, of the old barn at the back of the quarry though Lucy, Tom and Freddy went too. She loved to play in the loft, but when you had to go home it was a dare to slide down the rope that hung in front of the door under the eaves. Lucy did it; but she was afraid. Freddy and Tom once when Lucy wasn't with them tied her with ropes to a tree in the woods for a scaredy-cat. Tom's father found her, and was kind and angry; but her father only laughed.

If only she had let her father make her brave when he wanted to. She had tried about Prancer but her father didn't even think of her after that when he went out riding. Perhaps if he knew it wasn't really being afraid he wouldn't not like her so much, but she couldn't explain it as not actually being afraid, but something else, something in things outside her that she had nothing to do with their being like that. She would so like explaining she wasn't to blame. She liked doing things. It was only she was scared of how they were made to seem. Things by themselves were lovely. But he didn't like her to tell him that.

The sound came again. Deborah's eyes flew to the ceiling, her mind clutching back the terror in her throat lest it betray her. The low vibrated beating intensified. Then it ceased.

She tried to make her heart stop pounding. Her father would laugh at her, then walk straight into the attic and find out.

Deborah held her breath. Her thought came enormous and complete. It would be the bravest deed of all her life if she went straight into the attic as he would want. Everything would be made different. Deborah sat, believing hard. She could tell him it was just nothing in the attic. And he would like being her father.

The silence abruptly shattered. The sound went on and on, this time, as if it would overpower the emptiness of the house. Deborah leapt to her feet with a gasp. But she stood still until it stopped, tense with her decision, her hands stretched open along the lightness of her slanting gingham skirt.

She made herself aware of all her body, then went to the bed. She put her toy bear, Nicholas For Christmas, under one arm and moved to the bedroom door. Silently, she opened it toward her until the space was big enough to go through.

The windowless corridor of dark stretched before her, greyed only where her mother's and father's bedroom door was ajar. The sudden crescendo of the falls, opened into the house by her father's window facing the river, roared at her ears. She paused to make it lessen—then moved into the dark before her. She tried to be brave. Balancing on the tips of her sandals, avoiding the boards which creaked, Deborah walked to the door at the end. The knob filled all her hand but she soundlessly made the door wide enough. The mustiness in the room smothered at her nostrils. She went quickly past the stripped bed where her grandmother had been dead, waited in the far corner by the window, her heart thumping so that she felt ill. She listened, but there was nothing. The low moon shone pale and ineffectual at the dusty glass.

Then she pressed down the latch of the attic door. Putting Nicholas high on the fourth step around the right-angle the stairs made at the bottom, she got down on her hands and knees. The attic stairs creaked worst of all, but she hardly made any sound the house might not have made by itself. The stairway mounted steeply between two walls, and from above was just an oblong space in the floor. She lifted Nicholas up beside her with each rise.

When her head reached the level of the attic floor, Deborah stopped. If the sound came now she wouldn't be able to help it and it would come at her with the scream and the noise she had to make. She closed her eyes tight against the panic. Images she made at night tumbled green and monstrous through her mind.

Gripping her fingers flat on the board which edged the side of the stairway, she raised her head, then looked.

The attic stretched away before her the length of the house.

Slopes of white, torn with blackness where the plaster had fallen, leaned against each other hugging the silence. In each gable, and out of sight in the wing of the attic, were narrow windows muffled by the eaves. Under the leaning walls great shadows accumulated.

Forming vaguely in the long dimness, the confusion of shapes and objects were made themselves by Deborah's memory—the wooden cupboard projecting from the wall, whose lower shelf could contain Deborah herself; the white skeleton of the iron bed naked in the distance; along the walls the castaway trunks and boxes; the anonymous piles of books and pictures between.

It was Deborah's own territory of loneliness and reality, forbidden and secure—but now, as she crouched within the stairway, alien with terror and intrusion.

It came first as a swerve of greyness out from the wing against the yellow cupboard opposite. Screams tore from Deborah's throat and her terror scrambled for flight. But she had seen what it was.

The sound the wings of the pigeon made against the cupboard was the same rapid beating she had heard from below. The bird fluttered forward along the top, then with a thump against the farther wall. Its burst of desperation slanted to a stop and the pigeon dropped to the floor.

Deborah straightened up on her knees, raising her head above the floor. Her fingers still clutched the edge but slowly the panic in her faded away.

The bird stood, plump, on its two red threads of legs, unmoving, a few feet in front of Deborah's nose. Her eyes widened and she held her breath; now not because of herself but lest she frighten the bird. The shadows of the attic untangled from menace, were familiar and could be forgotten. Their seclusion and protection returned around her.

The pigeon swallowed a dry spherical coo, then took a step, its jab of neck like an iridescent afterbeat, the feathers shifting colours in a smoke of grey.

Deborah made a soundless Oh, and it stopped still, the soft

round of head perched a little, ready for instant discovery. She clucked her tongue, making the sound gentle and friendly. Its head tipped the other way—then it stalked off, delicately and wobblingly, across the attic floor.

Deborah got to her feet, and, arms balancing her tiptoe, followed, at a distance. Never before had she seen a pigeon so close-to nor such a beautiful one. She would keep it for her own, she decided, and wouldn't let anyone know they lived in the attic together and she would learn to talk its language so it would like to stay and she would know things no one else in the world had ever been told.

The pigeon walked into the shaft of moonlight that slanted the space before the windows in the wing of the attic. It stopped in the edge, uncertain. Carefully, Deborah bent over to take it in her hands. But before her fingers touched it the bird flew wildly upward. Deborah jumped away with fright. The bird struck against the angle of the ceiling, then beat down the ridge to the windows. Deborah looked in alarm. They were closed—except the window in the front of the attic. She ran to the nearest box, dragged it beneath the window and got up on it. The blind had been raised and the upper sash pulled down. She put the heels of her hands against the top of the frame and pushed. It stuck. Desperately, she wiggled the sash from side to side with all her might. The weight gave and the window slammed.

She jumped down and went to the angle of the wall. She peeked round, but it wasn't in sight. She came out into the moonlight. The pigeon had disappeared. A great hollow longing filled her—then she saw it. It was standing in the narrow space between the two piles of double-windows against the wall.

She got one of the cushions stored in the cupboard, placed it on the floor in front of the pigeon, and looked to see if it was all right. "You stay there," she told it.

She ran to the well of the stairway and down the steps, banged open the door at the foot, ran down the hallway and down the front stairs.

She switched on the light in the kitchen, got a bottle of milk from the ice-box and poured some into a saucepan. She took two crusts from the bread-box, then switched off the light. Picking up the saucepan of milk, she carefully carried it upstairs, along the hall, and into the attic.

Placing the saucepan and crusts beside the cushion, she sat down, her legs under her, and watched. The pigeon just stood. Slowly she stretched out her hand toward the bird. It couldn't fly up where it was. She let the tip of her forefinger gently touch the top of its head. It was feathery soft and smooth as milk. The pigeon huddled in so that its neck was gone.

"What are you afraid for?" Deborah asked it. "No one is going to hurt you. I wouldn't hurt you — ever." Out of the loneliness within her a vast affection welled. "I love you!" she told it. "I love you!" She took her hand away, shoved herself back two times on the floor, and pushed forward the pan and the crusts. She made a soft sound with her lips. The pigeon looked up askance. "Drink your milk," she urged. "Don't you want your milk?" In reply the pigeon took a step, then a tentative peck at the crust. Deborah watched, fascinated, furiously planning their being together in the attic. Tomorrow she would hold it and it would eat from her hand and wouldn't be afraid of her.

Then, faintly reflected on the plaster, she saw the sweep of light.

Her body tensed even before her mind reacted to its meaning. The apprehension and guilt came suddenly all at once. She looked at her pigeon. She would never let them find out! She scrambled to her feet and ran across the attic to the stairs. She slammed the door at the bottom and the one into her grandmother's room, ran down the hall and shut her bedroom door behind her.

She wriggled out of her clothes, kicking off her sandals, got her nightgown. She heard her mother coming over the lawn, but she was in bed before she entered.

She clenched the top of the covers, following the sounds below her. Her mother went to the kitchen first. She would let her father in from the garage, and they would come upstairs. She pictured God then prayed over and over: "Please don't let the pigeon make a noise! Please don't let it make a noise!"

Her mother came up to her bedroom. Deborah shut her eyes and lay perfectly still. Her door opened for a moment then softly closed. "Is she asleep?" her father asked as he went down the hall to the bathroom.

Deborah didn't let herself move until they both were in their bedroom and their door shut.

She tried frantically to think what to say why she was in the attic if they found out and asked when she knew she mustn't play there. Her father's gun! Deborah's mind leaped in panic. That was what he would do! He would shoot the pigeon, she knew he would, if he found out and saw it. He would never let her keep it, even if it wasn't in the attic and would take it out and shoot it! She thought of the laugh he made after he shot at something. The laugh wasn't because he liked things or there was fun.

She lay thinking desperately, staring at the leaf-shadows across the ceiling, listening, two fingers of each hand crossed.

But the sound didn't come. There was only silence and the hush of the falls and, sometimes, with long stillness between, the brush of leaves as night moved within the trees outside. Perhaps it was asleep. She crossed her heart for it to be asleep. Then wonder began if the pigeon had really and truly been a real live pigeon in the attic. Perhaps it was thirsty and was drinking the velvet white milk that made no sound with its silvery bill and the rainbow around its throat. But when she climbed, climbed a million stairs to the attic it was gone. She ran looking everywhere and flung open the trunks and the boxes and turned over the shelves. But they only grinned at her and shook their heads from side to side together and she had to run back down the million stairs pleading she'd do anything only don't let it die but when she got to the bottom of the beetling stairs with a million steps and into the woods she had to look down the black gun to where the pigeon was, tiny, oh tinier than the smallest bird, held struggling.

Deborah sat up, the scream at the top of her throat. But her mind had tightened herself not to. For a minute the images moved, vivid, then melted. It was twilight outside and she heard the sparrows in the bushes.

She jammed away the cover crumpled on her feet, put on her gown and slippers. Her panic told her to race against each terrible second to set her pigeon free, away from her father's gun—but she made herself not do it until the top of the stairs. Then she ran the length of the attic to the front window, clambered on the box and pulled at the sash with her hands. It didn't move. She beat at the frame with her fists. Then she stopped and pressed with her fingers where the crack was between the two sashes. It shifted and she pulled the window wide open by the slit made at the top.

She ran where the pigeon was but it was gone. She leaned over the double-windows and felt down the space with her arm. She became frantic.

"Pigeon!" she cried, not caring about the sound.

She went to where she had first watched it, then to the bed, and to the cupboard. Great sobs choked into her throat. She began looking behind the trunks and boxes, shifting them forward so she could see down the wall. In the tin edging of the blue trunk her cloth belt caught and she had to pull it off until it tore. But she thought only of getting the pigeon away from the attic, outside. Trailing the belt in her hand, she ran again to where the pan and crusts were—then she saw it in the corner, behind the framed pictures.

She went to the bird, the tears blurring her eyes. "You've got to get out. You've got to," she told it. She reached over to pick the pigeon up. It backed wildly, then thrashed up out of the corner over Deborah's head, its wings striking her face. It flew madly against the ceiling, pushed itself along the slope.

"Go out! Go out!" she screamed. She lashed at the bird with the belt in her hand.

Suddenly the pigeon dropped away and flew across to the

cupboard, beating violently against the cardboard boxes shoved on top.

Deborah ran after it, sobbing, hitting at the bird, reaching as high as she could.

The pile of shallow boxes gave way, tumbling forward, knocking the bird under them as they fell. The photographic plates spilled, scattering to the floor. The pigeon lay shivering, its neck half severed by the fragment of glass impaled in it.

Deborah stared at the scarlet opening with its spurting blood.

Then her mind went blind. She gave scream after scream as she watched, then tore herself from it. She stumbled down the attic stairs and down the hallway to her mother's door. Twisting the knob she pushed it open with her body and ran to her mother flinging herself against the side of the bed.

Her mother had raised herself when Deborah reached her.

"Debby! What is it?" She put her arms around her and pulled her to her. "Debby!"

"I killed it!" Deborah shrieked. "I killed it." Then the tension gave, and she broke into violent sobs.

Her father in the other bed propped himself up by his elbow. "Miriam! What's wrong?"

"It's Deborah. A nightmare."

He let himself fall back.

Deborah checked the violence that shook her. "It's dying! Oh do something, do something!"

Her mother straightened Deborah up. "There," she soothed her. She took the handkerchief from Deborah's robe and wiped under her eyes. "Now. Tell mother. What's dying?"

Deborah forced her sobs to leave her alone so her mother could go. "In the attic!" she told her. "The pigeon!"

"The pigeon! Darling, there's no pigeon in the attic. You only *dreamed* there was a pigeon."

Deborah felt the terror surge back. "I didn't dream it! I didn't!"

Her mother turned toward her father. "George. Can't you *do* something? You can see the state Deborah's in."

He groaned and sat himself up. "For heaven's sake! What do you expect me to do? Scare nightmares away?"

"At least you might go into the attic and prove to the child nothing's dying."

He clenched his lips to get his disgust across, looked at Deborah, then swung his legs out of bed.

Deborah watched him, wanting to tell him Oh hurry—please! but she couldn't tell him, not her father who was cruel.

He shoved his feet into his slippers, trailed his dressing gown and left the room.

Deborah held in balance all her existence. Her mother patted her and brushed back the hair from her face. She heard her tell her that her father would make everything all right but she knew he never would. He would find the pigeon dead and she would have to explain to him the wrong things that were not her fault that they happened. She stood in agony, the horror smouldering, staring at the open bedroom door.

Then he appeared in it. Deborah's eyes went down to the dead pigeon dangling from his hand.

"What have you been doing in the attic?" he asked her.

Her mother gave a gasp as she saw what he held.

The guilt, familiar but now complete, whelmed Deborah's mind. "I *didn't* do it! I *didn't* do it!" she told him.

"Stop yelling," he ordered.

"George!" Her mother turned to Deborah. "It isn't your fault, I'm sure, darling." She looked back at her father. "Can't you see the child's hysterical?"

"Then she better get over it," he said.

Deborah looked up from the pigeon to her father's face. The hate seared alive.

"I *never* will! I *never* will!" she screamed at him.

DAVID WALKER

DAVID WALKER was born in Scotland on February 9, 1911, and educated at Shrewsbury School and the Royal Military College, Sandhurst. He served as an officer in the Black Watch Regiment from 1931 to 1947. From 1932 to 1938 he was on duty in India and the Sudan, and came to Canada in 1938 as A.D.C. to the then Governor-General, Lord Tweedsmuir. He married Miss Willa Magee of Montreal in 1939. During most of the war he was a prisoner in Germany, and after his release in 1945 served briefly at the Camberley Staff College and as Comptroller to the Viceroy of India. Since 1947 he has made his home in St. Andrews, New Brunswick, and devoted his energies to the writing of novels and short stories.

David Walker has published seven novels—*The Storm and the Silence* (1949), *Geordie* (1950), *The Pillar* (1952), *Digby* (1953), *Harry Black* (1956), *Sandy Was a Soldier's Boy* (1957), *Where the High Winds Blow* (1960)—and short stories in *The Atlantic Monthly, The Saturday Evening Post* and other magazines on both sides of the Atlantic. His work varies from physical adventure to psychological analysis, from intense conflict to light humour. *The Storm and the Silence,* for example, is a superior thriller; *Geordie,* on the other hand, is a quiet, gently humorous regional idyll. In all that he writes, however, David Walker reveals a gift for precise and suggestive natural description, for strong atmospheric effects and for the deep understanding of characters under stress. The story which follows appeared first in *The Saturday Evening Post.*

Storms of our Journey

THE AIR-BRAKE GASPED and the door opened and Orville Palk got down. "Be seein' you, then, Orville," the driver said.

"Thanks, Jim." The bus blattered away. He swung the bag

up to his left shoulder and walked along the dirt road. It was just after noon. He would go down and wait till the tide was off the bar.

Be seein' you, then, Orville. Well, home in two miles, and nice weather for the walk. It was very mild for early March. The ditches were abrim, and there was a soft flop of rotting ice. It was not the true spring yet, but spring was speaking.

Orville Palk topped the rise and started down. The bay was muddy-looking, and the sky was muddy. It would be a bad sky with the wind from the south, but the wind held south-west. He had been watching winds and tides, the makers of weather, for sixty years or thereabouts out of his sixty-seven, and sometimes he could be right about them.

The pain started up again, so he put down his bag and sat on a rock beside the road in his good blue suit and heavy coat and grey fedora, and in a minute or two it stopped and he shouldered his bag and went on. He noticed pussy-willows among alder and he heard busy chickadees in tamarack and he heard snow-water seep and gurgle.

He was half an hour early at the bar. He sat down to his two cold hot-dogs, but he could only manage one. He noticed the last high-water mark, four feet or more above mean. He remembered that the springs of this March month were the biggest tides of the year, and he remembered that it was new moon today.

He looked across to the island, which was an island for six hours in each twelve. The charts called it Shoulder Island; the people of the Way called it Palk Island; but to him it was the Island. It was the place he had been born, a low-lying place with a wooded hump. It was nothing special in looks except for the red rocks which were pretty, but it was home, and he had been away a month and he had been thinking about it and he had been thinking: *Just let me get home and things will be better.* Now he was nearly home, and things were not better. He couldn't see where it led you. He couldn't see there was any kind of object in it.

Of a sudden the breeze fell off and the air was as still and dead as in a house. But the edges of the sea were not quiet. They were loud with gulls; bickering down after the ebb for clams.

It started up again and after a while it stopped and then he forgot about it because the wind puffed gentle and balmy. It puffed this time from the south-east, and the sky was a heavy yellow, and the air was as moist as a blanket on the line, and the gulls were in thousands. The wind had backed a full ninety degrees. "It's going to be weather," Orville said.

The line of the bar showed now, first as riffles in smooth water, then as a breaking point of wavelets. It came out slow and quick and sure like everything had to happen—pools sinking, wet gravel. The tide was off again.

It was Orville's road, and he took it. He walked firm, although he was a man who faltered in spirit. There were no other men to watch him. He crunched across while gulls cried harshly and wheeled to give him passage, closing behind to feed at the bar.

He was home now, but not home to the cabin. He followed the road above shore. The woods were on his right side. Another puff came out of stillness from the south-east. It surely was going to storm.

He passed above his first fish weir, The Sandbar. He looked at the circle of stakes showing now at half-ebb, at spindly marlin poles rising from them, at the long wing-fence that guides herring to the mouth. *A weir's a simple-looking rig,* he thought, as if he had never seen one before. And he smiled at the notion of it being simple.

The winter's damage wasn't too bad. He began to figure out what it would cost to build this season. But then he remembered again, and said a loud bad word and walked faster.

He came soon to Old Palk. It was a weir of feast and famine, of many bad years, of a few great times in the fall when silver hake hunted schools of herring up the bay and around Palk Island. He could see the screaming harry of gulls. He could see the herring run themselves ashore to drown. He could see a hundred hogsheads from one tide; and sometimes a good sardine price and sometimes a small fertilizer price and sometimes no market at all.

These pictures flashed in the eye of Orville's mind. But with his own eyes he saw Old Palk stripped and derelict at the end of winter, no life anywhere about it except in the furrows of ebb cutting away from barnacle-encrusted stakes.

Now it was nearly time to build again, and he must talk to his nephew Hazen, who had a half-share. They would work out something. Build weir in spring, and tend weir in summer, and make a good living or not make expenses, and strip weir in the fall, and mend nets in winter, and cut brush and start over, and where did it get you? It got you to the end of the road with a storm cooking.

Snap out of it! he told himself, and he rounded the corner to see white-bottomed boats pulled high and Mary Palk's old sedan and the frame house and his cabin and chimneys smoking and everything as he had thought of it while he was away, but without the pleasure. That light in the sky was certainly queer, more like the light of a candle than the bare light of day.

Linda was playing around outside the house. "Linda!" he called in the hollow air.

"Granka!" she yelled, and she came down into the dip and up this side all legs and arms and mop of hair. He dropped his bag. He gave her a hug.

"And how's my Lindy Lou?" She might have been shy of him but she wasn't. She was ten years old, still young enough to be a grandad's pal. It was good.

He put the bag on his left shoulder and they walked the way to the house. "Let's have it," he said. "What's been cookin'?" Which reminded him of the queer-looming sky, but Linda was full speed ahead into telling him her mother was taking her to the Skating Carnival at Rockhaven tonight and she was to be Robin Hood in a green costume and so on, and they would spend the night in town at Aunt Mabel's and so forth, and they might stay for church in the morning, etcetera.

"Well now!" he said, snowed under. Linda's thoughts and

plans and hopes and sorrows, they bubbled forth like the ever-rolling stream in the hymn that bears all its sons away.

"Mummy! Granka's home, Mummy!"

Here came Mary to the door. She dried her hands and she kissed her father-in-law on one cheek and then the other, and her eyes were wet. "Dad!" she said. "My, it's good to have you back. How d'you feel? You're thinner."

"I feel fine," Orville said. "The food was nothing to write home about is why I'm mebbe thinner." He turned away to look south-east where cloud was heavy as a yellow drape, or more mustard, but the shore of mainland to the south was sharp and clear and cut out with a knife. "What kind of a day is this for me to come back to?"

"It does look queer," said Mary. "Go and dry the dishes for me, Linda dear." She shut the door after Linda. "What did they say, Dad?"

"They said I was fine. They said it was nothing but the indigestion, and I was to take things easy for a month and sleep plenty and eat plenty."

"They said eat plenty with the indigestion?"

"That's what they said." Orville Palk looked at Mary. She was the widow of his son killed at sea in war. Mary would talk your head off like a real woman, and Mary was impatient with her boy Tommy, but she was a woman able to give man comfort. "They said to me: 'Palk,' they says. 'You got a woman back home can cook worth a damn?' So I says I lives in a cabin on my lonesome but there's a woman next door can cook not too bad when she puts her mind to it. 'Well, Palk,' they says. 'How's her deep apple pie?'"

Mary laughed and he laughed. "Oh, I'm glad," she said.

"Come on in," he said. It was unnatural how warm the day was, nearer sixty than fifty. Just then it started up again, but he was busy opening the porch-door and it only lasted a very short time.

"Hullo, Tommy boy," he said at the parlour.

Tommy was flopped out in an easy chair. He looked over

the top of his comic. "Hi, Granka." He smiled and went back
to reading as if Orville Palk had been away five minutes.

"Stand up, Tommy! Is that a right way to behave when your
Grandfather comes home?"

The boy uncoiled himself to stand. He was tall for fourteen.
He must have grown even in the month. And it seemed like
yesterday he was out in the boat with you every chance he got,
and to seine at four in the morning if you would have let him,
and hanging on every word you spoke. Now he stood by order,
awkward and fed-up.

"Take Granka's bag down to the cabin, Tommy, and put a
log on the stove while you're there." Mary sent Linda away
too. "He's so difficult, Dad," she said. "He reads those comics
nights, and all Saturdays and Sundays and if I suggest things
for him to do, he just gets the sulks. . . ."

"It's growing pains," said Orville. "Nothing to worry about.
He'll snap out of it."

Mary sighed. "I guess so," she said. "But now even take the
Carnival tonight, first he was for going and then he said he
wouldn't, and now he won't say either way. Comics and
hockey, although he's good at his lessons, I must say, and when
it isn't those things he's off in a day dream, and half the time
he forgets his chores. I don't know. Sometimes he's a mystery
to me."

"Just wait till the mystery is girls."

Mary laughed. "Oh, it's lovely to have you back, Dad. It's
just lovely. A man makes things seem easy."

"It's good to be back," he said. It was good to be back with
his gentle Mary, and with the kids, and to be home. But it
wasn't good altogether. "Speakin' of girls," he said, "there was
some trim numbers up there. Oh boy, oh boy, in their stiff
little dresses. They did my heart good."

"Did it bad, I bet. Were they nice?"

"They were," he said without a joke. "Real kind. It was a
surprise to me."

"Anybody would be kind to you."

A bluster struck the house. It was a small first buffet of wind.

Orville went to the window. "If I were you," he said, "I'd take Tommy along for the night. Mabel got plenty beds?" Mabel was her sister.

She nodded. "There's a couch in the parlour. Why?"

"Because it'll be a rough night on the island, the way things are shaping." Things were shaping now in a way he did not remember ever quite before in winter. You got a mauve-coloured light in the summer storms, and you got a brownish sky before snow; but this particular mustardy shade, hazy far off and clear close at hand and hanging so heavy—this was new. And a twenty-eight-foot tide with a storm from that quarter was something else again. "Take Tommy," he said, making it strong. "I'll ride out the blow in my old caboose; but the boy's too young to be alone in the house on a rough night. You take him."

Now Orville was fully and strongly determined to have the island to himself this night.

"O.K., Dad," she said. "We're leaving at four-thirty. I got you a grocery order in, and there's a piece of pie left over. Would you fancy something to eat now?"

"I had a bite on my way," said Orville Palk. "Here you've been talking a blue streak about everything but yourself. What's new? Are you still giving the brush-off to those fellas?" Mary was comely, and it wasn't natural her without a man. It wasn't right her slaving away alone all summer at the cut-flower garden, not that she didn't love it and make a good thing of it too.

"Go on, Dad!" she said, pleased. "Well, I got my seed catalogues and I sent the order, and I did four oils while you were away." That was a side-line she had taken up these last winters. She painted snow-scenes and sold them to the summer visitors, and there was an artist last year said she had a real talent, untrained. Orville himself thought the pictures were too rough and splashy with colour and he told her so. Mary could do most anything except mebbe know how to manage young Tommy. She couldn't sit quiet like a man either.

"I'll lie down a bit," he said. "Then I'll eat plenty like they

told me. Have yourselves a good time and don't get a sore
throat gassing with that Mabel and don't hurry back tomorrow." He let himself out and the door tugged at his hand and
he walked to his cabin in a gusty breeze from the south-east.

Mary watched him go. He was a middle-sized man with a
saltwater toed-in walk, and a face cragged and creviced by
years and sea. He was a wise and simple man whom she loved
as a father, but beyond that too because of her husband,
Orville. "I wonder," Mary said. "Oh dear, I wonder."

He rode a borderland of sleep where wind rose and fell and
rose again. Then it climbed to a new place too high altogether
and he was wide awake with a bad taste at five minutes of five
in his log cabin, and the kettle wheezed lightly on the stove
and the chimney moaned and he knew now what he had felt
in his dreams—that a big storm was fast on its way.

Orville listened a while, then leaned over to switch on the
radio. The weather man could be wrong, too. But what he said
now at five o'clock—cyclonic storm, winds of hurricane force,
warnings to shipping, warnings to low-lying coastal areas,
Fundy tides—what the weather man said now with an edge of
urgency in his radio voice, *"Warn everyone,"* he said, did not
leave any doubts about right and wrong, and it took Orville
Palk out of his bunk as quick as he was able. Teeth in, work
pants off the hook, thigh boots and so on. *Why didn't you get
a weather report earlier? Why not? Because you were too
taken up about yourself.*

He was dressed. He did not feel good. He was not hungry.
He put two spoonfuls of instant coffee in his mug, poured from
the kettle, stirred it, knelt at the floor-trap and drew out his
illicit jar of Navy. It was a gallon fruit-syrup jar, but not fruit-
syrup. He laced the coffee till it was cool enough to swig down.
The fifty-over was strong even diluted that way, and the
molasses-black coffee tepid taste was terrible, but it bit right
into his blood and bones.

He felt better already as he stepped outside into the murk
which had lost a yellow tinge of warning and now was plain

grey storm. It was much colder, and the wind was strong, but it was not a gale, nor even half a gale. Rain smacked at him from the south-east.

He could not winch the boats higher, but he could check the lashings, which he did; and then he double-lashed them— the scow, the dinghy and the scale-boat. Then he uncoiled the long painters and tied each to a spruce tree. When he had done that, he crouched in the lee of the big upturned scow, and he considered what he could do while the wind drove harder.

It's never happened, he thought for encouragement. *It's never happened in a hundred years and more.* Yet he had always known that a freak storm and a great tide together might just possibly make it happen, because once it had nearly happened—in the Saxby Gale of '69.

Shoulder Island, they called it on the charts; but it was more like a kid's snowman in shape—a big oval of land for the snowman's body, a small round of land for the snowman's head, nipped in to join at the shoulders.

The island ran east and west, bar on the north side, a shelter of bay across the south. Only at the south-east tip and only with a south-east wind did Palk Island face the drive of open sea. Even that sea was itself a closed sea, but it was fifty miles of Bay of Fundy where great tides flow and ebb. And the east end of the island—the snowman's head—was the lowest-lying part. The Loyalist Palks had settled there because they could find fresh water nowhere else on their island grant. So they built the frame house and they sunk a well and they made a rough sea wall, and the sea was close but it never harmed them; and in the sleep of time that threat dwindled to the remote unlikelihood which fishermen, above all men, disregard.

Orville knew the levels. A twenty-eight foot tide would just trickle over the narrow neck of the island. This happened occasionally, and it did no harm except to scour gravel from the road. Where he now sat on the level of cabin and well and house and boats was a good six feet higher, and the sea wall behind him gave another two, making thirty-six. So it could reach the buildings from the neck by rising to thirty-four—which it had never quite done. But if it rose that much and then some more, and if the waves were extra big, it would come another way altogether—it would storm over the sea wall with a gale of wind behind it.

He remembered what his father had said: *"The Saxby Gale veered from the east as it grew, and the last hours before high water it was a south wind near as dammit. That's what saved us, son. That's what stopped the flood right at this doorstep. If that gale had piled that tide at us from the south-east the length of this shallow bay, I wouldn't be here to tell the tale."* It had been Dad's great yarn, greater at each spinning.

He did not think it was possible, but he considered the possibility, and he considered what else he could do, and he could not see what was to be done but to batten her down and ride it out alone, which he was going to do, and enjoy doing, and love doing. He was home and he was staying right here at home.

The rum was wearing off. He shivered. Perhaps the chills made it start up again, and just then he saw a light come on in the house. Orville Palk cursed, and the wind blasted round his ears and plucked profanities away downwind. The wind took him trot-and-walk past his cabin where a snatch of music sounded and was gone, and a pair of black-duck whipped low overhead from the sea to shelter. He heaved at the door of the house. It was hot inside. "What the hell are you doin' here?" he demanded in a tone he had hardly ever, no never, used to his grandson, Tommy Falk.

The boy was still at those damn comics. "I didn't want to go," he said in a way that told you he had had a row with Mary, not just fresh sulky at rough words.

"Didn't want to go!" said Orville. "It's always what *you* want. You never think of your Mum."

"Why should I go, Granka?" said the boy hotly, no sulks. "Why do I have to watch a lot of kids in fancy dress not even able to skate?"

"Because . . ." Orville began. He was going to say: *because your Mum wanted you to.* But that wasn't the reason. The real reason was that Orville Palk needed the island to himself tonight. "I'll tell you why," he said. "Because there's a bad storm comin' up, and you'd be better in town." A stronger blast of wind shook the old house, and a hard slatter sounded through double windows. It must be hail. "Listen!"

"We get storms all the time," said Tommy. He stood his lanky fourteen-year-old length, and went to look out. It was dusk, although sunset was half an hour off.

"Not like this one," Orville said. What was to be done? Send the boy on foot into town? The bar would be up for another hour. But three miles in the dark in this weather on a tree-lined road? No. Send him across to shelter in Mary's glasshouse on the higher land? Without heat? Not now. Mebbe later. "I'll move in here for the night," he said. "Come on to the cabin and help me with my gear."

"Okay, Granka." Tommy was over his mood, whatever had blown up between Mary and him, and not bearing grudges against Orville either. He sounded eager, like his old self, or his young self. He was only a kid yet, a high-strung nervous boy with good in him. He slipped supple as an eel into the oilskins, and they went out together.

It was dusk, but not much darker. The dusk held on, and hail and rain had stopped for now, and the gale was solid. "Some wind!" shouted Tommy, a man's voice breaking into a child's voice.

Orville loved this storm growing. It was his own storm and he wanted it for himself and he did not want the boy. But the boy was here. In the cabin the radio crackled and it sang deep and strange and lazy: "A burly bum came hikin'—down a shady lane—Through the sugar cane—He was lookin' for his likin'."

He took his big flashlight from the shelf. "I'm going up to the sea wall a minute," he said. "You draw the fire from the stove, Tommy. Roll my bedding in that canvas. Get everything off the floor. Put it on the bunk and the table. Wait here for me."

"Okay, Granka." He looked a bit puzzled at all this fuss.

Orville turned south-east and he plodded step by step into the teeth of the wind like in books, into the wind's teeth he thought of it. He heard a big branch crash, but it was away on the right beyond the low ground, somewhere up at Mary's flower garden and greenhouse. Here he was, coming to the dim-white boats, and then the storm started up again, and for the first time he did not mind it starting up now and it was good how he could wait in the lee of the scow till it stopped. He struggled once more into his storm to the sea wall which was not a solid wall but jumbled piles and heaps of granite blocks from the quarry and boulders from the cleared land, as much to stop the sea from eating away the land as to stop it mounting over the land.

He crouched behind a chunk of granite and looked at the sea twenty feet below. The sea was boiling down there, but not worse than many other times he could remember. He could see it coming, churning brown mud close to shore. He could see it coming and rising, and the waves flew into nothing as they broke, and the salt-spume drummed on his sou'wester and pitted grains at his eyes and cheeks. *What did I come for?* He had come to meet the storm and not for anything he could do.

He wished he could get rid of Tommy. And then he worried about the boy being safe because the wind had risen from strong breeze to gale in the space of an hour, and it was piling on every minute. He remembered the August storm of '27 which had caught them in the fishing boat, the *Clara P.*, him and Ves Thomson and old Tom Palk, his own father. And he remembered now strangely the calm nights of summer weather, first nights when he and his bride Clara had shared the bed. He remembered many things.

The wind hustled him back to the cabin on a path he knew blindfolded, and he went in.

"Gee, I heard it on the radio, Granka." Tommy's eyes were just a bit wild. "He said it was the biggest tide of the year, and the gale could put it plenty higher."

Which was what Orville had meant to keep from young

Tommy, because what was the use of scaring him till the time came or the necessity arose to send him over to Mary's greenhouse for shelter?

"Could be," he said. "But there's been plenty big winds and tides together before this and no harm done. I guess it'll come to nothing." For the boy, son of his well-loved son, he hoped it would come to nothing. For himself, in his guts, he wanted it to come to something.

"Go on, Tommy," he said, turning off the radio. "Take the bedroll to the house and come back to the wall. I'll be there."

The two things Orville had waited to get were his wife Clara's picture and young Orville's picture, although Orville would have been forty now. They were small pictures and nice. They fitted into his pocket inside, and that was that and he switched off the light and stepped out to God's strong tempest. *Oh God*, he thought, for God did often lurk about him and around him on the sea and on the land, although God was not a Thing he was sure and certain about like some luckier folk. *Oh God*, he thought. *Make me strong.* He meant strong in his body, because for this storm he was strong in the courage of his mind. He did not remember now about the weakness.

He took a tarpaulin and cord from the shed by his cabin. He went to the well. It was boxed-in because they had had the blessing of an electric pump, but it was still an open-topped well inside the housing. The tarpaulin blew out like a sail and snatched, stiff and alive, and he nearly lost it. But he waited as he had long been able to wait, knowing what he could and could not do, and soon Tommy came to help him. They lashed her while he remembered things about the well that had never failed nor ever been polluted by salt water. It was their well, and their life in part. He and his grandson made it safe from anything but direct attack.

It was night now at seven o'clock, at half-flood, and it was very cold, and the wind had a greater voice. The wind cried: *Here I am! Here I come again! Here I come and I bring my sea and I flatten my land. Here I come, small beasts and trees and man.*

But Orville Palk was not this wind's small man. He loved this wind. He was the tired brother of this strong young wind. "Come on!" he shouted.

There was one more thing to do. He could not be sure it was a good thing to do, for in this thing he did not have experience. He and Tommy went back to the shed. He gave Tommy the flashlight. He opened his jack-knife and ripped burlap off the coil. He took the end of the lead-rope—an inch and a half diameter, fifty fathoms—and he walked off, and the wind made it easy for a while but not for long. Then he went back uprope upwind and Tommy helped him with the rest, all three hundred feet in a flat letter S not visible on the flat dark ground.

They hauled right around the house and back front into tempest and he tied a running knot and took the strain, sending Tommy round once more to place the rope as high as possible. They tightened, then dragged, the spare end off to two white pines which murmured in lightest airs and sounded in wind but now were small players in the tumult. They had been old trees in the days of the first Palks from Connecticut (they had been spared by the King's Navy; they had been shade trees not felled for a quick dollar); they were the pride of an unprideful place. The larger of them now served as mooring for the Palk house. Man and boy heaved; boy held; man knotted. The rope sagged. The tree was slightly east of wind; the rope could be unnecessary; or it could be useless; or it could be better than nothing.

Orville Palk had finished. As soon as he had finished, he thought of yet another thing. "Go in, Tommy!" he shouted. He turned his back to the lights of the house and gained a yard and lost a foot and gained and lost and fought against the wind and against a new weapon of the wind. It was sleet, wet-fingered, driving in the light-beam, stabbing. It was sleet freezing up. He made his cabin.

He knelt on the floor and it started up again. It was a long one, and it stopped him from reaching down for his jar of rum. It went away. He got the rum, which he needed not for spirit but for body to serve Tommy Palk his grandson. He took a nip and mouthed it because of the fiery burn and he felt it pouff and let it trickle down slowly. *I was drunk often in my time*, he thought. *I was ugly drunk in my time. But my drunk times are long past. I'm a sober old fella and not so old at that in years if it was years. I'm a sober old fella taking nips.*

He laughed loudly although he could not hear his laughter, and he trotted downwind in thigh boots and oilskins like a lumbering work-horse off the hill. The biggest of all blasts pinned him against the door of the house. He cherished his jar of rum. He could not move. He heard a tree pile down to crash somewhere. He heard another noise, high, brittle, long-drawn, almost music in it, tinkle, splinter tinkle through and above and keyed different from the wind. He knew what it was. It was Mary's precious greenhouse on the slope beyond the island's neck. Mary's glass house had set sail. *I guess a big glass box would sail pretty*, he thought. He was a great joker.

The squall eased on him and he put down his jar and managed the door with both hands and wedged it till he had himself and the jar inside, and he thought now of something which was not funny or a good joke. He thought now that the upland shelter for his grandson Tommy had sailed away and rolled over and over into slivers of glass. He was resentful at his grandson, who had been the apple of his eye and the pride of his heart, and now was a stranger at the age of puberty, off in his own new-troubled world with no time to waste on grandfathers.

He took his jar into the parlour. Tommy sat wrong way round on a straight chair with his chin on the backrest. He was close to the Franklin stove and he was shivering a bit although the fancy scrollwork on Franklin glowed red. The Franklin was shut but it roared and whistled. They said Benjamin Franklin invented lightning conductors and a hundred gimmicks including stoves. Old Ben might have had some idea about the tides. Mebbe he thought up the Quoddy scheme too. *My head's light*, Orville thought. It was nearly eight, which was seven hours and more since his cold hot-dog. He was not hungry, but he needed food.

"We'd better eat. What is there?"

"I don't know," Tommy said. Something loud and heavy hit the roof overhead, and Tommy gave a start and he looked up then over his shoulder at the window where the weather came from, and back. He edged closer to Franklin.

"Go and look," Orville said hardly. He knew a bit about fear in other people, and he couldn't wonder if the boy was scared, but he did not like it. "Cold meat if there's any, or a can, and bring bread too. Quick now."

He stowed his dark-swilling jar on top of the bureau, and he took off sou'wester and dripping coat and he listened to the house. Creak and groan and grind and grumble. She creaked in her stout timbers top to bottom and bow to stern like a sound boat. But she was not a good sea-going boat. *I never went to sea in a house,* he thought. Then he thought of a crazy rhyme his mother used to tell them, she was a woman from the Old Country. The rhyme was: *Few and far, far and few, are the lands where the Jumblies live. Their heads are green and their hands are blue. And they went to sea in a Sieve.*

He went through into the kitchen because he had thought of coffee. The storm roared over and round and about the Palk house. It bashed her and buffeted her and she stood like the house in the Bible built on rock. But she was not built on rock. Her sills rested on granite blocks set four feet down in gravel, which was not the same thing.

Tommy was carrying out orders. He had a slab of cold pork and a knife and a loaf of Mary's bread and some country butter on a tray. They kept one cow and they kept twenty hens. *Oh hell*, Orville thought. *I didn't think to shut those damn chickens.* The cow was in her barn back of the house, and the henhouse was back of that again, sheltered, and he did not see there was need to close the door to the run because coons and skunks and foxes and weasels would not do much hunting this night; and if the rooster and the barred-rock pullets and the cow sailed away too, well that would be just too bad, that would give old cockalorum something to crow about come cockcrow. The water was boiling for coffee.

"Granka!" said Tommy in the boy's half of his voice. He was better with having a small job to do, but he was not good. "How much could this wind put up the tide?"

Orville had a picture of the way he always saw it; of the wind like a giant shovel or dozer-blade pushing the sea ahead and higher. It wasn't quite a whole picture—they said a low barometer had a hand in the business too. "Don't know, Tommy," he said. "Mebbe five-six feet. Then there's the waves on top of that." *Stop it!* he told himself. *Cut it out, Palk! What kind of behaviour is that, scaring the kid, your grandson? That's cruel.* But he felt spite and reproached himself and said: "It'll be all right, though, Tommy. It won't come to nothing."

"That's high enough to come over the sea wall, Granka." The wind still grew. The noise was shrill, yet thunder, and peaceful times were not to be remembered. Tommy went over to the sink and drew himself water and gulped it. "Can't we go over to the high ground, Granka, before we're cut off?"

"The greenhouse is gone," said Orville. "I heard it. And that wind would freeze Scotch whisky. We'll stay here, boy." He was impatient. "Come on up forrard, then."

They went through to the parlour and they ate little, the one because of fear, the other because food was not easy. But they ate. It was eight-thirty, two hours to high water, and this wasn't Saxby veering south. This gale held true from the south-east. This gale waxed mighty.

I'm a wicked old man, he thought, although he thought also that perhaps not more wicked than God made every man with spunk in him. "Take your mother's pictures up the stair," he said when he had chewed a slice of dry bread to clean the greasy porkness out, and had drunk coffee. Mary's canvases were stacked against a wall, five or six of them, untidy.

Mary had a fault of untidiness and slapdashness. It worried Orville, being neat himself, but he admired it too. He wished now when Tommy was upstairs, and while he was getting the rugs up off the floor, he wished that he could go away out to be with his friend the storm again. *I wonder if I ever in my life heard a wind like that?*

The lights dipped to a glow for some seconds, and came too bright and went out for keeps. He sat on the chair beside Franklin who needed more wood. Franklin was a he and the house was a she and the storm was alive, and Orville Palk was the liveliest of the lot. "Tommy!" he shouted: "Where's the lamps?" No answer. But the boy was coming down. "Where's the lamps, Tommy?"

Tommy blundered against him. Tommy sighed. It was a lonely discernible sound, and Orville was sorry but not sorry. "Dunno, Granka. Out back in the pantry, I guess."

"Here, take the flashlight." He pushed up the slide and handed it over. He sat alone again beside fading gleams in the slits of Franklin. He went to the window, feeling his way. It started up again. He closed his eyes to redness and green-ness and purple flashes, and he pressed his fingers and thumbs, all nine of them being short of one by saw, against the cold glass till it stopped. He looked out and there was no pale hint of snow, but the panes were iced-up so it was freezing rain now.

As he stood there, he felt a new thing. He did not exactly feel it, but he sensed it. He sensed her ease on her windward sills and drop back at the end of gust. It was a stir, no more. They said that down in the hurricane countries like the West Indies and Florida and those places, the houses were bolted to foundations, but here none of the old ones were and none of them blew over. She stirred that one time and not again now on her granite blocks, and the breaking strain of his lead-rope was twenty-one thousand pounds more or less, he remembered. There were no figures of experience to figure it out, and he wouldn't have bothered.

I should be helping Tommy find a lamp, he thought, but he did not move. He stood in blackness at the thrumming window while that boy fumbled around some place, he supposed. *Used to be a great kid,* he thought. *Now he reads the comics. The modern generation picking and choosing what kind of soft jobs they might take after school. Life's too easy, and show me one that does an honest day's work, and what does a dollar buy, that's what I want to know. You old fool, he told himself. They're no different in below from what you were or from what your son Orville was. Life's different is the difference.*

Tommy brought the lamp. It was cold. Orville put two lots into Franklin. They flamed into destruction with violent draught and backblow, and it was quite cozy, more light than heat. The Palk house was the eye of the hurricane you read about, but they said the eye of the hurricane was quiet, and here it was not quiet. Here, Franklin roared small, and the house shook larger, and the storm had changed from a multitude of voices to one Goliath voice. "I never heard a wind like that," Orville said. "Never in all my life." He had not been sure before, but now he was sure and he was pleased about it, and he was pleased about the wind's direction.

"When is high water, Granka?"

"At ten twenty-four," he said. "In sixty-three minutes."

"How soon will the flood come, if it's coming, Granka?"

Orville Palk did not answer his grandson's question. He did not have time to answer.

The crash ended. It was a thing he had not thought possible, one of the many things. He stood in the guttering light of the lamp. He was not afraid. He looked at Tommy. Tommy was crying. Orville took the flashlight and went out of the room. The porch door was easy. The outside door was iced-up. He kicked and shouldered to free it, and used all his strength and wedged his boot in. Cold violence struck at him. He shone the flashlight out half-left. He could see which one had gone. It was the bigger of the two white pines, his mooring.

He knew what he was going to do and he wanted to do it alone but he did not think he could do it alone. All this time he had longed to be out with his storm, and now his chance and excuse was here, but something else was here which he had seen at the foot of the doorstep. The tide was here. The Atlantic ocean was lapping at his family doorstep with an hour to go before high water, and his grandson snivelled by the Franklin stove. Tommy was undone. He was undone by the earthquake of that falling tree which God's wind had smashed upon the earth beside this house. *The tree was alive,* Orville thought. *The old pine was alive like you and me. It had a good long life and now it's dead, although not sharp dead because life dies slower in them.*

He thought this in the time of looking at Tommy and of unscrewing the cap of his gallon jar on the bureau and taking straight sips or nips of rum. It was fierce and alive too. He was happy. "Outside, Tommy!" he said, putting on the sou'wester and oilskins. "We'll have to moor to the other tree."

Tommy came over. He was slow and heavy but he began to put on his oilskins and he said; "We can't, Granka."

"It's not what we can," Orville said. "It's what we've got to before the tide comes over the sea wall. Listen to it!"

They listened. It came from below at the west side of the house, a lapping smacking slap under the chorus. Never in a century and a half had a tide reached the house; but it was here now, and rising.

Orville took the flashlight and went to the door. Wind whined and whistled in the ice-free cracks. Wind thundered. The world was wind, and the house trembled with life of wind, and she teetered. *I love the wind,* he thought. Then he thought that his mooring-rope idea was crazy anyways, because if the sea found space underneath to gouge and suck at gravel, or if plain wind should take her, what the hell use would a rope be? *I have to do it because I have to, and I have to do it for the boy, and I have to have him along.*

He broke out. He was clever and careful. He stood on the icy step and held the door-edge into wind, and wind pinned him against door-edge. "Crawl!" he ordered.

Tommy did not crawl out. He stood in the doorway, raised both hands and dropped them. The parlour light went out. Tommy did not come. Orville let go the door. It swung wide open. Then a gust-vacuum whipped it back to strike him on the shoulder. He grunted, and dropped down the steps into water.

I must keep the flashlight dry, he thought. The water was a foot deep. There was ice below it. He crawled. The water came in over the tops of his boots. Rain jabbed at his cheeks and iced on his eyebrows and he did not have a spare hand to shield his face. It was solid salt rain, spray driven flat in long slivers of flatness from the sea wall south-east at his electric beam, needles of coldness till his face numbed and he felt nothing except cold pain in his legs and eyes and crotch, and he crawled on.

It's great, Orville Palk thought. *It's the best thing ever happened to me.*

He reasoned that the sea had not yet broken over because the water was less deep here at the inching rise of ground nearing his pine trees.

He crawled. He could see his trees, one up one down. They were not dark pines tonight. They glistened pale. *It's hard on that old tree,* he thought. *It's downright mean of God to help the wind with a load of ice. God helps them, but how can a poor old iced-up white pine help itself?*

He reached the tree, and he could get at the knots, and just for the fun of it first he swept his light down north where trunk and boughs lay as tall as the house against the house. *I guess God didn't mean that one to get us. I guess that wasn't the big old bullet labelled Palk.*

He needed both hands. He put the light in his pocket. It was black night. It was altogether howling darkness. His hands were numb. They slid over the ice-laden tree whose trunk was five foot thick or more. He fought with the loose end of rope; but it was not loose; it was hard and solid and stiff as a wire hawser of like size. *I knew it all along,* he thought. *I knew I couldn't do it by myself. What did I want to do?*

He could not break the ice-coat, but he would keep on. He would fight on. He would never say die. He heard a new sound. They were like a band, all the sounds making one clashing tune together, the deep horns and the high flutes and the pluck and sob of fiddles. But this was another sound. It was the voice of waves. It was the surge and rasp and smash of waves come over the sea wall. He no sooner heard it than here the ocean came, foaming and churning to swallow him in darkness.

The storms of his mind died down. He stopped struggling with the rope. *I must get back. I must get back to Tommy now this minute. I was crazy. How long to high water?* But he had no idea how long it would be till ten twenty-four and the height of this tide. *It's a record,* he thought. *Everything's a record some way when you come down to it.*

He turned to slide along his rope which was as slippery as any fireman's pole. Just then it started up again. It did not start up in the usual way with a tightness then a flutter then a jabbing tick-tock stab. It did not start that way. It started full force hammer hammer hammer with a hard steel hammer. It beat him down and pulped him up while his body knelt. It was all. No other thing could be, and Orville Palk had never been in any other place or time but on his knees in the attacking sea at night in tumult.

Then he sailed away. His heads were green and his hands were blue, and he went to sea in a sieve, he went to sea he did, he and Father with elegant beard, he and mother with rings on fingers, he and Clara where bobolinks sing with warm earth smells and sky-showing eyes, he and his seine and a teeming harvest, he and young Orville and Mary in her garden and sweet Lindy Lou, he and a yo-ho barrel of rum, he and a lifetime on a calmer sea. It was his voyage at the chosen time.

"Granka! Granka!"

"Leave me be," he muttered.

But Tommy would not leave him be. "You've got to come, Granka." Tommy sobbed for breath, heaving at him.

"Go to hell!" He had been happy on his knees with God's storm after it had stopped. He had been strong and weak joined together, and now he abused his grandson. But he stood in water that sank to his knees and surged. He slithered and stumbled in waterlogged boots along his lifeline to the Palk house. *I'm a tough old nut,* he thought happily again.

They made it together, the old one and the young. They made it together and with flood which swilled inside like water in the bilge. Tommy lit the lamp. Tommy had a new face on him. Bits of kindling floated around the floor.

Orville did not feel so bad. *I won't catch cold,* he knew. *I won't even catch my death of cold, goddammit.* His dentures chattered. His torn fingers came to life.

Something joined them. A white bullet cracked through double windows, hit the far wall and fell. It did not stir. It did not bleed. It was airborne flotsam, a herring gull in adult plumage, unruffled, only the life smacked out. It lay among the kindling. Soon it floated, no longer glossy. The wind made a piecemeal job of shattered panes. The wind had a foothold in the house.

Tommy sloshed to the bureau and turned the lamp up smoky and fetched the rum and poured some into a cup. "Drink it!" he said.

Orville drank and the good false heat piped through him. *I'm pickled with rum,* he thought, watching Tommy stoke Franklin. "Good man," he said in fairness. "Good man, Tommy!"

Tommy smiled. "I guess you must a fainted," he said deep man in his boots. "I could feel you sort of slumped across the rope. Are you okay, Granka?"

"I'm okay," said Orville. "A bit tired." He was more than a bit tired. He thought of what had hit him out there. And he thought of how he had gone to the sea always and now here was the sea come to him and coming, and everything coming.

He looked at his watch. It still went. It was a reliable old waterproof timepiece which, if it broke down, could be fixed. He listened at ten-twelve p.m., twelve minutes to go like the disciples. *Christ was good,* he thought. *Christ was good enough for us without there being a God, but Christ was sure about it and He seemed to know it was okay for sure. I guess*

Christ would have a reason too why my boy Orville had to be taken and me left.

He listened to the storm in its two elements. He heard and felt foundation-shudder as breakers struck at and down and into space below the house, and he felt her rock. He listened to the plundering sea and he listened to the devouring wind. Water sloshed at the old iron sides of Franklin who hissed now and blew steam and sent ash-dirted eddies around Mary's floor. Franklin made bad gases.

"Come on, Granka," said the boy. "Up the stair!"

They sat side by side on the fifth step. The house quivered. She was not afloat, but she was easy on her sills. "You're the skipper, Tommy boy," he said. "Any orders for the mate?"

They laughed at this. *I wonder the next time it starts up will it be like last time?* he thought. And he thought: *We should pray. I ought to pray for Tommy.* "Let us pray," he said. "Oh God," he prayed. "Give us strength for the storms of our journey. Amen."

"Amen," said young Tommy, his friend beside him. "I never knew you had much religion, Granka."

"I don't have, son," he said. "I just remembered it. That was a prayer my mother used to say, your great-grannie. She was a woman from the Old Country."

"It's a good prayer," Tommy said. "I like it."

The hour was half-past ten. The Palk house heaved in the belly of the storm. She heaved and trembled and leaned. She leaned as a blade of winter grass might lean below the wind for immeasurable wilful undecided time. Then she climbed back like the brittle blade of grass.

They sat on. "It's ebbing, Granka," Tommy said.

I wonder will he be a fisherman? Orville thought. *I wonder with his cleverness would it be right? Now take me, I never had no learning or the head for it. Mebbe I would be better if I'd had some learning to be wise. Mebbe I wouldn't just be an ignorant afraid old man.*

"The wind's veering south," he said. He knew that this storm was dying. His grandson helped him with his boots. He rubbed his chilled body. He saw to it that Tommy did likewise. He made Tommy take a drink of rum, and he had a last good swig himself. He took out his teeth and lay down in his son's wife's bed.

The old house stood. The grandfather slept. The grandson slept.

He was awake and not yet awake. But it crowed. It kept on moo-ing. The rooster and the cow forced him out of sleep, and he was right back.

His wet clothes lay on the floor. The morning was sunny. It was quiet too, except for that bird and that animal. It was unnatural, the stillness after storm. *I'll stay here,* he thought. *Why wouldn't I just stay here in bed?*

He got up and found clothes of young Orville's which Mary had kept in the cupboard these eight years. It didn't seem right having them ready that way, but it was her business what she did with them. He and young Orville used to be a fit. The pants hung big. *I hope she doesn't mind me wearing them,* he thought.

He drew his wet boots on. He left the room without looking out the window, called: "Wake up, Tommy!" and went downstairs. It was a mess of stains and puddles and dirty ashes. The power would be off for days if he knew anything about it. Coffee was all he wanted, and there was enough water in the kettle for that. He lit the stove.

Tommy thudded down and busted along to the kitchen. "Gee, Granka! Have you looked out? It's terrible out there. One of the boats is gone too." Tommy was excited and pleased about it, as a kid would be, he supposed.

He shook his head. "Not yet," he said.

"You look kind of tired. Do you feel okay, Granka?"

"Yes," he said. "I feel okay. I'm fine." He ate bread and plum jam and drank coffee and watched the boy's appetite.

"It's a good thing the barn and the henhouse stayed put. The storm could have been worse, Granka."

"It was bad enough," he said. "It was the worst there's been since our people come here."

"Could it be because of the atom bomb, Granka? These huge gales and tides all over, I mean. And I was reading where it said the mild winters. . . ."

"You never can tell," he said patiently enough. You never could. He stood up. "I'll go out," he said. "Better milk the cow and feed the chickens now, Tommy. That cow sounds like she missed a milking. Or did you do it in the afternoon?"

"I didn't have the time," Tommy said, huffy more like himself.

Orville Palk went out. He saw what had happened to the foundations of the house. He stepped over driftwood, cans and bleached trash, and he stepped on rockweed. He stood by the live and the dead white pines. He looked at his cabin but did not go in. The scale boat had vanished; the scow had stayed; the dinghy was stove-in, lying against a spruce tree. The tarpaulin was still lashed to the well-housing.

There were many blown trees across on higher ground. The greenhouse—it had cost him three hundred and thirty-six fifty when a dollar was still worth something—the greenhouse had sailed or rolled a hundred yards to be a tangled skeleton.

It was a perfect morning with a nip and a touch of breeze from the west, and a March sun warming up, and with destruction. It was seven-thirty and near to half flood.

He came to the sea wall. He came to it gradually, for the breakers had picked up ton-blocks of granite and tossed them on ahead. The sea had reached down through quarried granite to boulders brought from the first cleared-land, and it had gouged them out. It had dug gulleys to the bedrock.

He sat down with his back to it, and he looked at the calm blue sea. The tide edged up innocent as be-damned across the mudflats. The air was washed clean and crisp. It was peaceful. It was a pretence of peace, and he thought; *it means nothing and it comes to nothing.*

He sat alone a while until he heard footsteps. His hearing was still sharp. He did not want company.

"I saw the scale-boat, Granka. It's bottom-up on the north shore, halfways along to Old Palk."

"Good," he said.

"Two of the pullets were dead. They must have fallen off the perch and drowned, I guess."

"Chicken dinner," he said for a joke to the boy, but it was not much of a joke.

"I was thinking, Granka . . . ."

Tommy sat on one rock and he sat on another. What kind of a bright thought was it going to be next?

But Tommy did not go on. Orville looked at him. It was a face heavier in the brow than in the chin, more from Mary's side than from the Palks, a boy's nice moody half-made face with fuzz on it and a pimple or two, a face that life might harden into strength, or not. Then he noticed that Tommy's face was moving, lips and muscles. Tommy was in distress.

"Gee, I was awful scared last night, Granka," he blurted out. "I'm sorry, Granka."

Orville forgot his troubles. He started to put his right hand out to touch the boy's hand on the left knee, and he took it back. It was seamed and dirty, short of one finger, blotched by the barnacle-scars of fifty seasons. It was not a hand a boy would like to feel the touch of. "Listen, son," he said. "You did good last night. You came out alone to fetch me in. I was real proud of you." But he thought: *I didn't like it when he was scared, and then I didn't like it when he saved my life. I never even gave him a build-up after.*

"But I was scared first, Granka. I was too chicken to go along out with you."

He frowned. "I don't like that word. It's not a man's word. A chicken can't help its nature, but we're different. There's nothing bad in being afraid, Tommy, not if you beat it. Then it's a good thing. That's what you did." And he thought: *What is this I'm saying?*

"It's funny, Granka. When we got back in last night, I forgot I'd been scared. And then just now I saw that tree almost on top of the house, well then the crash and everything came right back at me." Tommy looked round, eyes wild with

the remembering. "I don't think I've been afraid before," he
said. "Never at hockey. I guess hockey's different."

"Yes," he said. "Hockey's different."

"Is it as hard every new time, Granka?"

Orville tried to speak well about what he did not know.
"It's easier every time you face it, and harder every time you
don't. I think that's right, son, but I don't know."

"I guess you've never been afraid, Granka."

"*Me* never afraid?"

It started up again. It was the first one since that one last
night beside the tree. He had been expecting it, and it had not
come. It was not as bad as the other, which had been an
all-time high, but it was bad enough. The pain dug into the
guts of his right side. He shut his eyes and leaned forward
into his knees and he sweated in the cool morning. Soon it
steadied back to the quiet thing that grew less quiet with him.
"What's wrong, Granka? What's the matter?" Tommy knelt,
arm across his shoulders.

He had meant to keep it from them till the time for going
away. He had meant to tell his nephew Hazen, who was in
the weirs with him, and no one else. He had meant just to
come home for a while and it would be easy; but it was
harder. And last night in the storm he had seen a way out,
but there had not been a way out. Now this morning he saw
destruction.

"What is it, Granka?"

He looked at his grandson. "You're the man of the family,"
he said. "I'll tell you, Tommy." He told him plain and blunt.
". . . They wanted me to stay, but I said I was for home. So
they said come home till it was bad, then they'd have space
for me in the hospital. I guess I should have stayed. I'd have
bin less trouble to other folk."

Tommy did not speak. He wept for a short time with
restraint.

"It's nothing, son. It's got to happen, and sixty-seven is a
fair good life." Now he did put his hand on his grandson's
hand. He thought: *What right have I to tell him or anybody*

and hurt them because I can't face it myself alone? Yet he felt comfort in telling the boy.

"Granka," asked Tommy in a while, looking out to sea. "What was that good prayer of my great-grannie's you said?"

"Oh God," said Orville Palk. He began again. "Oh God," he prayed. "Give us strength for the storms of our journey. Amen."

"Amen," Tommy said, and he said: "It was lucky for me you came back, Granka. I mightn't have known about you being so brave."

"I'm not brave, Tommy," he said. "I've been scared stiff off and on ever since they told me."

"I guess it's like what you said about facing it, Granka."

"I didn't earn the right to tell you that." But Orville felt better. He felt peace now for this moment until next time. He saw a gleam of God's manifold calm purpose.

He stood up. He did not feel so good in his body. "Come on then, Tommy," he said. "There's work to be done. We'll take a look at that scale-boat first."

"Are you able for it, Granka?"

"Now look, boy," he said. "I'm an old fella and I know what I'm able for better than any young fella knows it."

Tommy laughed. They went down past blocks and boulders, and scow and bashed dinghy, and log-cabin and well and pine trees, and the Palk house which needed attention, and he had nine thousand odd in bonds saved-up, and they came to the north side of the island and walked along the shore.

It was two hours to high water. It would be a big calm tide. Old-Squaws gabbled a wild sad merry-squawing music. In the vault of the sky one sea-gull soared, white and lazy at its own devices. Church bells pealed beyond the hill. Boots crunched mussels and sucked mud. Orville was happy this Sunday morning.

IRVING LAYTON

IRVING LAYTON, although best known as a poet, has also written a
good deal of prose. Born in Roumania of Jewish parents on March
12, 1912, he was brought to Montreal in the following year and
has lived there ever since. He attended Baron Byng High School,
and was coached in Latin by A. M. Klein who has remained a lifelong friend. After matriculating, Layton supported himself for four
years by teaching English to immigrants, and then entered Macdonald College, receiving a B.Sc. in Agriculture in 1939. During
the war he served briefly as a member of the Canadian Army, and
began to publish his poems in John Sutherland's magazine *First
Statement*. In 1946 he received the degree of M.A. from McGill,
writing his thesis for the Department of Economics and Political
Science on Harold Laski. Since then he has taught English and
History at the Herzliah High School in Montreal, and now con-
ducts evening classes in Modern Poetry and Creative Writing at
Sir George Williams College.

Layton has published some twelve books of verse, from *Here
and Now* (1945) to *A Red Carpet for the Sun* (1959), and, most
recently, a book which consists mainly of short stories, *The
Swinging Flesh* (1961). His poems and stories have also appeared
in many magazines in Canada and the United States.

Layton is now recognized as Canada's leading poet. The most
outstanding qualities of his work are vigour and variety. Whether
in anger or in love, in blame or in praise, he writes always with
force and candour. His stories do not have the natural raciness
of his poems, but like the latter they are made out of the direct
observation of the life about him and proclaim the values of the
imagination amidst a world in which materialism is dominant.
The story which follows appears in *The Swinging Flesh*.

A Plausible Story

AFTER THE FIRST WEEK in school my colleagues ceased to
interest me. Their ambitions were commonplace, their concerns trivial, their outlook—well, I couldn't say really what

it was. As high priests of education they genuflected mystically every three months in front of an oblong strip of blue pasteboard; for the rest there was no nonsense to them. After a time, to make them bearable, I invented for each of them an afterschool existence in which, suburban avatars, they lived intense, extravagant lives. Miss Raymond, maths, kept house for thirteen black dwarfs; dainty Miss Lerose, the French instructor, was a flea-catcher with an international reputation; and Mr. Sloper, a tall bony man who taught chemistry to the older boys, was at work on a powder for shrinking headmasters. When I met them hurrying along the corridors it lifted me to know that each of them had a preposterous story to tell me. Of course they never breathed a word to me; they were too closemouthed and secretive for that, or perhaps they suspected I already knew. In any event, their secretiveness was an item in the absurd circumstances I'd woven around their lives.

Bored, and sometimes desperate, I tried yet another expedient. During school hours I engaged upon a long stupendous blasphemy—I played Creator! I don't remember exactly when I first began to copy the Omnipotent; probably at the beginning of my career as a pedagogue. Foolproof, this expedient was also simple. I merely imagined that whatever happened during the hours of school happened solely by my permission. In the courtyard, in the classrooms, in the Headmaster's office, my writ ran everywhere; and my rule, like that of the Creator himself, was as sweeping as it was not-to-be-seen. No one ever rose to challenge it and no one, as far as I can recall, ever complained. My colleagues innocently did my bidding; they accepted without a murmur their prescriptive existence. They diverted though they had long ago ceased to astonish me. Unfortunately even omnipotence sometimes began to pall. By frequently amnestying my subjects and redistributing the main roles, I learned to cheat monotony of its inevitable triumph. My mood at last became serene and complacent. It had the winging pinion, the charming hauteur of the poet baylaurelled with success.

If you can imagine a bacchanalian satyr squeezed into a forty-two-fifty business suit you have a picture of Mr. Porlick. He was the school's Headmaster and one of my most remarkable creations. No other made me feel as omnipotent as he did, for he never voiced an opinion but I knew beforehand what it would be. He was balding and paunchy. On bad days I thought my colleagues had been condemned to rotate in hell around the naked infernal rotundity of Mr. Porlick's belly. He was egotistic, sentimental, and good-natured. He suffered from headaches and frequent attacks of depression; this, he said, was because he was an intellectual and read too many improving books. Porlick's routine for dealing with a misbehaving boy never changed. He'd hurl himself out of the chair, lean his overfed torso to one side, and pumping his arm frantically, demonstrate to his stenographer his famous technique of puff and bluster. If the boy cried—good! Porlick, an embarrassed smile on his face, would begin to comfort him, appearing to be surprised and happy that anyone should have taken his words so seriously.

Another creation was Mr. Edwards. Edwards wore the same deprecatory smile which I had given him three years ago. An unfortunate rigidity in his makeup prevented my acting more generously towards him. I mean that in the matter of character parts he was stuck with the one his mediocre talents made the most suitable for him. I did the best I could, however. I saw to it that he mistook his irresolutions for the promptings of a fastidious conscience and his futile explosions for the rampings of a lion. The squint in his right eye, nevertheless, was not of my doing; nor the queer look in that orb when he removed his glass, as though astonished at its own misplacement.

I had made Edwards' afterschool endowment an exercise in wish fulfilment. His skin was fresh and rosy; his figure athletic; his hair black and abundant; and his squint was gone. Or rather his squint was not gone. But now he dwelt in a land where a squint-eyed person had never before been seen. His defect was a defect no longer. On the contrary, it possessed all the appeal of an intriguing singularity. Women with lovely white skins, their bodies scented with subtle, oriental perfumes, pursued him everywhere. He held them at bay with brilliant epigrams, which only inflamed them the more until, touched by their despairing entreaties, he removed his glass to let them catch a glimpse of his abnormal, voluptuous eye. After that they fainted at his feet, and he strode over their bodies triumphantly.

But here in school Edwards was a failure. He was loquacious and bitter. His pupils despised him; on lavatory doors they rang changes on his name. One of them even penned an ode to him, ingenious and metrically correct—on toilet paper! They made fun of his person, imitated his gait and mannerisms, encouraged one another to new hilarious feats of mimicry. His appearance in the classroom was a signal for an artillery duel of bagbursting, popping noises that sent him scurrying for the Headmaster. Mr. Porlick, lines of worry appearing on the fat orgulous face, averred that Edwards was "unable to keep discipline". When Edwards was gone, the Headmaster would address himself briefly to his circle:

—Dope!

And raise his voice and add:

—The Dope gave a course in Educational Psychology at the Teachers' Seminary. His students revolted. They threw him out. Ha! Ha! Some teacher of psychology! Ha! Ha! Ha!

They listened fearfully while the caves of hell seemed to the farthest phospor-gleaming crag to fill with his laughter. When the walls had stopped echoing, they broke into self-conscious snippets of mirth to erect a wall, however fragile, between them and him. The words "unable to keep discipline" rang menacingly in their ears. They were dismayed, and in hell they shivered.

Edwards, drawing his lips back, was preparing to speak to me, when the morning bell began to ring. That was the signal. Children tumbled into the corridor, doors banged and shivered in their frames, the floor under us trembled. The noise was earsplitting. As if by command, the circling around the Headmaster's belly stopped. This was the first monitory bell. The teachers looked at one another sadly, ruminatively, without speaking. They were bracing themselves for the day's work.

Was it Edwards or another who said:

—Animals! Dirty little animals!

I'm not sure. But one of them did say:

—Animals! Dirty little animals!

I guess it was Edwards. He was the more likely to say it. He was the failure, the despised one, the sole inspirer of lavatory odes.

Edwards placed his nicotined fingers on the back of my wrist. He puckered his face, stretched his rubbery lips over his teeth, and smiled. Glaucous bubbles appeared in the corner of his mouth. He was expecting me to enter into his mood at once. When I kept silent he searched about in his mind for something more to say, perhaps a joke to cover up his indiscretion. Since I hadn't endowed him with ready wit— except in my afterschool fantasy—he searched in vain. The failure made him bitter, and he fairly hissed at me:

—You don't like me much, do you?

What had made him say that? Those were not his lines. Where had he gotten them from? Who or what had put them into his head? Had he rebelled, insanely resolving in a flash of defiance to be out-of-character? Milton's opening chord, organ-booming, vibrated in my brain:

> Of Man's First Disobedience, and the Fruit
> Of that Forbidden Tree whose mortal taste
> Brought Death. . . .

Mr. Edwards, too, should not go unpunished. Heretical impromptus—in my position I could not suffer them!

To uncover the source of his black rebellion I said:

—I don't know what makes you say that.

The second bell cut short his reply. I think he was relieved, preferring to let my question hang in the air unanswered. One word leading to another I might have admitted to disliking him. Edwards was no fool and knew perfectly that once such words are spoken there is seldom a retreat from them. People acquire a vested interest in their stated prejudices, utterance robing them in the false rags of objectivity.

My next thought was a queer one. It had nothing to do with what had gone before. It was of brussels sprouts. Edwards' face was like a cooked brussels sprout, flabbily round, its pale-green steamy leaves ruffled.

Were brussels sprouts merely cabbages without ambition?

The bell's fevered crackling died away. A young straggler, panting and happy, dashed into the open classroom next to us. Taking out some foolscap and my attendance book, I folded the brown annunciatory wings of the cupboard. I curved my arm over my back and raising the coatjacket over the nape of my neck said affably to Mr. Edwards:

—Well, let's put on the harness, shall we?

He made a face and shook his head.

—We must eat, mustn't we?

And saying this, he stepped aggressively in front of me into the long wide corridor. It led to our respective classrooms and for me, alas, to Ava Rickstein.

Little Ava was my masterwork, a figure I'd raised from the depths to tease my brain with hints of man's illimitable perversity. When I came into the classroom her frail body stiffened, and I saw the beleaguered look in her wide mocking eyes. Little Ava, I'm afraid, hated me. She hated me with all the fanatical vigour of a fourteen-year-old adolescent. She was a brilliant pupil who, by irony and composure, overawed her more boisterous classmates. She read eagerly everything she could put her hands on—histories, biography, travel, fiction. Her poise was astonishing. I thrilled to see her, sitting upright in her seat, so close I might have rapped on her desk with my pointer. Like the Arch-Creator Himself I'd insured myself against the sin of pride. I, too, had made someone in my own image, sensitive, perverse, and intractable.

For a few seconds I looked at the expectant faces.

—Take out your history books, I said when the room was quiet.

The twenty faces disappeared, reappeared. There was a clatter of books and pencils, a banging of desk seats.

The day's work was starting.

—Melvyn, what's the date for the execution of Charles I?

—1649, Sir.

—Good. Very good, boy.

—David, what great Englishman besides Charles was called king?

—Pym, Sir. "King" Pym.

—I see you've prepared your lesson. Good.

—Alan, what was the name of the persecuting Archbishop?

Silence. A helpful whispering in the aisles.

—Well, Alan?

—I . . . I . . . Archbishop Laud, Sir!

—Did neighbour Joey help you?

—No, Sir.

Fibbing little wretch. My eyes fell on Ava.

—Ava, give the dates of the English Civil War.

She moved her knees noiselessly out of her seat and stood up erectly.

—1642 to 1646, Sir.

—As usual you are quite right, I smiled.

Her face was unanswering. I began to drum on the desk with my forefinger.

—What were the causes of that war?

—You said, Sir, it was because Charles had sold the soap monopoly to a court favourite for a sum of money he badly needed. This favourite now controlled the supply of soap in the entire kingdom. He charged whatever price he wished since as you once said, Sir, that is the *raison d'etre* for possessing a monopoly. The court favourite raised the price of a bar of soap so high the English people didn't bathe themselves more than two or three times a year. Finally they gave up bathing altogether. And this—as you said, Sir—at last caused an awful stink in the country.

The class began to titter.

I cut short her triumph.

—Silence, I commanded.

There was silence, instantly.

I got up from my seat and sat down on the edge of the desk, facing her.

—Were you trying to be disrespectful, Miss Rickstein?

—No, Sir.

—Then why all the as-you-saids?

—Oh, I don't know, she said indifferently.

—I feel that you were trying to parody me, Miss Rickstein.

She was probably the only pupil in the class who knew the word's meaning.

—I wasn't parodying you. I only repeated what you told us the last history lesson.

—Was that all I told you?

—No, Sir. You told us a great deal more. Do you wish me to tell you the rest?

Bold little Ava, exasperating worm.

—No, Miss Rickstein. You have said enough. In heaven may you have your reward, suitably. Sit down.

—Thank you, Sir.

I returned to my seat and sat down. Looking at Ava sitting in front of me, I began for the hundredth time to compare her to her sister Evelyn. I had taught Evelyn in this same classroom three years ago. The girls were alike in almost everything but their attitude towards me. Evelyn had revered me, and hung upon my lightest word. I'd played my best roles for Evelyn. I'd been Shelley, Lincoln, Debs, Papineau, and no actor could have striven harder than I to win her silent applause. Each day I lived through a masquerade of noble roles. Occasionally I tried for new subtleties and nuances of character; her perspicacity pleased and chagrined me. No one had ever come to take her place.

I asked the class several more questions, went through the lesson for the day, and then told them to write a synopsis of the history chapter. I glanced at my wristwatch. Noon was still a long way off. I reached my hand into my briefcase for a book I had taken along to read. The time passed slowly. Ava

was writing carefully into her looseleaf. Why did she hate me?
I could think of no reason. Was I a stone left in her path by
her older sister, a challenge which she coldly and proudly
declined to accept? Was that the answer?

The class was growing restless. They had finished their task
and were waiting for the next lesson, which was literature, to
begin. I told them to take out their verse books.

—Who wrote "The Gift of Tritemius"? I asked.

Several hands shot up in a Roman salute. I saw myself
with a sunburnt furious bald head, an apron of balcony about
my waist. The voices in the room were plaintive, straining,
eager.

—Me. Oh, please, teacher, me. Me, teacher. I know the
answer.

I thrust out my jaw and looked stern.

—Bramson, do you know?

—John Greenleaf Whittier, an American poet.

—Good. That's the idea.

In the third row a boy was playing Sink My Battleship with
his neighbour.

—Stand up, Joey.

The boy got to his feet slowly, his fearstricken face turned
to his grinning classmates.

—Give me a full summary of the poem, I said.

—I don't know what you mean, the boy replied.

—By what? By summary?

—Yes, Sir. Do you mean the moral of the poem?

—No, I mean the story.

—It's about this here Abbot, the boy began painfully. A
woman comes to a mon . . . a mon-stry and asks for help.

—Why, why does she come to him asking for help? I
prodded. He had come to an abrupt stop.

—Because her son's a slave . . . a galley slave with the
Moors.

—That's better, I said. Now tell us why he's a galley slave.

The boy inclined his ear blotterlike to soak up the whispered
noises about him. He shifted his weight from leg to leg and

began ritually to scratch his head and elbow. The faces up-raised to him were as blank as his own. No one was waving his hand wanting to answer. He took courage.

—It don't say in the poem why, Sir, he blurted.

—True, Joey, I said with a laugh. It doesn't. But haven't you an imagination? Couldn't you think up a likely story to explain how the son came to be a galley slave? Or am I asking too much of you?

Joey grimaced to show that he thought I was. I had manifestly been unfair. I sensed that the mood of the class supported him and did not press it further.

—Go on, I said kindly.

—Well, this here Abbot offers the beggar woman his prayers, but she says what are you mocking me for? I need money to ransom out my son.

—What does ransom mean, Joey?

—It . . . it means . . . .

Hands began to wave in front of me, plantlike.

—Please, Sir, I know.

—Please, please, Sir. O-oh I know, Sir.

—You never ask me, Sir.

—Quiet, class, I made myself heard. Let Joey answer if he can. If he can't, I shall ask someone else. Well, Joey, do you know?

—I . . . . I know it. But I can't say it in words.

Ava's eyes were on me, self-assured, ironical. I was impatient to have the story finished.

—You tell the class, I said to her, what ransom means.

She rose to her feet silently.

—Ransom means to redeem, she said slowly. To redeem from captivity or bondage, or the like, by paying a price.

—That's right out of the dictionary, I laughed.

—That's where I got it from, she said coolly. May I sit down now, Sir?

—No, I said, finish our little story for us. Sit down Joey. You have acquitted yourself handsomely.

The boy made an ugly face and sat down noisily.

—Go on, Ava, I said softly.

—The woman persuaded the Abbot to give her the two silver candlesticks which were on the altar. His hands trembled as he gave them to her.

—Why, Ava, why did the Abbot's hands tremble? I interrupted.

—He wasn't sure he was doing the right thing.

—And was he doing the right thing? I asked.

—Yes. That same day when the Abbot arose from his evening prayers he saw the chapel lit up with golden candlesticks. It proves that God loves mercy more than sacrificial gifts.

—Excellent, Ava, I said hypocritically. How Evelyn had ridiculed Whittier's banal homiletic three years ago! Ava was disappointingly conventional.

—Now, class, I said, after telling Ava to take her seat, I want you to use your imaginations. That is, if you have any. We have seen that the hand of the Abbot shook as he gave the silver candlesticks away. Was it because he was worried and afraid? Or was it for another reason? Supposing his hands trembled because the woman was his wife, long believed to be dead. Supposing the son in the Moor's galley was his. Supposing. . . .

I lowered my voice.

—Tell me, children, a plausible story.

But at that point someone knocked at the door. I went to open it, knowing beforehand it would be Mr. Edwards. His words also did not surprise me.

Remember, I was omnipotent.

—I want you to do something for me, he began nervously.

—Sure, I said, feigning ignorance. What is it?

He closed the door and led me towards the staircase.

—You're the only one that can help me, he began again. You've heard of the Teachers' Seminary?

—Yes, I nodded.

Edwards did not look at me.

—Porlick is gone, he said after a time. He's gone for his

cigars and won't be back for the rest of the morning. We all know how well you keep discipline in your classes. I've got a free period. I thought if you could observe me giving a lesson, you . . . .

I waited for him to finish the sentence.

—You might give me a few pointers, he brought out in a low voice, his face reddening.

—Say no more, I said.

Poor Edwards. How ashamed and dilapidated he looked.

How different from his afterschool self!

I told him we had been doing "The Gift of Tritemius" before he knocked at the door. Did he know the poem? Yes, he knew it; and fortunately he knew the children also, having been their class teacher the year before. He would simply continue with the lesson, since if there was one subject more than another which he liked teaching it was English Literature. As we entered the classroom the children looked at us wonderingly and asked each other what was up. I explained to them humorously that they had so tired me out with their puerilities this morning I had asked Mr. Edwards to relieve me. There was a groan when I finished. I silenced it by staring hard at an inoffensive boy in the far corner of the room, an effective method I'd discovered for ending a disturbance in the class. When I turned my head, I saw Edwards' white face, and his hand was shaking.

Edwards remained standing. He looked nervous but resolute. I tiptoed to the back of the room where out of sight of the children I could observe the lesson. There was a chair near the cupboard. I sat down on it and felt as a dramatist might at the premiere showing of his play. The curtain was about to go up on the first scene.

Well, there could be no two thoughts about it. Edwards wasn't Nature's gift to the profession. His voice was not right, he spoke too often, and he lacked the sense of drama that makes the really good teacher. His movements were awkward and unconvincing. He couldn't find the words that would take him right to the hearts of the children, and so remained a gesticulating, slightly absurd stranger to them all the time he was talking to them. When he saw they were growing restless, he attempted to hold their attention by a sprightliness he did not feel; that was perhaps the most pitiful thing of all. It was a heartbreaking spectacle to watch. He picked up the verse book from the desk and began to turn the pages unsurely:

—Stephen, can you tell me who the Abbot was? he asked in a defeated voice.

Stephen was the class jokester. He was a short, swarthy-looking boy, with an irritating smirk on his face. A day seldom passed without my reprimanding him.

—He plays shortstop for the New York Giants, he said in a loud unabashed voice.

His impudent answer was the wanting spark. There was an explosion in the room.

—Naw, he's the prime minister of this country.

—Yer crazy, he's the minister for defence.

—Wanna bet?

—Ah, yer crazy!

I sprang to my feet, but the uproar subsided as suddenly and as quickly as it had arisen.

Edwards held his temper. He waited till perfect quiet had been restored to the class. When he had everyone's attention again he began to harangue them on the importance of litera-ture. He spoke softly and persuasively. He almost surprised me. His performance for the past thirty-five minutes had been anything but inspiriting. Now he began by telling them that literature was one of the humanities. Did the children know where the word came from? It came from the Latin *humanitas*. It was a beautiful word. It signified all that pertained to a human being. Literature helped you become more truly human. It did this by enlarging your imagination and your sympathy for your fellow men. He was a human being, and they were human beings. Through sympathy and imagination they could understand and talk to one another. Without these human qualities the world would be a poor place indeed. If they wished to grow into real men and women they must take their literature lessons seriously. Their teachers were here to help them.

Edwards had spoken almost eloquently. I could only suppose that something deep, something that never came to the surface, had stirred in him. While he was speaking I had gotten up and walked over quietly to the side of the room and leaned my back against the edge of the low windowsill. I could see Ava's fascinating profile. What was she thinking about? Many times I had said the same things about literature, glowing words intended for her sensitive ears alone. The other children I knew were unconvinced. They were barbarians. They had attended to Edwards because it amused them to see a grownup so earnest about words, about what to them meant merely a number of pages of homework.

When Mr. Edwards stopped speaking, he seemed pleased with himself. There was a flattering stillness in the room. Even Stephen was attending. The autumn sun spilled like a light sauterne over the yellow desks and collected into irregular patches on the floor. There was a friendly, industrious atmosphere in the room. Mr. Edwards' eyes sought my face. He smiled at the class and for the first time that morning he seemed to be at ease.

—Now, Ava, I heard him say comfortably, what have you gotten from a study of the English gems? Your teachers tell me you're an omnivorous reader. What do you say literature does and is?

Ava did not leave her seat.

—I think it's bunk, she said decisively.

The class roared and several children started a violent hand-slapping on their desks. Mr. Edwards, a green look returning to his face, bent his shoulders helplessly and waited. He was after all used to that sort of thing. He had deliberately called upon little Ava, thinking she would help him to intensify the warm mood he had by his little speech produced in the classroom. With one ill-tempered sentence she had swept it all away.

The tumult quieted down quickly because the children were

eager to hear what Edwards' answer would be. I sensed their excitement. Edwards shook his head at Ava sorrowfully.

—Miss Rickstein, he said at last, have you a reason for saying what you just did? I feel you must have.

Ava looked wretched. I now saw something which a few hours ago I would have declared to be impossible. The girl's lips were trembling and her black eyes, their mocking beleaguered look gone, were slowly filling with tears. Her famous composure was beginning to crumble. Yet her voice was steady.

—It makes people think too much of themselves. It makes them selfish and egotistic. I like honest, unaffected people. Not a brilliant showoff with no heart in her.

I hadn't missed a word of what she said. I, the omnipotent, was at last beginning to understand.

—That's quite an indictment, Miss Rickstein, Edwards said rather sharply, wishing to seize the helm again. And how do you know all this?

Ava had half-turned towards me. She seemed to be pleading with me. Her face was intense.

—Oh don't ask me, she cried. I know. I just know! They're snobs. They're insincere. They think they know everything because they know what a metaphor is . . . .

Mr. Edwards, who had been pacing back and forth while the girl was speaking, halted. His patience was used up.

—You're talking foolish, he said, interrupting her. I am very disappointed.

But Ava was no longer listening to him. She had buried her small proud head in her arms and was sobbing quietly. Her classmates were bewildered, and were watching her in deep silence. They were no more astonished than I was. Little ladylike Ava crying! I glanced up from her heaving back to Mr. Edwards' face. He was not very far from tears himself. What had he done? In heaven's name, what was the matter with the girl? He looked at her helplessly, at one moment putting out his hand as if to remonstrate with her, the next moment drawing it irresolutely back. Poor Edwards, squirming and flailing about on the implacable hook of his own incompetency. I could not bear to see his deep misery and humiliation and began to walk to the back of the room. I heard the door open and then shut with a loud noise. When I turned around Mr. Edwards was not to be seen anywhere. He had fled. Ava was still crying. I made no attempt to comfort her.

—Put your books away, class, I said from the back of the room.

But no one stirred.

HUGH GARNER

HUGH GARNER was born at Batley, Yorkshire, England, on February 22, 1913, and came to Canada as a boy of six. He spent his boyhood and youth in Toronto, where he was educated in the public schools and at Danforth Technical High School. During the depression years of 1929 to 1939 he worked at a great variety of jobs, including newspaper copy-boy, relief camp labourer, telegraph messenger, harvest hand, hobo, door-to-door salesman, packer, buffer, shipper, clerk, machine-operator and public relations director. In 1937 he served as a machine-gunner in the Abraham Lincoln Battalion of the International Brigade in Spain. On the outbreak of World War II, he served for six months in the Royal Canadian Artillery and from 1940 to 1945 in the Royal Canadian Navy. He was married in 1941, has two children, and now makes his home in Toronto and his living as a free-lance writer. He was awarded a Senior Arts Fellowship by the Canada Council in 1959.

Mr. Garner's first writings appeared in *The Canadian Forum* in 1936 and 1937, but he did not write again for publication until 1946. He has subsequently published four novels—*Storm Below, Cabbagetown, Present Reckoning* and *Waste No Tears*—a collection of short stories, *The Yellow Sweater and Other Stories,* and many articles and stories in Canadian and American magazines. He has had seven television plays produced, and is currently at work on a fifth novel and a second collection of short stories.

Mr. Garner's writings reflect his deep knowledge of and sympathy for those people who exist on the lower levels of the social structure. His early life in a poor section of Toronto, and his experiences as a manual and itinerant worker during the depression, provided him with a first-hand knowledge of such people, and his work is always packed with authentic detail. The story which follows is taken from *The Yellow Sweater and Other Stories* (1952).

One, Two, Three Little Indians

AFTER THEY HAD EATEN, Big Tom pushed the cracked and dirty supper things to the back of the table and took the baby from its high chair, carefully, so as not to spill the flotsam of bread crumbs and boiled potatoes from the chair to the floor.

He undressed the youngster, talking to it in the old dialect, trying to awaken its interest. All evening it had been listless and fretful by turns, but now it seemed to be soothed by the story of Po-chee-ah and the Lynx, although it was too young to understand him as his voice slid awkwardly through the ageless folktale of his people.

For long minutes after the baby was asleep he talked on, letting the victorious words fill the small cabin so that they shut out the sounds of the Northern Ontario night: the buzz of mosquitoes, the far-off bark of a dog, the noise of the cars and transport trucks passing on the gravelled road.

The melodious hum of his voice was like a strong soporific, lulling him with the return of half-forgotten memories, strengthening him with the knowledge that once his people had been strong and brave, men with a nation of their own, encompassing a million miles of teeming forest, lake, and tamarack swamp.

When he halted his monologue to place the baby in the big brass bed in the corner, the sudden silence was loud in his ears, and he cringed a bit as the present suddenly caught up with the past.

He covered the baby with a corner of the church-donated patchwork quilt, and lit the kerosene lamp that stood on the mirrorless dressing table beside the stove. Taking a broom from the corner he swept the mealtime debris across the doorsill.

This done, he stood and watched the headlights of the cars

run along the trees bordering the road, like a small boy's stick along a picket fence. From the direction of the trailer camp a hundred yards away came the sound of a car engine being gunned, and the halting note-tumbles of a clarinet from a tourist's radio. The soft summer smell of spruce needles and wood smoke blended with the evening dampness of the earth and felt good in his nostrils, so that he filled his worn lungs until he began to cough. He spat the resinous phlegm into the weed-filled yard.

It had been this summer smell, and the feeling of freedom it gave, that had brought him back to the woods after three years in the mines during the war. But only a part of him had come back, for the mining towns and the big money had done more than etch his lungs with silica. They had also brought him pain and distrust, and a wife who had learned to live in imitation of the gaudy boomtown life.

When his coughing attack subsided he peered along the path, hoping to catch a glimpse of his wife Mary returning from her work at the trailer camp. He was becoming worried about the baby, and her presence, while it might not make the baby well, would mean there was someone else to share his fears. He could see nothing but the still blackness of the trees and their shadows interwoven in a sombre pattern across the mottled ground.

He re-entered the cabin and began washing the dishes, stopping once or twice to cover the moving form of the sleeping baby. He wondered if he could have transmitted his own wasting sickness to the lungs of his son. He stood for long minutes at the side of the bed, staring, trying to diagnose the child's restlessness into something other than what he feared.

His wife came in and placed some things on the table. He picked up a can of pork-and-beans she had bought and weighed it in the palm of his hand. "The baby seems pretty sick," he said.

She crossed the room and looked at the sleeping child. "I guess it's his teeth."

He placed the pork-and-beans on the table and walked over

to his chair beside the empty stove. As he sat down he noticed for the first time that his wife was beginning to show her pregnancy. Her squat form had sunk lower so that it almost filled the shapeless dress she wore. Her brown ankles were puffed above the broken-down heels of the dirty silver dancing pumps she was wearing.

"Is the trailer camp full?" he asked.

"Nearly. Two more Americans came about half an hour ago."

"Was Billy Woodhen around?"

"I didn't see him—only Elsie," she answered. "A woman promised me a dress tomorrow if I scrub out her trailer."

"Yeah?" He saw the happiness rise over her like a colour when she mentioned this. She was much younger than he was —twenty-two years against his thirty-nine—and her dark face had a fullness that is common to many Indian women. She was no longer pretty, and as he watched her he thought that wherever they went the squalor of their existence seemed to follow.

"It's a silk dress," Mary said, as though the repeated mention of it brought it nearer.

"A silk dress is no damn good around here. You should get some overalls," he said, angered by her lack of shame in accepting the cast-off garments of the trailer women.

She seemed not to notice his anger. "It'll do for the dances next winter."

"A lot of dancing you'll do," he said, pointing to her swollen body. "You'd better learn to stay around and take care of the kid."

She busied herself over the stove, lighting it with newspapers and kindling. "I'm going to have some fun. You should have married a grandmother."

He filled the kettle with water from an open pail near the door. The baby began to cough, and the mother turned it to its side in the bed. "As soon as I draw my money from Cooper I'm going to get him some cough syrup from the store," she said.

"It won't do any good. We should take him up to the doctor in town tomorrow."

"I can't. I've got to stay here and work."

He knew the folly of trying to reason with her. She had her heart set on earning the silk dress the woman had promised.

After they had drunk their tea he blew out the light. They took off some of their clothes and climbed over the baby into the bed. Long after his wife had fallen asleep he lay in the darkness listening to a ground moth beating its futile wings against the glass of the window.

They were awakened in the morning by the twittering of a small colony of tree sparrows who were feeding on the kitchen sweepings of the night before. Mary got up and went outside, returning a few minutes later carrying a handful of birch and poplar stovewood.

He waited until the beans were in the pan before rising and pulling on his pants. He stood in the doorway scratching his head and absorbing the sunlight through his bare feet upon the step.

The baby awoke while they were eating their breakfast.

"He don't look good," Big Tom said as he dripped some brown gravy sauce from his plate with a hunk of bread.

"He'll be all right later," his wife insisted. She poured some crusted tinned milk from the can into a cup and mixed it with water from the kettle.

Big Tom splashed his hands and face with cold water and dried himself on a shirt that lay over the back of a chair. "When you going to the camp—this morning?"

"This afternoon," Mary answered.

"I'll be back by then."

He took up a small pile of woven baskets from a corner and hung the handles over his arm. From the warming shelf of the stove he pulled a bedraggled band of cloth into which a large goose feather had been sewn. Carrying this in his hand, he went outside and strode down the path towards the highway.

He ignored the chattering sauciness of a squirrel that hurtled up the green ladder of a tree beside him. Above the small noises of the woods could be heard the roar of a transport truck braking its way down the hill from the burnt-out sapling-covered ridge to the north. The truck passed him as he reached the road, and he waved a desultory greeting to the driver, who answered him with a short blare of the horn.

Placing the baskets in a pile on the shoulder of the road, he adjusted the corduroy band on his head, so that the feather stuck up at the rear. He knew that by doing so he became part of the local colour, "a real Indian with a feather'n everything", and also that it helped him sell his baskets. In the time he had been living along the highway he had learned to give them what they expected.

The trailer residents were not yet awake, so he sat down on the wooden walk leading to the shower room, his baskets resting on the ground in a half-circle behind him.

After a few minutes a small boy descended from the door of a trailer and stood staring at him. Then he pushed his head back inside and spoke, pointing in Big Tom's direction. In a moment a man's hand parted the heavy curtains on the window and a bed-mussed unshaven face stared out. The small boy climbed back inside.

A little later two women approached on the duckboard walk, one attired in a pair of buttock-pinching brown slacks, and the other wearing a blue chenille dressing gown. They circled him warily and entered the shower room. From inside came the buzz of whispered conversation and the louder noises of running water.

During the morning several people approached and stared at Big Tom and the baskets. He sold two small ones to an elderly woman. She seemed surprised when she asked him what tribe he belonged to, and he did not answer in a mono-syllable but said, "I belong to the Algonquins, ma'am." He got rid of one of the big forty-five cent baskets to the mother of the small boy who had been the first one up earlier in the day.

A man took a series of photographs of him with an expensive-looking camera, pacing off the distance and being very careful in setting his lens opening and shutter speeds.

"I wish he'd look into the camera," the man said loudly to a couple standing nearby, as though he were talking of an animal in a cage.

"You can't get any good picshus around here. Harold tried to get one of the five Dionney kids, but they wouldn't let him. The way they keep them quints hid you'd think they was made of china or somep'n," the woman said. She glanced at her companion for confirmation.

"They want you to buy their picshus," the man said. "We was disappointed in 'em. They used to look cute before, when they was small, but now they're just five plain-looking kids."

"Yeah. My Gawd, you'd never believe how homely they got, would you Harold? An' everything's pure robbery in Callendar. You know, old man Dionney's minting money up there. Runs his own sooveneer stand."

After lunch Big Tom watched Cooper prepare for his trip to North Bay. "Is there anybody going fishing, Mr. Cooper?" he asked.

The man took the radiator cap off the old truck and peered inside.

"Mr. Cooper!"

"Hey?" Cooper turned and looked at the Indian standing there, hands in pockets, his manner shy and deferential. He seemed to feel a vague irritation, as though sensing the overtone of servility in the Indian's attitude.

"Anybody going fishing?" Big Tom asked again.

"Seems to me Mr. Staynor said he'd like to go," Cooper answered. His voice was kind, with the amused kindness of a man talking to a child.

The big Indian remained standing where he was, saying nothing. His old second-hand army trousers drooped around his lean loins, and his plaid shirt was open at the throat, showing a grey high-water mark of dirt where his face washings began and ended.

"What's the matter?" Cooper asked. "You seem pretty anxious to go today."

"My kid's sick. I want to make enough to take him to the doctor."

Cooper walked around the truck and opened one of the doors, rattling the handle in his hand as if it were stuck. "You should stay home with it. Make it some pine-sap syrup. No need to worry. It's as healthy as a bear cub."

Mrs. Cooper came out of the house and eased her bulk into the truck cab. "Where's Mary?" she asked.

"Up at the shack," Big Tom answered.

"Tell her to scrub the washrooms before she does anything else. Mrs. Anderson, in that trailer over there, wants her to do her floors." She pointed across the lot to a large blue-and-white trailer parked behind a Buick.

"I'll tell her," he answered.

The Coopers drove between the whitewashed stones marking the entrance to the camp, and swung up the highway, leaving behind them a small cloud of dust from the pulverized gravel of the road.

Big Tom fetched Mary and the baby from the shack. He gave her Mrs. Cooper's instructions, and she transferred the baby from her arms to his. The child was feverish, its breath noisy and fast.

"Keep him warm," she said. "He's been worse since we got up. I think he's got a touch of the flu."

Big Tom placed his hand inside the old blanket and felt the baby's cheek. It was dry and burning to his palm.

He adjusted the baby's small weight in his arms and walked across the camp and down the narrow path to the lakeside where the boats were moored.

A man sitting in the stern sheets of a new-painted skiff looked up and smiled at his approach. "You coming out with me, Tom?" he asked.

The Indian nodded.

"Are you bringing the papoose along?"

Big Tom winced at the word papoose, but he answered, "He won't bother us. The wife is working this afternoon."

"Okay. I thought maybe we'd go over to the other side of the lake today and try to get some of them big fellows at the creek mouth. Like to try?"

"Sure," the Indian answered. He placed the baby along the wide seat in the stern and unshipped the oars.

He rowed silently for the best part of an hour, the sun beating through his shirt and causing the sweat to trickle coldly down his back. At times his efforts at the oars caused a constriction in his chest, and he coughed and spat into the water.

When they reached the mouth of the creek across the lake he let the oars drag and leaned over to look at the baby. It was sleeping restlessly, its lips slightly blue, and its breath laboured and harsh. Mr. Staynor was busy with his lines and tackle in the bow of the boat.

Tom picked the child up and felt its little body for sweat. The baby's skin was bone dry. He picked up the baling can from the boat bottom and dipped it over the side. With the tips of his fingers he brushed some of the cold water across the baby's forehead. The child woke up, looked around at the strange surroundings, and smiled up at the man. He gave it a drink of water from the can. Feeling reassured now, he placed the baby on the seat and went forward to help the fisherman with his gear.

Mr. Staynor fished for half an hour or so, catching some small fish and a large black bass, which writhed in the bottom of the boat. Big Tom watched its gills gasping its death throes, and he noted the similarity between the struggles of the fish and those of the baby lying on the seat in the blanket.

He became frightened again after a time and he turned to the man in the bow and said, "We'll have to go pretty soon. I'm afraid my kid's pretty sick."

"Eh! We've hardly started," the man answered. "Don't worry, there's not much wrong with the papoose."

Big Tom lifted the child from the seat and cradled it in his arms. He opened the blanket, and shading the baby's face,

allowed the warm sun to shine on its chest. If I could only get
him to sweat, he thought, everything would be all right then.

He waited as long as he dared, noting the blueness creeping
over the baby's lips, before he placed the child again on the
seat and addressed the man in the bow. "I'm going back now.
You'd better pull in your line."

The man turned and felt his way along the boat. He stood
over the Indian and parted the folds of the blanket, looking at
the baby. "My God, he is sick, Tom! You'd better get him to a
doctor right away!" He stepped across the writhing fish to the
bow and began pulling in the line. Then he busied himself
with his tackle, stealing glances now and again at the Indian
and the baby.

Big Tom turned the boat around and with long straight
pulls on the oars headed back across the lake. The fisherman
took the child in his arms and blew cooling drafts of air against
its fevered face.

As soon as they reached the jetty below the tourist camp
Tom tied the boat's painter to a stump, and took the child
from the other man.

Mr. Staynor handed him the fee for a full afternoon's work.
"I'm sorry the youngster is sick, Tom," he said. "Don't play
around. Get him up to the doctor in town right away. We'll
try her again tomorrow afternoon."

Big Tom thanked him. Carrying the baby and unmindful
of the grasping hands of the undergrowth he climbed the path
through the trees. On reaching the parked cars and trailers he
headed in the direction of the large blue-and-white one where
his wife would be working.

When he knocked, the door opened and a woman said,
"Yes?" He recognized her as the one who had been standing
by in the morning while his picture was being taken.

"Is my wife here?" he asked.

"Your wife? Oh, I know who you mean. No, she's gone.
She went down the road in a car a few minutes ago."

The camp was almost empty, most of the tourists having
gone to the small bathing beach farther down the lake. A car

full of bathers was pulling away to go down to the beach. Big
Tom hurried over and held up his hand until it stopped.
"Could you drive me to the doctor?" he asked. "My baby
seems pretty sick."

There was a turning of heads within the car. A woman began talking in the back seat. The driver said, "I'll see what I
can do, Chief, after I take the girls to the beach."

Big Tom sat down at the side of the driveway to wait. After
a precious half hour had gone by, and they did not return, he
got to his feet and started up the highway in the direction of
town.

His long legs pounded on the loose gravel of the road, his
anger and terror giving strength to his stride. He noticed that
the passengers in the few cars he met were pointing at him and
laughing, and suddenly he realized that he was still wearing
the feather in the band around his head. He reached up, pulled
it off, and threw it in the ditch.

When a car or truck came up from behind him he would
step off the road and raise his hand to beg for a ride. After the
first ones passed without pausing he stopped this useless, time-
wasting gesture and strode straight ahead, impervious to the
noise of their horns as they approached.

Now and again he placed his hand on the baby's face as he
walked, reassuring himself that it was still alive. It was hours
since it had cried or shown any other signs of consciousness.

Once, he stepped off the road at a small bridge over a
stream, and making a crude cup with his hands, tried to get
the baby to drink. He succeeded only in making it cough,
harshly, so that its tiny face became livid with its efforts to
breathe.

It was impossible that the baby should die. Babies did not
die like this in their father's arms on a highway that ran fifteen
miles north to a small town with a doctor and all the life-saving
devices to prevent their death. . . .

The sun fell low behind the trees and the swarms of black
flies and mosquitoes began their nightly forage. He waved his
hand above the fevered face of the baby, keeping them off, at

the same time trying to waft a little air into the child's tortured lungs.

Suddenly, with feelings as black as hell itself, he knew that the baby was dying. He had seen too much of it not to know, now, that the child was in an advanced state of pneumonia. He stumbled along, his eyes devouring the darkening face of his son, while the hot tears ran from the corners of his eyes.

With nightfall he knew it was too late. He looked up into the sky, where the first stars were being drawn in silver on a burnished copper plate, and he cursed them, and cursed what made them possible.

To the north-west the clouds were piling up in preparation for a summer storm. Reluctantly he turned and headed back down the road in the direction he had come.

It was almost midnight before he felt his way along the path through the trees to the shack. It was hard to see anything in the teeming rain, and the water ran from his shoulders in a steady stream, unheeded, soaking the sodden bundle he still carried in his arms.

Reaching the shanty he opened the door and fell inside. He placed the body of his son on the bed in the corner. Then, groping along the newspaper-lined walls, he found some matches in his mackinaw and lit the lamp. With a glance around the room he realized that his wife had not yet returned, so he placed the lamp on the table under the window and headed out again into the rain.

At the trailer camp he sat down on the rail fence near the entrance to wait. Some light shone from the small windows of the trailers and from Cooper's house across the road. The illuminated sign said: COOPER'S TRAILER CAMP — Hot and Cold Running Water, Rest Rooms. FISHING AND BOATING — INDIAN GUIDES.

One by one, as he waited, the lights went out, until only the sign lit up a small area at the gate.

He saw the car's headlights first, about a hundred yards down the road. When it pulled to a stop he heard some giggling, and Mary and another Indian girl, Elsie Woodhen, staggered out into the rain.

A man's voice shouted through the car door, "See you again, sweetheart. Don't forget next Saturday night." The voice belonged to one of the French-Canadians who worked at a creosote camp across the lake.

Another male voice shouted, "Wahoo!"

The girls clung to each other, laughing drunkenly, as the car pulled away.

They were not aware of Big Tom's approach until he grasped his wife by the hair and pulled her backwards to the ground. Elsie Woodhen screamed and ran away in the direction of the Cooper house. Big Tom bent down as if he was going to strike at Mary's face with his fist. Then he changed his mind and let her go.

She stared into his eyes and saw what was there. Crawling to her feet and sobbing hysterically she limped along towards the shack, leaving one of her silver shoes in the mud.

Big Tom followed behind, all the anguish and frustration drained from him so that there was nothing left to carry him into another day. Heedless now of the coughing which tore his chest apart, he pushed along in the rain, hurrying to join his wife in the vigil over their dead.

DESMOND PACEY

DESMOND PACEY was born in Dunedin, New Zealand, on May 1, 1917. His father, an engineer, was killed in World War I. After spending seven years at school in England, he came to Canada in 1931, and attended Caledonia High School and Victoria College, Toronto. From Toronto he went to Trinity College, Cambridge, as a Research Student in English Literature, receiving the Cambridge Ph.D. in 1941. From 1940 to 1944 he was Professor of English at Brandon College, Manitoba, and since 1944 he has been head of the Department of English in the University of New Brunswick. He is also Dean of Graduate Studies at U.N.B.

Dr. Pacey is the author of *Frederick Philip Grove* (1945), *Creative Writing in Canada* (1952; 1961), *Ten Canadian Poets* (1958) and of two small books of children's verse of which the better known is *The Cow with the Musical Moo* (1952). His stories have appeared in magazines in Canada, Switzerland and Germany, and have been broadcast by the CBC and the BBC. They were collected in the book *The Picnic and Other Stories* (1958). The story which follows first appeared in *Queen's Quarterly* and was reprinted in *The Picnic and Other Stories*.

The Boat

THE BOY Gerald pushed back his plate across the brown oil-cloth, nearly upsetting his empty milk glass.

His aunt glared at him with cold grey eyes. "Watch yourself!" she said in her thin, edged voice.

His uncle looked up from his dish at the end of the table. "What's he up to now?"

"Nearly broke another glass. We'll soon have none left."

His uncle grunted and went on eating his rice pudding in large spoonfuls.

The boy caught the eye of the hired man across the table, and a slight smile passed between them. The aunt noticed the smile and looked at them suspiciously, but the boy spoke to the man in spite of her.

"Don't forget what you promised to do today," said the boy.

"I haven't forgotten. We'll go as soon as I'm finished."

The aunt, quick and sharp as a pecking bird, picked it up. "What's that? What are you going to do?"

The hired man lifted his round, ruddy face and answered her. "Make a boat," he said slowly. "I promised I'd make him a boat today. Then we'll sail her in the creek."

The woman was silenced for a moment by the man's frankness, but the uncle spoke up. "A boat?" he said. "What are you making boats for? Has he been pestering you? I should think you'd have enough to do without making boats."

"It's no trouble," said the man. "I like making boats."

"Huh! More fool you then, that's all I can say. Rest while you can, I say. We get little enough of it." He pushed his chair back noisily and went off into the parlour with his weekly farm magazine.

"Boats!" muttered his aunt disdainfully, as she began to gather up the dishes before the hired man was quite finished. "I wonder what next? And on the Lord's Day, too."

The hired man and the boy went out of the kitchen together, into the warm glow of the summer sunshine. They walked heavily across the strip of lawn to the barnyard and past the heavily fragrant stump of last year's straw-stack. Some grey hens lay sunning themselves in the straw; others were vigorously dusting themselves in pockets of sand beside it. The boy had to take quick steps to keep up with the slow steady stride of the man's long legs.

They came to the machine-shed, and the man pulled back the heavy sliding door. Inside it was cool and dark and the air smelt of old leather and rusty iron. On the packed earth floor, between drill and mower and other out-of-season implements, were tins of nails, boxes of nuts and scraps of broken harness, scattered pieces of wood left from various repair jobs.

Tom began to rummage among the debris, searching for a bit of wood suitable for the boat-making. Gerald sat on an upturned empty nail-keg, watching. They did not speak. They had had enough of sharp, pecking chatter from the woman in the house.

Tom found a rectangular piece of wood about a foot long, and held it up for Gerald to see. Then he began to carve it with his big horn-handled clasp-knife. Magically the boat took shape, moulded patiently to form under Tom's skillful fingers. He worked at it until he had shaped a tapering keel, a pointed bow, and a gently rounded stern. Then he sand-papered the hull all over, until it was silky smooth. Last of all he made three holes in the middle of the deck and cut three thin masts to fit them. He regarded the finished boat carefully and then handed it to the boy.

"Isn't she a beauty?" said Gerald. "What shall we call her?"

"You name her," said Tom. "You're better with words than I am."

"How about the *Good Hope?* That sounds like a three-master to me!"

"Good enough," said Tom. "The *Good Hope* she is."

They went out again into the sunshine, walking down the lane towards the back of the farm. The boy clutched the boat in his hands, feeling its rounded smoothness beneath his fingers. They passed lines of stooks, stretched across the stubble fields, the grey-green surfaces of cleared hay-fields, the tall dark green stalks of the growing corn. In the full heat of the August afternoon, the landscape lay tranquil and silent.

They came then to the back pasture, where the black and white cows were chewing their cuds in the shade of the hickory trees. "Better get a stick," said Tom. "We'll need one to steer her along the creek."

They each selected a long stick, and then went on to the bank of the narrow winding stream which cut diagonally across the pasture.

"The bridge'll be the best place to launch her," said Tom.

They walked along the bank until they came to the home-made plank bridge, slung across the creek so that the cows might cross from one section of the pasture to the other.

Gerald held out the boat. "You launch her," he said.

"No, you do it! Just lean over the water and give her a little push."

The boy knelt on the planks, holding the boat as if it were made of thin glass, then leaned over and let it slide into the water. Its bow dipped for a moment: then it began to glide smoothly forward in the current.

The man and the boy, one on each side of the creek, followed the course of the boat as it nosed its way downstream towards the river. Most of the time it ran freely, but occasionally it was caught by a water-weed. When this happened, the sticks came into play, and the boat was quickly dislodged and started onward again. Tom walked soberly on his side, but the boy danced along his bank, waving his stick in the air, cheering the *Good Hope* on. He imagined the boat now as a Spanish galleon, its crew lusting for gold and spices; now as the craft of Drake, seeking honour and wealth for the Virgin Queen; now as a pirate ship seen hull-down, laden with treasure and with Long John Silver numbered amongst its crew.

The creek broadened and ran more swiftly as it neared the broad river which marked the rear boundary of his uncle's farm. The boat began to move more rapidly, racing in the swift current. The boy's excitement grew, and he cheered the vessel on more loudly than ever. But suddenly, before they were aware of the danger, the boat was swept out into the current of the river itself. Swiftly it was drawn farther and farther from shore, beyond the reach of their outstretched sticks.

"Oh, Tom," the boy cried, "we've lost her."

"No, we haven't," said Tom. "I'll fetch her back." He had already pulled off his shoes and socks, and was rolling up his Sunday trousers above his knees. In less than a minute he had begun to wade out into the river.

The boy watched carefully as the man waded still farther out into the swift brown river. The water was up to his knees already, and he was not halfway to the *Good Hope*. In the boy's eyes now the proud three-master was only a tiny, bobbing brown speck. But Tom kept wading after it, yet farther out into the current, until the water was well up above his rolled trousers. It was around his waist now, and still the boat was out of reach. It seemed to the boy that at any moment Tom must lose his footing in the strong current.

"Come back, Tom!" he called. "Come back! Let the boat go!"

He was startled by the sound of his own voice in the tense silence of the afternoon, but if Tom heard the shout he paid no attention. Man and boat now were both beyond the boy's reach, and he stood helpless on the bank, his fists clenched and his face set.

Tom waded steadily on, in water which now almost reached his armpits. At last he grasped the boat and, turning, held it up triumphantly for Gerald to see.

But, as he held it aloft, he suddenly lurched forward, as if his foot had struck a submerged rock. For one long horrible moment it seemed that he must be swept away and be carried under the water, which, even in the glare of the hot summer sun, looked cold and dark and evil.

Then somehow the man recovered his balance and began to edge his way towards the shore, clutching the precious boat carefully against his chest.

Once he was safe again, Tom dried his clothes in the sunshine. "Don't say anything to your aunt about this," he said.

"Of course not," said the boy. "But weren't you scared, Tom?"

"Nothing to be scared of in a bit of water, is there?"

They took the boat up to the bridge again, and launched her as before. This time, however, they were more cautious, and took her out of the creek before she could reach the treacherous river.

The summer holidays had come to an end, and now the first term of a new school year was more than half over. Already Gerald was looking forward to the Christmas holidays, and hoping that Tom would be better by then and able to make him the sleigh he had promised.

For the hired man was very ill. His aunt wouldn't often let Gerald in to see him, but when he did get into Tom's room he was scared by the man's flushed cheeks and strangely bright eyes. His face had lost its round fullness, and was thin and drawn.

One evening in late November, an unseasonably mild day when the grey rain had washed the light covering of snow from the fields and had left them brown and bare, the boy was sitting at the supper table with his aunt and uncle. His aunt had just come down with a tray from Tom's room.

"A fine thing this is," she said sharply. "Me waiting hand and foot on a hired man every day. It's nearly two weeks now he's been stuck in bed. I've enough to do around here without playing the nurse all the time."

"How does he seem?" asked the uncle.

"Looks about the same to me. Still running a high fever, and he eats hardly enough to keep a sparrow alive."

"Doctor in today?"

"Yes. He didn't say much. More pills, and keep giving him lots of liquids till the fever goes down."

"Did he say anything about the hospital?"

"He said it would be better not to move him the way he is now, but he may have to if he's not improved in a day or two. I don't like the look of him, I can tell you. His eyes are so bright they fair frighten me."

The conversation went on, but the boy took no part in it.

He felt as lost and helpless as he had felt that day on the bank of the river.

Suddenly the door from upstairs opened, and the boy caught a quick terrifying glimpse of the hired man, his eyes wild, his nightshirt dangling grotesquely about his knees. Before Gerald could move or even speak, the hired man had run across the kitchen and had disappeared through the back door into the wet darkness.

All sense of living had fled from the boy, and he heard his aunt and uncle as if from a great distance.

"What . . . ?" said his aunt, in a curiously muffled voice. She looked helplessly towards her husband.

His uncle had jumped from his chair. "Delirious," he said. "It's the fever." His wife ran towards him, but he pushed her aside and followed the hired man into the night.

The boy had come to himself again. "I must go too," he said, starting for the door..

"Oh, no, you don't," said his aunt, seizing his arm and holding him with all her strength. "It's no place for a nine-year-old boy."

He stood staring at her furiously, his will hard set against hers. She let go of him, and then, in a soft, tired voice quite unlike her usual sharp tone, she said: "I know you want to help, but you'll only hinder. Your uncle will find him if he's to be found. Do your home-work and see how your uncle makes out."

Mechanically he cleared a place for his books and tried to concentrate on his home-work. His aunt was at the sink doing the dishes.

His uncle returned at last, alone, his soaked shirt plastered against his arms and back, the rain-water streaming from his black hair. "Not a trace of him," he said wearily. "I was too late to see which way he went, and it's pitch black out there. I've called all through the barns and about the garden, but there was no answer. Light a lantern for me, Esther."

"Are you going out again?"

"Yes. We can't leave him out on a night like this. I'll call some neighbours, too. Between us we might find him."

The boy watched and listened as his aunt lit the lantern and his uncle made the telephone calls. When he took the lantern and started for the door again, the boy asked, "May I come with you?"

"No, lad, it's no job for you. Get on with your home-work!"

He turned again to his books, but they meant nothing to him tonight. He kept straining his ears for a sound from outdoors, but heard nothing.

At ten o'clock, when there was still no sign of his uncle, his aunt sent him up to bed. He fled swiftly up the narrow stairs and undressed with quick, fumbling fingers. The dim light of the coal-oil lamp left shadowy, fear-filled corners in his small room. And then, propped against the small mirror of his pine dresser, he noticed the boat. He took it in his hands, blew out the lamp, and dived into the damp bed. He pulled the covers over his head, and hugged the smooth boat tightly to his chest.

They did not find Tom that night, nor the next day, Saturday. The rain had washed away his footprints: it was impossible to tell which way he had gone.

The men of the neighbourhood had split into two groups, one to search the fields and the patches of bushland, while the other, led by the boy's uncle, dragged the river.

His uncle forbade Gerald to join either group and warned him especially to stay away from the river. All day Saturday he wandered about the fields alone, clutching the boat.

Another night passed; Sunday dawned dull and clear. A slow, unceasing wind mourned around the house, and sent the branches of the elms into a melancholy dance. Again the boy slowly circled the fields, but he knew it was no use looking there and in spite of his uncle's warning drew closer and closer to the river.

He came to the pasture and to the creek where he and Tom had sailed the boat. In the grey light of the November afternoon he stood on the plank bridge where they had launched her, and looked towards the river. He could see his uncle and the three neighbours, dragging the dark water from an old rowboat.

Suddenly he heard a shout from the boat, and saw the seated men spring to their feet. They were hauling something from the water. They began to row toward the shore, and he ran down beside the bank of the creek to meet them. He stood on the shore of the river and waited, as he had waited when Tom waded after the boat. The men did not notice him, so intent were they on the object in the bottom of their boat.

The rowboat scraped to a halt, and the men began to lift out the drowned body of the hired man. The striped nightshirt still clung to the cold limbs.

Again the boy had that timeless sensation of paralysed helplessness. It was his uncle who broke the spell. As if he had realized for the first time that Gerald was there, he suddenly shouted, "What are you doing here? Didn't I tell you to stay away from the river? Get back to the house and stay there!"

The boy turned and ran stumbling along the bank of the creek. He did not stop until he came to the bridge. There he paused and looked back at the small group of men, still bending about the body of the hired man.

When he saw that he held in his hand the boat which the hired man had fashioned for him he fingered a little the smooth curves of her hull and felt her three tiny graceful masts. Then he lifted his arm and threw the *Good Hope* with all his strength down the stream towards the dark river.

BRIAN MOORE

BRIAN MOORE was born in Belfast, Northern Ireland, on September 25, 1921, and was educated at Saint Malachy's College, Belfast, and at the University of London. After service in World War II, he emigrated to Canada in 1948 and has subsequently made his permanent home in Montreal. For four years he was a reporter on the *Montreal Gazette* but he now makes the writing of fiction his full-time occupation. He was awarded a Guggenheim Fellowship in Creative Writing in 1951 and a Senior Arts Fellowship by the Canada Council for the year 1961-62.

Mr. Moore is the author of three novels and many short stories. His first novel, *Judith Hearne* (1955), received very favourable reviews on both sides of the Atlantic, and won The Authors' Club Award in Great Britain for the best first novel published during the year. The Canadian edition of *Judith Hearne,* published in 1956, won the Quebec Literary Competition first prize for the best work of fiction in English in a four-year period. His second novel, *The Feast of Lupercal* (1957) was equally well reviewed in the United Kingdom, the United States and Canada, and was chosen as one of the best novels of the year in several newspaper polls. *The Luck of Ginger Coffey* (1960), his third novel and the first with a Canadian setting, was also widely and favourably reviewed. His short stories have appeared in such magazines as *The Atlantic Monthly, The Cornhill, Transatlantic Review, Northern Review, The Tamarack Review* and *The Gentlemen's Quarterly.* His work has also been broadcast by both the CBC and the BBC.

Mr. Moore's fiction is distinguished by its sensitivity of style and feeling. He is fascinated by those who are in some way crippled or deprived, and must seek to survive in spite of their handicap or their limitations. The world he presents is often a bleak and narrow one, but it is made interesting by his obvious faith in man's tenacity and by his capacity to find comedy amid distress. The story which follows appeared first in *The Atlantic Monthly.*

Lion of the Afternoon

THE FOUR non-professionals in the men's dressing room wore blue blazers with white tin buttons in the lapels. On the buttons, like a profession of faith, were their names and the name of the Kiwanis branch they represented. All four stared at Tait when he and his partner walked in.

Jack Tait was an achondroplastic dwarf, twenty-four years old, with a handsome head and normal torso, but tiny arms and legs. His partner, Davis, was a melancholy young man, six feet six inches tall. They were billed as The Long And The Short Of It, and were to be paid twenty-five dollars for this afternoon's work.

As Tait squatted on his tiny legs to unzip his overshoes, a man wearing a magenta suit with silver lapels straightened up on the bench opposite and put a yellow balloon in his mouth. He blew the balloon into a long sausage shape until it reached across the aisle and gently patted Tait's brow. Tait looked up, smiling.

"Hi, Len. Haven't seen you around lately. Lots of work?"

Len let the yellow balloon deflate and stowed it carefully in his pocket. "Been up in Kwee-bek City," he said. His pronunciation of Quebec told the listening Kiwanians he was an American.

Tait stood on the bench, unbuckled his belt, and let his cut-down flannels fall, revealing thick, dwarfish thighs. "How was it there?" he asked.

"Great, just great," Len said. "I had this one-week guarantee, see? But after the first night, the manager comes in with a contract for a full month. That's the good thing about this act, the jokes don't count. Just blow and smile. You see, this was a French audience in Kwee-bek. Worse than here in Montreal. None of them speak English good."

"What club was it you were in?" one of the Kiwanians asked.

Len ignored the question. He turned to them politely. "You in the show today?" he asked.

Four faces smiled as one. "Yes," one said. "We're a barber-shop quartet."

"Matter of fact, we've been a regular feature at this crippled kids show for the last five years."

"Six years, Howie."

"Yes, by gosh, it has been six years, come to think of it, Frank."

"Say—what do you do with those balloons, anyway?"

Len obliged. He took a green balloon out, blew it up, then blew up a yellow one. Smaller balloons appeared and were inflated. With great dexterity, he began to bend and tie them. He held up a multicolored, balloon dachshund for the Kiwanians' edification.

"That's cute," one said.

The others nodded. But, sidelong, their eyes were on Tait. He had dressed himself in baggy check pants, yellow blouse, and a comically cut, tiny tailcoat. He opened a box of paints and began to make up his face, white cheeks, wide clown grin, and star-shaped dimples. Childishly, he hopped down from the bench and began to shoo the Kiwanians away from the center of the room. "Would you mind?" he asked, his face serious beneath the painted grin. Curious, not knowing whether to smirk or look grave, they obeyed, instinctively dressing them-selves against the wall in their quartet positions.

"Thanks, fellows," Tait said. He turned his back and walked with dwarfish toddle to the end of the room. Then he ran towards them, little legs flying. Up he went and over in a forward flip, his acrobat shoes thudding squarely on the bare boards.

The Kiwanians were surprised. Being a dwarf was enough, they felt. What they had seen, the fact that he did somersaults, somehow lowered their stature. They were not athletic.

Tait, loosening up, walked on his hands for a moment.

Then he did a standing somersault, leaping off the floorboards like a trained terrier in a dog act. His partner, meanwhile, began to dress himself in a Superman costume, a black and white suit of cotton tights which clung to his lumpy muscles like shrunken underwear. Dressed, he took out a pocket mirror and began to comb his pompadour of black hair into a series of mounting waves, designed to make him seem even taller. Tait relaxed, flexing his fingers. Len carefully concealed his folded balloons in the pockets of his magenta suit.

Someone knocked on the door. Tait went to open, reaching up childlike for the door-knob.

"Hello, Shorty," a woman's voice said. She looked over Tait's head into the room. "Haven't seen Arnoldi, have you?"

"No, Doris," Tait said.

"He was supposed to come in and help me," she said. "I'm all alone in that dressing room next door. Say—do me up, will you, Shorty?"

She turned her back to Tait, dropping her rose dressing gown, revealing long, black-meshed legs, black-spangled hips. Her costume lay open in a deep V all the way down her back. Tait reached up, grasped the material firmly at the opening, and quickly zipped it shut, black spangles blacking out white nakedness. The Kiwanians looked at the woman and then at the dwarf. It was an interesting speculation.

"Excuse me," a voice said.

"I'm sorry." Doris hastily pulled her dressing gown up and moved out into the corridor. The newcomer bowed graciously. He entered the dressing room. He wore a gray hopsack suit and a white clerical collar.

"Hello there, gentlemen," he said. "Everything going all right, I trust?"

The Kiwanians, restored like fish to a tank of water, swam up at once to greet the minister, handshaking, talking. Tait backed into a corner and did some knee bends. Then he bounced over in a somersault. The minister was interested.

"Hard work, eh?" he said. "Never could do that trick myself. Although I used to be a great man for gym. Yes."

"It takes a lot of practice," Tait said, stopping, looking serious.

"Keeps one wonderfully fit, though, doesn't it?" the minister decided. Then, slightly embarrassed—the little chap might take a remark of that sort amiss—he held up his hands for attention.

"Well, gentlemen," he said. "We have eight hundred crippled children waiting for us in our auditorium. They're all terribly thrilled and I'm sure we won't disappoint them. I say *we* because I'm afraid you'll have to put up with me as your master of ceremonies." He smiled headmasterishly. "Now, we'll start with Tommy Manners, one of our local entertainers. The children love his singsongs. And after he's warmed things up, we'll bring on our friends the clowns, here" —he gestured at Tait and David—"and then we'll follow with our singing quartet, and then the gentleman with the balloons, and finally, of course, the magician. Now, how does that strike everybody?"

"We're not a clown act," Davis said. "We're acrobats."

"Oh, I see." The minister looked at Tait. "I thought the little chap here. . . . ?"

"So, we're on second, then. Okay?" Tait asked, hurrying over the rough spot.

"Yes. If that's all right with you, gentlemen."

"But don't bring us on as acrobats neither," Davis warned. "Just leave the intro vague."

"I see," the minister said doubtfully.

As though on cue, a voice cried in the corridor. "Ready there, Reverend?"

The minister opened the door. Outside, a very fat man was buckling an accordion against his heavy paunch. He stared into the room, his eyes finding Tait at once. As he and the minister went off up the corridor, his voice could be heard, asking: "Who's the midget?"

The Kiwanians looked over at Tait. But Tait was using his eyebrow pencil, his clown face stony, unhearing.

A sound of accordion music drifted back from the stage. Then, gathering force, hundreds of childish voices faltered and followed the accordionist into a popular chorus. A tall man in evening clothes hurried into the dressing room, shutting the door, muting the singing sound. He took an empty pint bottle of whisky out of his tailcoat pocket, slid it under the bench, then opened a large trunk in the corner of the room. From the trunk he took a white, silk-lined cape, an opera hat, and a paper bouquet. He laid these on the bench. Then he removed several silk scarves, four metal containers, and a collapsible card table. He laid these on the bench too, placing them very close to Tait.

"Move over, Tiny Tim," he said.

Tait turned, eyebrow pencil poised, clown face white and hideous. "So you're drunk again, Arnoldi," he said. "Doris will love that."

Arnoldi aimed a mock blow at the dwarf's head. Tait jerked his head back. The eyebrow pencil smeared his cheek. He put the pencil down, then very deliberately scattered an armful of Arnoldi's scarves to the floor. He hopped off the bench, fleeing Arnoldi's anger.

"You little runt! So you tell Doris I'm drinking?"

Tait dodged his head out from behind his partner's thighs. "Tell her? She don't have to be Dunninger to find that out herself!"

"Arnoldi?" a woman cried.

"Here, here, stupid!" Arnoldi yelled, abandoning his pursuit of the dwarf.

Doris came in. She wore elaborate stage make-up and had removed her dressing gown. The Kiwanians watched her black-meshed legs and comely hips as she bent, picking up the scarves from the floor, folding them in a complicated layer arrangement. Arnoldi, ignoring her, carefully hid the paper bouquet in the pocket of his tailcoat.

"Acrobats?" a voice cried in the corridor. "Acrobats next!"

David stood up at once, his head higher than the naked light bulb in the centre of the room. He picked up a fake bar bell and signaled to Tait. Tait toddled across the room and they went out together, the long and the short of it. Single file they moved along the corridor, Tait close on his tall partner's heels to avoid having to push and tug at the church workers and Kiwanis officials who might not notice him, child-small in the crowd. In the wings they paused, waiting like wound-up toys.

"Look—about Arnoldi" Davis said. "I'll tell him to lay off you."

"Who asked you?" the dwarf said angrily. "Mind your own goddamn business."

Rebuffed, the tall man looked out at the footlights. Beside him, his tiny partner scuffed his feet, studying the stage for loose floorboards. Tommy Manners was finishing his act, the accordion shaking like a jelly cake on his huge paunch as he urged the children through a final chorus. He began to back towards the wings, panting like a tired dog, but the minister came out, leading him to the footlights for a bow, a long burst of applause.

When Manners finally backed off, his great rump bumped against Tait's forehead. He did not seem to notice, but stood sweating and happy as the minister hushed the children's applause and announced the next act. When the minister had finished, Davis stepped out into the lights, rolling the fake bar bell carefully in front of him. The children were silent, their eyes on the strong man.

At centre stage, Davis bent double, his melancholy face contorted, his big hands gripping the bar bell, trying to raise it up. He lifted it about a foot, then falsely collapsed, letting it sink back to the floorboards. In the darkness, beyond the foot-lights, the children watched. Spastics, polio victims, the congenitally deformed: all knew what it was like to be defeated by the physically difficult. They waited, with the patience of experience, as Davis tried a second time.

In the wings, Tait raised his arms above his head and came out on a handstand, the ridiculous tailcoat rucked up his back, his silly clothes a Catherine wheel of spinning color. Davis dropped the bar bell, ears pricked for laughter. It came. Tait, moving with an exaggerated, circus-dwarf swagger, walked to the centre stage, looked at the bar bell, rolled up his sleeves, picked the bar bell up, and twirled it above his head.

They were off then, off on a drum roll of laughter, into the hard work, the pratfalls, the somersaults, the running and the catching; awkward in spots when the adult hint of obscenity must be stripped from the routine, covering up by more outrageous antics than an adult audience would have stomached. And Tait, the children's favorite, commanded the stage. The curiosity, the smiles that met his every waking moment were assets now, turned to triumph by his willing acceptance of the dwarfish role. In the dark sea of the auditorium, the children's heads moved like weeds drawn back and forth by the tide of the tiny man's movements.

In front, close to the empty orchestra pit, were two rows of tightly ranged wheelchairs, attended by four white-uniformed nurses. In these chairs, mouthing and twitching soundlessly in an unpleasant parody of old age, the spastic children sat. When Tait, perched high on Davis' shoulders, fell thumping to the footlights for a final pratfall, nurses and children cowered back, on guard against familiar injury. But Tait bounded up, smiling, spat out a set of fake false teeth, waved at the cheering children, and went off on a handstand while the children made the auditorium shudder with their applause. Back he came to their frantic cheers, admired, a wonder man, the lion of the afternoon.

At the last bow, the hall lights bloomed and the minister stepped forward, hands raised in benediction on the cheering children. In the wings the Kiwanians waited, fussing with their bow ties, their minds already in close harmony as the acrobats passed them by. Tait lowered his head as he followed Davis along the crowded corridor. As always, he felt let down when, the act over, he was returned to normal stares. He dodged the patting hands of pleased officials, glad to reach the dressing-room peace.

The non-professionals had gone. The professionals had taken over. Doris and Arnoldi sat side by side on one bench while Len, the balloon blower, drank from a bottle of rye.

"How was it?" Doris asked, with an angry side glance at Arnoldi, who had seized the bottle.

"Kid stuff," Davis said. "They'll go for anything."

He sat down, tired Superman, on the bench beside Doris. Arnoldi drank, then passed the bottle to her with a malicious smile. Angrily, she took it, did not drink, but passed the bottle on to Davis. The tall man tilted it towards the ceiling as he drank, then lowering the bottle, leaned forward to hand it to Tait, who waited his turn, childlike, standing in front of the big people.

But Arnoldi, in a swift magician pass, flicked the bottle from Davis' fingers. "Not for the louse," Arnoldi said. "This stuff is for people."

"Go on, give him a drink," Len said.

"It's my booze," Arnoldi told him. "And I say no."

Tait turned away. He hopped onto the bench and began to scrub his clown face clean. Arnoldi put the bottle in his trunk and then he and Doris began moving their magic props into the corridor. Davis sat silent, his great head drooping, as he watched his tiny partner change into street clothes: windbreaker, ski cap, flannels.

"You in a hurry, Shorty?" he asked.

"Yes."

"Wait, and I'll come with you." He stood up, beginning to unbutton his Superman uniform.

"I don't want you. I got something to do downtown. I'll see you later at the hotel, okay?"

"Okay. See you later, Shorty."

Tait went into the corridor. "See you, Shorty," Doris said. He did not answer. He went down the fire escape stairs to avoid the crowd and emerged at the back of the auditorium, pausing to look up at the stage where the Kiwanians rocked in humming unison. Moving behind the rows of watching children, Tait came to a door marked EXIT. He opened it and entered an ill-lit stone corridor, leading to the street.

"Wait! Where are you going?"

Tait turned. A woman, a tall woman wearing glasses, held the door open, calling him. She came out and put her hand on his shoulder. "Looking for the washroom?"

"No," Tait said. "I'm leaving."

She tightened her grip, guiding him further down the corridor. She opened a door. "Wait here a moment," she said. "I have something for you."

Tait allowed himself to be pushed inside. He looked up at her face, wondering. She couldn't be that shortsighted. But then he saw the other small figure in the room and decided that with these particular children she might be excused her ignorance.

"Now, just wait here," she said. "I have to go and get it."

She shut the door. The small boy swung around stiffly to face Tait. His left leg was a withered miniature, supported by a heavy, stilt-like, iron brace. His features were bloated and coarse.

"I got a little car in mine," he said.

Tait stared at him for a moment. Then asked: "Did you see the show?"

"No, I got sick," the boy said. "Did you get sick too?"

"I was in the show."

"Stupid," the boy said. "Only grown-ups are in the show."

"Well, I'm—look, I can do a somersault," Tait said, and did.

The boy watched him somberly. Then sat down, stiff-legged, on the floor. It was obvious he had difficulty in standing up. Tait felt embarrassed.

"I can crack my knuckles," the boy said. He pulled at his fingers.

Tait squatted on the floor beside him. He took the boy's hand. "You have strong fingers," he said.

"Want to feel my grip?"

They gripped hands and the boy squeezed. Tait made a grimace.

"You have big hands yourself," the boy said. "You should practice a grip like mine."

"I will," Tait said, seriously.

When the woman came back they were sitting on the floor, looking over the contents of the boy's gift package. She handed Tait a cardboard box, wrapped in green tissue paper. "Now, this is yours," she said. "You can play with it here until the others are ready to go home. It won't be long." She smiled at them. Tait kept his head down so that she only saw the top of his ski cap. When she had gone, he unwrapped the green package. Inside were a small rubber ball, a paper hat, a bag of candy, and a small metal automobile.

"Your car is better than mine," the boy said.

"Here." Tait held it out. "You can have it."

The puffy white face turned to stare. The weak eyes watered. Slowly, unsure of himself, the boy reached out and took the metal car.

"You can have the other junk too," Tait said. "Except the ball."

"My name is Kenny," the boy said, watching Tait.

"Mine's Sh—Jack."

"You're sure you don't want this stuff then. Only the ball?"

"Yes, just the ball," Tait said. He put the ball in his pocket and picked up his club bag. The iron leg brace made a scraping sound on the floor as the boy turned, white, coarse face tilting upwards. The boy said, "Why are you going away?"

"I better," Tait said. "I'm not supposed to be here. So long, Kenny."

"So long. Thanks for the car and stuff."

"That's okay."

In the corridor outside three women were talking, their backs to Tait. They wore armbands marked OFFICIAL. Tait moved down the corridor in rubber-soled silence. He reached a steel door marked EXIT TO STREET. Opening it, he found himself at the top of a flight of steps. It was snowing and the street lamps were lit. Across the street, a line of school buses waited for the children.

Tait paused at the head of the steps. He took out the rubber ball and looked at it again. It was like the one he had owned as a boy. The snow-whitened steps, the waiting school bus, the rubber ball: they touched on memories of his childhood.

He thought of the cripple on the floor. Remembered the iron brace, the tiny, withered leg. Did the leg never grow? It must be funny to be a cripple. How did they get in and out of bed, for instance? What happened to them if they fell in a lonely place and no one could hear them? Did women shrink from that tiny, withered leg?

Above him, the snow clouds had blackened to night. Like a baseball pitcher he wound his arm and skied the ball high into the darkness above. It fell, faraway, beyond the street lamps. Gaily, Tait ran down the steps.

HENRY KREISEL

HENRY KREISEL was born in Vienna in 1922, and left Austria in 1938. From 1938 to 1940 he lived in England, but was interned and sent to Canada soon after the outbreak of war. After his release from internment in 1941, he entered the University of Toronto and eventually earned the degrees of B.A. and M.A. Since 1947, with an interval of two years (1952-1954) during which he earned the doctorate at the University of London, he has been a member of the Department of English at the University of Alberta. In 1961 he was appointed head of that department.

Dr. Kreisel has published one novel, *The Rich Man* (1948), and short stories and articles in *The Tamarack Review, Queen's Quarterly, Prism, The Canadian Forum* and the *University of Toronto Quarterly*. Some of the stories have been translated into Italian and German, and one story, "The Travelling Nude", published in *Prism,* was awarded the President's Medal for the best Canadian short story of 1959.

Dr. Kreisel is particularly interested in the problems and tensions that beset immigrants to Canada, and in the relations of these immigrants to the lands from which they came. He writes of these persons always with a mixture of warm sympathy and ironic detachment, and has a quick eye for the revealing detail of mannerism or gesture. The story which follows appeared first in *Queen's Quarterly*.

Two Sisters in Geneva

IT HAD BEEN RAINING all day. Once or twice it had looked as if the rain might let up, and Warren had paid for his coffee and gone out into the street, but the sky was leaden and the rain never stopped at all. That's how it was in Geneva, a waitress told him when he sought refuge again and ordered a glass of beer, once it started to rain like this, it just wouldn't stop for two days or maybe three.

Warren was on his way from Italy to England. He could only stay a day in Geneva and he'd hoped to be able to take a little trip on the Lake, but that was out of the question. In spite of the rain, however, he tried to see as much as he could of the city which John Calvin had made famous, and where the League of Nations had debated in vain. For Warren was studying history at Oxford.

His train left at midnight. By ten o'clock he was tired and wet and worn out and he walked to the station and went into the waiting-room. There were a lot of people there already. The air was damp and steamy-smelling. He sat down beside an old man who was stuffing newspaper into his shoes. The old man said something in French, but Warren couldn't understand him and merely nodded pleasantly, and then pulled a pocket-book out of his over-night bag and started reading. After a while the old man got up with a weary sigh and left, and as he opened the door of the waiting-room two elderly ladies were coming in, followed by a porter carrying their suitcases. The old man held the door open for them, smiling gallantly. The smaller one of the two pushed past him without seeming to notice him, but the other one, who was quite tall and was wearing a broad-brimmed black Italian straw hat, stopped and smiled at him. They exchanged a few words, and then the old man left and closed the door behind him.

"There's room over there," said the smaller of the two ladies. "Over there, Emily."

She walked over and sat down beside Warren. One of the suitcases, Warren noticed, had Canadian Pacific Steamship labels. She took off her felt hat and then her raincoat, and spread her raincoat over on of the suitcases. Then she straightened her beige cardigan and leaned back against the bench. When the other lady joined her she said, "You should take your hat and coat off, Emily. You're all wet. You don't

want to come to England and first thing you know you'll have
to go to bed with pneumonia."

"I'm tired," the other one said. "I feel almost as if I had
pneumonia already." She talked very slowly and her voice
was low and had, thought Warren, a melodious, Italian
rhythm. As she talked, she pulled a long pin out of her hair
and took the straw hat off. She had black hair, gathered
together at the back of her head in a bun. Now that he could
see her face plainly, Warren noticed how pale she was.

"I tell you what, Emily. You better go and get something
to drink over in the restaurant. Something hot. A cup of tea
will do you good. You go and I'll look after the luggage. And
then you come back and I'll go. How'll that be?"

"Yes. That will be fine."

"Have you got enough money?"

"Yes, I think so."

"Well, here is some more." She pulled out a purse from her
handbag. "Here. This is Swiss money, I think. Yes, it is. All
this foreign money!" she exclaimed. "Liras! Francs! It gets a
person all confused."

"Ah, well," said the other one. "It's not foreign money to
the people who live here." She got up and walked out of the
waiting-room.

Warren read a few pages, but he was always conscious of
the woman sitting beside him. She fidgeted about on the
bench and kept looking over to him, and at last she said, "Oh,
you're reading an English book. Then you speak English."

"Yes," said Warren. "I'm a Canadian."

"Are you now, really," she exclaimed. "Well, what a
coincidence. I'm from Canada myself. What part of the
country do you come from?"

"Toronto," he said.

"How nice," she said. "I live in the West myself. In
Edmonton now. But we used to live up in the North. In the
Peace River country. Oh, it's wonderful country, it is. Mr.
Miller—that's my husband—he got land up there after the
first war, and we homesteaded there. We lived up there for

thirty-three years. Until my husband died. Two years ago it is nearly. Well, there wasn't much point me staying there alone. My son and my daughter were gone, so I sold the farm and the car and moved down to the city and got a place not far from my daughter. Thank God Mr. Miller left me well provided for."

"Yes," mumbled Warren. "That's fortunate."

"Oh, he was a good man," said Mrs. Miller. "I met him in England during the war. He was stationed in Yorkshire near where we lived, and we had a real whirlwind romance." She smiled, remembering. "Homesteading sounded very romantic, then. But it wasn't let me tell you. Irene, my first child, why, she was born during a blizzard in January and you couldn't get a doctor for love nor money. Even if there'd been one nearby. Which there wasn't. Oh, but Mr. Miller—he wasn't scared. Not much, anyways. He helped right along as if he'd been a midwife all his life. She was born all right. As healthy a baby as you'd ever want to see. Oh, it was backbreaking work, all right, but we made out. Had good years and bad years. It's the good times you really remember, though. And in the end, Mr. Miller left me very well provided for. I thank God for that. . . . Stomach. That was always his trouble. It kept getting worse and worse, and finally he died of it."

"I'm sorry," said Warren.

"Isn't that rain awful?" she said. "Still, it's better than that awful heat in Italy. Oh, I couldn't stand that heat. I nearly died of it. I don't know how my sister stood it all these years. I'm trying to persuade her to come and live with me in Canada."

"Is the other lady your sister?" Warren asked, for he would not have thought it.

"Yes," said Mrs. Miller. "Yes. We don't look much alike, do we? She's the Eyetalian branch of the family." Mrs. Miller gave a little high-pitched laugh. "I'd never have believed that Emily would up and marry an Eyetalian. That was after I'd left for Canada. It must have been—oh— about 1920. My brother Ronald wrote to me and said Emily'd married an

Eyetalian and had gone to live in Italy. Well, you could have knocked me down with a feather. Fancy that, I thought. Our Emily an Eyetalian! She'd met him in London, where she'd gone to work after the war. He was a painter, like—an artist. I don't think they ever had much money, and he didn't leave her hardly anything when he died. She's just got enough to live in a furnished room, you know. I was a bit shocked when I saw how she has to live, poor thing. I thought she'd at least have a house. But he didn't leave much. I thank God Mr. Miller left me well provided for. I bought a little house in Edmonton and she'd be most welcome to come and live with me."

"Is she going with you to Canada now?" asked Warren.

"Not just now," said Mrs. Miller. "I only managed to talk her into coming to see the family in England. We've got two sisters and two brothers living in Yorkshire and this'll be the first time in—" she stopped for a moment and calculated silently—"in thirty-six years that we'll all be together. She's never been back in all that time, and neither have I. Only it'd've been easier for her to go back. She had no children and it's not so far. Oh, but I'm sure she'll come and live with me now. There's nothing to keep her in Italy that I can see, and here she'd be with her own flesh and blood. Wouldn't you think it stands to reason?"

"It seems like it," said Warren.

"Where are you coming from now?" asked Mrs. Miller.

"Well, I've just been to Italy, too," he said.

"Oh, have you? Did you go to Florence?"

"Yes," he said, "as a matter of fact, I did."

"Fancy that," said Mrs. Miller. "I might have seen you there. I just spent two weeks there. That's where my sister lives."

"Lovely city," said Warren, but he saw Mrs. Miller shake her head skeptically, and asked, "Didn't you like Florence?"

"Well," she said, "I can't say I really did. Now, mind you, there are some nice things there, all right. I wouldn't deny that. Statues and fountains and churches, like. And my sister took me through some of the museums they have there and I saw some very pretty pictures. But it's all a bit too Papish for me, if you want the truth." She stopped short and looked sharply at Warren. "You're not a Catholic by any chance?"

"No," said Warren, smiling. "Old Presbyterian stock."

"Oh, that's good," she said. "Not that I have anything against Catholics, God forbid. I believe in each person believing as he wants to. But still I must say some of those statues they have—and right out in the open, too—well, I wouldn't have liked it if my daughter had seen them when she was a young girl. And then the heat, too. Oh, it did affect me. But it's a nice enough city otherwise. I'll be glad when I get back to a place where you can understand what people are saying, though. It's a weird feeling hearing people jabbering away and you not understanding a word they're saying."

Neither Warren nor Mrs. Miller noticed her opening the door to the waiting-room, so that she seemed suddenly to be standing there before them.

"Oh, Emily," said Mrs. Miller. "You're back. Did you have some tea?"

"As a matter of fact," she answered, and Warren thought that her eyes glinted ironically, "I had some brandy. It's better than tea."

"Oh, well," said Mrs. Miller tolerantly. "Once in a while it's all right. That's what my husband always used to say. But he never held with drinking. Oh, Emily. There's a young Canadian gentleman here. Mr.—"

"Douglas," he said. "Warren Douglas."

"Mr. Douglas. And that's my sister. Mrs. Emily Bun— . . . Bun— . . . Oh, I never can remember how to pronounce that name."

"Buonarroti. Emilia Buonarroti."

"Well, I never can get over it," said Mrs. Miller. "It never does sound like our Emily."

Mrs. Buonarroti sat down and, turning to Warren, she said quietly, "Buonarroti was the family name of the great Michelangelo. My husband belonged to a branch of the same family." She had taken off her coat, and Warren saw that she was wearing a black silk dress which looked very old-fashioned.

"I think I'll go off and have a cup of tea myself," said Mrs. Miller. "If you'll excuse me."

Warren watched her walk out of the waiting-room. Her shoes were sturdy and new, and she wore a good worsted skirt and beige cardigan over a frilly white blouse.

"You are a student?" said Mrs. Buonarroti.

"Yes," said Warren. "How did you know?"

"My husband taught for many years. The history of Renaissance art—that was his subject. So I knew many students. All students look alike," she said and smiled at him.

"That's very interesting," he said. "Your husband being a scholar, I mean. I thought he was a painter. I mean, that's what your sister said."

"Oh, yes, he painted, too," she said. "But he was not a professional painter. He was a good painter, but not a professional painter." She sat there thinking for a while, and then she said, "My husband was a very interesting man. And to live with him was, yes, a great privilege. You know, Mr. Douglas, I was an ignorant girl when I married, and my husband taught me such a lot. Of course, when you live in Firenze—in Florence—you have to learn something. Art, religion, history—it is all preserved around you."

"I am reading history now at Oxford," Warren said.

"But my sister said you are from Canada."

"I am, but I am studying at Oxford."

"It is strange speaking English again after so many years. I hardly talked English at all for years and years, and when my sister came, I could hardly speak it any more. I had to practice first." She laughed. "My husband could speak English, but after the first year or two we always talked in Italian. . . . He was a wonderful man—my husband. But the war—it was too much for him. He was never too strong, and it was hard to get the right kind of food and in the winter you could never get enough coal. It was too much for him. He died only a few weeks before the end of the war." She began to cough, at first lightly, and then more violently, until her whole body trembled and Warren was quite concerned.

"Is there—is there anything I can get you?" he stammered, not knowing what to do.

She shook her head and gradually she stopped coughing. "I'm sorry," she said. "It's this terrible rain and this dampness. I can't stand all this wet. As soon as we left Italy I began to feel it, you know. Perhaps I was only imagining things at first, but as soon as we came to Geneva it was very real. I hate rain and dull, cloudy skies. And this is all just a foretaste of what it will be like in England. Gray skies and rain and rain and rain." She shuddered. "And what will I say to them all when I am in England? To my brothers and sisters?" She seemed for a moment to be talking to herself alone, for she dropped her voice and her eyes looked across the waiting-room in the direction of the station restaurant where Mrs. Miller would now be drinking her tea.

She turned again to Warren. "We have been living in different worlds," she said. "Much too different. My sister is such a good woman. So kind and so well-meaning. But after two days, Mr. Douglas—well, we didn't have anything to say to each other. She told me about how they built their farm, and about blizzards, and how her children were born, and how they became well off, and I—well, I tried to show her Florence, and I'll never forget how shocked she was when I took her to the Piazza della Signoria and she saw in the Loggia statues of nude figures—famous works by Cellini and Giambologna. It was quite funny, really, but also sad. And it will be the same thing when I meet the others. It will rain and we will all be crowded together in a room and I will long to go back home to Italy. I wish now I was waiting for a train to take me back to Florence. . . . Do you know Italy, Mr. Douglas?"

"A little," he said. "I've just been in Florence and Venice. I love them both, but especially Venice."

Mrs. Buonarroti turned her pale face to him and looked

musingly at him. "Yes," she said. "Yes. At first it is always Venice. In Venice everything is out in the open, and you—you are so—so—well. . . ."

"Overwhelmed." Warren supplied the word.

"Yes," said Mrs. Buonarroti. "Overwhelmed. Your eyes cannot take it all in at once. But Florence opens herself only slowly, until you see her full beauty. My husband didn't like Venice. Not enough secrets, he said. Of course, he was a Florentine, and that explains a lot. But really there is nothing in the world that is so beautiful as to look down at Florence from Fiesole just when the sun goes down, and to see the hills and the mountains and the cypress trees and the wonderful city in the plain. Nothing."

"You will miss all this," said Warren, "if you go to Canada."

She looked at him quickly. "To Canada? Why should I go to Canada?"

"Oh, but Mrs. Miller—your sister. . . ."

Mrs. Buonarroti shrugged her shoulders and smiled. "My sister is such a kind person," she said, "but she doesn't understand. From the room where I live I can look out and see the wonderful campanile, and I can walk along the Arno, and once a week I take a bus to Fiesole. Florence is my city, Mr. Douglas. . . . I don't know whether you understand."

"I think I do," said Warren.

"To live in a strange land and in a strange city with my sister would be—well, not exactly like the Inferno, but like Purgatorio."

They both laughed.

A minute or two afterwards Mrs. Miller returned.

"Well," she said, "that was nice and hot. Mind you, they don't know how to make a cup of tea here. Or in Italy. The water's never boiling when they pour it. That's the trouble." She turned to her sister. "Well, I hope the young gentleman's been telling you all about Canada."

"I'm afraid Mrs. Buonarroti has been telling me about Italy," said Warren.

"I knew it," said Mrs. Miller. "Emily does love talking about Italy. Oh, well. You just wait till you see the wide-open prairie, Emily, and the Rocky Mountains. Once you live there, you'll never again want to live anywhere else. I know I wouldn't. Why, I couldn't live in England again, let alone in Italy. Everything's all crammed together so."

Just then Mrs. Buonarroti began to cough and she had to get up to catch her breath. Warren and Mrs. Miller both jumped up and supported her, and after a while the fit subsided and she sat down on the bench, exhausted.

"The dry climate out West will do her the world of good," said Mrs. Miller to Warren. "It will clear this up in no time."

Over the public address system there came an announcement. The express to Paris and Calais was arriving.

"That's our train," said Warren. "Should I go and get a porter?"

Mrs. Miller nodded.

When she returned with the porter, the ladies put on their coats and hats. Mrs. Buonarroti took hold of Warren's arm and they walked out on to the platform. The rain was still coming down in steady, thin strings.

"How I hate this rain," said Mrs. Buonarroti, speaking very softly, "and how I wish I was back in Florence."

JACK LUDWIG

JACK LUDWIG was born in Winnipeg on August 30, 1922, and was educated at the University of Manitoba, receiving the degree of B.A. in 1944. He then proceeded to the University of California at Los Angeles and completed a Ph.D. in English Literature. He has lectured at Williams College, Bard College and the University of Minnesota, and in 1961 accepted an appointment as professor of English in the Graduate Division of the new State University of New York, Long Island Centre. He is a co-founder and co-editor of the periodical, *The Noble Savage*.

Mr. Ludwig's stories have appeared in *The Noble Savage, The Tamarack Review, The Atlantic Monthly* and in several anthologies: Robert Weaver's *Ten for Wednesday Night* (1961), Martha Foley's *The Best American Short Stories of 1961*, and *The O. Henry Prize Stories, 1961*. He received an "Atlantic First" award for "Requiem for Bibul" and a Longview Foundation Award for "Thoreau in California". He has completed a novel which is scheduled for publication in 1962.

The story which follows was read over CBC "Wednesday Night", published in Robert Weaver's *Ten for Wednesday Night* and, in a slightly different form, in *The Atlantic Monthly*.

Requiem for Bibul

ONCE UPON A TIME—if we counted time not by calendars but by assimilated history and scientific change I'd be tempted to say four or five thousand years ago: before total war and all-out war, before death camps, Nagasaki, before fusion and fission, jets, moon shots, cosmonauts, Luniks in orbit, before antibiotics, polio vaccine, open-heart surgery, before TV, garburators and other wonders of automation, before dead-faced hoods on motorcycles, dead-faced beatniks on malde-cycles—once upon *that* kind of time lived a boy and his horse.

The year was 1939. This is no pastoral tale. The boy and the horse are both dead.

Twenty years late, counting time by the calendar, I write you of this boy Bibul and his horse Malkeh, of Bibul's ambition and his sad sad end. In time-sorrowed perspective I record for you the imprint Bibul left on my mind and feeling—his tic-like blink, his coal-black hair in bangs over his fore-head, his emerycloth shaver's shadow, his ink-stained mouth, his immutable clothes that wouldn't conform to style or the seasons: always black denim Relief-style pants whitened by wear and washing, always a brown pebbled cardigan coiled at the wrists and elbows with unravelled wool, always a leather cap with bent visor, split seams, matching the colour and texture of Bibul's hair. And old ruined Malkeh, scorned before lamented, making her daily round under Bibul's urging, dragging his creak of a fruit-peddler's wagon through Winni-peg's "island" slum north of the Canadian Pacific Railway Yards.

Bibul peddled while my time burned: in 1939 all of us high-school boys owlish with sixteen- and seventeen-year-old speculation, almost missed seeing this B i b u l foxy with world-weary finagling. We were out to save the world, Bibul a buck. Hip-deep in reality, trying to beat tricky suppliers, weasely competitors, haggling customers, Bibul couldn't believe in us vaguesters. Peddling had forced him to see, hear, and judge everything. By his practical measure we were simply unreal. We'd speculate: Bibul would respond with *yeh-yeh* —the Yiddish double affirmative that makes a negative. He didn't have to say a word, or raise a sceptical eyebrow, or even frown with that tic. His smell alone argued a reality out of reach of our politely neutral Lux, Lifebuoy, Vitalis middle-class sweetness: "effluvium Bibul" we called that mixture of squashed berries, bad turnips, dank pine applecrates, straw, chickens, sad old horsey Malkeh. Bibul had a grand gesture to sweep away our irrelevance, a sudden movement of the

hand like a farmwife's throwing feed to chickens, his nose
sniffing disgust, his sour mouth giving out a squelching sound,
"aaaa." Sometimes he sounded like a goat, other time a baby
lamb—just "aaaa," but enough to murder our pushy preten-
tions.

We were a roomful of competitive sharks—math sharks,
physics sharks, English, Latin, history sharks, secretly, often
openly, sure we surpassed our teachers in brain and know-how.
Joyfully arrogant we shook off the restricting label of high-
school student, considering ourselves pros—mathematicians,
scientists, writers, artists. In our own minds we had already
graduated from the University, had passed through Toronto or
Oxford, were entangled in public controversies with the great
names in our respective fields, ending right but humble,
modestly triumphant. But where was Bibul in this league? As
loud as we pros hollered Bibul heard nothing. He only yawned,
slouched, even snoozed, gave out with that killing *yeh-yeh*,
poked his greyish nose into his peddler's notebook red with
reality's ooze of tomato.

"Bibul," we'd say in the break between classes, "do sem-
antics mean nothing to your knucklehead? An intellectual
revolution's coming. You've got to stand up and be counted.
What'll it be? Are you *for* Count Korzybski or against him?"

"Aaaa," aaed Bibul, and his chicken-feeding motion sent
us back to ivory towers.

"You' nuddin' bud gids," he'd say haughtily whenever we
disturbed his audit of fruit-and-vegetable reality, "a 'ell of a
lod you guys know aboud live."

Though we jeered and mocked, treated him like a clown,
he was one of us, so how could we disown him? Kings of St.
John's High, lording it from our third-floor eminence over
the giants and dwarfs living the underground life in the
school's basement ascreech with whirling lathes and milling
machines, or those second-floor, salt-of-the-earth commercial
students dedicated to bookkeeping, typing, the sensible life,
we of course wanted to pass our nobility on to Bibul. We ran
the yearbook and could have established him there—but on

the "island" English ran a poor second to Ukrainian, Polish, German, or in his case, Hebrew. We could have made him captain of the debating team, but peddling wrecked that: wrought up he stammered, angry he slobbered, no way to win arguments. Being a businessman, like his breed he had no time for politics; being tone-deaf he was a flop at glee-club try-outs. At sports he was dreadful. He couldn't swim a stroke, or skate, was flubbyknuckled at baseball, slashingly pigeon-toed at soccer, truly kamikaze going over a hurdle. And women? He had no time for them in his practical life: his old mare Malkeh and the ladies who haggled with him were the only females Bibul knew.

In recognition of his memo-book involvement we made Bibul our room treasurer.

After classes we theoreticians sprawled on the school green and took pleasure from long-limbed, heavy-thighed, large-breasted girls thwarting an educator's pious wish that the serge tunic neutralize the female form. Bibul was never with us. At the closing bell he'd run off to his horse and wagon, set to run the gauntlet of his customers (*shnorrers,* pigs he called them); and early on a morning, when we theoreticians-turned-lover, weary after a long night of girl-gaming, sat in Street Railway waiting houses knocking ourselves out over noisy reading of Panurge's adventure with the Lady of Paris, Bibul, up and dressed since 4:00 a.m., struggled at the Fruit Row for bruised fruit and battered vegetables in competition with wizened peddlers and their muscular sons.

Lost in abstraction, and me, I thought little of Bibul in those days. He was a clown. A mark. A butt. The peddling was part of the sad desperate struggle for money every family in the depression knew. Bibul was the eldest of four children, his widowed ma supporting them on what she could make out of a tiny grocery store, doing the best she could, the dear lady, known throughout the "island" as "The Golden Thumb" and the "Adder," the latter reference ambiguous, meaning either snakes or computation, Bibul's ma being famous for a mathematical theorem that said $5 + 6 = 12$ or 13, whichever was higher.

Not till the year of our graduation did I discover why Bibul peddled with such dedication, why he rode out like a teen-age Don Quixote to do battle with those abusive, haggling, thieving *shnorrers*.

And what a riding-out that was! His paintless wagon listed like a sinking ship, sounded like resinless fiddles in the hands of apes, each wheel a circle successfully squared. Bibul sat on a tatter of leatherette bulging at the ends like a horsehair creampuff; over his wilted greens and culled fruit Bibul's faultless-in-his-favour scales made judgment, his battered tin scoop more dented than a tin B-B target. And what was more fitting than a nag like Malkeh to drag that crumbling wagon on its progress?

As grim as Don Quixote's Rosinante would look next to elegant Pegasus, that's how Malkeh would have looked next to Rosinante: she was U-shaped in side view, as if permanently crippled by the world's fattest knight lugging the world's heaviest armour. She sagged like a collapsed sofa with stuffing hanging low. She was bare as buffed mohair, her shoulders tanned from the rub of reins, her colour an unbelievable combination of rust, maroon, purple, bronze, found elsewhere only in ancient sun-drenched velvets. Her tail was a Gibson Girl's worn discarded feather boa, its fly-discouraging movements ritualistic, perfunctory, more to let flies know that Malkeh wasn't dead than that she was alive. Her legs, like a badly carpentered table, were of assorted lengths, which made Malkeh move by shuffling off like a pair of aged soft-shoe dancers in a final farewell. Her hooves were fringed with fuzzy hairs like a frayed fiddle-bow abandoned to rain and sun, her horseshoes dime-thin, rusty as the metal hinges on her wagon's tail-gate. To encourage Malkeh to see Bibul covered her almost-blind eyes with a pair of snappy black racing-horse blinkers trimmed with shiny silver rivets, a touch to her decor like a monocle in the eye of a Bowery bum.

Out of compassion, out of loyalty to this wreck of a horse,

Bibul let his wagon go to ruin: wood could be camouflaged with paint or varnish but where was covering to hide or revive sad old mortal Malkeh?

One day I came to school early, and saw her.

She was the horse version of "The Dying Gaul." On Bibul's "island" Malkeh suffered no invidious comparisons, but on a main thoroughfare like St. John's High's Salter Street Malkeh was exposed to the cruelty of horse hierarchy, and her sub-marginal subproletariat hide was bared. High-stepping, glossy-flanked, curried and combed T. Eaton Company horses, middle-class cousins of aristocratic thoroughbreds seen only on race tracks, veered their rumps sharply as they passed, hooves steelringing, traces white as snow. Their tails were prinked out with red ribbon, their wagons chariots sparkling in red, white, gold against blue-blackness that could mean only good taste. These bourgeois horses had the true bourgeois comforts—warm blankets, stables with hay wall-to-wall, feed-bags that offered privacy and nourishment. Their drivers looked like sea-captains, neat contrast to a slop like Bibul. And their commercial feed was gastronomical compared with the bad lettuce, wilted carrot tops, shrivelled beets Bibul shoved at Malkeh in a ripped old postman's pouch.

Malkeh took their snubs without flinching. It was part of the class struggle. What hurt was the heavy powerful working-class Percherons and their stinking garbage scows, when *they* avoided kinship with Malkeh, acting like a guest at a high-toned party ignoring a waiter who's a close relative.

Pity old Malkeh's vengeful heart: the only pleasure she got from her enforced station on Salter Street came from knowing flies used her as an aerodrome from which to launch vicious attacks on the elegant department-store horses passing.

I saw her. The Principal too saw her, slouched with resigna-tion, a "Don't" in an SPCA exhibit, her right foreleg flatteringly fettered by a cracked curling stone to give Malkeh the impression she had the vim and youth to turn runaway horse. Malkeh died a long time ago, but years before she did the Principal had her one visit gnomically memorialized and

graven in metal: early next morning, where Malkeh had stood,
this marker went up: "No Parking At Any Time."

Bibul never again brought her to school.

Which is not to say that life on the "island" was without
its grim side: what accounted for an almost-blind horse
wearing blinkers? *Shnorrers!* Those women with bare feet
stuck hurriedly into their husbands' outsize felt slippers, their
hair uncombed, faces unmade, women in nightgowns at four
on a sunshiny afternoon, hands clenching pennies and silver
Bibul had to charm away from them with hard-sell and soft-
soap. Singly they waited, in concert plotted, en masse moved
in on him. Their purpose was simple—*get much, pay little.*
To the victor went Bibul's spoiled spoils.

"Giddy ahb, Malgeh," Bibul would holler from his high
seat on the wagon, and his cry sounded to a *schnorrer's* ears
like a warring clarion.

Into the lists Malkeh dragged the keening wagon, onto the
"island" in ruins like a mediaeval town (Canadian history is
short but our buildings add spice by getting older faster).
Foundationless hovels kids might have built out of assorted-
sized decks of cards sagged, leaned at crazy-house angles to
astound Pisa. Gates tipsy as Malkeh's wagon swung on one
hinge from a last lost post; dry, cracking wood fences leaned
in surrender towards the ground, begging like old men in sight
of a grave to be allowed to fall the rest of the way; windows
were tarpaper-patched, like pirates' eyes, ominous as the
blackness left in the streets by uninsured fires.

Behind every window or screen opaque with dust, behind
every door splintered from kids' kicking waited the *schnorrers*,
trying to make Bibul anxious, make him sweat a little, a cinch
for persistent hagglers.

"Ebbles, ebbles, den boundz f'a quadder." Bibul shouted.

Crafty with stealth the *schnorrers* didn't bite.

Unflustered, unfooled, Bibul took advantage of the phony
war, biting off the only three unspotted cherries in his entire
stock while Malkeh dragged the exposed tin rims of the
wagonwheels into the frost heaves and back-lane crevices.

That cramped stinking back lane was mutually agreeable as a Compleat Battlefield—for Bibul because the solid pall of chicken droppings and horse dung was fine camouflage for the imperfections Time and Decay wrought his produce, for the *schnorrers* because the narrow quarters made tampering with the scale easier, detection harder, filching a hot possibility.

"Whoa beg, whoa der Malgeh," Bibul ordered, oblivious of the spying women.

There, among rusted bedsprings hung up like huge harps, torn mattresses resembling giant wads of steel wool, in a boneyard of Model T's, Malkeh and the wagon rested. Dogs scooted in darts of nervous yapping, cats hissed down from rust-streaked corrugated rooftops, pigeons wheeled high above Bibul's untroubled head, returning to perch on overhanging eaves like fans anxious to get close to a scene of scuffle.

The *schnorrers* tried to read Bibul's face: the text was that Sphinx-like tic of a blink. Stalling he made entries into that memo-book, peeled an orange, scratched himself with casual but maddening thoroughness.

The *schnorrers*' united front crumbled. A foot slipped out from behind a door. Then a head.

"Wha' you gonna cheat me on t'day, Bibul?" rasped out of an impatient throat.

The war was on! Horseflies, the depression having made pickings so sparse they dropped their high standards and declared Malkeh a host, left the depressing fare of uncovered garbage cans (each lid long ago commandeered to be targe in the minor-league jousts of the *schnorrers*' unknightly kids), and, hiding behind the *shnorrers* sneaking up to do Bibul battle, launched assault on old Malkeh's flat weak flanks.

The siege began, swiftly, deftly: a red-haired old woman flipped two-cent oranges into the one-cent bins, her other hand pointing up at the sky to make Bibul raise his eyes and predict weather.

Her accomplice brought Bibul back to reality, picking the bargains up before they'd even stopped rolling.

"Boyaboy Bibul, you god good tings in y'usually stinkin' stock, look here, Mrs. Gilfix, at such oranges."

Bibul's tic-like blink snapped like a camera shutter on their mischief.

"Give over here dem oniges," he reproved them, "*yoisher,* show a liddle resdraind," and the sad old innocents watched the two-cent numbers fall back into the two-cent bins.

On the other side of the wagon a pair of raspberry hands crushed away at lettuce greens.

"Hom much off f'damaged goods?" the criminal hollered, wiping lettuce juice on her gaping nightgown.

But the red-haired old woman hadn't given up on oranges.

"Black head means black heart, robber," she cried out. "Perls d'fruit man who has a white head and eight kids and supports two unmarried sisters in Russia, from *him* I get fresher cheaper by two coppers—ha come, ha? Ha come?"

"My oniges are Sundgizd, Blue Gooze," Bibul, a sucker for brand names, came back huffily, "Berls' oniges grow on ebble drees."

One man's quarrel is another woman's smoke screen. The *schnorrers* moved in, squeezing the fruit, poking, tapping, complaining with shrieks and curses that sent the pigeon-hearted pigeons high off their perches. Like a bucket brigade the ladies passed fruit up and down the length of the wagon, each nose an inspector, those with teeth taking their duties more seriously, tasters whose opinions Bibul could live without.

"*Schnorrers* dad youz are," he hollered, holding up a nipped apple, a chewed-up orange, "you god no gare vor my brovids?"

"Look how he's independent," mocked the red-haired one, lunging fruitless after a fistful of cherries, "look how he holds hisself big! His fadder's a doctor, maybe? Or the mayor?"

Bibul was a lone guard defending his fortress from desperate pillagers; ubiquitous as Churchill, many-handed as Shiva, he had to be compassionate as Schweitzer. Though *I* didn't know what Bibul's dedication to peddling was all about, the *schnorrers* did: Bibul was saving up to become a Rabbi. Bibul immersed himself in the practical, pedestrian, material life because of a Great Cause—the Yeshiva in New York, eventual immersion in a spiritual life dedicated to comfort suffering mankind.

How the *schnorrers* used that Great Cause in their war with Bibul! It was all double: in sincerity they poured out their hearts to him—an educated boy, soon to be a Rabbi, maybe he'd understand *their* side—the husband who had taken off and never come back, the bad-hearted rich relatives, the ungrateful kids, the treacherous friends, root, trunk, branch of a Jewish Seven Deadly Sins. They dizzied him with complicated stories, unsettled his strong stomach with demonstrations of human frailty—missing teeth, crossed eyes, wens, tumours, needed operations.

As a bonus to sincerity they hoped the tales would divert Bibul long enough for their aprons to fill with filched fruit.

Crying real tears Bibul would free an apricot from a fist already stained with cherry.

"A religious you call yourself?" the caught thief howled. "God should strike me dead if I stole ever in my life one thing!"

Glancing up at the sky she moved closer to the other ladies: who knew what kind of pull with God a boy-studying-to-be-a-Rabbi had?

"Bibul, sveedhard," cooed one Mrs. Itzcher, blemished but bleached, "give off ten cents a dozen by oranges and Tillie'll show plenty appreciation."

Bibul used his chickenfeed gesture to ward off temptation.

The *schnorrers* prayed God to give Bibul good enough ears to hear their laments but to compensate with a little dimming of the eyes so he wouldn't catch them stealing. When they lost they cursed in tones loud enough to be heard above the world's fishwifery in action.

No wonder Bibul considered us sharks irrelevant. After those *schnorrers* poured it on what was left to be said?

"My brudder's second wibe's kid wid da hump in back, Rabbi Bibul, has already her third miscarriage."

In the midst of haggle they rained down proofs of suffering and absurdity—banged heads, cut knees, singed eyelashes, hands caught in wringers, slippery floors, broken steps, toppling ladders. The compensation they asked was meagre. Pity, a buy on a busted watermelon.

When we sharks, hot for culture, cool for Schoenberg, long on judgements, short on facts, turned our abstract expressions Bibul's way how else could he respond but with that "aaaa"? What did our books and ideas have to compete with a *shnorrer's* lament? Now when I think of that "aaaa" I translate it "When I was a child I spake as a child . . ." (may Bibul forgive me for quoting Saint Paul); "aaaa" said "vanity of vanities; all is vanity"; in explanation of the term for Mammon so that the rest would be with Abraham, Isaac, and Jacob; "aaaa" said "To everything there is a season, and a time to every purpose under the heaven."

On St. John's High School's Graduation Day Bibul was already at least half a Rabbi. The cardigan was gone, so too the denims and the black leather cap. He wore a fancy blue serge suit so new it still smelled of smoke. His sideburns were growing religiously into side curls, his emerycloth shadow was now a beardlike reality. But it was Bibul's eyes I remember, excited, gay, snapping under that tic. He looked incredibly happy.

"Bibul," I said seriously, "you look beautiful in that suit!"

"Damorra, Joe," he said low and secretive, "damorra I go d'Noo Yorick an' d'Yeshiva."

I talked to him without clowning. He told me what he wanted, explained the peddling.

"Bibul," I said as we were walking out to our waiting parents, "doesn't the idea of a city the size of New York scare you? You'll be strange. Winnipeg's a village—"

"Wadz t'be asgared?" Bibul said with that wave of his hand. "Beoble iz beoble. I zeen all ginds aready."

He told me he'd sold Malkeh to Perls the peddler. His mother walked proudly towards Bibul as we reached the street.

"Bibul," I shouted as parents came between us, "you'll be a terrific Rabbi! Good luck!"

He gave that chickenfeed flourish, but with new style, and with modesty.

"Aaaa," I heard above the shouting congratulations of parents, the last time I heard or saw Bibul.

That fall we sharks entered the University, and Canada the war. Winnipeg was transformed, full of aircrew trainees from places I knew about before only through postage stamps, men with yellow skins, red, brown, black, Maori tribesmen from New Zealand, bushmen from Australia, strange-sounding South Africans, carved-faced Indians thronging the streets and beer parlours. But far off in New York, Bibul, who had known war with the *shnorrers,* paid little attention to this latest struggle. He studied Torah and Talmud. He made his spending money selling fruit to Lower East Side *shnorrers* at the Essex Street Market.

Bibul's old Winnipeg customers haggled half-heartedly with old man Perls and old horse Malkeh, the one mercifully deaf, the other nearly blind. The depression seemed over: money came easier.

Once in a long while I checked in at Bibul's mother's store and, gleaning news of Bibul, let her weigh me up a light pound of corned beef. She wore her hair Buster Brown, carried a huge buxom body on little feet in grey-white tennis shoes.

She shoved a letter at me.

"Look how a educated boy writes?" she said, pugnaciously proud. "Who but a Rabbi could understand such words?"

She pulled it back before I could answer.

"See him only, just look," she pushed a picture at my eyes.

Bibul huddled against a bare Williamsburg wall grinning the same grin as the three other Bibuls in the picture, all of them bearded and wild as Russians, in black beaver hats bought with money they had earned tutoring the Americanized grandchildren of rich Chassidim.

"Some boy, my Bibul," his mother called to me as I was leaving.

Winter passed and the war grew grimmer. Spring was beautiful, the war more dreadful. Summer was hot, particularly in New York where Bibul divided his time between the Yeshiva and Essex Street's *shnorrers*. For days the temperature was in the high nineties. Bibul had never known such heat. He couldn't study, sleep, sell. In desperation he took himself one evening to the "Y," forgetting in the heat that he'd never learned to swim.

An attendant, going off duty, warned Bibul away, told him not to enter the pool. Who can be blind to Bibul's response?

"Aaaa," and that gesture.

He drowned.

His *shnorrers* on the "island," being told, wept and lamented. We sharks, even in the midst of war's casualties, were moved and stricken. Bibul was the first of us to die.

I cannot find Bibul's like in Winnipeg today.

Somebody waved a T-square wand over the old "island," bringing in the ninety-degree angle unknown in Bibul's far-off day. Progress pretends Bibul's "island" never really existed: the lanes are paved, the rot-wood of wall and fence has been sloshed over with paint. A few sneaky signs of the old world are around: a clothesline pole, exhausted from long years of soggy fleece-lined underwear to support, seems ready to give up the ghost; an outside staircase, impermanent as a hangman's scaffold, mocks the fire commission that asked for greater safety and got greater danger.

Malkeh is dead. The wagon is all bits and crumble.

Motorized peddlers in trucks like Brink's Cars zoom through the reformed "island" late at night with the remnants of produce picked over by ringed and braceleted hands on the day route—River Heights, Silver Heights, Garden City, places of Togetherness, Betterness, Spotlessness, the polite answers Comfort has given to the sad old questions of Civilization.

"Apples, apples, two pounds for a quarter," the peddlers call, but not too loudly, and the women once poor enough to be *shnorrers* (few are still alive), the women who have replaced the departed *shnorrers* in remodelled rebuilt houses, look over the fruit and vegetables (ironically like Bibul's old rejects and reduced-to-clears because of prior though elegant pawing), buy a little, haggle not at all, or withdraw with a snub at peddling, a bow in favour of the superior refrigeration of supermarkets.

Through the streets old Malkeh drew that creaking wagon urged on by leather-capped Bibul, chrome-trimmed cars speed in unending gaggle, their sport-capped, stylishly-hatted drivers in control of power the equivalent of four hundred un-Malkeh horses. The Mayor tells Winnipeggers to "Think Big," bid for the Pan-American Games, hang out more flags and buntings. Slums like Bibul's "island" and the City Hall are fortunately doomed: Winnipeg is obviously a better place to live in.

Who doesn't welcome prosperity?

But the fact remains: I cannot find Bibul's like in Winnipeg today.

And that is why here and now, in this, his and my city, I write you this requiem for Bibul, for his face, for his Great Cause, his tic, his wave, his "aaaa." In love and the joy of remembering I sing you this Bibul and all that's past and passing but not to come.

When the City Hall is torn down they will build Winnipeg a new one; but where, O where shall we find more Bibuls?

MORDECAI RICHLER

MORDECAI RICHLER was born in Montreal on January 27, 1931. In 1951, after completing two years of study at Sir George Williams College in Montreal, he left for Europe and lived for almost ten years in France, Spain and England. He returned to Canada in 1960, and will spend the year 1962 in the United States on a Guggenheim Fellowship. Mr. Richler had previously held junior arts fellowships from the Canada Council for the years 1959 to 1960 and 1960 to 1961.

Richler has published four novels (*The Acrobats*, 1954; *Son of a Smaller Hero*, 1955; *A Choice of Enemies*, 1957; *The Apprenticeship of Duddy Kravitz*, 1959) which have been very well received on both sides of the Atlantic. He has also published articles and stories in such magazines as *The New Statesman, Commentary, The Spectator, Maclean's* and *The Tamarack Review*, and has had television plays produced by the BBC, the CBC and ITV. He has written two film scenarios, and is at work on a book of non-fiction to be entitled *Their Canada, and Mine*.

Richler's work is distinguished by its abounding vitality, its accuracy and fullness of sensory impressions, its capacity for quickly sketching in eccentric characters of various kinds and its constant search for stable values in a shifting society. He is at his best in rendering the life of the Jewish section of Montreal with a mixture of warm sympathy and angry satire. The story which follows appeared in *The Montrealer*.

Benny, the War in Europe, and Myerson's Daughter Bella

WHEN BENNY was sent overseas in the autumn of 1941 his father, Mr. Garber, thought that if he had to give up one son to the army, it might as well be Benny who was a quiet boy, and who wouldn't push where he shouldn't; and Mrs. Garber

318

thought: "My Benny, he'll take care, he'll watch out"; and Benny's brother Abe thought "when he comes back, I'll have a garage of my own, you bet, and I'll be able to give him a job." Benny wrote every week, and every week the Garbers sent him parcels full of good things that a Jewish boy should always have, like salami and pickled herring and *shtrudel*. The food parcels were always the same, and the letters—coming from Camp Borden and Aldershot and Normandy and Holland —were always the same too. They began—"I hope you are all well and good" — and ended — "don't worry, all the best to everybody, thank you for the parcel."

When Benny came home from the war in Europe, the Garbers didn't make much of a fuss. They met him at the station, of course, and they had a small dinner for him.

Abe was thrilled to see Benny again. "Atta boy," was what he kept saying all evening, "Atta boy, Benny."

"You shouldn't go back to the factory," Mr. Garber said. "You don't need the old job. You can be a help to your brother Abe in his garage."

"Yes," Benny said.

"Let him be, let him rest," Mrs. Garber said, "What'll happen if he doesn't work for two weeks?"

"Hey, when Artie Segal came back," Abe said, "he said that in Italy there was nothing that a guy couldn't get for a couple of Sweet Caps. Was he shooting me the bull, or what?"

Benny had been discharged and sent home, not because the war was over, but because of the shrapnel in his leg, but he didn't limp too badly and he didn't talk about his wound or the war, so at first nobody noticed that he had changed. Nobody, that is, except Myerson's daughter Bella.

Myerson was the proprietor of Pop's Cigar & Soda, on Laurier Street, and any day of the week, you could find him there seated on a worn, peeling kitchen chair playing poker with the men of the neighbourhood. He had a glass-eye and when a player hesitated on a bet, he would take it out and polish it, a gesture that never failed to intimidate. His daughter, Bella, worked behind the counter. She had a club foot and

mousy hair and some more hair on her face, and although she
was only twenty-six, it was generally supposed that she would
end up an old maid. Anyway she was the one—the first one—
who noticed that the war in Europe had changed Benny. And,
as a matter of fact, the very first time he came into the store
after his homecoming she said to him: "What's wrong, Benny?
Are you afraid?"

"I'm all right," he said.

Benny was a quiet boy. He was short and skinny with a long
narrow face, a pulpy mouth that was somewhat crooked, and
soft black eyes. He had big, conspicuous hands, which he
preferred to keep out of sight in his pockets. In fact, he seemed
to want to keep out of sight altogether and whenever possible,
he stood behind a chair or in a dim light so that people
wouldn't notice him — and, noticing him, chase him away.
When he had failed the ninth grade at Baron Byng High
School, his class-master, a Mr. Perkins, had sent him home
with a note saying: "Benjamin is not a student, but he has all
the makings of a good citizen. He is honest and attentive in
class and a hard worker. I recommend that he learn a trade."

And when Mr. Garber had read what his son's teacher had
written, he had shaken his head and crumpled up the bit of
paper and said—"A trade?"—he had looked at his boy and
shaken his head and said—"A trade?"

Mrs. Garber had said stoutly, "Haven't you got a trade?"

"Shapiro's boy will be a doctor," Mr. Garber had said.

"Shapiro's boy," Mrs. Garber had said.

And afterwards, Benny had retrieved the note and smoothed
out the creases and put it in his pocket, where it had remained.
For Benny was sure that one day a policeman, or perhaps even
a Mountie, would try to arrest him, and then the paper that
Mr. Perkins had written so long ago might prove helpful.

Benny figured that he had been lucky, truly lucky, to get
away with living for so long. Oh, he had his dreams. He would
have liked to have been an aeroplane pilot, or still better, to
have been born rich or intelligent. Those kind of people, he
had heard, slept in mornings until as late as nine o'clock. But

he had been born stupid, people could tell that, just looking at him, and one day they would come to take him away. They would, sure as hell they would.

The day after his return to Montreal, Benny showed up at Abe's garage having decided that he didn't want two weeks off. That pleased Abe a lot. "I can see that you've matured since you've been away," Abe said. "That's good. That counts for you in this world."

Abe worked very hard, he worked night and day, and he believed that having Benny with him would give his business an added kick. "That's my kid brother Benny," Abe used to tell the cabbies. "Four years in the infantry, two of them up front. A tough hombre, let me tell you."

For the first few weeks Abe was very pleased with Benny. "He's slow," he thought, "no genius of a mechanic, but the customers like him and he'll learn." Then Abe began to notice things. When business was slow, Benny — instead of taking advantage of the lull to clean up the shop—used to sit shivering in a dim corner, with his hands folded tight on his lap. The first time Abe noticed his brother behaving like that, he said: "What's wrong? You got a chill?"

"No. I'm all right."

"You want to go home, or something?"

"No."

Then, when Abe began to notice him sitting like that more and more, he pretended not to see. "He needs time," he thought. But whenever it rained, and it rained often that spring, Benny was not to be found around the garage, and that put Abe in a bad temper. Until one day during a thunder shower, Abe tried the toilet door and found that it was locked. "Benny," he yelled, "come on out, I know you're in there."

Benny didn't answer, so Abe got the key. He found Benny huddled up in a corner with his head buried in his knees, trembling, with sweat running down his face in spite of the cold.

"It's raining," Benny said.

"Benny, get up. What's wrong?"

"Go away," Benny said. "It's raining."

"I'll get a doctor, Benny. I'll . . . ."

"Don't—you mustn't. Go away. Please, Abe."

"But Benny . . . ."

A terrible chill must have overcome Benny just then for he began to shake violently, just as if an inner whip had been cracked. Then, after it had passed, he looked up at Abe dumbly, his mouth hanging open. "It's raining," he said.

His discovery that afternoon gave Abe a good scare, and the next morning he went to see his father. "It was awful spooky, Paw," Abe said. "I don't know what to do with him."

"The war left him with a bad taste," Mrs. Garber said. "It made him something bad."

"Other boys went to the war," Abe said.

"Shapiro's boy," Mr. Garber said, "was an officer."

"Shapiro's boy," Mrs. Garber said. "You give him a vacation, Abe. You insist. He's a good boy. From the best. He'll be all right."

Benny did not know what to do with his vacation, so he tried sleeping in late like the rich and the intelligent, but in the late morning hours he dreamed bad dreams and that made him very frightened so he gave up that kind of thing. He did not dare go walking because he was sure that people could tell, just looking at him, that he was not working, and he did not want others to think that he was a bum. So he began to do odd jobs for people in the neighbourhood. He repaired bicycles and toasters and lamps. But he did not take any money for his work and that made people a little afraid. "Isn't our money good enough for him? All right, he was wounded, so maybe *I* was the one who shot him?"

Benny began to hang around Pop's Cigar & Soda.

"I don't like it, Bella," Mr. Myerson said, admiring the polish of his glass eye against the light. "I need him here like I need a cancer."

"Something's wrong with him psychologically," one of the card players said.

But obviously Bella liked having Benny around, and after a while Mr. Myerson stopped complaining. "Maybe the boy is serious," he thought, "and what with her club-foot and all that stuff on her face, I can't start picking and choosing. Beside, it's not as if he was a crook!"

Bella and Benny did not talk much when they were together, afraid, perhaps, that whatever it was that was "starting" up between them, was rich in delicacy, and would be soiled by ordinary words. She used to knit, he used to smoke. He would watch silently as she limped about the store, silently, with longing, and burning hope and consternation. The letter from Mr. Perkins was in his pocket. He wanted to tell her about the war —about things.

"I was walking with the sergeant. He reached into his pocket to show me a letter from his wife when . . . ."

There he would stop. A twitching would start around his eyes and he would swallow hard and stop.

Bella would look up from her knitting, waiting for him the way a mother waits for a child to be reasonable, knowing that it is only a question of time. But Benny would begin to shiver, and, looking down at the floor, grip his hands together until the knuckles went white. Around five in the afternoon he would get up and leave without saying a word. Bella would give him a stack of magazines to take home and at night he would read them all from cover to cover and the next morning he would bring them back as clean as new. Then he would sit with her in the store again, looking down at the floor or at his hands, as though he were in great pain. Time passed, and one day instead of going home around five in the afternoon he went upstairs with her. Mr. Myerson, who was watching, smiled happily. He turned to Mr. Shub and said: "If I had a boy of my own, I couldn't wish for a better one than Benny."

"Look who's counting his chickens already," Mr. Shub said.

Benny's vacation continued for several weeks and every morning he sat down in the store and stared at his hands, as if he expected them to have changed overnight, and every evening he went upstairs with Bella pretending not to have heard the remarks, the good-natured observations that had been made by the card-players as they passed.

Until, one afternoon she said to him: "I'm going to have a baby."

"All right," Benny said.

"Aren't you even going to say luck or something?"

Benny got up and bit his lower lip and gripped his hands together hard. "If you only knew what I have seen," he said.

They had a very simple wedding without speeches in a small synagogue and after the ceremony was over Abe slapped his younger brother's back and said: "Atta boy, Benny. Atta boy."

"Can I come back to work?"

"Sure, of course you can. You're the old Benny again," Abe said. "I can see that."

And when Mr. Garber got home, without much more to expect but getting older, and more tired earlier in the day, he turned to his wife and said: "Shapiro's boy married into the Segals."

"Shapiro's boy," Mrs. Garber said.

Benny went back to the garage but this time he settled down to work hard and that pleased Abe a good deal. "That's my kid brother, Benny," Abe used to tell the cabbies, "married six weeks and he's already got one in the oven. A quick worker, I'll tell you."

Benny settled down to work hard and when the baby was born he even laughed a little and began to save money and plan things, but every now and then, usually when there was a slack period at the garage, Benny would shut up tight and sit in a chair in a dark corner and stare at his hands. Bella was good with him. She never raised her voice to say an ugly thing, and when he woke up screaming from a dream about the war in Europe she would stroke his neck and say tender things. He, on the other hand, began to speak to her confidentially.

"Bella?"

"Yes."

"I killed a man."

"What? You what? When did you. . . ."

"In the war."

"Oh in the war. For a moment I — a German you mean. . . ."

"Yes, a German."

"If you ask me it's too bad you didn't kill a dozen. Those Germans I. . . ."

"I killed him with my hands."

"Go to sleep."

"Bella?"

"Yes."

"Are you ashamed that I. . . ."

"Go to sleep."

"I saw babies killed," he said. "What if. . . ."

"There won't be another war. Don't worry about our baby."

"But. . . ."

"Sleep. Go to sleep."

The baby grew into a fine, husky boy, and whenever there was a parade Benny used to hoist him on his shoulders so that he could see better. He was amazed, truly amazed, that he could have had such a beautiful child. He hardly had nightmares at all any more and he became talkative and somewhat shrewd. One night he came home and said: "Abe is going to open a branch on Mount Royal Street. I'm going to manage it. I'm going to be a partner in it."

So Benny finally threw away the paper that Mr. Perkins had written for him so long ago. They bought a car and planned, the following year, to have enough money saved so that Bella could go to a clinic in the United States to have an operation on her club foot. "I can assure you that I'm not going to spend such a fortune to make myself beautiful," Bella said, "and plainly speaking I'm not doing it for you. But I don't want that when the boy is old enough to go to school that he should be teased because his mother is a cripple."

Then, a month before Bella was to go to the clinic, they went to see their first cinemascope film. Now, previous to that evening, Bella had made a point never to take Benny along to see a war film, no matter who was playing in it. So as soon as the newsreel came on — it was that special one about the hydrogen bomb tests—she knew that she had made a mistake in bringing Benny with her, cinemascope or no cinemascope. She turned to him quickly. "Don't look," she said.

But Benny was enthralled. He watched the explosion, and he watched as the newsreel showed by means of diagrams what a hydrogen bomb could do to a city the size of New York— never mind Montreal.

Then he got up and left.

When Bella got home that night she found Benny huddled up in a dark corner with his head buried in his knees, trembling, with sweat running down his face. She tried to stroke his neck but he moved away from her.

"Should I send for a doctor?"

"Bella," he said. "Bella, Bella."

"Try to relax," she said. "Try to think about something pretty. Flowers, or something. Try for the boy's sake."

"Bella," he said. "Bella, Bella."

When she woke up the next morning he was still crouching there in that dark corner gripping his hands together tight, and he wouldn't eat or speak—not even to the boy.

The living-room was in a mess, papers spilled everywhere, as if he had been searching for something.

Finally—it must have been around noon—he put on his hat and walked out of the house. She knew right then that she should have stopped him. That she shouldn't have let him go. She knew.

Her father came around at five o'clock and she could tell from the expression on his face that she had guessed right. Mr. and Mrs. Garber were with him.

"He's dead?" Bella asked.

"Shapiro's boy, the doctor," Mr. Garber said, "said it was quick."

"Shapiro's boy," Mrs. Garber said.

"It wasn't the driver's fault," Mr. Myerson said.

"I know," Bella said.

ALICE MUNRO

ALICE MUNRO was born in Wingham, Ontario, in 1931. She published her first short story while a student at the University of Western Ontario. She was married in 1951, and moved to Vancouver with her husband. She is at present a housewife in West Vancouver, and has two children.

Mrs. Munro's short stories have appeared in most of the leading Canadian literary magazines, including *The Canadian Forum, Queen's Quarterly, The Tamarack Review* and *The Montrealer.* Her stories have been read over the CBC network, and she was represented in Robert Weaver's anthologies *Ten for Wednesday Night* (1961) and *Canadian Short Stories* (1960). The story which follows appeared first in *The Canadian Forum.*

Sunday Afternoon

MRS. GANNETT CAME INTO the kitchen walking delicately to a melody played in her head, flashing the polished cotton skirts of a flowered sundress. Alva was there, washing glasses. It was half-past two; people had started coming in for drinks about half-past twelve. They were the usual people; Alva had seen most of them a couple of times before, in the three weeks she had been working for the Gannetts. There was Mrs. Gannett's brother, and his wife, and the Vances and the Fredericks; Mrs. Gannett's parents came in for a little while, after service at St. Martin's, bringing with them a young nephew, or cousin, who stayed when they went home. Mrs. Gannett's side of the family was the right side; she had three sisters, all fair, forthright and unreflective women, rather more athletic than she, and these magnificently outspoken and

handsome parents, both of them with pure white hair. It was
Mrs. Gannett's father who owned the island in Georgian Bay,
where he had built summer homes for each of his daughters,
the island that in a week's time Alva was to see. Mr. Gannett's
mother, on the other hand, lived in half of the red-brick
house in a treeless street of exactly similar red brick houses,
almost downtown. Once a week Mrs. Gannett picked her up
and took her for a drive and home to supper, and nobody
drank anything but grape juice until she had been taken home.
Once when Mr. and Mrs. Gannett had to go out immediately
after supper she came into the kitchen and put away the dishes
for Alva; she was rather cranky and aloof, as the women in
Alva's own family would have been with a maid, and Alva
minded this less than the practised, considerate affability of
Mrs. Gannett's sisters.

  Mrs. Gannett opened the refrigerator and stood there, holding the door. Finally she said, with something like a giggle,
"Alva, I think we could have lunch—"

  "All right," Alva said. Mrs. Gannett looked at her. Alva
never said anything wrong, really wrong, that is rude, and
Mrs. Gannett was not so unrealistic as to expect a high-school
girl, even a country high-school girl, to answer, "Yes, ma'am,"
as the old maids did in her mother's kitchen; but there was
often in Alva's tone an affected ease, a note of exaggerated
carelessness and agreeability that was all the more irritating
because Mrs. Gannett could not think of any way to object to
it. At any rate it stopped her giggling; her tanned, painted
face grew suddenly depressed and sober.

  "The potato salad," she said. "Aspic and tongue. Don't forget to heat the rolls. Did you peel the tomatoes? Fine—Oh,
look Alva, I don't think those radishes look awfully attractive,
do you? You better slice them—Jean used to do roses, you
know the way they cut petals around—they used to look
lovely."

  Alva began clumsily to cut radishes. Mrs. Gannett walked
around the kitchen, frowning, sliding her fingertips along the
blue and coral counters. She was wearing her hair pulled up

into a topknot, showing her neck very thin, brown and rather sun-coarsened; her deep tan made her look sinewy and dried. Nevertheless Alva, who was hardly tanned at all because she spent the hot part of the day in the house, and who at seventeen was thicker than she would have liked in the legs and the waist, envied her this brown and splintery elegance; Mrs. Gannett had a look of being made of entirely synthetic and superior substances.

"Cut the angel-food with a string, you know that, and I'll tell you how many sherbet and how many maple-mousse. Plain vanilla for Mr. Gannett, it's in the freezer—There's plenty of either for your own dessert—Oh, Derek, you monster!" Mrs. Gannett ran out to the patio, crying, "Derek, Derek!" in tones of shrill and happy outrage. Alva, who knew that Derek was Mr. Vance, a stock-broker, just remembered in time not to peer out the top of the Dutch-door to see what was happening. That was one of her difficulties on Sundays, when they were all drinking, and becoming relaxed and excited; she had to remember that it was not permissible for her to show a little relaxation and excitement too. Of course, she was not drinking, except out of the bottoms of glasses when they were brought back to the kitchen—and then only if it was gin, cold, and sweetened. But the feeling of unreality, of alternate apathy and recklessness, became very strong in the house by the middle of the afternoon. Alva would meet people coming from the bathroom, absorbed and melancholy, she would glimpse women in the dim bedrooms swaying towards their reflections in the mirror, very slowly applying their lipstick, and someone would have fallen asleep on the long chesterfield in the den. By this time the drapes would have been drawn across the glass walls of living-room and dining-room, against the heat of the sun; those long, curtained and carpeted rooms, with their cool colours, seemed floating in an underwater light. Alva found it already hard to remember that the rooms at home, such small rooms, could hold so many things; here were such bland unbroken surfaces, such spaces—a whole long, wide passage empty, except for two tall Danish vases standing

against the farthest wall, carpet, walls and ceiling all done in
blue variants of grey; Alva, walking down this hallway, not
making any sound, wished for a mirror, or something to bump
into; she did not know if she was there or not.

Before she carried the lunch out to the patio she combed
her hair at a little mirror at the end of the kitchen counter,
pushing curls up around her face. She re-tied her apron, pulling its wide band very tight. It was all she could do; the
uniform had belonged to Jean, and Alva had asked, the first
time she tried it on, if maybe it was too big; but Mrs. Gannett
did not think so. The uniform was blue, the predominant
kitchen colour; it had white cuffs and collar and scalloped
apron. She had to wear stockings too, and white Cuban-heeled
shoes that clomped on the stones of the patio—making, in contrast to the sandals and pumps, a heavy, purposeful, plebeian
sound. But nobody looked around at her, as she carried plates,
napkins, dishes of food to a long wrought-iron table. Only Mrs.
Gannett came, and rearranged things. The way Alva had of
putting things down on a table always seemed to lack something, though there, too, she did not make any real mistakes.

When they were eating she ate her own lunch, sitting at the
kitchen table, looking through an old copy of *Time*. There
was no bell, of course, on the patio; Mrs. Gannett called, "All
right, Alva!" or simply, "Alva!" in tones as discreet and
penetrating as those of the bell. It was queer to hear her call
this, in the middle of talking to someone, and then begin
laughing again; it seemed as if she had a mechanical voice,
even a button she pushed, for Alva.

At the end of the meal they all carried their own dessert-
plates and coffee-cups back to the kitchen. Mrs. Vance said
the potato-salad was lovely; Mr. Vance, quite drunk, said
lovely, lovely. He stood right behind Alva at the sink, so very
close she felt his breath and sensed the position of his hands;
he did not quite touch her. Mr. Vance was very big, curly-
haired, high-coloured; his hair was grey, and Alva found him
alarming, because he was the sort of man she was used to
being respectful to. Mrs. Vance talked all the time, and seemed,

when talking to Alva, more unsure of herself, yet warmer, than any of the other women. There was some instability in the situation of the Vances; Alva was not sure what it was; it might have been just that they had not so much money as the others. At any rate they were always being very entertaining, very enthusiastic, and Mr. Vance was always getting too drunk. ✳

"Going up north, Alva, up to Georgian Bay?" Mr. Vance said, and Mrs. Vance said, "Oh, you'll love it, the Gannetts have a lovely place," and Mr. Vance said, "Get some sun on you up there, eh?" and then they went away. Alva, able to move now, turned around to get some dirty plates and noticed that Mr. Gannett's cousin, or whoever he was, was still there. He was thin and leathery-looking, like Mrs. Gannett, though dark. He said, "You don't happen to have any more coffee here, do you?" Alva poured him what there was, half a cup. He stood and drank it, watching her stack the dishes. Then he said, "Lots of fun, eh?" and when she looked up, laughed, and went out.

Alva was free after she finished the dishes; dinner would be late. She could not actually leave the house; Mrs. Gannett might want her for something. And she could not go outside; they were out there. She went upstairs, then, remembering that Mrs. Gannett had said she could read any of the books in the den, she went down again to get one. In the hall she met Mr. Gannett, who looked at her very seriously, attentively, but seemed about to go past without saying anything; then he said, "See here, Alva—see here, are you getting enough to eat?"

It was not a joke, since Mr. Gannett did not make them. It was, in fact, something he had asked her two or three times before. It seemed that he felt a responsibility for her, when he saw her in his house; the important thing seemed to be, that she should be well fed. Alva reassured him, flushing with annoyance; was she a heifer? She said, "I was going to the den to get a book. Mrs. Gannett said it would be all right—"

"Yes, yes, any book you like," Mr. Gannett said, and he unexpectedly opened the door of the den for her and led her

to the bookshelves, where he stood frowning. "What book
would you like?" he said. He reached toward the shelf of
brightly-jacketed mysteries and historical novels, but Alva
said, "I've never read *King Lear*."

"*King Lear*," said Mr. Gannett. "Oh." He did not know
where to look for it, so Alva got it down herself. "Nor *The
Red and the Black*," she said. That did not impress him so
much, but it was something she might really read; she could
not go back to her room with just *King Lear*. She went out of
the room feeling well-pleased; she had shown him she did
something besides eat. A man would be more impressed by
 King Lear than a woman. Nothing could make any difference
to Mrs. Gannett; a maid was a maid.

But in her room, she did not want to read. Her room was
over the garage, and very hot. Sitting on the bed rumpled her
uniform, and she did not have another ironed. She could take
it off and sit in her slip, but Mrs. Gannett might call her, and
want her at once. She stood at the window, looking up and
down the street. The street was a crescent, a wide slow curve,
with no sidewalks; Alva had felt a little conspicuous, the once
or twice she had walked along it; you never saw people walking. The houses were set far apart, far back from the street,
behind brilliant lawns and rockeries and ornamental trees; in
this area in front of the houses, no one ever spent time but the
Chinese gardeners; the lawn furniture, the swings and garden-
tables were set out on the back lawns, which were surrounded
by hedges, stone-walls, pseudo-rustic fences. The street was
lined with parked cars this afternoon; from behind the houses
came sounds of conversation and a great deal of laughter. In
spite of the heat, there was no blur on the day, up here; everything—the stone and white stucco houses, the flowers, the
flower-coloured cars—looked hard and glittering, exact and
perfect. There was no haphazard thing in sight. The street, like
an advertisement, had an almost aggressive look of bright
summer spirits; Alva felt dazzled by this, by the laughter, by
people whose lives were relevant to the street. She sat down on
a hard chair in front of an old-fashioned child's desk—all the

furniture in this room had come out of other rooms that had been redecorated; it was the only place in the house where you could find things unmatched, unrelated to each other, and wooden things that were not large, low and pale. She began to write a letter to her family.

"—and the houses, all the others too, are just tremendous, mostly quite modern. There isn't a weed in the lawns, they have a gardener spend a whole day every week just cleaning out what looks to be perfect already. I think the men are rather sappy, the fuss they make over perfect lawns and things like that. They do go out and rough it every once in a while but that is all very complicated and everything has to be just so. It is like that with everything they do and everywhere they go.

"Don't worry about me being lonesome and downtrodden and all that maid sort of thing. I wouldn't let anybody get away with anything like that. Besides I'm not a maid really, ✳ it's just for the summer. I don't feel lonesome, why should I? I just observe and am interested. Mother, of course I can't eat with them. Don't be ridiculous. It's not the same thing as a hired girl at all. Also I prefer to eat alone. If you wrote Mrs. Gannett a letter she wouldn't know what you were talking about, and I don't mind. *So don't!*

"Also I think it would be better when Marion comes down if I took my afternoon off and met her downtown. I don't want particularly to have her come here. I'm not sure how maids' relatives come. Of course it's all right if she wants to. I can't always tell how Mrs. Gannett will react, that's all, and I try to take it easy around her without letting her get away with anything. She is all right though.

"In a week we will be leaving for Georgian Bay and of course I am looking forward to that. I will be able to go swimming every day she (Mrs. Gannett) says and—"

Her room was really too hot. She put the unfinished letter under the blotter on the desk. A radio was playing in Margaret's room. She walked down the hall towards Margaret's door, hoping it would be open. Margaret was not quite

✳

fourteen; the difference in age compensated for other differ-
ences, and it was not too bad to be with Margaret.

The door was open, and there spread out on the bed were
Margaret's crinolines and summer dresses. Alva had not known
she had so many.

"I'm not really packing," Margaret said. "I know it would
be crazy. I'm just seeing what I've got. I hope my stuff is all
right," she said. "I hope it's not too."

Alva touched the clothes on the bed, feeling a great delight
in these delicate colours, in the smooth little bodices, expens-
ively tucked and shaped, the crinolines with their crisp and
fanciful bursts of net; in these clothes there was a very pretty
artificial innocence. Alva was not envious; no, this had nothing
to do with her; this was part of Margaret's world, that rigid
pattern of private school (short tunics and long black stockings), hockey, choir, sailing in summer, parties, boys who
wore blazers. . . .

"Where are you going to wear them?" Alva said.

"To the Ojibway. The Hotel. They have dances every
weekend, everybody goes down in their boats. Friday night is
for kids and Saturday night is for parents and other people—
That is I *will* be going," Margaret said rather grimly, "if I'm
not a social flop. Both the Davis girls are."

"Don't worry," Alva said a little patronizingly. "You'll be
fine."

"I don't really like dancing," Margaret said. "Not the way
I like sailing, for instance. But you have to do it."

"You'll get to like it," Alva said. So there would be dances,
they would go down in the boats, she would see them going
and hear them coming home. All these things, which she
should have expected—

Margaret, sitting cross-legged on the floor, looked up at her
with a blunt, clean face, and said, "Do you think I ought
to start to neck this summer?"

"Yes," said Alva. "*I* would," she added almost vindictively.
Margaret looked puzzled; and said, "I heard that's why Scotty
didn't ask me at Easter—"

There was no sound, but Margaret slipped to her feet. "Mother's coming," she said with her lips only, and almost at once Mrs. Gannett came into the room, smiled with a good deal of control, and said, "Oh, Alva. This is where you are."

Margaret said, "I was telling her about the Island, Mummy."

"Oh. There are an awful lot of glasses sitting around down there Alva, maybe you could whisk them through now and they'd be out of the way when you want to get dinner—And Alva, do you have a fresh apron?"

"The yellow is so too tight, Mummy, I tried it on—"

"Look, darling, it's no use getting all that fripfrap out yet, there's still a week before we go—"

Alva went downstairs, passed along the blue hall, heard people talking seriously, a little drunkenly, in the den, and saw the door of the sewing-room closed softly, from within, as she approached. She went into the kitchen. She was thinking of the Island now. A whole island that they owned; nothing in sight that was not theirs. The rocks, the sun, the pine trees, and the deep, cold water of the Bay. What would she do there, what did the maids do? She could go swimming, at odd hours, go for walks by herself, and sometimes—when they went for groceries, perhaps—she would go along in the boat. There would not be so much work to do as there was here, Mrs. Gannett had said. She said the maids always enjoyed it. Alva thought of the other maids, those more talented, more accommodating girls; did they really enjoy it? What kind of freedom or content had they found, that she had not?

She filled the sink, got out the draining-rack again and began to wash glasses. Nothing was the matter, but she felt heavy, heavy with the heat and tired and uncaring, hearing all around her an incomprehensible faint noise—of other people's lives, of boats and cars and dances—and seeing this street, that promised island, in a harsh and continuous dazzle of sun. She could not make a sound here, not a dint.

She must remember, before dinner-time, to go up and put on a clean apron.

She heard the door open; someone came in from the patio. It was Mrs. Gannett's cousin.

"Here's another glass for you," he said. "Where'll I put it?"

"Anywhere," said Alva.

"Say thanks," Mrs. Gannett's cousin said, and Alva turned around wiping her hands on her apron, surprised, and then in a very short time not surprised. She waited, her back to the counter, and Mrs. Gannett's cousin took hold of her lightly, as in a familiar game, and spent some time kissing her mouth.

"She asked me up to the island some weekend in August," he said.

Someone on the patio called him, and he went out, moving with the graceful, rather mocking stealth of some slight people. Alva stood still with her back to the counter.

This stranger's touch had eased her; her body was simply grateful and expectant, and she felt a lightness and confidence she had not known in this house. So there were things she had not taken into account, about herself, about them, and ways of living with them that were not so unreal. She would not mind thinking of the island now, the bare sunny rocks and the black little pine trees. She saw it differently now; it was even possible that she wanted to go there. But things always came together; there was something she would not explore yet—a tender spot, a new and still mysterious humiliation.

ALDEN A. NOWLAN

ALDEN NOWLAN was born at Windsor, Nova Scotia, on January 25, 1933. He left school when he was in Grade V, and worked at a variety of occupations, mainly manual, during his early youth. In 1952 he moved to Hartland, New Brunswick, and became news editor of the weekly paper of that town, the *Observer*. In 1961 he was awarded a junior arts fellowship by the Canada Council to enable him to travel to other parts of Canada and to confer with other poets and critics.

Mr. Nowlan is one of the most promising young Canadian poets, and has already published three small books of verse—*The Rose and the Puritan* (1958), *A Darkness in the Earth* (1958) and *Under the Ice* (1961)—and poems in a host of magazines in Canada and the United States. He has also published short stories in *The Fiddlehead, The Canadian Forum* and *Queen's Quarterly*, and is at work on a novel. His work so far has dealt almost exclusively with the more sordid aspects of life in rural Nova Scotia and New Brunswisk: with a fearless honesty he portrays the suffering and cruelty that result from prejudice and bigotry, from ignorance and poverty. Without a trace of sentimentality, he evokes our sympathy for the victims of these crippling forces. The story which follows appeared first in *The Fiddlehead*.

True Confession

SHE COULD REMEMBER how pleased Arleigh had been when she'd told him, soon after they'd started going together, that he reminded her of a western gunfighter, she wasn't sure who: maybe George Montgomery, certainly somebody younger than John Wayne and tougher than Audie Murphy; he'd walked with that easy slouch, his arms not swinging much, hands never moving far from his hips, stooping a little, his eyes half shut, and he'd drawled, wrinkling his nose, making his voice sound more casual and throaty than usual when he got angry.

All the boys wanted that look. But none of them could do it so well as Arleigh. Barbara thought of this now as he came into the kitchen and threw the black lunch pail, on which he had scratched his initials with a spike, on the chair nearest the door.

He walked straighter now. Over the past two years she had watched the tension increase in him, his body stiffen, his shoulders grow hard. She had seen him coming to look more like his father, like her father, like all the men at the sawmill, and the transformation baffled and rather frightened her.

He sat down and swung his chair around, away from the table. Bending forward he unlaced his gum rubbers, then kicked them under the chair and stood up in his wool socks. All the mill-hands wore wool socks at work in summer because the wool absorbed the sweat from their rubber-smothered feet.

Barbara rubbed her palms on her faded jeans, shook salmon from a can onto a plate.

"Hot, ain't it?" she said shyly.

Every day she grew more shy with him.

"Yeah. I guess so."

He undid the two top buttons of his plaid shirt and pulled it over his head. At the sink he washed himself in cold water, his eyes closed, grunting.

"I guess every summer gits a little hotter than the one before, somehow," she said.

"Yeah." He rubbed his face briskly with a towel. Yellow flecks of sawdust were shaken out of his hair. Despite the scrubbing, bits of sawdust were still entangled in his two day's growth of beard.

He put on his shirt and sat down at the table. She filled his plate with potatoes, canned peas and salmon, hurrying because he did not like to be kept waiting for his food, and poured strong black tea into his cup. Then she sat down opposite him. He bent low over his plate, a slice of bread in his left hand, his right wielding the fork, his eyes focussed on nothing, his mouth to be kept full from now until he finished.

"You have enough stuff in your lunch pail today?" she asked.

He looked up.

"What?"

"You have enough stuff in your lunch pail today?" she repeated.

"Yeah. Sure. I guess so. Why?"

His voice was muffled and distorted, his cheeks puffed out with food.

"Oh, no reason, especially. Jist wonerin', that's all."

"Oh."

He bent back to his plate, forgetting her again.

They completed their supper in silence. She wished he would talk to her, although she knew there was nothing to say. He was not irritable, she knew. His silence was matter-of-fact and masculine. It was a silence that she had watched expand and envelop him since he had married and gone to work in the mill.

It means that he is a man, no longer a boy, she thought. But she could not accept it quite, not yet. The memory of his loud braggadocio and boisterous, insolent laughter was too fresh. She felt something curiously similar to jealousy, as though the mill, the men with whom he worked, the whole ritual of manhood as they knew it, had somehow seduced him and robbed her. But she pushed such thoughts away, because all deep thoughts disturbed her. She was not equipped to control them: they distracted and confused her, and she was mortally afraid of being pretentious or over-imaginative, what she believed to be "odd" or "queer" or "foolish".

He finished eating, cleaned his plate out with bread, and crossed the floor in his socks, loosening the belt of his denim pants and patting his belly. While she washed the dishes and cleaned the oil cloth table covering, brushing crumbs onto the floor to be swept up later, he lay on the couch smoking a hand-rolled cigarette, staring sightlessly at the smoke as it curled up toward the ceiling.

"How was everythin' at the mill today," she prodded him, resenting the complacency with which he withdrew from her.

"Same as it allus is, I guess," he said, not sullenly but as if the question were meaningless and unnecessary.

Not George Montgomery, she thought. Maybe it was Myron Healy. He's the fellow who always gets killed. He's gotten killed whenever I've seen him in the movies, every single time.

"Arleigh," she said suddenly.

"Yeah?"

"Mebbe we could go to the movies in town this Saturday night. I hear they're showin' a real good movie."

"Mebbe."

"You mean we'n go?" Her voice became tense with eagerness and excitement.

"I dunno, Barb. Movies are kinda kid stuff, ain't they? I mean a man works all week he wants to kinda see the boys, you know—have a few beers. You know how it is, Barb."

"Yeah." Her excitement died.

"Mebbe we'n go. We'll see what happens between now and then. O.K.?"

"Yeah."

Her work done she took a magazine from the shelf which held the radio and sat down at the table again. The first story was entitled *I Couldn't Help Loving Him*. Opposite the title there was a photograph of a man and a girl locked in one another's arms, his mouth crushing hers. They were standing under a street light in the city and the man wore a suit, the girl a beautiful white dress, its neck cut low, his trenchcoat thrown over her shoulders.

She glanced at Arleigh. Already he had fallen asleep.

She began to read, her lips moving tenderly.

QUESTIONS FOR DISCUSSION

GENERAL

1. What qualities do you look for in a good short story?
2. What do we mean by the "plot" of a short story?
3. What do we mean by the following terms when they are applied to the short story: singleness of effect, climax, economy, sincerity, structure, theme, setting, atmosphere, mood?
4. How does the short story differ from (a) the novel? (b) the play? (c) the narrative poem?

THE LOCKSMITH OF PHILADELPHIA / *Joseph Howe*

1. Why is Joseph Howe considered one of the most important figures in early Canadian history?
2. Howe was known as a champion of the common people. What evidence of his popular sympathies do you find in this story?
3. What humour do you find in the story?

SAM SLICK THE CLOCKMAKER / *Thomas Chandler Haliburton*

1. (a) Why is the first paragraph of a story very important? (b) Does this story have a good beginning? Why is this a good beginning?
2. (a) What is a pun? (b) How many puns can you find in this story?
3. Haliburton deliberately used North American dialect in his writings. What examples of dialect can you find here?
4. (a) Write a character sketch of Sam Slick. (b) Does Haliburton admire or despise him? Give reasons for your answer.
5. Haliburton wrote to impress certain lessons on his fellow Nova Scotians. What lessons is he teaching here?
6. Why do we consider Haliburton a master of anecdote?

OLD WOODRUFF AND HIS THREE WIVES / *Susanna Moodie*

1. Why does Susanna Moodie begin her story as she does, rather than at the chronological beginning?
2. What do we learn of pioneer conditions in Canada from this story?
3. What examples of humour do you find in this story?
4. Vivid descriptive details add much to a story. What especially good descriptions do you find here?
5. Write a character sketch of "old Woodruff".

THE PRIVILEGE OF THE LIMITS / *Edward W. Thomson*

1. What do we learn of the lives and characters of the early Scottish-Canadian settlers from this story?
2. What is "the privilege of the limits"?
3. (a) What is a "tall tale"? (b) How does this story resemble a "tall tale"?
4. Why does Thomson have this story told by old Mrs. McTavish?

5. Relate any similar, amusing or interesting yarns that you might have heard about your own ancestors.
6. What similarities do you see between this story and Haliburton's "Sam Slick the Clockmaker"?

"THE YOUNG RAVENS THAT CALL UPON HIM" / *Charles G. D. Roberts*

1. (a) "You can tell that this story is written by a poet." Do you agree? (b) How can one tell?
2. "If a story has fine description and suggestive atmosphere, it needs only a very simple plot." Do you agree? Support your answer with examples from the story.
3. How does Roberts manage to make us so interested in his animal characters?
4. "Roberts is the master of the exact word." What examples of exactitude of expression do you find in this story?
5. Do you think that the last two paragraphs of this story are particularly effective? Why?

PAUL FARLOTTE / *Duncan Campbell Scott*

1. In what ways do Scott's poems resemble this story?
2. What examples of symbolism do you find in this story?
3. Write a character sketch of Paul Farlotte.
4. Paul Farlotte was fond of reading Montaigne. Who was Montaigne, and what did he write?
5. Has Scott captured the atmosphere of rural Quebec in this story? How?
6. (a) Do the characters in this story strike you as too "odd" to be believed, or do they arouse your sympathy and quicken your understanding? (b) Have you known anyone like old Paul Farlotte or his neighbours? If you have, write a character sketch of this person.

THE SPECULATIONS OF JEFFERSON THORPE / *Stephen Leacock*

1. Leacock is considered a master of irony. (a) What is irony? (b) What examples of irony do you find in this story?
2. Does Thorpe strike you as a typical small town barber? Why?
3. (a) Do you think Leacock wrote this story just to be funny, or did he have some important and serious idea too? (b) If the latter, what is the idea?
4. "Humour of character, humour of incident and humour of expression: Leacock was master of them all." Discuss this statement with reference to this story.
5. "For all its faults, Mariposa was a town beloved to Stephen Leacock." Do you agree, or do you think Leacock is holding the town up to ridicule? Support your answer.
6. Why are Leacock's books enjoyed throughout the world?

THE FRUITS OF TOIL / *Norman Duncan*

1. What do we learn from this story of the lives of our east coast fishermen?
2. (a) What is a parable? (b) Does this story seem to you to resemble a parable in any way?
3. Some people consider this story bombastic and rhetorical. (a) What do you think? (b) Do you think its unusual style is justified by the effect it produced?
4. What is the theme of this story?
5. Duncan had obviously read the Bible carefully. What examples of Biblical phrasing and rhythms do you find here?
6. Do you find the death scene of Solomon effective, or is it an example of sentimentality? Why?
7. What is the significance of the repeated references to "the seven thunders"?

SNOW / *Frederick Philip Grove*

1. (a) What similarities do you see between this story and Norman Duncan's? (b) Which is the more convincing story, and why?
2. "Grove keeps us aware, at every turn, of the intense cold of a prairie winter day." Comment on the means he uses.
3. Why does Grove so often emphasize the men's silence?
4. What effect is gained by Grove's precise, detailed descriptions of persons, places and things?

THE WORKER IN SANDALWOOD / *Marjorie Pickthall*

1. What similarities are there between this story and that by D. C. Scott? Which do you think is the better story? Explain your answer.
2. "There are annoying touches of sentimentality in this story." Do you agree? Explain your answer with reference to the story.
3. What hints does Miss Pickthall give us to suggest that the visitor is Jesus Christ?
4. What similarities are there between this story and Miss Pickthall's poems?

COME FLY WITH ME / *Mazo de la Roche*

1. Miss de la Roche's gift for similes and metaphors is often admired. What examples do you find here?
2. What does this story have in common with the Roberts' story?
3. Would this story have been improved by omitting the middle section involving human life? What does that section add to the story?

HURRY, HURRY! / *Ethel Wilson*

1. Mrs. Wilson is known to be a close observer of bird and animal life. What examples of this are there here?
2. "The remarkable thing about this story is the way it moves irresistibly forward from innocent security through slight fear to a climax of sheer terror." Discuss.

THE MOVIES COME TO GULL POINT / *Will R. Bird*

1. Compare and contrast this story with Norman Duncan's "The Fruits of Toil." Which gives the more convincing picture of fishermen and the sea? Support you answer with examples from the story.
2. What other stories in the book have as their main theme the struggle of man against nature?
3. This story relies heavily on irony. What is irony? What examples of it do you find in this story?

THE STRAWSTACK / *Raymond Knister*

1. "To Knister words were not mere counters, but vivid signs of concrete things." What examples of this fresh use of language do you find in this story?
2. What evidence do you find in this story that Knister was a poet?
3. Compare and contrast this story with either "Paul Farlotte" or "The Lamp at Noon".
4. How does Knister suggest to us that the hero's mind is unbalanced?

THE AMULET / *Thomas H. Raddall*

1. Why does Raddall have this story told by an old minister to a young skeptic?
2. What other means does the author employ to make the strange story credible?
3. Why do you think Raddall wrote this story—to entertain us or to set us thinking? Support your answer by reference to the story.

THE BLUE KIMONO / *Morley Callaghan*

1. What does the blue kimono symbolize?
2. "Callaghan makes his stories out of the ordinary problems of ordinary people." Discuss.
3. "The style of this story is deliberately simple and unemphatic." (a) Give some examples of this. (b) Why do you like the style?
4. Why does the husband say, at the end, that the kimono does not matter?

THE LAMP AT NOON / *Sinclair Ross*

1. Compare and contrast this story with Knister's "The Strawstack".
2. This story records a conflict between man and nature. What other stories in the book have a similar theme?

3. Discuss Ross's descriptive powers.
4. Why does this story impress you as an authentic picture of prairie life?

THE FIRST BORN SON / *Ernest Buckler*

1. This story comes from the Maritimes. What special features of Maritime life does it reflect?
2. What is the main theme of this story? What other stories or poems do you know with similar themes?
3. Discuss the style and structure of this story.

THE PIGEON / *Ralph Gustafson*

1. What means does Gustafson employ to build up the tension here?
2. Discuss the author's choice of words, metaphors and similes.
3. What is the real source of the tension between father and daughter?

STORMS OF OUR JOURNEY / *David Walker*

1. Compare and contrast this story with either Norman Duncan's "The Fruits of Toil" or Will R. Bird's "The Movies Come to Gull Point".
2. (a) Are the many detailed descriptions in this story justified? (b) Could the story have been improved by condensation? (c) If so, what might be cut out?

A PLAUSIBLE STORY / *Irving Layton*

1. The author of this story, Irving Layton, is also a poet. What evidence of his poetic talent do you find in the story?
2. What do you consider to be the theme of the story?
3. Prove that this is or is not a convincing account of a school situation.

ONE, TWO, THREE LITTLE INDIANS / *Hugh Garner*

1. What does this story suggest about the status of the Indian in Canada? What steps could be taken to improve his status?
2. What is the significance of the title of this story?
3. Show how the style of this story is appropriate to its material and theme.

THE BOAT / *Desmond Pacey*

1. Why does the story begin with the scene at the supper table?
2. Discuss the use made of weather and physical description in this story.
3. Why does the boy throw the boat away?
4. Show how the style of this story is appropriate to its theme and characters.
5. Compare this story with the others which deal with children. Which is the most effective? Give reasons for your choice.

LION OF THE AFTERNOON / *Brian Moore*

1. It has been said that the outstanding quality of Brian Moore's work is his compassionate understanding of the misfit. How does this apply to this story?
2. What is the significance of the title?
3. Why did the dwarf run gaily down the steps?

SUNDAY AFTERNOON / *Alice Munro*

1. (a) What is Mrs. Munro implying about Canadian society in this story? (b) How far do you think this story is a true picture of our society?
2. What is the "new and still mysterious humiliation" referred to in the last line?
3. Write a character sketch of (a) Alva, (b) Mrs. Gannett.

TWO SISTERS IN GENEVA / *Henry Kreisel*

1. Compare and contrast this story with "Sunday Afternoon".
2. Write character sketches of the two sisters.
3. What is the theme of this story?

REQUIEM FOR BIBUL / *Jack Ludwig*

1. (a) Discuss Mr. Ludwig's handling of the setting of this story. (b) How authentic a picture of a modern Canadian city is this?
2. What is remarkable about the style of this story?
3. Compare and contrast this story with "Lion of the Afternoon".
4. Write a character sketch of some striking fellow-student of your experience.

BENNY, THE WAR IN EUROPE, AND MYERSON'S DAUGHTER BELLA
/ *Mordecai Richler*

1. "Richler has a brilliant gift of mimicry. He catches the exact shades of speech, gesture and behaviour of his characters." Discuss this opinion.
2. Compare the picture of Montreal in this story with the picture of Winnipeg in the previous story. Which is more convincing?
3. It has been said that Richler writes of the Jewish section of Montreal in a style that mingles irony, anger and compassion. Discuss this view in relation to this story.

TRUE CONFESSION / *Alden A. Nowlan*

1. Alden Nowlan seems to be fascinated by characters who are stunned by a narrow environment. How does he bring out the narrowness of Barbara's environment?
2. "This story is very simple, but very true to life." Discuss.
3. Of which other story in the book does this most remind you and why?